An Epic Joy

A NOVEL

BASED ON THE LIFE OF RUBENS

Books by Donald Braider

THE PALACE GUARD

PUTNAM'S GUIDE TO THE
ART CENTERS OF EUROPE

COLOR FROM A LIGHT WITHIN

RAGE IN SILENCE

AN
EPIC JOY

A NOVEL
BASED ON THE LIFE OF RUBENS

by Donald Braider

G. P. PUTNAM'S SONS, *New York*

For Helen and Christopher Braider

WITH GREAT LOVE AND BENIGN ATTENTION

AN EPIC JOY

One

N June 27, 1587, the eve of his tenth birthday, Pieter
Paul Rubens departed from Cologne with his mother, Maria
Piepelinx, his two older brothers and a sister who was also his
senior. After almost two decades of exile, the Rubens family
was finally returning to Antwerp.

Behind them in the Rhenish city of Cologne, in Siegen, and
in the dungeon of the castle at Dillenburg, the Rubenses were
leaving many memories, most of them unhappy. They were
leaving, above all, the remains of Jan Rubens, husband and father, who had died the previous March and who had been
responsible for all the misfortunes he and those who survived
him had been made to suffer—none more resolutely or more
bravely than his widow, the loyal, strong-willed Maria Piepelinx. Before them, in the great Flemish city of Antwerp, lay a
future which Maria had often depicted to her children in the
most glowing terms—her descriptions gathering color as the
years of separation grew more numerous.

To Pieter Paul, as he rode in the diligence that followed the
irregular course of the Rhine, it was all rather confusing. He
looked forward with enormous eagerness to a new life in Ant-

9

werp. How could he help it? His mother had made the prospect so dazzling. Yet he alone of his family regretted the departure from Cologne, the town where he had spent almost all his years, where his beloved, slightly raffish father was buried in a soil he had never adopted, where the child himself had made friends, learned the Lutheran liturgy, and acquired the fundamentals of a quite astonishing education.

Of all the perplexities that now disturbed this slender, thoughtful, energetic boy, the one most baffling was his mother's admonition, reiterated several times each day since the death of Jan Rubens, "You're Catholics now, all of you. Philip and Pieter Paul must forget that they were ever Lutherans. In Antwerp, you're never to whisper a word of that to *anyone*."

Philip, three years older than Pieter Paul, professed to understand what Maria meant by this warning. "In Antwerp," he explained with his usual earnestness and lack of humor, "*everyone* is Catholic. That's the law. Protestants are garroted. Do you want to be garroted?"

This seemed to the youngest child a most inadequate summary. Yet when he so protested to his mother, she dismissed him curtly. "The less you know about it, the better."

Maria's sharp rejection of Pieter Paul's inquiries was characteristic. There were many topics which she refused to discuss with any of her children. And, of course, her suppression of the facts served to stir their natural curiosity. In the absence of reliable information, the Rubens progeny thrived on a sort of family folklore of their own devising. Blandine, next in age to Philip, was the most imaginative. She had been four when her parents left Antwerp in 1568, and had been with her mother during Jan Rubens' "difficulties," as Maria chose to call them. Jan-Baptiste, four years older than Blandine, had spent these years with his mother's relations and was therefore a hopelessly ill-informed witness—for to his own guesses he could only add the lies recounted to him by aunts and uncles anxious to avoid scandal and its possible consequences.

Blandine had it that Jan Rubens had been exiled from Antwerp because of his unshakable fidelity to the great Prince Wil-

10

liam the Silent, of Orange, hero of every Protestant in the Low Countries, organizer of the first coherent resistance to the Spanish Fury, who was eventually martyred by an assassin's bullet. At the prince's request, Blandine went on, Jan Rubens had gone to Cologne to watch over the interests of the Princess Anne of Saxony, the great man's second wife. Cologne, in Catholic Westphalia (a possession of the prince's), had soon proved hostile to Jan and to his importance in the princess' entourage. Therefore, the authorities had imprisoned him for more than two years, releasing him only when he had sworn never again to meddle in the affairs of state and never to leave the town of Siegen (and later, Cologne) on pain of death. Furthermore, because of his loyalty to the Protestant Prince William, Jan Rubens had been excommunicated. That was why his two younger children had been baptized into the Lutheran faith.

As is customary with legend, Blandine's garbled account contained elements of the truth, but they were few. Only Maria Piepelinx could disabuse her children of their fantasies, and this she wasn't inclined to do. The permission to return to Antwerp, which she had obtained only weeks before her husband's death, had been much too difficult to secure; not for worlds would she place herself and her young in any further jeopardy by giving them information which, in her opinion, could only make them unhappy and, if given general circulation in the city from which she had so long been absent, might very easily endanger their future.

So his father's tale remained a mystery for little Pieter Paul —or, more precisely, a kind of myth. As a matter of fact, all the years he could remember of his brief life were marked by similar befuddlements. Inexplicable events were constant features of the Rubenses' existence—all suggestive that out there, beyond the walls that enclosed the garden of the house they had leased in Cologne, there was a strange and rather menacing world; this he knew from what both his mother and father said or made vague allusions to. It was a hostile world, filled with dangers to which they declined, in his presence, to give names

11

—people, ideas, "forces," whose nature he attempted to divine, or to pry out of Philip or Blandine, without appreciable success. And as for Jan-Baptiste, he was altogether beyond the boy's reach—a figure alone and aloof, pretending, as much as was possible in the circumstances, that he really didn't belong to the Rubens clan, and refusing to share whatever he knew with the younger members of the family.

Maria Piepelinx was that most formidable of all God's creations—a supremely competent woman. It was not the role for which she had been prepared by her prosperous parents in Antwerp. It had been thrust upon her by marriage to Jan Rubens. Yet it was a part which she quickly learned to enjoy, in a perverse way. To be indispensable to her husband, to be invincible, to be courageous—these were qualities that society admired, particularly in a woman, because a woman of the sixteenth century was not expected to possess them. And if the admiration she received from the world (a world which she claimed so to fear and despise) was at the expense of Jan Rubens, in whose direction much sniggering laughter had been directed, Maria Piepelinx was not so Christian in her charity that she failed to relish the considerable advantage it gave her over him. In a social order established by men, for men, she stood out in dramatic contrast—a strong woman. She had ideas. She made plans. She was indomitable.

To say that she had the careers of her sons methodically plotted would be an exaggeration. Had their father not played the fool, it would have been logical for at least one of them to follow him in the legal profession. Jan Rubens had been, at the time of his unseemly flight from Antwerp, an *échevin*, a magistrate, an alderman of the city; he might even have become the burgomaster. Such a career was now out of the question for Jan-Baptiste; he was too old, at twenty-five, to establish himself on his initiative (of which he had no great natural endowment, in any case) in a profession. So she must try to arrange for him an advantageous marriage—just what she planned for Blandine.

For the two younger children, Philip and Pieter Paul, the

12

future could be brighter—though God alone knew how she would manage for them. A dowry for Blandine would take most of the capital that had been restored to her by the amnesties accorded Protestants and others who had supported Prince William of Orange. Yet Maria was certain that God *did* know how she would manage. Had she not been an optimist, she would long since have hurled herself into the Rhine out of frustration or anguish or despair. Somehow, she would see to it that Philip and Pieter Paul had opportunities—though opportunities to do just what, she couldn't say yet. Something, she was confident, would present itself at the proper time.

This buoyancy of temperament was Maria's most attractive trait. Even Jan Rubens, who had more than once been lacerated by her savage tongue, had had to wonder at his wife's spirit. It had almost surely saved his life. He could argue, as he certainly had done, that she had rescued him only to preserve the family fortunes and to upbraid him; but the very fact of proving herself capable of mastering the complexities of courtly diplomacy and clerical bureaucracy was evidence enough of her genius and tenacity. To have accomplished these things without ever seeming to lose heart or patience or self-confidence was miraculous.

Jan Rubens, scapegrace and scapegoat, had been neither at the time of his marriage with Maria Piepelinx. The bride's father had assured her that this young man was the most promising *bourgeois* of his generation in Antwerp; there could be little doubt that Jan would go far, almost as far as he wished. It seemed an accurate prognosis. Jan Rubens enjoyed every advantage of birth and education except those that nobility could offer. There had been Rubenses of at least some importance in Antwerp since official records had been kept. The young man's father was the city's most prosperous apothecary. Jan himself had gone first to the University of Louvain, and later to Padua in Italy, to learn the law and foreign languages. He had been a faithful servant of the Spanish regents, had become an *échevin*, a husband, a father.

To all of these commendable attributes and achievements, he

13

brought a nature that was easygoing—too casual by far, it later seemed to his wife; though during the first seven years of their married life he had never given her occasion for thinking so. If he womanized a little now and then, he did no more than his colleagues; he never caused a scandal. The women with whom he consorted were the socially countenanced courtesans—creatures whose reputation for accomplishment and beauty was rivaled only by those of Venice.

No, Maria Piepelinx had later observed wryly, it had not been solely Jan Rubens' folly that had brought him low; it had also been the gravity of the times. The times had brought nearly every important Netherlander low, in one way or another. The period from 1567 on through this present year of grace, 1587, had been one of the cruelest generations in the annals of Christendom. It had been witness, in fact, to the very sundering of Christendom—that conception of western Europe so long cherished by popes and worshipful Catholic monarchs. There was now loose on the Continent a force that gave itself the name of Reformation. It was not a new idea, this movement to alter the nature and practice of religion; it had been born almost a century before. But only with the conclusion of the Councils of Trent, in 1563, had the Church of Rome at last officially recognized the extent to which Protestantism in its proliferating forms had eroded papal authority in matters temporal as well as spiritual. The Edicts of Trent, promulgated a year later, proposed a Counter Reformation which, as it was given effect in countries divided by theological differences, occasioned a series of civil wars that would continue sporadically through the end of the seventeenth century.

Maria Piepelinx didn't understand, at the outset, what the fundamental argument was about. As a well-raised daughter and wife and mother, it didn't occur to her to inquire of her husband. Worldly matters were exclusively the concern of men. As a man about Antwerp, it didn't occur to Jan Rubens to explain to her that in the Netherlands, as elsewhere, a dispute that had its theoretical origins in religion had assumed a far greater significance through the addition of questions of politi-

14

cal power. National self-interest, a sense of regional cohesiveness quite independent of the matter of faith, was a development of the post-feudal epoch; its continued and gathering strength had made an honest woman of the Reformation in many parts of Europe—especially in Scandinavia, the German principalities, Great Britain, and the Low Countries. The injunctions of John Calvin had riven his native France.

To Jan Rubens, raised in the tepid Catholic tradition of Flanders, the religious question was of very little concern. Like his father before him, he inclined to the amiable toleration inspired by the Hollander Geert Geerts who, under the fashionably Latinized name of Desiderius Erasmus, had traveled and lectured in France and England, rubbed elbows with hospitable kings and future saints, and preached a doctrine of humanism that was finally rejected by Catholic and Protestant alike as too infirm to survive in a period of accruing religious fanaticism. When Protestant-nationalist tempers in the Low Countries flared in the face of the attempts of Philip II, King of Spain and hereditary ruler of the Netherlands, to enforce the Edicts of Trent, Jan Rubens rode the fence—by conviction as well as by predilection. It truly didn't matter to him which religious faith dominated so long as all faiths were tolerated, all individuals respected.

In 1567, when Philip II's bastard half-sister, Margaret of Parma, was replaced as regent by the bloodthirsty Duke of Alba, this temperate outlook was very unhealthy. Alba, author of a reign of terror that came to be called the Spanish Fury, set about erasing all traces of Protestant heresy and opposition to the rule of that most Catholic of kings, Philip II. A year later, though emigration was prohibited and dreadfully punished, almost all Lutherans and Calvinists and Anabaptists had fled (or been slaughtered). They found refuge in Germany, Switzerland, or Britain. Though Jan Rubens remained a faithful Catholic according to his own lights, his nationalist sympathies with Prince William of Orange were no secret. The prince himself, still nominally embracing the faith of Rome, was married to the Lutheran Anne of Saxony. He was declared by Alba to be an outlaw, all his properties were confiscated; he might be killed by anyone with impunity—nay, with honor—not because he opposed the Catholic Church, but because he opposed the Spanish hegemony.

When the name of Jan Rubens appeared on a list of persons suspected of having cordial relations with the heretics—a term, under Alba's rule, that applied equally to nationalists and Protestants, the young *échevin* deemed it wise to follow his many friends and acquaintances into exile. He selected Cologne, for it was here, as Blandine Rubens had rightly explained to her younger brothers, that Anne of Saxony was installed. Jan's reasoning was that since he had been compelled to leave his native city because of his devotion to her husband's cause, he should join his court abroad.

As it proved, Prince William established no court at Cologne, or anywhere else. He had no time for the pomp and ceremony of that sort of life. He was busy at the wars, or off at the courts of the Protestant German princelings seeking funds with which to continue his battle against the Duke of Alba. The princess, however, was very much present at Cologne. Jan Rubens, who had frequently been presented to her in Antwerp, soon found himself a comfortable situation in her entourage—as her legal adviser. The ugly, self-centered, bibulous young wife of the great Orange prince had many legal problems—most of them concerned with the rights to property which had been threatened with confiscation because of her religion or her husband's rebellious activities.

Jan Rubens attended to Princess Anne's financial affairs. Within a few months of his arrival with Maria and their children at Cologne, he had become her closest confidant—and her lover. Maria Piepelinx was aware from an early date that her husband was attending to more than Anne of Saxony's estates, for he rarely performed the physical role of spouse anymore, electing, she inferred, to reserve all his powers for his mistress. Maria's opinion of this arrangement was equivocal—quite in the spirit of the age. On the one hand, she was certainly not pleased to have a rival for Jan's affection; on the other, if she

16

must have a rival, the princess was a worthy one. Further, Jan's intimacy with Prince William's wife, as long as it remained discreet, was a most useful form of protection for a family in exile in his lands.

But the law of averages caught up with the guilty couple within less than two years. By the early months of 1571, Princess Anne was noticeably pregnant, a condition she couldn't very well ascribe to the attentions of her husband—for she had refused to see him on the one occasion he had visited Cologne. The problem thus posed was an extremely delicate one for everyone concerned—for it came at a time when Prince William, though thoroughly revolted by his wife's deception and by her as an individual, had good reason to wish to avoid anything resembling a public scandal. He was trying to raise money to finance yet another military adventure against the Duke of Alba. Nevertheless, the development was not, for different causes, wholly unwelcome, for it furnished the prince with an opportunity to rid himself permanently of a woman in whom he was no longer interested. The princess was dispatched at once to the Westphalian town of Siegen to await the birth of the unwanted child. Thereafter, she was confined to the same rooms until her death, in 1577, of chronic alcoholism.

The infant girl, fruit of the illicit relationship, was turned over to foster parents and vanished from the public eye. The prince didn't follow the custom of waiting for his wife to die before remarrying. After becoming a Protestant in 1572, he ordered five prominent Calvinist theologians to declare his union with Anne of Saxony annulled. As his new bride, he took three years later the Protestant daughter of the Prince de Condé, hereditary Constable of France. Yet his marriage with Anne had produced four children, one of whom would, on balance, be a far greater man than his father; this was Prince Mauritz of Nassau, who succeeded in 1584 to the title of Stadholder of Holland and ruler of the United Provinces of the Protestant Netherlands.

Jan Rubens' fate was, for a time, much more parlous than that of his former mistress. Adultery was punishable by death,

17

and Maria Piepelinx had no reason to suppose that such a penalty wasn't to be meted out in this instance. Had her husband embraced a less important matron, it is likely that he would have been executed, according to the law. But, for the same reason that protected Anne, he too was spared. After imprisonment for more than two years in a dungeon cell of the medieval castle at Dillenburg, Jan Rubens was given a conditional release. He was made to post a bond of 6000 thalers. He must promise not to leave Siegen, and not to attend mass. He had ample grounds for imagining that he would have been left to rot in his dank cell at Dillenburg had his wife not interceded, moving heaven and earth to obtain his freedom.

She wrote letters to bishops and archbishops, and to Count Jan of Nassau, a younger brother of Prince William, entreating them to spare her husband's life and, later, to give him his release. What she contrived to convey in all her correspondence, whether with public figures or with Jan (for she knew that her letters to him would be pored over by his jailers), was a curious blending of abject remorse and veiled blackmail. She heaped upon herself a great share of the blame for his present plight, to which she alluded in the most careful terms, and allowed it to be inferred that if her husband were not freed, she wouldn't know how to explain it to her children—except, of course, by telling them the terrible, scandalous truth. Then, heaven only knew how many people would eventually be privy to the facts. No ambassador ever negotiated so strongly from a position of the most vulnerable weakness as did Maria Piepelinx. She made her point supremely well. In May of 1573, a pale, weakened Jan Rubens joined her in the house she had leased in Siegen. They commemorated this joyous occasion by creating a child, Philip, who was born the following year. Maria was faithful to her oath. She never confided her husband's true story to a mortal soul—and though rumors circulated, the facts were not unearthed until after her death.

Only after the birth of Pieter Paul, in 1577, were the Rubenses permitted to move back to Cologne, where Jan was able to resume his practice of the law. No longer was the family dependent for its livelihood on the good nature and generosity of Maria's German relations. They were still prohibited from returning to Antwerp, but their lands and other assets in the Netherlands were restored to them. Life, after almost a decade of anguish and penury, grew softer. Yet Maria was unwilling and constitutionally unable to accept the compromise of the new conditions as definitive. She wanted a total restitution of the *status quo ante,* and she labored for it with the same zeal she had earlier demonstrated in behalf of Jan's release from prison. She made frequent trips to Brussels, seat of the regency, to petition the authorities for permission to bring her family home again. Until January, 1587, these demands were rejected with monotonous regularity. It was a fitting irony that Jan Rubens should have died before her dream was realized. He would never see the great city he had so vividly and so frequently described to his young sons.

But the Antwerp evoked by their father was not the town that Philip and Pieter Paul discovered for themselves on July 1, 1587. What they found was a ghost town, its cathedral and churches gutted and pillaged, nearly half its population disappeared; its commerce, once the greatest of northern Europe, was all but throttled by the blockade of the Scheldt's estuary by the combined fleets of the Protestant Netherlanders of the United Provinces and the British. It seemed cheerless by comparison with Cologne—the more so because there was no affable Jan Rubens to carry his sons over the shock of the reality which confronted them.

Like every sizable town of the Low Countries, north or south, Antwerp had been ravaged alternatively by Catholic and Protestant vandals in approximately equal measure. It was difficult, perhaps impossible, for any but a Solomon to ascribe responsibility in suitable proportion. For both sides were guilty of abuses, some of them atrocious, committed in the interest of creed and/or loyalty to the Spanish crown or the independent nationhood of the Netherlands. The issues, which now appear reasonably clear cut, didn't seem so during the later decades of the sixteenth century, and certainly not to those who were directly involved in the prolonged conflict. Simplistic apothegms flew thick and fast in both directions, but slogans—no more then than today—were inadequate substitutes for understanding; they heated the blood without clearing the mind.

The struggle, which occupied the best brains and the best troops and the best naval fleets of western Europe, was characterized by the popes as a battle to save men's souls. By this the pontiffs meant that it was a battle to preserve the single religious and temporal authority of the Church of Rome—an integrity which had been increasingly questioned since the beginning of the century. The sparks of religious rebellion, scattered somewhat heedlessly by Luther and Calvin and Zwingli— and even by such differing Catholic personalities as Erasmus and Savonarola, had ignited grass fires all over Europe. Where monarchs had been slow to respond to the cries of alarm that emanated from the Vatican, for reasons of their own that had little or nothing to do with theology, the flames in the dry grass had set fire to great forests. So that by the middle of the present century, that medieval entity that had once been Christendom, a front unified against the incursions of the infidel that had begun in the eighth century and continued still, was disintegrating to such a degree that it could scarcely be recognized any longer.

The papacy, in its panic, invoked those powers it could still muster to strike back against the equally hellish and more insidious flames of internecine heresy. Only one great ruler answered the papal call with enthusiasm—Philip II of Spain. Some heads of state ignored the pleas altogether, for they weren't in the least unhappy to see the influence of Rome curtailed; too long had they and their predecessors watched the Church fatten herself on the tithe without contributing more than moral support to the defenses of the menaced Catholic crowns of the west.

When the Edicts of Trent were first circulated in 1564, there seemed a genuine possibility that the Counter Reformation

20

they proclaimed might succeed. There was a call for a total cleansing of the Catholic house of worship and administration, which was badly needed. Unfortunately, a thorough reform of the convents and monasteries, the parish houses and the diocesan palaces, simply couldn't be accomplished overnight. A complete generation of clerics had to die off before a total alteration could be effected, and a more foresighted pope had to ascend the throne of St. Peter—a possibility even more remote, since he must be appointed by cardinals who were very well pleased with their own positions and perquisites and wanted *their* prerogatives to remain sacrosanct, though they were perfectly willing for lesser clerical lights to be dimmed or extinguished. Time and inertia in high places were running against the spiritual monopoly that the True Church claimed but refused to support wholeheartedly. What the popes were unable or unwilling to do within the Church, they demanded that Catholic rulers achieve outside it, by force of arms and the exercise of purely secular authority. Only the Jesuits proved exceptions to clerical indifference.

In 1570, two years after Jan Rubens and his family fled from Antwerp, Pope Pius V, who prided himself on his life of poverty, assured with a single stroke of his pen the ultimate permanence of the Reformation. In that year, he circulated a bull in which he excommunicated Queen Elizabeth of England, calling her a bastard, and absolving all Britons of the obligation to accord the lady their allegiance. This interdict was not preached from parish pulpits in either Spain or France—for the kings of those two countries were seeking ties of friendship with the British queen. A copy of it did, however, reach Westminster. The infuriated Elizabeth made it limpidly clear to her many Catholic subjects (perhaps a majority of the total population of the British Isles) that if they followed the pope's advice, she would have them hanged, or worse, and would confiscate all their property.

Given the alternative of an eventual and not wholly demonstrable damnation promised as a consequence of disobedience to Rome and the immediate and quite certain scourge assured

21

by Queen Elizabeth, British Catholics forswore their religious creed in droves. Some of them, it is true, did so with marked mental reservations. Some even refused and, for reasons of state, were spared punishment. But Elizabeth's purpose was attained. The Vatican had declared spiritual war against her and been vanquished. Elizabeth's arrogant defiance of the pope's authority, like that of her father, Henry VIII, before her, had proved to all wavering rulers that whatever the ultimate price in the hereafter, a king could govern his own people in spite of all the pope, on his own, might do. It was a lesson not lost elsewhere, but one less easily put into practice on the Continent.

For Britain's insular position was chiefly responsible for her impunity. Philip II, who had done his very best to restore that nation of barbarians to the true faith by marrying Bloody Mary Tudor, daughter of the original heretic Henry VIII, would occasionally make war against Elizabeth (after proposing marriage to her), and more often threaten to. But in 1588, after the disaster that befell the Spanish Armada, he was compelled to admit defeat—something he did with infinite reluctance.

Such was not the case with the Netherlands. This territory could be reached by land—though at times the passage was hindered by hostile rulers of France and the German states. A succession of Spanish armies, under the redoubtable Duke of Alba, under Don Juan of Austria (heroic author of the victory of the Holy League over the Infidels at Lepanto in 1571), and under the Italian Alessandro Farnese, had swept into the Low Countries and sought to impose by force and terror a perfect acceptance of the Spanish authority and the Roman faith. Their failure to achieve either goal was due almost entirely to Philip's policy of unconditional surrender.

History frequently finds the spirit of nationalism to be a virtue, and thus tends to ascribe to it very miracles of heroism. So it is with accounts of the Low Countries' continuing resistance to the rule of Spain. However, as with the American rebellion against Britain two centuries later, the real issues at stake were ones of commerce and taxation. Had the Spaniards not exacted confiscatory levies from the Netherlander subjects, and had

22

they agreed to a policy of reasonable religious toleration which these people wore very naturally, the outcome of a war that lasted eighty years would probably have been reversed. Indeed, there would probably have been no war at all.

No one knew how many victims, innocent and guilty, were tortured and executed between 1567 and 1587. Alba acknowledged the loss of 12,000 soldiers during his seven-year regency —the period of the greatest violence. He claimed, on his departure, to be responsible for the deaths of 18,000 heretics. This figure didn't include the enemy troops who had perished in the conflict. Nor did it comprehend the irreparable destruction of the treasures of the Church and of private property. Three thousand Catholic churches were sacked by successive waves of Protestant and Catholic armies that comported themselves like street mobs. The methods of torture inflicted on heretics, real or merely suspected, had been initiated by the Spanish Inquisitor, Torquemada, in the previous century, and perfected by Pieter Titelman, a Netherlander.

By July 1, 1587, a good deal of the steam had gone out of the rebellion in the Low Countries. The assassination of Prince William of Orange three years before had crushed, for a time, the spirit of his followers. His son, Prince Mauritz, was yet to prove himself the brilliant successor he would eventually be. The foolhardy adventure of a British expeditionary force led by the poetic, courtly Sir Philip Sidney and the queenly favorite, the Earl of Leicester, had failed to release the Spanish grip over the northern regions, and had been abandoned in the autumn of 1586.

The United Provinces, as the Protestant maritime sector of the northern Netherlands called themselves, survived the English departure, mainly because the Spanish forces, now led by the Duke of Parma, were preoccupied with the impending attempt to invade and conquer Britain for the Church—a military operation that called for the participation of Parma's troops once the British fleet had been disposed of. The republic (for so the United Provinces were constituted, more or less on the model established by Venice and Genoa) controlled the entire Netherlands seacoast. Therefore, it controlled a large proportion of the commerce.

Amsterdam had long since replaced Antwerp as the capital of banking in northern Europe—though most of the bankers were Flemings who had emigrated during Alba's Spanish Fury. (A significant phenomenon of the era was that Philip II, who had already declared himself bankrupt once in 1571, and would repeat the process twice more before his death in 1598, depended heavily on the very Flemish financiers his regents were persecuting—nor was he the only Catholic monarch to make use of Protestant gold.) Under the ingenious political guidance of Jan van Oldenbarneveldt and the growing military wisdom of young Prince Mauritz, a state of stalemated equilibrium had been reached. The Spaniards couldn't suppress the republic, though they would keep trying for another sixty years. The republic couldn't eject the Spanish from all of the Netherlands, but they would keep trying and, after sixty years, would succeed—but by treaty, not by war.

Antwerp was caught in the middle of this seemingly endless conflict. When the Rubenses resumed possession of the Piepelinx family house in the city's most fashionable square, the Meir, in the summer of 1587, it appeared probable that the largest town in Flanders would never again enjoy its cultural and financial preeminence. Nevertheless, because man is Sisyphus, the *Anversois* were rebuilding and refurbishing with just the same degree of fervor they had given only a few years before to the destruction of their city.

To young Pieter Paul Rubens, the vestiges of devastation to be seen at every hand were at once alarming and exciting. He discovered in himself a quality he had not been aware of, a capacity to adapt easily to new circumstances, new surroundings. As the family belongings were carried into a strange house in a strange, desolate town, Pieter Paul became an *Anversois*, a Fleming. He found that he liked the idea of novelty, that he was not—as are most children—a reactionary. He remembered everything about Cologne, especially treasuring memories of his father's laughter; but here, in Antwerp, he felt he was be-

24

coming a new person to be shaped by the new circumstances he encountered.

When he tried to explain this sensation to his brother Philip, he met a stone wall of incomprehension. Philip was stolid in his personality, endowed with none of Pieter Paul's mercurial flights of feeling. His intelligence, which was considerable, inclined itself to method, not to inspiration. He was, at thirteen, what Pieter Paul thought he would always be—reliable, tenacious, but very sparing of his shows of emotion. Philip found it difficult to take seriously much of what his younger brother said to him. The difference in age between thirteen and ten was an enormous gulf. Worse, he suspected his brother of being frivolous—a description of him he had heard Maria Piepelinx utter more than once when referring to Pieter Paul. "He's just like his father," she was wont to observe. It was a kind of curse, in the opinion of anyone who took a poor view of frivolity.

The boy always met this accusation with a strong denial— yet, to himself, he conceded that it had a touch of the truth in it. He enjoyed laughter, and couldn't believe, no matter what his elders told him, that a love of joy was evidence of a love of folly. Was he not, after all, as dutiful and diligent as Philip in the fulfillment of the few obligations assigned to him? Did he not excel in his lessons? Was he not neat, respectful, honest? What the older members of his family took for mockery in his manner was, in reality, ebullience.

Pieter Paul was imbued with an energy that threatened to defy exhaustion. And to accompany this apparently boundless power, he rejoiced in an eagerness, a quickness of understanding, a passion for knowledge—as well as for novelty. Until his arrival in Antwerp, he had thought this zeal confined to learning—but now he understood that it was, like his energy, not confined at all. When he entered the room of the house in the Meir that Maria told him was to be his, he felt certain that one day he was going to move the earth—not out of ambition for wealth or power, but simply because he was so strong, so energetic, so filled with a passion for life, and because, like his mother, he sensed that he was invincible.

There wasn't a trace of mystery or mysticism in this conviction. It was rather that he appreciated, intuitively, the possession of a force that couldn't be contained—one that he had no desire to contain. When he tried to tell his brother about this exciting discovery, Philip turned away with a sigh of mock despair. "You'll run and you'll run, Pieter Paul, and all you'll finally do is to fall on your face, like papa." He and Philip were the tortoise and the hare. Pieter Paul had always doubted the accuracy of the fable and the lucidity of the moral; the race was almost always to the quick. All the tortoise could do was stop and hide within himself.

In addition to the house in the Meir, Maria Piepelinx was the proprietor of a number of other buildings in Antwerp. It was the rents from these holdings and the dwindling income from participation in a number of mercantile and banking ventures, which she had inherited from her father and husband, that were to support her and the children in their new life. From the moment of their arrival, Maria knew what she must do for her offspring; it was simply a question of management. And she was very good at that. She soon found Jan-Baptiste a wife whose dowry would keep them from utter destitution. She could anticipate nothing better for him, for he expected nothing better for himself; he was the least likely of her children. A husband for Blandine was less easily discovered—but she was certain that persistence would have its eventual reward. She persisted.

For the two younger boys, there had first to be further schooling. Though other masters offered education in Antwerp at less exorbitant rates, none was so highly considered by the right people as Rombaut Verdonck, an amiable despot who governed his classes as he governed his family of thirteen children, with generosity and a benign good humor. His combined home and school were near the cemetery of Notre Dame, a short walk from the Meir. There, each day, Philip and Pieter Paul absorbed with different but comparable ease Verdonck's burden of the classic tongues, of mathematics, philosophy, history, and

26

French—the language affected by the Catholic nobles of Flanders, who regarded Flemish as fit only for the peasants.

Philip made a friend, Balthasar Moerentorf (whose father, following the style of the epoch, had assumed the Latinized name of Moretus). Balthasar was a brilliant cripple; his whole right side was paralyzed. He dragged himself about with the aid of a crutch and was the object of derision to all his schoolmates, except for the newly arrived brothers Rubens who, because they were strangers, shared poor Balthasar's exclusion. Philip respected the handicapped boy for his dogged triumph over this curse of the flesh. He admired his good mind and his gentle temperament. But Pieter Paul, who was three years younger, became Balthasar's slave. This relationship was healthy for both of them—because Balthasar had given love all his life and received very little in return, and because Pieter Paul, so sure of himself, felt no ignominy in giving his affection unstintingly to this brave, soft-spoken boy.

It was not Balthasar's malady that Pieter Paul found so attractive at first; it was his aroma. The young Moretus carried with him from his home each day the distinctive odor of printer's ink. His grandfather was Christophe Plantin, the greatest printer of his day in all of Europe. Balthasar had inherited the family passion for everything connected with the comparatively new process of printing from movable type. When the two Rubens boys were first admitted to Maître Verdonck's classes and met Balthasar, both were immediately aware of the smell the rather pathetic-looking cripple carried around with him. Philip was too polite to ask its source. Pieter Paul had no such compunction. When he discovered that the young Moretus lived over a printing establishment, he begged to be shown it. The older boy, touched and amused by his new friend's almost feverish excitement, at once assented.

From that moment, during his first week with Verdonck, through the next three years, Pieter Paul Rubens passed an hour or two of every school day in the printing house of Christophe Plantin. The proprietor was well into his sixties, a

27

man of almost ethereal frailty now, who produced volumes of exquisite beauty from type of his own design, manufactured in his own small foundry, on paper he had himself developed, bound by his own craftsmen. The subjects of most of these works (except for those distributed by Maître Verdonck) were mainly scholarly, all in Latin, and of little interest to a boy just on the threshold of adolescence. But the wonderful toolwork of the vellum bindings, the etched or woodcut frontispieces, title pages, and illustrations were objects very nearly of devotion.

Old Plantin and his son-in-law Jan Moretus were moved both by Pieter Paul's affection for the wounded Balthasar and by his boundless enthusiasm for print. When the founder of the great and celebrated firm died, in 1589, Moretus gave Balthasar a set of printed illustrations to present to Pieter Paul in memory of Christophe Plantin, to whom he had brought great joy. The joy, of course, was mutual. In the workshops of Plantin, Pieter Paul Rubens discovered a corner of himself which, he afterward believed, he might not otherwise have discerned until too late—a concern and later a love for art. Not since the death of his father had the boy been so distressed as he was to learn that Christophe Plantin had died. He took a pained little pleasure in detecting, as he paid his final respects before the old man's coffin, the smell of printer's ink.

The end of the school term in the summer of 1590 marked the conclusion of Pieter Paul Rubens' formal education in the liberal arts. Maria Piepelinx's decision to withdraw him from Maître Verdonck's classes was not an impulsive one. Like everything she did for her children, it was for reasons she considered good and practical. After a search that had lasted for three years, she had found a husband for Blandine—which was no small achievement, given the fact that her daughter was, by the standards of the time, getting pretty long in the tooth for marriage. Better still, the prospective bridegroom was a young nobleman, Siméon du Parcq, with an inherited income that was modest but sufficient; he was, best of all, willing to wait for his wife's dowry until economic conditions improved in the Low Countries—though he demanded that interest be paid until the sum was finally handed over. Siméon du Parcq was just as hard-headed in the business of marriage contracts as was Maria.

The time had come for Philip to leave Antwerp for Louvain, at whose university he would, according to his mother's plan, pursue his study of the law and, thereafter, emulate his father's career—become an *échevin*, make a handsome marriage, and carry on the Rubens tradition, or at least that portion of the tradition considered proper. Blandine's wedding and Philip's higher education put stern demands on Maria Piepelinx's material resources. This meant that she must dispose of Pieter Paul, the youngest (and therefore the least important) of her sons, as best she could. She didn't consult him in the matter. She simply announced to him, one morning in September, that he was leaving the next morning for the castle of the Countess de Lalaing, widow of a governor of Antwerp, at Audenarde, on the outskirts of the city. There he would serve as her page.

Pieter Paul stared at his mother in disbelief. "A *page*, mama?"

"To improve your manners. You're much too brusque."

"I want to be an artist."

It was Maria's turn to be shaken. "To work with your *hands?*"

The boy shrugged. "*Mijnheer* Moretus does it. Balthasar will do it. What's wrong with it?"

"Gentlemen do not work with their hands," she said.

"Wasn't papa's papa an apothecary?"

"He *dispensed*. He was a merchant. It's not the same thing. Besides, there's never been a painter in my family or your father's."

Pieter Paul didn't press the issue. He knew his mother's tone well enough to recognize that, for the time being, the subject was closed. There was another reason for his silence. The prospect of living in a castle, in however lowly a situation, rather intrigued him. It had not been any sort of innate snobbishness that caused him to balk at Maria's dictum; it had been surprise. He knew the countess remotely, remembered that she had been an occasional guest of his parents at the house in Cologne, and had heard of her return to Antwerp at about the same time that the Rubenses had made the journey. But beyond these scraps of information, Pieter Paul was in ignorance of what lay in store.

Maria had of course discussed her youngest son's future with the countess on several recent occasions, repeating the complaint so often heard at home. "He's so like poor Jan. I don't know what's to become of him." It was the noblewoman who suggested that the boy be sent to her. It was difficult, during these tiresome times, to find suitable, reliable help. Pieter Paul could attend her and, in return, learn the manners his mother said he lacked. "Though heaven knows," the old countess was constrained to add, "if he's so like your dear Jan, I can't imagine what you have to worry about."

Maria Piepelinx didn't think an honest explanation in order. But she had, in fairness to her son, to admit to herself that as yet, Pieter Paul had shown no signs of inheriting his father's ardent interest in women. He was a little young for that. "He's too frivolous," she told the countess. "This is no time for anyone to be frivolous."

There were few aristocrats in all of Flanders with a more convincing claim than that of the Countess de Lalaing to any greatness that could be transmitted through the genes. Her masculine ancestors had been the Counts de Ligne, leading Flemish landowners and loyal Catholics. As a young matron, she had been presented to the promiscuous, gouty emperor Charles V, and had frequented his court in Brussels whenever that august personage saw fit to grace the city with his presence. During her late husband's tenure as governor of Antwerp, she had met at various times most of the leading figures of Europe —had even made her obeisances to the dour, much-married Philip II of Spain.

Despite their differences of age and station, she and Maria Piepelinx had much in common—notably a quality of iron determination that is so often found in widows who must fend for themselves. They got on well. The dowager countess was something of a bully, and like most bullies, she respected only those whom she was unable to intimidate. No one intimidated Maria Piepelinx. This was the basis of their friendship.

When Pieter Paul rode by himself in the countess' coach the short distance to Audenarde, just beyond the outer fortifications of Antwerp, where the old lady's battlemented castle stood, he tried to imagine what his new life would be like. But imagination was beggared by reality. He was ushered at once into the rather creaky and decrepit presence of his new mistress. He made an ungainly bow, and then gazed directly into her milky blue eyes—something he soon learned was thought uncommonly rude. Before she elected to speak, the lad took in the sight of her—an ancient, fragile body that seemed held together by a dress of dark brocaded silk so stiff that it could probably stand without support. She wore a tall, broad wimple of black wool, whose trailing bands were wrapped about her throat to protect it against the terrible drafts that coursed through the rooms and halls of the castle—hardly impeded by the thick stone walls and lead-mullioned windows. It was difficult, because she was seated on a low chair, to determine her height—and Pieter Paul's recollection of her in Cologne was distorted by the fact that, at the time, he had been much smaller than he now was. He remembered her as tall, but in fact, she was shorter than his fierce little mother.

Most remarkable about the countess were her face and hands —the skin wrinkled and ashen, the only trace of color furnished by bulging veins. The bent fingers were studded with rings—garnet, onyx, and amber stones, crudely cut, clutched by claws of gold. Her eyes, for all their cloudiness, were quick— though her range of vision was limited. Only when she finally spoke to him did he remark that she had lost most of her teeth. "Well, well," she said in a grating bronchitic voice. "You certainly *look* like your father. Yes, I think you'll do very nicely."

"Do *what*, madame?"

The old eyes widened with interest, then compressed themselves into a travesty of a smile. "What I tell you to do. That's what you're here for, isn't it?"

"I'm here, madame, because my mother has sent me to you."

31

"Just so," she murmured musingly. "And she wants you to learn how to behave like a gentleman. How do you feel about that?"

"I suppose it can do me no harm, madame."

The old woman started to chuckle, and then choked over her laughter. Pieter Paul hastened to her side and gently patted her bent old back. "Thank you, my son," she said when she had quite recovered. "Your candor does you credit. But a gentleman tries to say what he thinks his listener would like to hear." She paused, staring up at him with as much affection as her shattered features could register. "That is your first lesson."

"A gentleman must learn to lie, then, madame?"

"He learns to be sparing of the truth."

"Why should that be? Isn't it contrary to the teachings of Our Lord?"

"Our Lord, young man, was no gentleman. That's why they crucified him."

In the weeks that followed this first encounter, Pieter Paul came to love the old countess as he would an eccentric grandmother. For all that she railed against his propensity for excessive candor, she was herself the most candid of mortals. When he tactlessly commented to that effect, she brought him up sharply. "I'm too old to care what people say of me or think of me. But for you it's different. You're just beginning your life. Such things as the good opinion of others are important to you. Only people who have nothing to lose can afford to discard hypocrisy altogether. Isn't that why we always believe the confessions of those who think they're about to die?"

It was from the countess that Pieter Paul heard the first more or less dispassionate, though not disinterested, account of the troubles that had for so long beset the Netherlands. She was no intellectual, but in her cranky way, she possessed keen perceptions, especially of human frailty and folly. Few great personalities of her age escaped unscathed in her narrative. She was a brilliant gossip, and could hold the boy's attention for at least an hour at a sitting—something Maître Verdonck had rarely managed—without detecting the first signal of restlessness. Unlike Verdonck, the countess always ceased to speak when she observed that she was beginning to bore her listener. It was a lesson the lad learned from her without being aware of it.

The countess perceived as well, after he had been in her company for a few months, that Pieter Paul was wasting his time. She enjoyed a new guest in her house, particularly so handsome a youth whose charm and open eagerness and gentleness would, she was certain, take him almost anywhere he chose to go. But, as she explained to Maria Piepelinx, whom she summoned to her side, "The boy has to be on his way."

"On his way *where*, madame," asked Pieter Paul's mother somewhat querulously. "He says he wants to be an artist. Where is *that*, for any gentleman?"

The countess was scornful. "You insist that he be a gentleman, a toady of the court?"

"I certainly don't want him to be a tradesman."

"And if he wants nothing else? You want him to be like your Jan-Baptiste, a parasite, a cipher?" The old lady silenced herself, then shook her head slowly. "No, that's unjust, Maria. Forgive me. Your Pieter Paul is incapable of becoming a cipher. He's a man already, in a way. That's why he has to leave me, to get on with life, not to stay cooped up here with a vain, demanding old woman."

"Get on with what?" Maria persisted.

"With *art*, in heaven's name. If that's what he wants, let him have it."

The mother sighed. "It's all Jan's fault. What a foolish, frivolous notion."

The countess wagged an arthritic finger at the younger woman. "You're absolutely obsessed with that idea. Do you realize that? Pieter Paul has been with me for five months. I've watched him very carefully. He does have his moments of silliness. What child of his age doesn't? But he has many more moments of seriousness, of purposefulness. Have you seen his drawings?"

"He's not offered to show them to me," said Maria, smarting a little under this inquisition.

33

"Can you blame him? You know very well what you'd say. You've formed the wrong conclusions about him, Maria. You must think about him again, look at him some more. He's not at all what you take him for. Believe me."

"I only want what's best for him."

The old woman snorted. "Liar. You only want what you think is best for the impression you'd like the entire Rubens family to create. Maria, my dear, you're a snob. You can't afford that."

"I can't afford to have a second son who's a failure."

"*I* can."

"That's easy for you to say, madame. It's not your responsibility. You don't have to find the money for such nonsense," said Maria with some asperity.

"You're not following me," the countess replied calmly. "I mean, I'd be willing to help."

"But why?"

"Because I've learned to love your son, and because I think he has the makings of a very great man, perhaps even a hero."

Maria stared in wonder. "A hero? Little Pieter Paul? He's no more a hero than poor Jan."

"Much more. You just won't see."

"I can't see."

"You'll not even try. Let me help you. Let me help *him*. Find an artist who's willing to teach him. I'll provide the funds as long as they're needed."

"You believe in him that much?"

"More. I believe in him absolutely."

"Oh, madame, I only wish I had half of your faith in him."

"That's of no importance, Maria. Pieter Paul has faith in himself. That's what matters."

When he learned of the countess' handsome offer, Pieter Paul's self-confidence faltered. His months in the castle had so altered his outlook that he no longer knew who he was, who he wanted to be. He had made drawings of members of her household that had amused his patroness. *Her* pleasure gave *him* pleasure. But art as a career? He wasn't sure any longer. It wasn't the glamour of existence under the countess' aegis that had changed him; it was she herself. He had told her, several times, of his desire to become an artist. She had put the question to him, and his reply had been automatic; he could think of no other. But now, when the possibility was presented, he was suddenly indecisive. He felt that he must tell her of his misgivings. They failed to perturb her. But then, nothing could perturb her. "You'll never know unless you try."

"And if I should fail?"

"You'll not fail, Pieter Paul. I've never met anyone, and I've met *everyone*, less likely to fail at anything than you. You may find it's not what you want for yourself. But that isn't failure. That's discovery. No discovery of that sort can be a failure."

"And what if I *should* find that it's not what I want, madame?"

"You're like a horse that's trying to leap two sets of fences at the same time."

"But if I don't like it . . ."

"Then you'll not like it. It will have cost you a little time and me a little money. Each of us can spare that much."

Adam van Noort, in the early months of 1591 when Maria Piepelinx was seeking a place for her youngest son, was the most noteworthy painter in Antwerp, a leader of the city's Guild of Saint Luke (the local academy of fine arts), and reputed to be a skillful instructor. In a period when art and architecture in the Flemish town were still recovering but slowly from the depredations inflicted by the Spanish Fury and the Protestant counterblows, he stood out in a crowd that was relatively thin, even insignificant.

Himself a Catholic exile from Amersfoort in the Calvinist north of the Netherlands, he had come to Antwerp in the same year that the Rubenses had returned from Cologne. He found demand for his somewhat limited range of painting chiefly from the local clergy and from the independent Jesuits, those soldiers of Christ who were seeking, through alternative offerings of the carrot of joy and the stick of orthodoxy, to woo a wavering flock back into the arms of the True Church.

Van Noort had learned his craft originally from his father, and pursued his studies in Italy, considered the fountainhead of all wisdom in the arts and letters. If he was no better than a reasonably competent painter of portraits and landscapes and historical allegories, there was no one in the Antwerp of that year to prove him so.

When Maria Piepelinx dangled before him the temptation of the Countess de Lalaing's gold, van Noort never hesitated—even though the prepossessing little widow warned him that Pieter Paul was wholly untried, that so far as she was aware the only pictures he had ever drawn were of members of the countess' household and of figures he had found on the sculptured tombs of the Lalaing chapel at Audenarde.

"Madame," he announced with a grandiloquent gesture he had acquired in Rome, "I can teach an intelligent dog how to paint pictures." Maria assured him that her son was no dog. The artist, however, was paying no attention. He was thinking of the overdue bills he could pay with the fees he was to receive from his new pupil's patroness.

Pieter Paul liked Adam van Noort from the very beginning. Only in later years, however, long after he had left the man's studio, did he understand why they got along so well. It was because van Noort, in spite of his extravagant physical mannerisms, was without the least pomposity about himself, his position, or his profession. He regarded painting as a craft, a trade. "It's like learning to make boots or build houses," he told the boy on his first day with him. "The first thing you must do is understand the nature and properties of the materials you're going to be working with. Only when you've grasped those essential facts can you learn how to make use of them. That means, my child, that you'll spend the next twelve months grinding my colors, preparing my panels and canvases and," he added, after the slightest hesitation, "keeping my floors clean."

He was as good as his word. In the first year of his training under van Noort, Pieter Paul was required to learn only the function of the mortar and pestle, the palette knife, and the broom. His only contact with brushes occurred when he cleaned them. It was drudgery, purely and simply, not at all the sort of labor designed to attract anyone to art—for it had so little to do with art. And this was precisely van Noort's intent. "If, after a year of this," he explained to Maria, and later to the illustrious Countess de Lalaing when she magnanimously condescended to visit his studio, "the boy is still interested in becoming a painter, then I shall teach him."

Van Noort erred where the countess had not. He devoted very little of his time or thought to the youth in his charge during that first year of their association. He was therefore unaware that his every move was closely observed by Pieter Paul, was remembered and emulated to the best of his ability. The apprentice, whenever he was left to himself, duplicated his master's efforts. He began by copying van Noort's pencil and pen sketches. After several months, he dared even to make small watercolor or oil replicas of the artist's studies.

So what was meant to be a year of drudgery turned out to be one of discovery and growth; there was not a moment of boredom in it, for no experience could bore a boy who was constantly on the alert. When he heard his sister's lament that married life was a bore, Pieter Paul exclaimed incredulously, "How is it possible, Blandine? It's all new. Every day brings something new." He had no idea, at fourteen, that he was especially endowed by God with the greatest of all human resources—the capacity to amuse himself. Every door he came upon seemed to open outward. He was not in the least introspective. Nor did he ever feel hurried, ever lose patience.

Maria Piepelinx was perplexed by her youngest son. She saw him only occasionally, but whenever they were together, she felt herself in the presence of someone she knew at the same time terribly well and not at all. She complained of this to the countess—for by now Maria had come to regard the countess as Pieter Paul's exegete. The old lady assured her that the boy wasn't reserved, as his mother claimed him, for in his conversation with his protectress he was ever full of enthusiasm, usually over trifles. Nor was it, as Maria accused herself, that she was blind. Rather, explained the countess, was it that she was still looking for Pieter Paul in the wrong place—in her own mind rather than in his physical and intellectual presence. "You're still trying to find Jan in Pieter Paul. He's not there."

What baffled Maria most was that her son seemed so contented with his life in van Noort's studio. She had been certain that after a few months of hard labor, he would beg to be allowed to return home, or to the countess' drafty castle. *She,* she protested, would have been driven to distraction by so monotonous an existence. How could a child of hers, one whom the countess insisted on describing as "brilliant," find the onerous tasks assigned by van Noort endlessly attractive? The old lady was the first to confess that *she* could offer no explanation for it either.

Of importance, however, was Pieter Paul's own reaction to such questions. He never posed them to himself. The countess was wise enough to keep her peace. To his mother's frequent and strangely plaintive interrogation, he confined himself to a superficial observation: "I enjoy what I'm learning." This was not merely a diplomatic turning aside of Maria's query. The verb he selected was *le mot juste.* He certainly didn't *love* the life. He knew very well that he wouldn't die if, tomorrow, he was informed that he could no longer study with van Noort, that the possibility of his becoming a painter had been forever eliminated.

In the years since he had first told his mother that he wanted art for a career, he had learned this much about himself—that there was, in fact, nothing of life that didn't interest him at least a little bit. He was, van Noort said when he finally came across, by chance, the boy's little treasure of sketches and paintings, "a born painter." But Pieter Paul knew this wasn't true. He was a born observer. He could as easily become a priest, a lawyer, a carpenter, a herdsman—anything, except a soldier. For there was no hatred in him; he was sure he could never bring himself to kill. Beyond this single restriction, he felt he could do anything, learn anything. If he was particularly well suited, temperamentally and technically, to art, it was because he was so ceaselessly observant, so consciously a mimic, so hospitable to novelty, so quick to note what was new or odd in objects or actions or persons that were otherwise familiar to him.

Adam van Noort considered Pieter Paul's response to his compliment perverse. "I call you a born painter, and you merely hunch up your shoulders. What kind of thing is that?"

The lad shrugged again. "You taught me."

"I didn't teach you. You peeked."

"That wasn't fair?"

The heavyset painter tugged at his coarse, dark beard and chortled. "You got more than your countess paid for. *That* wasn't fair."

What van Noort really considered unfair was Pieter Paul Rubens, the prodigy. The incontrovertible fact was rendered more intolerable by the pupil's bland acceptance of it—as if there were nothing remarkable about being able to perform, after a year's exposure and without formal instruction, tasks that lesser creatures, like Adam van Noort, for example, had managed only after years of application. It was infuriating. It was unfair. Yet the master contained his feelings of injured remorse, for it was very difficult to be angry with a boy who offered no offense—apart from the totally unwitting offense that the pedestrian discovers in the presence of a man on horseback. Pieter Paul never pressed to learn more rapidly than van Noort chose to teach him. He never suggested that one day he would be a far greater artist than his present master—though both of them knew this very well.

Resent it though he certainly did, van Noort also knew that the day must come when he would have to say to Pieter Paul, "There, little one. I've taught you all I can. You'll have to go somewhere else now." The moment arrived in the late spring of

1594, shortly before the youth's seventeenth birthday. By then, the reputation of Adam van Noort had been eclipsed by the appearance in Antwerp of Octave van Veen—whose pupil Pieter Paul Rubens soon became.

During the summer that separated his departure from van Noort's tutelage and his entering the studio of van Veen, Pieter Paul enjoyed a rare holiday. Philip and Balthasar Moretus were home from their studies at Louvain, the older brother filled to bursting point with his achievements at the university, where he had received most of the highest honors. The crippled Balthasar, who had done nearly as well, saw no need to commend himself to a friend who, he knew, loved him without regard to his accomplishments or failures. Pieter Paul kept informally to his craft through the warm, long days of the summer by portraying his mother, his sister and her first baby, his brother, Balthasar, and the aged Countess de Lalaing.

He also had a chance to learn what had been happening in the world, events to which he had paid little attention during his four years with van Noort—for the great affairs of Europe were not a subject to which his former master often addressed himself, except to complain that the high rate of taxation discouraged potential patrons of the arts.

The most significant developments had been the brilliant culmination of Prince Mauritz's four-year military campaign against the forces of Philip II. The young stadholder had gained for the United Provinces most of the territories whose populations were predominantly Protestant. The Duke of Parma had died early in 1592, to be replaced as regent by the Archduke Ernest of Austria, who was now doing his best to maintain a most precarious tranquillity—a condition that was neither quite peace nor quite war. The archduke was, according to those who said they were close to him, not in the most robust health.

If one didn't seek to peer too deeply beneath the surface of Europe's ostensible calm, one might have been pardoned for believing that out of sheer exhaustion and financial depletion, the great rulers of France, Britain, and Spain were prepared, without actually saying so aloud, to accept not only the Reformation as a *fait accompli* from which there was to be no turning back but had agreed tacitly to settle for the present distribution of power on the Continent as well.

To the inquisitive, however, it was evident that there were stirrings, within certain national boundaries, that would soon cause more serious eruptions. The greatest single problem of the moment was France. In 1589, Henri de Navarre had become that country's king—though he had been born and raised a Huguenot. He remained unconsecrated because the Bishop of Reims, who alone had by tradition the right to proclaim a king by God's grace and in God's name, had quite understandably evinced reluctance so to declare an avowed heretic. In 1593, after four years of spasmodic civil and international war, Henri IV—far more interested in women and power than in theological questions—decided that Paris was worth a mass. He renounced his former faith; early in 1594, he was officially crowned before the high altar of the magnificent cathedral at Reims.

Nevertheless, the Low Countries were enjoying, because of the interest which had been focused on France, a period of comparative peace. With Philip II's waning powers of attention directed at his nearest neighbor, the gentle Erasmian tolerance of the Netherlands Catholics, which had flourished during the era prior to the publication of the Edicts of Trent, returned. It was reciprocated in kind by the well-disciplined ranks of Protestants of the United Provinces, in the higher interest of their mutual economy. The port of Antwerp was still blockaded; but slowly, commerce was increasing. This, in conjunction with the Church's efforts to restore the buildings and furnishings destroyed or desecrated during the long religious strife, made the *Anversois* hope for better times.

There could hardly have been two personalities more different from each other than Adam van Noort and Octave van Veen, Pieter Paul's new master. In his late thirties now, van

41

Veen had come to Antwerp in 1592, in the entourage of the Archduke Ernest, the new regent, whom he had once served as a page. Born in Protestant Leyden of a father who was an ardent supporter of the cause of Philip II—in a region where the very name of that king was anathema—he had fled first to Antwerp and then to Liège. But his life had been transfigured by a stay in Rome, where for five years he had been a pupil of the immensely popular Federigo Zuccaro, whose boasts were that he had once been commissioned to complete an unfinished painting by Michelangelo, that he had decorated the dome of the church of Santa Maria del Fiore in the Eternal City, and that Philip II had summoned him to Spain to make paintings for the Escorial.

Octave van Veen became Octavius Vaenius, and with his Latinized name he acquired a dense veneer of Italianate culture —in his style of work and in his manner. His affectations were almost too numerous to be catalogued. He claimed nobility because of a remote and illegitimate descent from Jean II, Duke of Brabant. He was proud of his skill and knowledge of the military arts and sciences, letting it be known that he had once been an adviser on fortifications and the placement of artillery to Alessandro Farnese during his unsuccessful campaign to reduce the Protestant resistance in the Low Countries. He was so sure of his command of classical Latin that he composed (and often read aloud) heroic verse in that tongue. He was, in his own opinion at any rate, a "Renaissance man," and he often compared his various interests and achievements to those of Michelangelo and Leonardo.

In September, Pieter Paul presented himself for the first time at the door of van Veen's studio in the Meir, almost directly opposite his mother's house on that great, beautiful square. The servant who confronted him was, in the manner of domestics, every bit as lofty as her employer, a hulking, somewhat surly woman in her forties. The visitor was brusquely informed that the master could not be disturbed, that Pieter Paul would have to make a special appointment. Not a bit flustered at finding himself thus put off, the youth handed her letters of introduction from Adam van Noort and the Countess de Lalaing and requested that Maître van Veen let him know when it would be convenient to receive him. Then he turned abruptly about and returned to his house across the Meir.

Pieter Paul had barely time to recount to his mother and Philip, much to their amusement, the cool reception with which he had just been greeted when one of Maria Piepelinx's servants appeared in the doorway of her sitting room to announce a visitor—"Maître Octavius Vaenius." A foppish, overstuffed figure with meticulously groomed hair, mustache, and beard, fairly burst into the room as soon as he was given leave, trailing on the floor a broad-brimmed hat with a long peacock feather which dangled from his left hand. He bowed in an egregiously courtly fashion to Maria, gave Pieter Paul the curtest of nods, and addressed himself with regretful graciousness to Philip. "My *dear* young man, I must ask you to forgive me, or rather to forgive my woman. She's only a peasant. She can't tell the difference yet between tradesmen and the gentry. I'm so very sorry to have inconvenienced you."

There was a moment of dead silence. Philip stared at van Veen with all the evidences of distaste the arrogant intellectual feels for the pretentious fool. "I believe," he drawled at last, "that you're mistaking me for my younger brother." He pointed to Pieter Paul.

Van Veen looked as if he had been stabbed. An expression of terrible anguish clouded his agile features as he turned his impeccable head very slowly, and with obvious dismay, toward Pieter Paul. "*You* are this cynosure the dear countess writes of so glowingly?" he asked with patent incredulity.

The youth nodded, trying to repress his laughter. "I don't know what she wrote of me, *maître,* but I *am* Pieter Paul Rubens."

It took the artist a long time to regain his composure. To be made a fool of twice in the same hour was plainly not an experience he relished, especially in the presence of well-connected strangers. "But you're so young," he said feebly, "to have had so much experience."

43

"I'm seventeen, *maître*," said Pieter Paul evenly. "Only women like to be told they look younger than they really are," he added softly, seeming to belie the malice of his words. He recalled the countess' admonition: "If you want to insult a man mortally, you have only to correct him, quietly, in public."

This gratuitous observation stunned the vulnerable van Veen. It surprised Philip, who had never before heard his brother speak harshly to an adult. But it was Maria Piepelinx who was most stirred. Pieter Paul had invested four years of his life; the Countess de Lalaing had invested a considerable sum of money in her son's career. That Pieter Paul should put all that in jeopardy with a remark so thoughtless seemed to her little less than criminal. "Apologize," she told him sharply.

"There is no need, my dear lady," said van Veen. "Actually, it was fair comment, and very witty."

"It was rude, *maître*," retorted Maria. "Pieter Paul knows better."

The artist smiled obliquely at Pieter Paul, his expression half angry, half admiring. "But exactly," he muttered.

"Apologize," repeated Maria.

"I apologize, *maître*," said Pieter Paul. But there was no regret in his tone.

"I think," van Veen said hastily, "that we've exhausted the possibilities of this line of conversation. Shall we address ourselves to the matter in the letters?"

An arrangement was rapidly agreed to. Pieter Paul would enter the master's studio as an apprentice-assistant, with a view to preparing him for admission to membership in the Guild of Saint Luke when he reached the age of twenty-one. As soon as van Veen left, Maria scolded her younger son for his impoliteness. But, unexpectedly, Philip came to his defense. "You did well, brother. His bladder needed puncturing."

Pieter Paul's initial and somewhat bruising encounter with Octave van Veen was entirely fortuitous. Though he hadn't planned it, the youth thereby established himself in the mind

44

of his new master as a person, a most singular individual, not merely an additional pupil whose main importance lay in a friendship with a rich and powerful aristocrat. The veiled hostility that had denoted their meeting didn't persist—but their mutual recollection of it did, and this served Pieter Paul well from time to time. He became the only apprentice in van Veen's studio to whom the master never tried to condescend, for he would never risk being wounded once again by the adolescent's precocious tongue.

Van Veen was startled and more than slightly awed by the boy's remarkable proficiency in the crafts of drawing and painting. Pieter Paul handled pen, pencil, and brush with most uncommon facility—by which, as he explained in terms most carefully couched to avoid any hint of reproval, he meant the style of work now fashionable in Rome—which was the style affected by the contemporary artists of Antwerp. Van Veen was himself an accomplished craftsman in that mode. His portraits, his landscapes, his paintings of religious themes were models of studied detachment—rather icy replicas of visions that had nothing whatever to do with Flanders. The jagged peaks, the narrow green valleys that were features of his canvases were scenes garnered from his travels in Italy; there was nothing in the flat Flemish countryside that resembled them.

This "Romanism" of van Veen's was an attribute that Pieter Paul greatly admired. From the master's reiterated dictum to all of his pupils that only in Italy could one fully comprehend the wonders of Raphael and Michelangelo, the young man gradually concluded that he must, somehow, some day, make a pilgrimage to Rome to see the masterpieces of which only copies existed in the Low Countries.

That so great a project could be realized, if it *could* ever be realized, only in the remotest future failed to dampen Pieter Paul's ardor. He knew very well how to wait, and he knew how to profit from the present. Perhaps the greatest lesson he learned from van Veen was one that had nothing to do with art. He learned to be skeptical. For no one so important as van Veen claimed to think himself would settle for a second-rate

45

existence and reputation—which was what a career in Antwerp in this final decade of the sixteenth century represented. Thus did the youth first discern that his master was not what he boasted of being; if he were, he would be in Rome or Madrid or Paris, not in an Antwerp still licking her wounds. The Countess de Lalaing had schooled her protégé in the art of posing the probing question, reminding him that where life and men were concerned, doubt was the only sound first position to assume. But until his exposure over a long period to van Veen, he had failed to make much sense out of his patroness' cynical advice; now he understood it perfectly.

Octavius Vaenius wasn't entirely a windbag. There was usually just enough truth in many of his claims to give them a certain dull luster. When the Archduke Ernest died, the year after Pieter Paul entered the artist's studio, van Veen was commissioned by the court at Brussels to design and supervise the construction of funerary ornament to decorate the principal streets and squares of Antwerp to commemorate the event. There was great excitement in his workshop as these traditional arches of painted wood and black crepe were assembled and adorned with portraits of the departed regent.

Van Veen's connection with the previous governor of the Spanish Netherlands gave him an *entrée* to his successor, the Archduke Albrecht of Austria, a former cardinal who had been released from his vows to marry the Infanta Isabel, younger sister of Philip II; their triumphal entry into Antwerp, in 1596, was the occasion for a further commission to see to the decoration of the city—this time in bright colors, to signify the joy this moment was intended to provoke.

The joy, at first, was less than spontaneous. Save for the most ardent, single-minded Catholics who dwelt in the portion of the Low Countries that the new regents would jointly and nominally rule, the population looked on them with instinctive apprehension—as they must on any official representative of the heavy-handed king of Spain. Philip II's instructions to his brother-in-law were most explicit. He was to arrest the cancerous spread of Protestantism and, if possible, to capture its in-

46

spirers, political and military, and restore ͺ
called United Provinces to Spain. If the A
bride meant seriously to pursue the latter goal,
tries could look forward to a revisitation of soͺ
Alba's Spanish Fury—and a comparable measure of
from the inhabitants of the north. What all but the mͺ
less fanatics on both sides aspired to was peace—permͺ
peace, if that were attainable, but an intermittent one at the very least.

It was not from Octave van Veen that Pieter Paul Rubens acquired what gradually became a second ruling passion of his life, an urgent love of peace. That artist was too much a creature of the court he so admired to hold opinions of his own on any subject even vaguely political. Rather did Pieter Paul find inspiration for his desire in the fear he read in the faces of the crowds that had lined the streets of Antwerp for the arrival of the Archduke Albrecht and his infanta in 1596. The young man, who had himself never experienced the horrors of war, only appreciated in his nineteenth year what an unmixed blessing peace must be.

He had been repelled by the Countess de Lalaing's fascination in describing, with meticulous attention to detail, the scourges that had devastated the Low Countries after 1567. He had seen countless illustrations—drawings, etchings, woodcuts printed by Jan Moretus' Plantin Press, and numbers of paintings, all of them depicting the rape and pillage that had attended the wars of religion. But it had been only when he perceived the anxiety in the faces of the people, those for whom there could be no escape from whatever course the new rulers chose to take, that he was moved by a sense of compassion that seemed almost crushing in its effect on him. Heretofore, his objections to violence had been merely moral, religious; they had no particular relevance to life as it was lived each day by people, by human beings whose names he didn't know, but whose victimization was all the more terrible to him for that very reason.

Pieter Paul knew better than to try to communicate this new-

...scovery to van Veen or his mother or the countess. He did bring it up rather tentatively with Philip, whose current occupation as secretary to the Archbishop of Antwerp should have softened the harsh angularity of his outlook. But Philip, more conscious than his younger brother of their unmentionable Lutheran upbringing, declined, even in intimate conversation, to allow himself what he imagined the luxury of charitable feelings. He was no Erasmian. "If we tolerate heresy merely because the people of the north have elected to go to hell, then we shall have elected to go to hell ourselves. There's no room for compromise, Pieter Paul, and you'd be wise to remember it." This was the official clerical viewpoint, and no amount of argument seemed likely to shake Philip's acceptance of it.

Balthasar Moretus, on the other hand, agreed with Pieter Paul. There was no need to employ arguments with him. Having suffered physical and emotional anguish all his life, he saw no virtue whatever in pain. "These disciples of the Counter Reformation sicken me," he said hotly. "They insist on thinking in terms only of absolutes. They have no mercy." That was precisely the point. If Pieter Paul had been a thinker, a philosopher, he would have written a treatise in praise of mercy. He was unaware that just across the North Sea, an English poet had only recently phrased all that needed to be written about the "quality of mercy."

Happily, the early years of the new regency demonstrated that the archduke was neither an enthusiastic nor an effective military commander. He made halfhearted attempts to turn back the forces of Prince Mauritz. The young stadholder, for his part, was disinclined to press his advantage too outrageously for fear that Philip II might supplant Albrecht of Austria with a master made of sterner stuff. Again, the state was one of armed stalemate. In the region fully under their control, the joint rulers were generous, even lavish, especially in their patronage of the arts and architecture. They liked to entertain a wide variety of subjects in their happy palace in Brussels—and they were extravagant in their praise of work that was, in the main, mediocre.

48

The year 1598 was one of enormous moment for the Spanish Netherlands in general and for Pieter Paul Rubens in particular. The great event of international importance was the terrible, agonizing death of Philip II in his apartment of the Escorial—his last, gout-stricken moments, it was said, given over to a contemplation of hell as that place had been conceived by the eccentric Flemish painter of the fifteenth century, Hieronymous Bosch—a master whose works the Spanish monarch had collected in considerable quantity.

What the king's death meant to the Low Countries was a topic of almost inexhaustible conjecture. He had bequeathed the land to his sister and her husband, with the single stipulation that it would revert to the Spanish crown should the couple die without surviving male issue. Thus, for the time being, the absentee rule from Madrid had ended. This was a cause for unmitigated rejoicing among those who had struggled so long for just this surcease. There would still be the shedding of blood and tears as Catholic warred against Protestant, but the frightening shadow of the implacable Philip II no longer brooded over the country bordering the North Sea.

It was too soon to say what his son and heir, Philip III, would turn out to be. First indications were not especially promising. He decreed a new style of clothing—wide, tightly pleated white linen collars, to be worn by both ladies and gentlemen of his court. It was not long before this became an affectation in both Brussels and Antwerp. The new king distressed all of Europe's major artists by canceling every commission authorized by his late father, and proved himself slow in paying for those that remained unpaid for on Philip II's death. He was interested, one learned, only in portraiture. The little heavy thinking that took place in any of the several royal palaces of Spain was the work of the Duke of Lerma—of whom no one as yet appeared to know very much, except that he was venal.

Venality, however, was not a monopoly of the Spanish. It was the rare public servant in any country who couldn't be induced to render a favor in exchange for gold or some other asset, tan-

49

gible or otherwise. Indeed, it was *expected*. Officeholders were miserably paid at every level of government. How else were they to make ends meet than by accepting, discreetly, an occasional bribe? So long as it didn't affect too adversely the interest of the state, such practice was countenanced with total equanimity.

Queen Elizabeth had no important minister during her entire long reign who failed to rob the public treasury. Partial responsibility for Spain's three bankruptcies during the era of Philip II could be attributed to the slips between the cup of the tax collector and the lip of the royal coffers. If the popes were innocent of actual theft it was because, as a poet would later observe, "the Church can sleep and feed at once." But nepotism was a creation of the papacy; the *nepoti* were papal nephews who enjoyed Vatican favors because popes, as a rule, had no sons to spoil. The single, shining exception to the general pattern of corruption in high places was the Duke de Sully, principal adviser to Henri IV, whose absolute probity was the more annoying to his contemporaries in France and elsewhere because he was a Huguenot. If that was what Protestantism boded, Catholics could only pray that its spread would not reach them.

For Pieter Paul, the year of Philip II's death was of immense personal meaning. He attained the age of twenty-one. He was duly declared a master painter and, as a consequence, was admitted to membership in the Guild of Saint Luke. He accepted his first pupil. And he was presented by his former master, Octave van Veen, to the regents in Brussels. It was at once the completely predictable culmination of eight years of steady application and, strangely, altogether unexpected. So habituated had he become to the life of the assiduous apprentice, the dutiful protégé, the obedient son, that suddenly to be acknowledged as a full-grown man, a master, and a teacher, was a shock —though a wholly pleasant one.

The only cause for regret was that the Countess de Lalaing was unable for very long to share the pleasure of a fruition to which she had contributed so faithfully and with such enduring affection. She died within a week of Pieter Paul's twenty-first birthday, bequeathing to the beloved young man "a modest sum with which, one day, I hope he will make the journey to Italy he has so often talked with me about."

Of the delights that marked that year, Pieter Paul's first appearance at the court in Brussels was the most important. Everything in his education and in his nature had prepared him for that moment. He had no need to pay close attention to van Veen's solemn counsel about his dress and deportment. He *knew* how to dress, how to behave. The dear dead countess would have been proud of him. He was far less nervous than his master when the moment of presentation came, and this aplomb was obvious to both the archduke and the infanta. The words exchanged were banal, because banality is the currency of people who have little or nothing in common. Yet Pieter Paul managed to convey to the regents an impression that transcended the inanity of their brief conversation.

Like the Countess de Lalaing, the Archduke Albrecht perceived in this handsome, lithe, graceful-mannered young man a quality that was intriguing. He wanted to know more of him, see more of him. What better way to accomplish this end than to commission young Maître Rubens to paint the portraits of himself and the infanta? It was this royal demand that bowled over Pieter Paul—and lost him the friendship of Octave van Veen. He rued his former master's ferocious envy—but he refused to permit it to intrude very deeply on his pleasure.

The portraits he made of the regents were workmanlike—better than their subjects had reason to expect from an artist just officially admitted to the practice of his craft. But the painter himself was an object of some astonishment, particularly to the archduke, who was a worldly, widely traveled European. What he found so startling about Pieter Paul was his easy bearing, his casual erudition. The young man spoke fluent French and German as well as the Flemish of the marketplace. He wrote Latin and Greek. He appeared to be well read in the classics and was perfectly conversant with the more urgent topics of the day. He had opinions which he willingly advanced when asked for them. Without seeming to wish to impose his will on the regent, he forcefully argued the cause that was now so close to his heart, that of domestic tranquillity. "You would have peace, no matter what the cost?" the archduke inquired.

"I can think of not a single institution, sire, for which I'd sacrifice one human life."

"That's an interesting and very dangerous viewpoint." The regent smiled. "But I may one day give you a chance to argue it again. It's extremely radical, you understand. Some would call it incendiary."

"I know, sire. My brother thinks me a menace to good order." Pieter Paul said this with a smile he believed, rightly, to be disarming.

"If you're not hanged, Maître Rubens, you may go far."

"Who would want to hang a painter, sire?"

The former cardinal looked at his wife. "My late brother-in-law, for one, if he heard a painter utter so terrible a heresy. But not I." The archduke paused. "You say you plan to go to Rome."

"I do, sire, as soon as may be."

"Before you leave, let me know. I believe I can be of some use to you. And that would give me great pleasure."

TWO

IN the middle of June, 1600, Pieter Paul Rubens was admitted to the terrestrial paradise that was Venice. The month-long journey that had brought him from Antwerp was filled with wonders, most of them by the hand of nature, for he had felt too pressed, too anxious to reach Italy, to dally along the way.

From numerous accounts he had received before his departure from the Low Countries, he knew that the Most Serene Republic on the Adriatic was not a community typical of the rest of Italy. From his first view of it, as he stepped into a gondola to cross over to the principal island from the mainland, he was certain that Venice must be unique.

Almost everything on the surface of Venetian life glittered with suggestions of limitless prosperity. The single notable exceptions were the quantity and variety of beggars who beset him on every hand as he and several porters made their way to the inn which had been recommended by Adam van Noort. But there were plenty of beggars in Antwerp too.

Pieter Paul was overwhelmed almost physically by the assault made upon all his senses from the moment he set foot on the cobbled pavements. His eyes were dazzled by the richness and diversity of architectural splendors. His ears rang with the cries of the gondoliers, the vendors, the mountebanks . . . and, of course, the mendicants who knew neither home nor time of day or night. His olfactory system was all but shattered by the sharply conflicting odors—of the food that was hawked in the overhanging arcades of the great buildings that lined the Piazzetta and the Piazza di San Marco; of the perfumed whores who brushed against him boldly with their shoulders and their half-bared breasts; and of the ordure flung into the canals and lagoons. The initial impression of Venice, therefore, was mainly of confusion, of great bustle, of great beauty, of great ugliness, of great emotions carelessly displayed. But of one thing he was perfectly sure: He was in Italy, not in the Netherlands.

The venture had been nearly a year in the arrangement. Maria Piepelinx had thought it, naturally, folly from the start. "You're already a master of the Guild of Saint Luke. Of what use is a long, expensive trip?" But Pieter Paul had the precious legacy from the Countess de Lalaing to point to. "Would it be honest," he replied with mock reproof, "to spend it on something else?" He did not, however, tell his mother of his firm decision to establish himself in Italy, preferably in Rome, and there to remain for the rest of his days—so brilliant was the picture of that peninsula in his imagination. As far as she was concerned, the journey was merely for self-improvement. He would return to Antwerp after a year or two.

Maria Piepelinx was gratified that, while away, Pieter Paul would earn some money; for he had been awarded by the Archduke Albrecht a commission to paint a triptych for the Roman church of Santa Croce in Gerusalemme, of which the regent was a patron and dean. He had also received from the archduke a letter of introduction and recommendation to Vincenzo Gonzaga, Duke of Mantua, who was to arrive in Venice in the middle of July. Whatever might evolve from this meeting, there was a month for Pieter Paul's comprehensive exploration of the superb floating city. He made admirable use of his time.

It required a full week for him to adjust to the vigorous Venetian tempo of existence and to the assorted wonders of its architecture. On foot and by gondola, he devoted these seven days merely to a contemplation of externals—the façades of the palaces, the confraternities, the astonishingly elegant warehouses of the Grand Canal, the magnificent churches of the previous six centuries with their coppered domes, and the soaring *campanile* with its thunderous bells. Most of the styles represented here were unknown in the Low Countries, where the clutch of the Gothic mode remained strong. He had as well to adapt himself to a different climate, where the sky's blue was several shades more intense than that over Antwerp, and where the slanting sun of morning and evening turned the light to a glaring gold that contrasted vividly with the blinding whiteness that predominated in the regions bordering on the North Sea.

He had a smattering of Italian on his arrival—enough to make his basic requirements understood and, when mixed with French and Latin words, even to carry on brief conversations with the proprietor of the inn where he was lodged. Endowed with a marvelous ear for language, Pieter Paul listened to the talk of the Venetians, watched with amused admiration as they substituted gesture for speech (recalling van Noort's emulation of this habit), and quickly augmented his vocabulary. By the time the Duke of Mantua reached Venice, the young Flemish master could defend himself reasonably well in the new tongue.

By that time too he had managed to see most of the important works still in the city by the hands of the Serenissima's greatest painters—the principal object of his visit here. These were the pictures of Giorgione, the Bellini, of Tintoretto, Veronese, and the most celebrated of Venetian artists, Titian. He had seen isolated examples of some of these masters' paintings in Antwerp and Brussels; and there were countless copies whose proficiency, he now understood, was questionable. But here, in the city where all of them had flourished, there was an abundance that took young Rubens' breath away. The wonder of Venetian painting, especially in the century just ending, was the easy juxtaposition of the sacred and the profane in religious art—something, in theory at any rate, specifically prohibited by the decrees on painting for churches promulgated at Trent.

In this somewhat eccentric manner did Rubens stumble over one of the more surprising aspects of the Venetian viewpoint—the republic's ample indifference to the admonitions of the Holy See. True, Paolo Veronese had been summoned to appear before a tribunal of the Inquisition to explain the presence of nude figures, male and female, in some pictures he had painted for a local church—and he had treated his interrogators with much due deference, seeming to implore their forgiveness for having so audaciously transgressed. But the fact remained that the offending works were never altered.

Wherever possible, the doges and members of the consiglio followed a similar course, giving lip service of agreement to everything the Vatican uttered but failing to make any of the significant changes that agreement seemed to dictate. In short, Venice would never permit the pope to interpose himself in matters that were of vital local or international interest, religious or secular—such as the designation of bishops or the enforcement of most of the Edicts of Trent. Like the Flemings, the Venetians were humanists and merchants first, Catholics second. As Pieter Paul was to learn, this impunity was the prerogative exclusively of the invulnerable and the well connected.

It would have been difficult for a dignitary of only minor military, geographical, or political significance in Italy (which was itself of only minor importance in a Europe where the nation-state had emerged as the major factor) to be better connected than Vincenzo I Gonzaga, Duke of Mantua. The blood of every notable ducal house of the peninsula flowed through his veins. His first wife had been a Farnese; his second and present one was Eleonora de' Medici, daughter of the richest banker in Europe and Duke of Florence. The Gonzagas had governed Mantua for nearly three centuries according to the despotic principles that still prevailed among the dukedoms and Papal States of the peninsula.

Vincenzo carried this ancestral burden with a minimum of obvious effort. He rarely gave this impressive heritage two consecutive thoughts. His concern was exclusively with the present; with life at its roisterous, exuberant, sensual, and aesthetic best. Granted the limitations of his treasury, Gonzaga was probably the most generous and all-inclusive patron of important artistic and scholarly endeavor in Italy. For all that some of his contemporaries thought him crude, his taste in most things was unerringly superb. Like his forebears, he was an omnivorous acquisitor, with a particular penchant for beautiful women—an interest he shared with many of his countrymen, but one which his fortune and position allowed him to indulge more lavishly than the average man's condition permitted. Gonzaga's passions and his purse ran an unequal race; he was constantly in debt—but a relative of the banking Medici, if only a connection by marriage, was not often at a loss for credit.

Just under forty, the duke was in the lusty prime of his career—an imperious, sentimental, childishly impulsive and demanding personage who was accustomed to have his way in all matters and with all the creatures he encountered, except for the handful of individuals whom he acknowledged as his masters—the pope in Rome, his father-in-law of Florence, the king of Spain, and the Holy Roman Emperor in Prague.

When he walked, he strutted. When he spoke, he thundered. The very ground beneath his feet was meant to tremble when he was angry. The servants who surrounded him (and everyone about him was a servant) were meant to sigh, to laugh, to cower, according to his tone or whim. Yet for all his bombast, there was a genuine magnetism about him that attracted men and captivated women. The essence of his power over others was his unshakable conviction that he possessed such a power. He owned the secret of demagogy.

Pieter Paul had learned something about the forceful Gonzaga from the duke's permanent emissary to Venice, to whom he had presented his letter from the Archduke Albrecht soon after his arrival. But this information, acquired at second hand and couched as it had been in terms of exquisitely abject deference, was not very illuminating. It was a favorable caricature of the man, not a serious portrait. When the duke reached the Serenissima on July 16 and had settled into his comfortable quarters, a large suite of rooms in a *palazzo* overlooking the Grand

57

Canal and Palladio's great new church on the opposite bank, he ordered Rubens to visit him.

Over a white silk blouse, the young Fleming wore a handsomely brocaded doublet—sleeveless, for it was hot in Venice. His breeches were dark, his stockings immaculately white and tight-fitting, his buckled boots just polished for the occasion. Apart from a neatness of appearance, the Duke of Mantua observed a slender young man of medium height, with splendid brown eyes that seemed quick and expressive of intelligence. His hair and beard were auburn, scrupulously combed and cropped. His manners were gentle, his voice clear and of middle range—not excessively masculine as were the tones of the Germans.

The painter from the Netherlands and the hard-living Mantuan exchanged amenities—the former with a solemn reserve that he hoped spoke well of his rearing, the latter in a series of impatient but incongruously high-pitched grunts. Gonzaga held in his left hand the letter from the regent in Brussels. He waved it briefly before Pieter Paul as if it were a handkerchief. "What do you want from me?" he demanded harshly.

"A post as painter in your court, excellency, if there's an opening."

The duke shook his curly head and grimaced wearily. "I already have a countryman of yours as painter to my court, the younger Frans Pourbus. Do you know him?"

"I know *of* him, excellency."

"You've seen his work?"

"No, excellency. I'm sorry to say I haven't."

"That's fortunate for you. I'd have asked your opinion of it."

Rubens grinned. "And I'd have lied to you if I hadn't liked it."

The older man eyed him with new curiosity. "Why should you do a thing like that?"

"In order not to offend you, excellency."

"Yet you might as easily have offended me by saying that you'd lie."

"I thought not."

58

"Why?"

"It was a surmise."

"Do you depend a great deal on surmises like that?"

"A great deal, excellency. I presumed that if you'd not been an admirer of Maître Pourbus, you'd not keep him in your employ. So it really wasn't a very wild surmise, was it?"

A look of reluctant pleasure crossed Gonzaga's features. "Where did you learn your Italian?"

"Mostly here in Venice, excellency. It requires polish, I know. But I've been in Italy only for a month or so."

The duke gave another grunt. "When it acquires polish, then, you'll be a diplomat."

"I know something of court life."

"So I gather from the archduke's letter. He thinks very highly of your several talents."

"He flatters me, perhaps."

Gonzaga once again considered his young visitor with interest. "You say 'perhaps.' You think he may *not* have flattered you?"

"Not knowing what he says of me, excellency, I can't very well answer that."

" 'Maître Rubens is the most gifted painter to come to my attention since my arrival in Brussels four years ago. He is as well potentially the most skillful and worldly man of affairs I shall ever know. In any case, I can assure you that there is, even today, no task with which I should not trust him absolutely. His honesty is a wonder to me,' " Gonzaga read. Then he paused and stared at Pieter Paul. "Now tell me, Maître Rubens. Is that flattery?"

"It's certainly most complimentary, excellency."

"You're being evasive."

The young painter smiled. "I've no way to give you a positive answer, excellency, because I don't know what task the archduke might have had in mind when he wrote that."

"What about your honesty, then?"

"I'm honest, excellency."

"You'll say no more about it than that?"

"What else is there to say, excellency? Honesty is absolute, like perfection." He brightened, coming across a simile he thought the duke would appreciate. "It's like virginity. One either has it or one doesn't."

Gonzaga nodded and grinned. "And having once lost it, one can never retrieve it."

"Precisely."

"What have you to say about the archduke's views of your art, that you're the most gifted painter?"

"I think that's true."

"Are there no great painters working in Brussels or Antwerp these days?"

"I thought there were some very good ones, excellency . . . until I came to Venice. My mind has been radically changed by what I've seen here."

"Ah yes, we have some great men. And in Mantua we have fine things too. But humility? I didn't expect that of you, Rubens."

"Not false humility, excellency. It's just that I'm aware of my limitations."

The duke sighed, and let the letter fall to the tiled floor. "You knew all along, of course, that I'd *have* to take you in, didn't you, at least for a time. The archduke has connections that are precious to me, you understand."

"I knew that you'd have to give the matter serious reflection, excellency, that you'd not be able to reject me out of hand."

Gonzaga appeared to ruminate for a moment. "Can you copy?" he inquired at last.

"I *can*, excellency, but I'll not pretend that it's the sort of work I'd choose."

"That wasn't the question. What I require, if I require anyone at all, is a competent copyist. If you're willing to do that for me, I'll take you under my protection and I'll pay you a hundred ducats a quarter. When I've seen what you can do in that way, we'll reopen the question. How does that strike you?"

Pieter Paul knew that he should be effusively grateful, but he didn't feel that way, and this seemed to him the moment for candor. "If I may make the single reservation, excellency, that you'll not condemn me exclusively to copying . . ."

Gonzaga pointed to the letter at his feet. "You have a commission from the archduke to make something for him in Rome. Do I understand that you're asking me to give you a commission as well?"

"In time, excellency, I'd certainly hope for one."

The nobleman uttered a small, stuttering laugh of admiring exasperation. "You certainly don't believe in settling for a single bit less than you believe you can get, do you?"

"Do *you*, excellency?"

"Of course not, but I don't have to."

"Why must *I* have to?"

Gonzaga's tone became avuncular. "Because, young Rubens, that is the way of the world. Because I'm rich and you're poor, because I'm important and you're insignificant, because I'm a duke and you're a commoner, because I'm powerful and you're powerless. How many reasons do you want? As I say, it's the way of the world, and neither of us has the means to change it —nor do I very much want to."

On a peninsula of comparatively high ground in the broad, low Lombard plain, surrounded by three brackish lagoons of the river Mincio, the fortifications of Mantua presented to Pieter Paul Rubens, when he first saw them late in July of 1600, a most doleful prospect, totally bereft of the wonders of Venice, sharing with the magical city on the Adriatic only an aspect of insularity. Mantua was a fastness, a fortress town still girding itself against possible siege—a condition it had known many times during its long and tumultuous history. Everything seemed forbidding—the fortified bridges, the battlements, its isolated situation. He felt certain that he would not be happy here.

Mantua's austere exterior was belied by the great beauty its walls concealed. As the ducal cortège drew closer to one of the entry gates, Rubens was happily startled to remark a truly magnificent building of quite recent construction, which he later learned to be the Palazzo del Te, the work of Raphael's most illustrious pupil, Giulio Romano. And once the great portal leading to Mantua proper had been traversed, the young painter's gratification was greatly augmented by the sight of many treasures protected by the awesome walls—as a mother protects her offspring in a close embrace.

There were villas, churches, public buildings, and palaces of surpassing splendor. What he gradually discovered was that Mantua possessed some of the most magnificent works of Renaissance art and architecture in existence accumulated by Gonzagas since they had first gained sway here in 1328. Duke Vincenzo's ancestors had from the outset attracted to this city of ancient Etruria (Virgil had been born, it was thought, not far away) many of the finest painters, sculptors, and builders of their epochs.

Of all the brilliant artistic names associated with Mantua, only one came close to rivaling that of Romano—Andrea Mantegna, whose contributions to the building and decoration of the town were dazzling, exceeded in number but not in quality solely by his earlier work in Padua. Dead almost a century now, and buried in a chapel of his own design in the Mantuan church of San Andrea, Mantegna had mastered the techniques of fresco and oils and caused them quickly to evolve, making of him the first northern Italian Renaissance painter of unquestionable genius.

Mantegna's stay of more than forty years in Mantua was more than adequate testimony to the wonderful judgment of Duke Ludovico Gonzaga. No single work of Mantegna's was more characteristic nor more glorious than the frescoes he created in the vaulted Camera degli Sposi of the Palazzo Ducale, which could be ranked only with Raphael's and Giulio Romano's *stanzi* in the Vatican and Michelangelo's decoration of the Sistine Chapel. But Mantegna's frescoes antedated these glories by almost half a century. When Pieter Paul Rubens was introduced to the room by a Vincenzo Gonzaga who was bursting with delight, he thought for a moment that he might never be able to breathe again. It was as if he had emerged from a dank cave to find himself on the edges of a garden of purest delight. And this, he perceived with time, was probably what Mantegna himself had felt; he had brought painting out of its rigid, hieratic shackles and given it the freedom of profanity. The room, whose every inch had been decorated by Mantegna's own hand, was a song of delirious joy.

But the man who had transfigured Mantua was Giulio Romano. He had been brought here by the widow of Giovanni Francesco III Gonzaga, the brilliant and beautiful Isabella d'Este—supporter as well of Giovanni Bellini (Mantegna's brother-in-law), Leonardo, and Michelangelo, and collector of Roman antiquities. When Romano was sentenced to death and saw himself burned in effigy by the inquisitors of the Holy Office in Rome, the duchess invited him to take refuge in Mantua. He spent sixteen years here, occupying himself with an extraordinary variety of ambitious projects. He dammed the flow of the Mincio, protecting the town against flood and dispatching to oblivion the annual crop of ferocious malarial mosquitoes that had long been hatched in its reedy banks. He restored the cathedral. He built houses. He painted a great number of fine portraits and many religious and secular pictures. Undoubtedly, however, his masterpiece was the Palazzo del Te, that immense pile that Rubens had seen just outside the walls. The Mantua of 1600 was largely the creation of Giulio Romano.

The aura of elegant festivity that denoted the achievements of Mantegna and Romano was a somewhat refined reflection of life in the ducal court of Vincenzo Gonzaga—whose appetites were not circumscribed by the dictates of elegance. The figures with whom he surrounded himself represented every aspect of his bizarre personality. He loved secular music; the composer-in-residence when Pieter Paul Rubens came to Mantua was Claudio Monteverdi, who was engaged in the composition of a work he called *Orfeo*, in a form hitherto unknown outside of

63

Florence—opera. Gonzaga maintained for Monteverdi, or vice versa, a complete chamber ensemble to entertain the ducal guests during evening meals and post-prandial galas.

Fancying himself something of a poet, like Octave van Veen, Vincenzo wrote occasional sonnets in the gallant Italian style to one or another of his several current mistresses—but never to his buxom Medici wife. He always contrived to find room in his eccentric household for versifiers whose production was more capable and more regular than his own. The demented Torquato Tasso, greatest Italian poet of his age, had spent his last paranoiac years under Gonzaga's affectionate protection.

The duke respected scientists in an era when these investigators into the unknown were generally regarded with misgiving and great suspicion. He especially admired the mind of Galileo Galilei, with whom he carried on a steady correspondence which, he confessed, was mostly way over his head. Galileo, then at Padua, wrote with reserved skepticism about matters in the heavens that had theretofore been taken as explicable only in terms of God's majesty and will. The scientific tone of questioning and doubt disturbed Gonzaga now and then, so it was a comfort to have nearer at hand charlatans who expressed doubts about nothing—an omniscient astrologer, an alchemist, and several quacks who passed themselves off as specialists in various branches of the medical arts.

Of all the features of Mantuan court life, the one to which Pieter Paul found it most difficult to accommodate himself was the plethora of readily available women. It wasn't that he was a prude. No one who had painted the female human form from life as often as he had done could be prudish. Rather was he shocked by the women's easy access not only to the beds of the duke and his courtiers but to the business of the state. The intrigues of the courtly ladies of Italy were totally dismaying to a Fleming who was accustomed to a definite separation between the obligations of the sexes. The women of Antwerp knew their place; those of Italy seemed not to. More incomprehensible, the men didn't care.

Conversely, what Vincenzo Gonzaga found most perplexing

about Pieter Paul Rubens was his patent distaste for the flesh of the ladies whose proximity the duke himself cherished above everything else. The young painter's explanation failed to solve the riddle for his new master. "A woman's place?" he bellowed. "A woman's place? A woman's place is beside her man, wherever he happens to be. What's the *matter* with you? That fellow Pourbus finds nothing strange about it. Do you imagine yourself superior?"

"Perhaps, excellency, when I've been in Mantua as long as Maître Pourbus, I'll find nothing strange about it either."

"By God, Rubens, you *do* think yourself superior, don't you?"

"No, excellency. I expect it's just that I'm a little more reserved . . . The climate, perhaps."

"You prefer to make love to men, perhaps?" the duke inquired without a trace of disapproval in his voice. "It can be arranged." He leered. "We have something for every taste in Mantua. That's one of our boasts."

Rubens was scandalized, but kept his outrage to himself. "No, excellency, but I thank you all the same," he responded calmly.

"*What,* then? You have your choice." Gonzaga spread out his arms and splayed his fingers, then brought his hands together and clasped them, beginning to rock to and fro on his ample hams. "You have your choice, I say. There's nothing else, you know. There are women and there are men. That's all the good God has seen fit to give us." He froze in the middle of a forward motion and looked up into the painter's eyes, his mouth agape, as a horrendous thought crossed his mind. "You're *not,* for God's sake, a *virgin.*"

Rubens lost a fraction of his composure. "I am not, excellency. I promise you I am not," he murmured a little hastily.

"Tell me," said the duke, all eagerness. "Tell me about losing your virginity."

"I'm afraid it wasn't very spectacular, excellency. Boccaccio tells a better story."

"But those were *inventions*. This is *truth*. Tell me," he insisted warmly. "Every detail."

Pieter Paul shrugged. "She was a model. We were alone. That's all there was to it."

The duke leaned back in his chair, shaking his head in disappointment. "Is that how you spend the long winter nights in Antwerp? Is that how they tell stories? My God, what a man. And you're supposed to have imagination. 'She was a model. We were alone. That's all there was to it.' God in heaven, Rubens. How much more do you think there was to the Annunciation? I suppose the way you'd tell it, while Joseph was out, his wife cuckolded him with a bird."

"*Excellency!*"

The duke raised a hand. "I know. I know. You protest. But there's not a priest within earshot. Don't worry. I'm going to hell anyhow." He sighed. "No wonder poor Alessandro Farnese, my former brother-in-law, you know . . . no wonder he brought his whores along with his army. You Flemish have no emotions. You're sticks of wood. Don't you have *any* feelings?" He threw his braceleted arms in the air. "Have you no joy, no sorrow?"

"We do, excellency, but we've learned to conceal our feelings."

"Why?"

The painter grinned and shrugged—in the Italian manner, a grotesquery lost on his master. "As I said, it may be the climate."

"The climate, the climate. *We* have snow in Mantua every winter, you know." He pointed to the north, where the Alps, on a clear day, could be seen to rise mightily in the distance. "We have blizzards. The Mincio sometimes freezes solidly. It's *not* the climate, Rubens. It's the blood. You have cold blood up there, Norman blood. We of Italy feel things in our bowels."

There was only one character in the colorful and voluble entourage of Vincenzo Gonzaga who impressed the young Rubens

66

as being perhaps capable of bringing a semblance of superficial order out of the chaos in which the profligate duke appeared to revel. This was his secretary of state and general *factotum*, Annibale Chieppio, a gentleman of a certain antiquity who had served the previous duke in a lesser capacity and who attended the present ruler of Mantua with a fidelity that was nicely tempered by discreet disdain.

Chieppio said that he had modeled his long and successful career on two books which he heartily commended to the newly arrived Flemish artist—*The Prince* and *The Courtier*, both volumes which, as it happened, Pieter Paul had read with care in their Plantin Press editions before leaving Antwerp. He conceded that they were instructive, but he was unable to go along completely with the secretary who described them as containing "all anyone needs to know in order to prosper in this world."

"That depends," Rubens retorted respectfully, "on how one chooses to define one's world, I should think."

The old Italian snorted at this. "The world defines itself. Power defines it."

"But surely, *signore*, power is redefined very frequently."

"It shifts, I agree. But it's not redefined. It is an absolute."

"And yet as it shifts, it seems to me that power takes on different aspects . . . What one pope decrees another can abrogate. Isn't that so?" He hesitated, wondering whether or not he should argue the point, then proceeded—for it was his experience, albeit restricted, that Italians enjoyed debate, especially on themes unlikely to be resolved by argument. "In my country, during my father's time, it was generally accepted for people to tolerate Protestantism. That was the position of established power. Then, after the Edicts of Trent were made known, the position was altered."

"I don't disagree. I merely point out that he who has the power *has* the power. The power can change hands. It can change purposes. But power is like an inexhaustible chunk of charcoal. It is energy that can be placed at the service of anyone who possesses it. Power knows no morality."

Rubens was impressed. "Do you suggest that this is right?"

Chieppio gave a toothless chuckle. "What has right to do with it? Vincenzo Gonzaga has the right to order my execution. He has that right because of his position. He may order my execution wrongly, in moral terms, but he'll not be brought to book for it on this earth. Yet if this same Vincenzo Gonzaga were to order the execution, let us say, of Pieter Paul Rubens, Fleming, subject of the Archduke Albrecht, he *could* be brought to book—because the archduke is more powerful than the duke."

"Ah," said the painter gleefully, "then power isn't absolute after all."

"It's relatively absolute," said Chieppio with a complacent smile. "And you must learn not to pounce so when you're discussing a question. It's very bad manners. You must make your point quietly."

"*Signore,* you are a casuist."

"I am simply a man who knows how to stay alive in a very hostile world."

Chieppio knew every skeleton in the Gonzaga closet and was equally familiar with the most damaging secrets of other important Italian households. He was a seasoned diplomatist who had traveled to most of the Continent's capitals as an emissary of Mantua. There was very little he confessed ignorance of—certain sciences and the method of loading and discharging firearms, weapons he deplored as having eliminated chivalry from the field of battle. "Gentlemen are not noisy," he declaimed.

He protested bitterly and often about his master's improvidence, intemperance, and promiscuity—but wholly on financial grounds. "He'll be the ruin of us," he told Pieter Paul with great relish. It was a favorite refrain, but not the only one. Chieppio spoke in clichés, like Polonius. And, like Polonius, he didn't imagine himself a figure of fun, a well-spoken buffoon. Yet even when his words had originality, his ideas lacked it. "Now that I'm wise enough to deal reasonably with women, I'm too old to deal with them at all," he observed. And he had similar epigrams on the subjects of wine, money, the harried life he was compelled to lead, and for the deplorable state of the earth's affairs—of which he swore repeatedly that he would soon wash his hands. No one, least of all Vincenzo Gonzaga, believed him.

As his views about power suggested, Chieppio was not overburdened with political or religious convictions, a condition endemic among Italian statesmen who were not always sure that the master they served the night before would be on hand the next morning. It was, given these circumstances, unwise to hold strong feelings about matters over which one had no control. "The principalities of this peninsula have been fought over by the great powers for so long a period that every major town in Italy keeps in reserve supplies of the banners of the kings of Spain, of France, of the Empire, and of the Holy See," he said. "But I think we might safely dispose of the papal banners now," he added. The remark amused Pieter Paul, but Chieppio had meant it seriously. He meant everything seriously, as did Polonius. He would have been terribly offended by the young man's laughter. Fortunately, Rubens kept it to himself.

Since he was, among other things, the duke's principal paymaster, Pieter Paul treated Chieppio with the deference the old man thought he merited. In this, the artist was unique. For other members of the court took their cue from Vincenzo Gonzaga, who showed the venerable gentleman a scorn not always obviously mitigated by affection, and who paid an imperfect attention to his complaints and admonitions—except when he wailed with weary rage, "There is no more money!"

Then the duke would plaintively inquire, "What must be done?" He knew very well what Chieppio's reply would be: "You must stop squandering." The ensuing economy wave would usually last a week—even a month if the pinch was particularly severe. Then Vincenzo would borrow from his father-in-law in Florence and decree a "temporary tax increase." Ducal pleasure took its toll, as was the custom, mainly from the poor—for they had no useful defenders in this world, least of all in the Church.

Chieppio saw in Pieter Paul Rubens not merely another artist gratuitously added to the Gonzaga retinue. If the young man had seemed only this to him, he would have paid him no attention at all. He perceived his own successor. It was his intention, when the moment appeared propitious, to begin his training in the rituals and principles of the craft of the minor state. That young Rubens was able to paint concerned Chieppio not at all, save that through painting he might gain entrées blocked to others. He wanted to guide his protégé in directions he thought suitable for one who might one day be Mantua's secretary of state. Of this, however, he said nothing; he wanted more time to be certain his choice had fallen on the proper shoulders. And Pieter Paul divined nothing. What he saw, or thought he saw, was a childless old man who had found a son. Fatherless, Rubens understood Chieppio's need and tacitly consented to play the designated role—or the role he imagined the secretary to see him in.

Without understanding that he was possibly Chieppio's chosen instrument, Pieter Paul allowed himself to be gently instructed in the Byzantine subtleties of Italian statecraft. It was, in any case, a subject that interested him almost as much as art. He had much to learn. In Italy, a nod was certainly *not* the equivalent of a wink. Tone was more significant than the words uttered. Expression, gesture, dress . . . all were calculated to give pleasure or offense. Certainly his pleasure was as great as his surprise when Chieppio announced that he was going to take the young artist with him to Florence for the great wedding.

The great wedding was the event of the year for all of Catholic Europe. Henri IV of France was to take as his second wife, Vincenzo Gonzaga's sister-in-law, Maria de' Medici. The king's first marriage, to Marguerite de Valois, had been dissolved by Pope Clement VIII because, for one thing, *la reine Margot* had borne her husband no children, leaving her practically the only pretty woman in France who had failed to conceive a royal infant. For another, marriage to a Medici carried with it a dowry that was almost irresistible—a substantial quantity of ready gold and the cancellation of France's immense debt to the Florentine banking family.

The famous nuptials were set for October 5, 1600. From all corners of the Continent where the papal authority was acknowledged the official guests jubilantly journeyed toward the magnificent Medici capital on the banks of the Arno to witness a ceremony that would combine the assets of the earth's most beautiful country and Italy's most prosperous house. None was more excited by the prospect than Pieter Paul Rubens. Few men of little importance could have been better placed than he to see and hear every detail—for his master's wife was to act as her sister's matron of honor and would travel with her as far as Marseille.

It was not the first time a Medici would be queen of France. Maria's ancestor Caterina had been the bride of Henri II to whom she gave four sons, three of whom acceded to the French throne, all of them thoughtlessly dying without male issue. Caterina had, on the whole, been a credit to her family and the Church. She had been the power behind the throne right up to the end of her life, which mercifully came near to coinciding with the death of her last royal son, Henri III. Though there had been times when Catholics thought her unduly soft on Protestants, they could forgive her much in the face of her achievement on Saint Bartholomew's Day, 1572, when every important Huguenot luckless enough to find himself in Paris was slaughtered at Caterina's order.

Those who were gathering for this second alliance of France and Florence considered the prospective bride with interest. Would she emulate her great aunt and try to bring the heretics out of the darkness? It seemed unlikely. Henri IV was a much more forceful character than any of his Valois predecessors. And his minister, Sully, was notoriously a Huguenot and even more notoriously inhospitable to financial blandishments.

It did seem churlish of the royal bridegroom not to put in an appearance at his own wedding. Henri IV's excuse was that he was occupied with great affairs of state that demanded his complete attention and his alone. Some alleged that his preoccupation was his current favorite, the delectable Henriette d'Entragues. Others, more plausibly, reasoned that the French king was reluctant to set foot on Italian soil, for he had legions of enemies there, as almost everywhere else—not the least the pope himself, who had not yet forgiven him for having been a Huguenot, for the indecent delay he had imposed before his conversion, and most grievous of all offenses, for the promulgation of the Edict of Nantes, in 1598, which accorded Protestants most rights of employment and at law, which had previously been the perquisites only of True Believers. The French king set a very bad example to his counterparts in other lands. It would take a very large hell to accommodate all the wicked works of which he was guilty.

The absence of Henri IV from the festivities was of little consequence to Pieter Paul. The confusion of pomp and panoply attending the wedding was, despite his anticipations, almost superfluous where he was concerned. From the moment when he started to descend the long hillside road that led to the gate of Florence, he was enthralled by everything he beheld. Here was the seat not of the Medici, but of Fra Angelico, of Giotto, Brunelleschi, Leonardo, Michelangelo . . . the list of artists who had made Florence the jewel of central Italy seemed infinitely long.

Inevitably, Rubens compared this city with Venice and Mantua and found that useful comparison was difficult. Venice was a great brothel of a city, open to every vagrant wind of culture from an early Christian date. Mantua had drawn great men to her during the past three centuries. But Florence had given them birth. It was this sense of being at the fountainhead of the Renaissance that caused young Pieter Paul tremors of delight. Fortunately, he had nearly a week before the wedding day to give to a scrutiny of the paintings and sculptures, the galleries and palaces, and to the churches—especially, of course, to the baptistery, *campanile*, and *duomo*, those masterpieces of polychrome marble that were the architectural glories of the Medici, if not of God.

Where was Antwerp now? How, after such an experience as

this, could he think of returning to that icy, damp drabness? He had to laugh that such a thought even crossed his mind. There wasn't a possibility of it. Here was his home now, in Italy. Here he would make a great place for himself.

The entourage of the Duke of Mantua was allocated a place of great honor in the wonderful cathedral which Giotto had so gloriously renovated and augmented. It was only as the bride made her appearance at the high altar of the *duomo* that Rubens had his first glimpse of her—and his first disillusionment. In such a setting as this, surrounded by such absolute magnificence, a sow was being offered to a hog. Maria de' Medici was, like her older sister of Mantua, apparently charmless, her face that had known twenty-seven summers empty of interest. The single distinction she possessed was the bearing of a queen—though even this might be illusory, for she was juxtaposed with a fastidious but vapid French duke who was standing as proxy for his king.

Nevertheless, since the only weddings he had to compare with this one were those in Antwerp, Pieter Paul was hugely impressed by everything that took place in the cathedral—and, later, by all that occurred in the splendidly garlanded banquet hall of the Palazzo Pitti, across the Arno, where hundreds of seated dignitaries (himself included) were served by more hundreds of scurrying domestics attired especially for the occasion.

The confusion of the repast bordered on the chaotic. But as the wine flowed continuously, none but the abstemious appeared to notice. Neither Rubens nor his companion, Annibale Chieppio, was inclined to stay the flagon whenever it was presented. Throughout the service of the wedding breakfast, which occupied the better part of three hours and carried the participants well into the glowing autumn afternoon, a company of musicians competed lustily with the assembled throng—and mainly lost; only the clarion of an occasional brass could be distinguished above the general clamor of shouts and laughter. "It's like an orgy out of Ovid," bellowed Rubens to Chieppio. The old man shrugged and withdrew a leg of newborn Abruzzi lamb from between his gums. "I've not seen a woman ravished on a table yet. Can't be a proper orgy without a rape, you know."

When the meal was over, a moment determined quite arbitrarily by the repeated sounding of a thunderous gong, the servants abruptly disappeared, after clearing the floor of the larger bits of broken crockery. The first group of musicians gave way to a second. The audience, most of it in various stages of extreme inebriation, found itself regaled with the initial public performance of *Euridice*, an opera composed by Jacopo Peri with a fanciful libretto by Ottavio Rinuccini. Though hardly anyone present was conscious of this or any other important fact, musical history was made that afternoon. *Euridice* was the first opera ever to be published, the first therefore to survive. On October 5, 1600, was initiated the second most popular of Italian indoor entertainments.

By nightfall, scarcely a soul in all of Florence was sober, except for the handful of the performers and musicians who had offered *Euridice* as a gift to Henri IV and his Maria. Many of them simply collapsed in the banquet hall and slept off the excesses of the long and exciting day. Though Pieter Paul had consumed a great deal more wine than was his habit, the stimulation of all the new impressions prevented him from succumbing altogether to the effects of the drink. When Chieppio disappeared, weaving unsteadily, in the direction of the quarters they shared in the palace, the artist took once again to the streets of Florence. He was hardly in a state to inform himself usefully, but he could wander at his leisure, smugly contemplating the pedestrians he encountered who were staggering helplessly, bawling irreverent toasts to the groomless bride who was spending her last fitful night beneath her father's roof. The next day, Maria, Queen of France, would be off to Marseille to meet the man she had married the previous morning.

As he strolled, Rubens gradually recovered possession of his faculties sufficiently well to consider not merely the spectacular event, of which he had been but an incidental participant, but all the sights and sounds and encounters he had experienced

74

during his months in Italy. Introspection didn't come readily to him. In this respect, perhaps, he *was* like his dead father. But at rare moments, as now, after something of enormous importance had taken place, even the most extroverted man must collect himself a bit, must ask himself a question or two—particularly if the man is young and still in the process of forming himself.

The question which posed itself first was one that had been lurking furtively at the edges of his consciousness since the day of his arrival in Venice. Could someone so temperamentally different from most of the Italians he had so far met be ever wholly assimilated in this land? He rather thought not. He also thought it didn't matter very much, was certain, indeed, that Annibale Chieppio regarded him highly in great measure *because* of this difference in nature. But Chieppio's patronage, valuable though it doubtless was, raised yet another question which was, perhaps, more fundamental. There was no hesitation in his mind about the desirability of his remaining in Italy. Therefore it was vital for him to establish permanent connections with the rich and powerful . . . but in what capacity? What he must do was to explore possibilities; and in order to accomplish this, he believed, he had to get away from Mantua for a time—without giving offense to Gonzaga or his secretary of state.

The obvious excuse was the best—the commission he had received before leaving Antwerp to paint an altarpiece for the church of Santa Croce in Rome. The fulfillment of this obligation would serve a dual purpose; for it would remind his masters in Mantua, particularly Chieppio, that his *official* role in the ducal court was that of painter. That he was a painter at all seemed to have escaped Vincenzo Gonzaga's notice completely. So preoccupied had Rubens been with the machinations of Italian society, he had done virtually no painting and, alarmingly, had felt no great desire to paint. The visit to Florence had changed all that, had affected him profoundly. He suddenly remembered that art was still his first mission. As he returned slowly in the cool October evening to the Palazzo

Pitti, he rehearsed the speech he would make to Chieppio and Gonzaga. Its burden was simple enough: "I must go to Rome as soon as possible."

The European earth had taken a number of curious turns before Pieter Paul Rubens reached Rome in July, 1601. The Spanish king, Philip III, emulating his late father, had assembled another great fleet with the intention of invading Britain to restore Catholicism to those islands. Like Philip II, he had seen the exploit fail because of bad weather and miserable seamanship; and like Philip II, the son was poorer but no wiser for the failure.

To the dismay of most right-thinking Netherlanders, the Archduke Albrecht, responding to great pressures from his lord the King of Spain, had begun a siege of the Protestant-held coastal town of Ostend. The possibility that full-scale war might ensue caused Maria Piepelinx to write her son in Mantua that he should, at all costs, remain in Italy as long as the danger lasted. No one knew just then what length of time was involved.

In early March, Queen Elizabeth suddenly took deathly ill. Some thought her afflicted by pangs of conscience over the execution of her whilom favorite, the Earl of Essex, for treason—a feature of the previous month. The queen disappointed her known enemies by making a smart recovery, and discovered some new ones who had hitherto concealed themselves behind protests of utter fealty.

Maria de' Medici was pregnant and would, before the calendar year was out, give birth to a son destined to become Louis XIII. The future of the Bourbon monarchy was assured, a condition that was greeted by Pope Clement VIII with mixed feelings, for he still cherished uncharitable thoughts about Henri IV's policy of religious toleration.

Rubens kept these facts of international life at the back of his mind when he journeyed in July to Rome. They were important, and he couldn't escape them. But he was determined to concentrate his energies on the artistic pursuits that had

76

brought him here. Vincenzo Gonzaga had yielded gracefully to the painter's request to be allowed to address himself to the Santa Croce commission for the Archduke Albrecht. He did better than that; he ordered the young painter of his court to make copies for him of some paintings he greatly coveted which now hung in private Roman collections. And with a view to facilitating Rubens' access to these works and to making life more pleasant for him in the Eternal City, Gonzaga had given him a warm letter of introduction to Cardinal Alessandro Montaldo, Grand Elector of the Collegial Conclave, the most influential prelate of the Church, except for the pope himself. Some went so far as to say that Montaldo, who was Clement VIII's uncle, was even more powerful than the pontiff, whose election he was supposed to have secured in 1595.

A celebrated collector of art, the cardinal had been, as a younger man, almost as great an admirer of women as the Duke of Mantua. Folklore had it that he had once declared himself willing to sacrifice his soul for one lovely countess and his tiara for another. Such were the inclinations of the men who proposed to cleanse the Church.

Cardinal Montaldo received Pieter Paul with some curiosity and, inevitably, a little advice. He would find two factions of painters who were vying desperately with each other for supremacy in this city. Supremacy in Rome, which was thought to be the center of western culture, implied domination of artistic endeavor everywhere in Europe—even in those portions of the Continent that were Protestant. It was consequently a struggle on whose outcome hung a lot more than mere artistic theory; it was a question of money and politics. Rubens was informed somberly by Cardinal Montaldo that he would be wise to side with those painters and sculptors who championed the work of the Carracci and Guido Reni as distinguished from that of Michelangelo Merisi, who was pleased to call himself Caravaggio, after the town of his birth. "Guido Reni," the cardinal soberly explained, "is a gentleman. Caravaggio is a savage." Pieter Paul listened to the old cleric with attention and respect, assuring him that he would take this counsel into consideration, but

adding, as courteously as might be, "I'm not sure that I understand, excellency, how a man's character or nature have very
much to do with his art."

"It is tainted," replied Montaldo severely. "If the man is
tainted, so is his work."

Pieter Paul thought it judicious not to pursue the subject
further. But he was more intrigued than put off by the cardinal's warning against Caravaggio.

Jan Richardot, the Archduke Albrecht's ambassador to the
Holy See, proved much more helpful in practical matters. He
had had a letter from his master in Brussels instructing him to
provide young Rubens with funds and, more important still,
with suitable living quarters while he painted the triptych. Richardot, a Fleming, was an amiable Catholic in middle age who
had little of surpassing interest to do with his time. Rubens' arrival was, as a result, something of a relief from the monotony
of his daily life. Nothing would do but the *Anversois* must take
up residence with him and his wife and children in his commodious house near the Piazza di Spagna. He even provided a
well-illuminated room in which Pieter Paul might work without disturbance.

He offered at once to show his fellow countryman about the
city, and was full of useful information about what he called
"survival." He described Rome as a battlefield. "The enemy is
everywhere, especially after dark." It was certainly a bold gentlemen who dared to venture alone in the streets of the city
after nightfall. The immunity officially accorded ambassadors,
like Richardot, was naturally ignored by the importunate
thieves and whores. Only the poor enjoyed relative security—
and fashionable people found this impunity at once repugnant
and gratifying; it gave them another cause for rationalizing
poverty. The propertied classes traveled in convoy, with torch-
bearers preceding and following them—and even this precau-
tion wasn't invariably effective. Springing from the shadows of
churches or elegant palaces, bandits had no qualms about slit-
ting the throats of guards or of those they protected if the
slightest resistance was offered. A man might be comparatively

78

safe if he restricted his nocturnal walks to the district where he lived and was known—going to and returning from a tavern; but recognition was no guarantee of a harmless stroll.

The reason their city was singled out for a reputation for violence was that it was the nominal seat of Christendom. Christians weren't supposed to be criminals. This argument didn't carry much weight with Jan Richardot, who gave it as his profoundly considered opinion that not even the present pope was a very good Christian. Had he not allowed the pitiable Beatrice Cenci to be burned at the stake for the "crime" of murdering an incestuous father? Had he not ordered the execution of the brilliant Giordano Bruno as a heretic? "With His Holiness as an example," he told Rubens, "the Romans can behave as they please, which is just what they do."

Yet despite the hazards of the Eternal City at night, by day it was even more glorious than Pieter Paul had been led to expect from the extravagant descriptions given him by van Noort and van Veen and the Archduke Albrecht. Of the Italian cities he had so far visited, Rome was remarkable for its comprehension of *all* the art and architecture that had been produced in western Europe since the days of earliest civilizations. Where Venice's most ancient structure was a product, perhaps, of the tenth Christian century, there were major evidences in Rome that antedated the birth of Christ by literally hundreds of years. If Mantua possessed Isabella d'Este's collection of ancient busts and statuary, Rome was crammed with far finer examples. If it had been the Florentines who first appreciated the beauties of such antiquities, they had made most of their discoveries in Rome, in the ashes of the Caesars—some of them, ironically, turned up during the rehabilitation of the city after the Emperor Charles V's fearful sack of 1527.

The artistic shintoism that characterized the cool, respectful painting of Guido Reni and the Carracci, whom Cardinal Montaldo had commended so strongly to Rubens, was the occasion of no surprise. That, after all, was the tradition in which the Fleming had been schooled by van Noort and van Veen; Reni, the Carracci, and van Veen's former master, Federigo Zuccaro, were the solidly established academicians of Rome and therefore of Europe. The challenge to their authority came from a man barely four years older than Pieter Paul—the Caravaggio who had been described as "a savage."

Not since the prolonged and unresolved dispute between the followers of the divine Michelangelo and those of Titian over the relative virtues of line and color had the city witnessed a quarrel of such bitterness. There were, however, important differences between this debate and its antecedent. Caravaggio's violence was not confined to the vigor with which he clung to his artistic opinions. When he was drunk, which was very frequently, he was angry; when he was angry, he wanted to fight; when he wanted to fight, he was as likely to feel like murdering his opponent as was any common criminal in Rome.

To the arbiters of social propriety in Rome, the cardinals and their relations whom they had enriched and ennobled, the contest was bootless; it wasn't a contest at all. Guido Reni and the Carracci were declared the winners. The difficulty was that Caravaggio refused to accept this decision, and the wonder was that he had a handful of powerful supporters, notably Cardinal del Monte, who obtained for the rebellious and irascible artist major commissions and who saw to it that he never languished for too long in jail after one of his escapades. Happily, Caravaggio had avoided murder so far, though he had been involved in more than one duel and in numerous scuffles where knives were brought into play.

This much Rubens learned from Richardot—who was nearly as informative and gifted a gossip as the dear Countess de Lalaing, whom he had been acquainted with in Antwerp. Where the Flemish diplomat was unable to elaborate, on questions related purely to the issue of art, Pieter Paul could of course find out for himself by consulting the pictures of the principal antagonists. He took under discreet advisement his kind host's caution against seeking out the "malevolent" Caravaggio in person. For the artist found it hard to believe that however contentious that tempestuous creature might be, he would lash

80

out, literally, at a quite disinterested stranger. "That," Richardot observed ominously, "remains to be seen, doesn't it?"

Michelangelo Merisi da Caravaggio's full, voluptuous mouth opened in an expression of excessive annoyance when Pieter Paul Rubens made his appearance in the church of San Luigi dei Francesi, where the Italian artist was helping to place a picture on the wall of the nave. His black beard was dense, cropped; his hair was shaggy and unkempt, as were his clothes. The aura, however, was not of an aboriginal savage, as Cardinal Montaldo and Richardot had suggested, but of a domesticated creature inexplicably gone feral.

"Well," he said hotly as Rubens stood and watched him at his work, "are you here to serve me with a paper?"

"Certainly not."

"For decorative purposes, perhaps?" When Rubens shook his head, he snarled, "Then you might offer a man some help."

Pieter Paul sprang forward and took a bottom corner of the enormous painting. Caravaggio, supporting the opposite end, bellowed to a pair of workmen who were standing on a scaffold above him. "Higher. It's got to go higher." All four hoisted mightily. The laborers groaned, for their position made it difficult for them to lift and maintain their balance at the same time. "There," said the artist after a minute or so, and taking a piece of chalk from a pocket, he made a mark on the wall at the base of the picture. "That's where you're to put the brackets." There were loud and profound expressions of relief as they lowered the heavy painting to the floor.

"Thanks, *signore*," said Caravaggio to Pieter Paul as he brushed his filthy hands against equally soiled breeches. "You came along at just the right time. Some other fellow was supposed to be here. You can depend on no one, no one."

The Fleming introduced himself, but he wasn't looking at the controversial Italian as he spoke his name. His eyes were on the large canvas propped against the wall. It was a vivid, theatrically illuminated representation of the martyrdom of Saint Matthew, a treatment made intensely dramatic by Caravaggio's clever use of light and shadow and by meticulous attention to details, a trait that adherents to Guido Reni's views considered of minor interest; to them, the human figure was all-important. To Caravaggio, plainly, anything worth painting at all should be rendered with great care. In such little attentions, Rubens was reminded of Flemish painting of a half-century before. He was touched.

"You like it?" Caravaggio inquired abruptly.

"I'm stunned."

The Italian gave a short, harsh laugh that was filled with fury. "They'll make me paint something else in its place, of course. 'The nudes are too naked,' they'll say. 'Everything is too natural, too warm,' they'll say. The fools." He took Rubens' arm and led him at a trot out of the church. The newcomer went with reluctance; he would have liked to stay a while and consider the picture with greater care. "Come, we'll have a glass of wine together."

There was an inn directly across the street from the entrance to the church of San Luigi, the memorial in Rome to France's canonized King Louis IX. Caravaggio forced Pieter Paul into a chair and sat down opposite him. "Well, what is it you want?"

"To drink?"

"To ask me. You sought me out, didn't you? For what reason?"

Rubens grinned. "Because I was so strongly advised against it."

Caravaggio's laughter was more gentle this time. "Good man. I like that. I know who you are, of course. There are no secrets in this cursed city of gossips. Are you a good painter?" He ordered a bottle of red wine while Pieter Paul measured his reply.

"A *good* painter, yes."

"But you seem to have reservations." The Italian filled their glasses.

"Not about painting, not about craft, I mean. But about where I stand with respect to manner."

82

"Ah yes, *manner*," said Caravaggio with heavy and sarcastic emphasis. "That's *the* question, isn't it? Shall we declare that with Michelangelo and Titian all advances should cease? Shall we go on painting from dead sculptures? Shall we worship the past and say that nothing can be improved on? Or shall we try to move ahead, or at least in some other direction?" He emptied his glass at a single gulp and replenished it. He seemed disconcerted by his guest's silence. "Well, Rubens, what do *you* say?"

"That you're the greatest living painter I know of."

"I'll drink to *that*." The violent, angry artist matched the words with a deed. "But you're evading the question."

"Not exactly. You can obviously do anything you please as a painter. I mean, there's no problem of craft for you."

"My problem is the Church. I won't follow that idiotic set of rules. The cardinals want paradise. I give them earth—guts, gore, life."

"But they pay."

Caravaggio snorted. "They pay, I agree, but do they have *taste?* Do incompetents have the right to dictate what we shall and shall not paint?"

"Payment, I should think, gives them that right." Rubens hesitated. "You say you'll be forced to make a new picture to replace the one over there." He pointed toward the church they had just left. "So you accept dictation too."

The Italian shrugged dramatically, and forced out his already prominent lower lip. "But I'll not replace it with something that looks like a Guido Reni, you understand. I'll make the nudes more seemly. That's all."

"Then why go to the trouble of giving them something you know they'll reject?"

Caravaggio thumped the table. "Education. I want to accustom their eyes to the kind of painting I'm going to make them accept from me eventually. And one of these days, they'll start seeing things my way."

"You're that stubborn?"

"I'm a revolutionary, Rubens." He drained his glass again,

and again refilled it. Pieter Paul had drunk barely half the contents of the one first poured for him. "How old are you?" asked Caravaggio aggressively.

"Twenty-four."

"My God, I'm twenty-eight. *You* should be more rebellious than I."

The Fleming shook his head and offered his new acquaintance an apologetic smile. "Rebellion isn't in my nature, I'm afraid."

"Of what cardinal are you the pet?"

"None."

"Nonsense. Every painter in Rome has managed to tame at least one cardinal."

"I've been presented to Cardinal Montaldo."

"Ah." Caravaggio ordered a second bottle of wine. "Montaldo." He refilled his glass. "You don't drink much."

"It affects me."

"It affects *me* too."

"Do you drink when you paint?"

"I drink when I piss."

"It doesn't harm your work?"

Caravaggio nodded in the direction of the church. "You can answer that question as well as I. That painting represents, I should say, a hundred bottles of wine."

Rubens laughed. "Is that how you price them?"

The Italian joined in the hilarity. "I'd never thought of that." He sobered suddenly. "How did you mean that?"

Pieter Paul lifted his right hand from the stem of the glass. "Peace," he said. "I'm a man of peace. I meant it as a joke."

" 'I bring not peace, but a sword,' " said Caravaggio grandly.

"If I bring anything," Rubens responded blandly, "it *will* be peace. I have no desire to stir people up about anything. That seems to me wholly superfluous in a world full of rage and hatred."

"You know what happens to the peacemakers," snarled the Italian, "according to our good Christian traditions? They get

84

themselves killed. That's why their reward is the kingdom of heaven. They arrive there ahead of the rest of us."

"I take it that you're speaking metaphorically—about art, not war."

"It's all the same battle, isn't it? Don't you see that? War, the Church, art, thought, manners, morality . . . all part of the same thing." The wine was beginning to reach Caravaggio. Pieter Paul, watching him, was certain that he had been drinking since morning; his heavy eyelids closed more languidly, and his mouth remained partially ajar, as if he had lost the power to shut it. It was familiar ground that the hostile artist was covering now; he was speaking from memory, from his subconscious, having no need for a clear head to express this viewpoint so often elaborated by himself and all who supported him. "The Philistines are inheriting the earth," he mumbled bleakly, and consulted his glass for a consolation that must elude him. "If you're not *for* me," he said with sullen, drunken anger, "you must be against me. There's no ground in the middle. Are you with me, or are you a Philistine?" he growled, and once again emptied his glass.

Rubens sighed. "I'm the peacemaker. Don't you remember? I have to occupy the middle ground."

Caravaggio swept the surface of the table clear of glasses and bottles with a single, savage, backhanded gesture of his powerful right arm. "There," he roared, causing the other patrons of the inn to look up in surprise. "*There.* Look at that." He pointed to the empty space between them. "There's your middle ground. That's peace. What do you see?"

"Nothing."

"Nothing. Exactly. Peace is nothing. Peace is the absence of mankind. It's unnatural. Don't you understand that? *That's* why the peacemakers are doomed. No one wants them. No one needs them." He stood up and flailed his arms loosely about. "I think I'd like to kill you—but in a fair fight, of course. You annoy me, sitting there all smug and self-contained, knowing how good you are, how right you are. Would you prefer knives or swords? I must warn you that I'm very skillful with both."

Rubens laughed uneasily. "Neither, if it's all the same with you . . ."

"Well, it's not." Caravaggio reached awkwardly across the table to grasp at Rubens' shoulder—and missed by several inches. He stumbled heavily against a chair and fell to the floor, a heap of relaxed muscles. Before the young Fleming could help him to his feet, he had risen with remarkable ease through his own efforts. He shook himself, as a dog does, concluding this strange ritual by flicking his fingers to restore feeling. As Pieter Paul approached, he raised a menacing hand. "Don't touch me," he roared. "If you don't agree with me, don't touch me." Then he careened precariously to the door of the inn, leaving his bemused guest to settle the account.

Though the impression made by Caravaggio the man was an exceptionally powerful one, it was the Italian's paintings that made the more lasting mark on Rubens' memory and intelligence. Given an ideal set of circumstances and sufficiently indulgent and understanding patrons, Pieter Paul felt certain that the *man* could be tamed. But the painter, the paintings? Never. He might not see Caravaggio again, and certainly would avoid him if it were possible, but the pictures that young master contributed to the churches of Rome were objects of pilgrimage to Rubens during the periods when he was visiting there. He agreed with Caravaggio's detractors that the artist's behavior was deplorable, his alcoholic truculence calculatedly intolerable. But by God, he did admire the work. If Cardinal Montaldo was unable to separate the artist from the art, Rubens had no such difficulty.

When he recounted to Jan Richardot his meeting with Caravaggio, the ambassador was not amused. "Are you always so foolhardy?"

"Almost never, excellency. But I daresay that there's only one Caravaggio."

"And more than one Rubens?"

"I'd not thought of it. But yes, perhaps there is."

* * *

86

Rubens spent the better part of ten months in Rome completing the triptych commissioned for a chapel dedicated to the memory of Saint Helena in the church of Santa Croce in Gerusalemme. The theme was no novelty to painters in Rome, for the Emperor Constantine's mother was credited with accomplishments that were heavy with import for Christianity. It was her son who legitimized Christendom by making it the state religion of a divided and perishing empire. After a lengthy stay in Palestine, she had returned with the Holy Steps of Jerusalem, which Christ ascended on His way to Calvary. And she was, according to the legend, among the throng who discovered the True Cross. A less reliable corollary was the assertion that Saint Helena had also found Christ's crown of thorns—a relic that Saint Louis of France also claimed to possess, and for which he caused to be built the Sainte-Chapelle in Paris, the most glorious reliquary ever conceived. Like an American President who uses a number of pens with which to sign a piece of legislation into law so they may be distributed among the interested, Our Lord may have worn several crowns of thorns on His way to Calvary.

The Rubens triptych was, by his own admission, a most eclectic work, its inspiration derived in some degree from what he had been taught before reaching Italy, and in some measure reflecting what he had seen and been able to make his own since his arrival. The theme of the central panel depicted Saint Helena's embrace of the cross which she had just discovered. Flanking it were renderings of the Crucifixion and of Christ being crowned with a wreath of thorns. He was sufficiently self-critical to appreciate, when the paintings were installed, that they were not all he would have wished them to be. Even in the month that had elapsed since their completion, he himself had changed so much that, were the opportunity to do the work over again presented, the result would be totally different. He was honest enough to confess as much to Jan Richardot.

The ambassador, who rightly professed vast ignorance about painting, considered Rubens overmodest. "I find them very pretty things," he protested mildly. "You've nothing to be ashamed of."

Since Pieter Paul had to leave almost at once for Mantua, where both Chieppio and Gonzaga had been summoning him for weeks, he didn't press the point. But he felt the triptych to be inadequate, and later concluded that its stiffness (its principal affliction) was the result of too much caution, too much care. He was not Caravaggio. Had he allowed himself to paint instinctively, impetuously, as he was learning only now to do, the pictures would have been more successful. If they served no other purpose, they were most instructive to their author—and that was a very important purpose, though it might not have seemed so to the Archduke Albrecht who, on Richardot's advice, authorized final payment for them.

April was well along before he reached Mantua, and hardly had he arrived before he was seeking permission to leave again. He learned in a letter from his mother that his brother Philip was at this very moment in Verona at the university, with a scholarly friend, Jan Wouverius, on his way to Rome where he hoped to find a post. Expectedly, two years had not done much to change Philip. His hairline had receded a bit more; his eyes were a trifle puffier, his pale northern flesh a little flabbier. But the essentials had been too securely established in him for too long to admit of substantial alteration. He remained as serious and as cautious as ever.

The major item of general information that Philip brought with him from the Low Countries was that after more than a year the Archduke Albrecht had failed to capture the besieged town of Ostend. "I don't think his heart is really in it," the older Rubens said with grave disapproval. "He's said to turn his back when food is brought in to Ostend from the sea. If it were more than a gesture to placate Philip III, he'd starve the people out. That's the proper way to conduct a siege."

Pieter Paul silently cheered his illustrious, humane patron. To his brother, he merely observed, "I don't think it behooves you to criticize. You're not a general, you know."

Neither brother was inclined to linger over such topics where

88

their disagreement was and would always be fundamental. More personal news was not altogether pleasant. Philip informed Pieter Paul that their mother had sold the house in the Meir in order to raise the money finally to pay off Blandine's dowry. "The interest was reaching the proportions of the principal," he explained when his brother expressed regret over the loss of the handsome, comfortable dwelling he had, until this instant, thought of as his permanent home. That he had for two years been decided on staying forever in Italy didn't alter this feeling of deprivation; the house in the Meir had been a symbol—the place to which he could, if the need arose, always return. Now it was no longer so. He couldn't visualize his mother installed in a smaller residence far from the city's center.

Philip's decision to go to Rome had been inspired partially by this change of circumstance in Antwerp. "It was a little demeaning," he said. "People thought less of me because of it."

Pieter Paul could readily understand his brother's feeling. In the restricted, almost incestuous society of the Flemish town, to have to sell property was nearly as desperate a confession of poverty as bankruptcy—in spite of the fact that nearly everyone had had to do it. Still, Philip was a little ashamed of having left his mother to fend for herself. "Blandine will care for her, of course, and she urged me to go. But I know all the same that I'm really in hiding."

He had, as had Pieter Paul, a letter from the Archduke Albrecht to Jan Richardot, and hoped to secure from the ambassador some sort of position, preferably as his personal secretary. The younger brother added a letter of his own, knowing he had left behind him in Rome a very happy memory of himself. He was certain Richardot would find something useful and interesting for Philip to do, and that Philip would do it well, whatever it proved to be. Though the emotional distance between the brothers had widened during their separation, Pieter Paul was surprised by his pleasure in thinking of Philip nearer at hand. They had almost nothing in common except blood; how very much that represented was startling.

During the week they spent together in Verona, the Rubens

89

brothers discovered that two years apart had subtly rearranged their relationship. Philip now perceived in Pieter Paul the qualities of what he had always thought his brother's faults. His access and accessibility to new ideas and new experiences had made him much more urbane. What seemed annoyingly precocious in a youth was very attractive in a grown man. Philip was not loath to say so.

"Oh, yes," responded Pieter Paul with a boyish smile. "I'm the darling of the court of Mantua, you know."

His reply shattered the illusion for Philip. "Can you *never* be serious?"

"But I'm always serious, Philip, even when I don't seem to be. In fact, I think I'm much more serious than you are, implausible though that may sound to you. The difference between us is that you look down all the time, pay attention only to what you're about. I pay attention to everything."

The brother was scornful. "You imagine I don't know how the world goes? I know much better than you do. That's what makes me gloomy."

Since their disparity of outlook was never to be reconciled, they avoided further exchanges in this vein. They agreed on their fundamental disagreement and proceeded from there as brothers, as intimates, but not as "twin ends of the same thought." Philip discussed at length the treatise he was composing to secure his doctorate in law. Pieter Paul described the paintings he had made in Rome for the Archduke Albrecht and the works he had copied for the Duke of Mantua. These conversations were hardly mind-bending, but they weren't superficial either. The trouble was that these two young men were like a pair of perfect spheres; when they came together, they could be tangent at only one point—their fraternity. This was enough, provided they needn't share the same air too frequently or for too long at one time. They parted tearfully, reassuring each other quite truthfully of their brotherly devotion—but both rather relieved to be going in different directions.

Not until his return to Mantua did Pieter Paul discover how very different a direction had been selected for him. As soon as

90

old Annibale Chieppio released the young Fleming from his paternal embrace, he said, "His Excellency, your master and mine, has agreed with me that you're the one to lead a special mission for him to the court of King Philip in Spain."

Caught completely off his guard, Rubens for once reacted impulsively. "I believe you really *are* determined to keep me from painting."

Chieppio looked wounded. "Why should I want to do a thing like that? But almost anyone can learn to paint. Isn't that what one of your masters told you? *You* have a gift for diplomacy." He brandished a document. "Cardinal Montaldo's praise is so glowing that I'll not let you read it. It would ruin you. He calls you, among other things, incorruptible." Chieppio eyed his protégé with interest. "What did he offer you that you refused?"

Pieter Paul was bewildered. "Nothing, *signore*. I can't imagine what he means." He paused. "He's a very old gentleman, you know. He may be confusing me with someone else."

"Ah, no. You don't believe that. Neither do I."

"I do want to paint, you know," said Rubens feebly, torn between two temptations of almost equal attraction.

"But think what a useful combination the two talents could be to you. You paint a king's portrait, let us say, and while you're doing it, you plumb his thoughts."

"I know no Spanish."

"That should present no problems. We've a teacher for you. With your capacity to learn languages, you'll probably be sounding more Castilian than the Castilians by the time you're ready to leave." The wily secretary of state allowed Pieter Paul to reflect on this for a long moment before continuing. "You've often talked about wanting peace between your country and Spain. Here's a chance for you to make the acquaintance, under the happiest possible auspices, of the very men who are responsible for making war against your people, no?"

Rubens smiled wryly. "You use your Machiavelli too indiscriminately, *signore*. You imagine anything *I* might say would be persuasive to a king? Who, after all, am *I*?"

"Without the distinctions of rank which are, after all, purely matters of accident and fortune, my young friend, who is *anybody*? You're *someone*, and you're someone who knows how to make his presence felt and remembered." Once again he waved Montaldo's letter. "Go. Make an impression. Can you possibly make things worse?"

Remembering now what Philip had told him only the day before about the continuing siege of Ostend and the apprehension that worse might ensue, Pieter Paul could only concede that there seemed little he could do to exacerbate conditions in his beleaguered little native land. "I hear and obey," he mumbled.

Three

THE caravan bound for Spain, with Pieter Paul Rubens as its leader, departed from Mantua on March 5, 1603. It was a surprisingly large convoy if one took into account the nature of the mission it was to implement—the reinforcement of Vincenzo Gonzaga's quest to succeed to the title and, more important, to the rich perquisites and emoluments of admiral in the service of Philip III—a post made vacant by the recent death of the celebrated Genoese seafarer, Andrea Doria. The duke had not a single qualification for the office. He wasn't even a very skilled military commander. His experience afloat was limited to one or two ceremonial voyages, in clement weather, across the Strait of Messina to visit Sicily. But in a culture where cardinals were named at the age of five, Gonzaga's ambition was not in the least farfetched. And even if the main purpose of Rubens' embassy proved fruitless, it was important for the ruler of Mantua to keep it clearly before the eyes of the Spanish king and his first minister, Lerma, that they had a good friend residing on the banks of the river Mincio.

The route selected for the passage of the caravan, which included a fine coach and six matched bay carriage horses for presentation to King Philip, was not the most direct; this would have followed a straight course to Genoa, from which port vessels sailed regularly for several Spanish harbors. Though Pieter Paul was not offered an explanation, he presumed that the avoidance of Genoa was intended to prevent the Spinola-Doria family from learning of Gonzaga's designs on the admiralcy.

He was ordered to travel to the coast by way of Florence and Pisa, and was prevailed upon to pause for two nights in both cities—to be entertained first by the Duke of Mantua's Medici father-in-law, then by the Grand Duke of Tuscany in the city of the Leaning Tower. In the first of a series of lengthy letters to Annibale Chieppio, Pieter Paul expressed himself as amazed by the detailed information in the possession of his host at Pisa, not only about the nature and purpose of the expedition and the gifts that were being transported, but about the young ambassador himself. If the stripling diplomat had any doubt about the speed and accuracy of Italian espionage, it was dispelled by the grand duke's casual enumeration and description of all the major items in the cargo. He was, as he indicated in his letter to Chieppio, more than a little puzzled that the Pisan ruler should have been so interested in what seemed to Pieter Paul an embassy of only minor importance.

After his departure in the direction of the port of Livorno, it occurred to the painter that in addition to deceiving the Spinola-Doria family, the circuitous journey had had a second point, in ostentatiously demonstrating to the dukes of Florence and Pisa how very insignificant the mission was. This elaborate and entirely Italian line of reasoning, bemusing though it was to him, had two effects on Rubens. It led him initially to wonder if, then, his assignment was not, in reality, much more vital than he had been led to believe by Gonzaga and Chieppio. And, second, it determined him to treat it as a mission of the greatest urgency and delicacy. This wasn't difficult; he wanted very much for that to be so. He was, he appreciated, beginning to think in a manner that no respectable Fleming would recognize.

The goods in Rubens' charge lay for nearly a week on a

94

quayside of Livorno before he was able to locate the captain of a ship out of Hamburg who was willing to transport him, his attendants, and his large and varied cargo to a Spanish harbor. Two problems arose. The German ship was bound for Alicante, very nearly the worst possible port of entry for an expedition destined finally to go to Valladolid. And the charges demanded seemed exorbitant, far in excess of Chieppio's estimate. Since delay might render the entire mission useless, Pieter Paul elected to agree to the terms.

It was early April before the ship reached Spain. There, contrary to all Rubens had been led to expect of the treatment normally accorded an ambassador, he was compelled by the customs officials to open every carefully packed case. This quite unwarranted violation of diplomatic immunity was but a foretaste of disappointments and disillusionments to follow—the first of which was a three-week journey from Alicante across half of Spain to Valladolid, a trip attended by repeated storms of wind and rain of a fury and duration unprecedented, or so he was informed by Annibale Iberti, the permanent Mantuan ambassador to the Spanish port, when he finally reached the city of Valladolid, newly designated Spanish capital.

The rain had certainly done nothing to improve an early impression of Spain which, Rubens was convinced, would not in any case have been a very happy one. The grim, barren, desolate, abandoned Spanish earth needed no torrents of rain to make it inhospitable. The sullen, suspicious innkeepers who greeted him and his little company along the tortuous route were, like the downpours, wholly superfluous too. Spain was not simply another country; it was another state of mind, existing in another world, in another and much earlier century. To the casual traveler, it appeared that there had been no rebirth of civilization in any way comparable to the Renaissance that had transformed the rest of western Europe. Here, the Middle Ages had been prolonged fully two hundred years, into the immediate present.

If this judgment wasn't entirely just, it surely applied to the immense majority of the Spanish people. Only in Ireland were the extremes of wealth and poverty so dramatically posited side by side—with the important difference that the Irish peasantry was exploited by the British occupant while the Spanish peasant was victimized by his own clergy and nobility. Thus, while the Irish could rightly focus their hatred on an enemy intruder, the enemy of Spain was Spain herself. Although Rubens had not yet added the word to his startlingly comprehensive vocabulary of the Spanish tongue, he was aware from the outset of his long trip to Valladolid of a quality of despair which the natives called *desengaño*—the certainty that life would never improve and, since this was the unalterable reality, it wasn't worth the effort of seeking to ameliorate conditions. All were doomed. There was and could be no ground for hope.

Malnourished, overtaxed, and ultimately dispossessed of the pitiable little tracts of scarcely arable land they had so miserably harvested, the peasant families were driven toward the nearest town. There they discovered the dubious comfort of slowly starving to death in the company of hundreds of others in exactly the same terrible and hopeless condition. To add to a burden of fiscal catastrophes that had thrice broken the back of the nation's economy during the past thirty years, there had been an epidemic of the black death which, in 1600, had literally decimated the Spanish population and been especially virulent in the richest of the country's provinces, Castile.

To pestilence and bankruptcy were added a pair of wars which couldn't possibly be won—against Britain and the United Provinces of the Low Countries. Their only effect in 1603 was to exacerbate, if that was possible, a set of conditions so appalling already that Rubens concluded he had come to a land whose entire population was being systematically martyred on the altar of royal and Catholic folly.

By the time he reached Valladolid he found himself in the ironic position of feeling sorrier for his country's enemies than he did for the Protestants of the northern sections of the Low Countries. The enormity of that conviction didn't impose itself on him all at once; rather did it work upon him as the rain had wrought its erosive devastation on the usually arid plains and uplands he had just been traveling through. He had arrived in Alicante with a determination to do what he could to bring about peace between Spain and the United Provinces by pleading the despair of his own people. When he arrived in Valladolid, he could as easily have argued the same cause from a purely Spanish standpoint and with equally fervent and cogent speeches. He had not known that life could be sustained on levels of such abject and grinding poverty. Indeed, it wasn't life; it was merest existence.

With Rubens' entry into the Spanish capital, the rains ceased. He hoped it was a good omen, but he was so profoundly depressed by what he had seen on the way from Alicante that it almost didn't matter. The Mantuan ambassador, Annibale Iberti, was a stern, rapacious little man who greeted the young man's arrival with liverish hostility. He professed at first to know nothing of the mission, though Pieter Paul had read Chieppio's letter informing him of it. Iberti claimed next that he had no accommodations for this special emissary and his precious cargo; he yielded only when Rubens offered to write Vincenzo Gonzaga in detail of the icy reception he had been given. Yet it remained evident that relations between the middle-aged Italian and the young man from Antwerp were going to be as difficult as Iberti could reasonably make them.

Pieter Paul, given Iberti's hostility, was anxious to present the gifts he had brought for the king and the Duke of Lerma as soon as possible. The prospect of a prolonged stay in agonized Spain under Iberti's provoking aegis seemed very bleak. The wish was not to be granted. The court of Philip III, following a custom established during the joint reign of Fernando and Isabel more than a century before, was wandering about the Spanish countryside to make a spectacle of itself for the benefit of the grandees of Castile; these great nobles, according to the Mantuan ambassador, were showing themselves to be much more intractable today than had been the case under Philip II, who would never have countenanced such resistance to the royal will.

At the moment, the king and his favorite minister were hunt-

ing. After a fortnight of this diversion, they would proceed to
Burgos. Only in late June or early July would they return to
Valladolid. Rubens' heart sank when he heard this news. The
realization that he would have to spend two months in the company of Iberti made very attractive the ambassador's suggestion
that he leave the gifts and return to Mantua. He rejected it on
the ground that he had been commanded by Vincenzo Gonzaga
to make the presentations personally to the king and to Lerma.
Moreover, having come such a distance, and in such circumstances, it seemed foolish not to wait for their return. It was
not, after all, every day that one had the opportunity of paying
homage to a king.

The issue of whether he would stay or go was made academic
the day after his arrival. Rubens ordered the unpacking of the
crates and boxes. Among the gifts was a group of paintings, copies of celebrated pictures in the Gonzaga collection. The canvases, which had been in pristine condition at the time of their
inspection in Alicante, were in various and terrible stages of de-
composition now. All had been damaged by the constant wind
and rain; two were totally ruined. When he learned of the
painter's predicament, Iberti had difficulty concealing his mali-
cious pleasure. "What will you do now?" he asked almost jubilantly.

"I shall write His Excellency the Duke at once," Pieter Paul
replied, "but there can be no doubt what his answer will be. I
shall have to repaint the damaged portions."

"You?" The Italian's tone of incredulity was meant to be
offensive. Rubens was offended.

"It's not the sort of work I enjoy, repainting another artist's
pictures, but you may rest assured, Signor Iberti, that I can do
it in such a way that no one but you and I will be the wiser."

"I forbid it."

The artist stared at him, astonished. "I don't see that you're
in any position to forbid it."

"I'm in charge here. So far as you're concerned, I am the
Duke of Mantua in Spain."

"Very well, *signore,* and just what do *you* propose to do?"

"I shall summon some local artists to make the repairs required."

"You have so much confidence in these men?"

"More than I have in *you*. I've seen *their* work. I've not seen yours."

Though infuriated by Iberti's manner and meaning, Pieter Paul couldn't repress a grin. "Ah, I see. And you know a great deal about painting?"

"I know what my eyes tell me."

"A pig knows as much as that, *signore*."

Iberti huffed. "Do I understand that you're comparing me to a swine?"

"Only in the sense that you and a swine share a knowledge of what your eyes can tell you. The only difference is that you're able to give words to your experience. A pig can't do that."

The ambassador was beside himself. "In my twenty years of service in His Excellency's diplomatic corps, I've never been told such a thing, even by an enemy of Mantua. To hear it from someone who pretends to be an ally . . ."

"And how often in those twenty years have you tried to set yourself up as an expert in painting?"

"You have no respect for a man who's old enough to be your father."

"I give respect, *signore,* where I think it due. The only reason we respect age is that the aged often have the power to compel respect. An old man can be just as foolish as a young one. In matters where I think you competent, I can respect you. Where the matter is painting, I think you foolish and ignorant."

"I've seen no sign of your respect," Iberti retorted icily.

"I've seen no sign of your competence, *signore,*" said Pieter Paul.

When the ambassador offered no reply, Rubens felt that he had won the day—though he was, in the aftermath, staggered by the presumptuous ferocity of his attack against Iberti. It was so out of character. He attributed his evil temper to the harsh atmosphere of Spain. He was certain he had gone too far, said too much, been carried away on the tide of pent-up indignation, not all of which had to do with poor Iberti. It had been very wrong of him, not the behavior to be expected of a man who wanted to be at least a part-time diplomat.

Nevertheless, the Italian had invited this assault by comporting himself with the arrogance of a pontiff. So they had both been mistaken. Somehow, the breach must be repaired. While he made with truly prodigious celerity the necessary restorations to the damaged canvases, and painted two new pictures to replace the pair that were irreparable, the ambassador kept looking in on him, all anxiety (whether feigned or genuine). Rubens turned over in his mind how best to effect a reconciliation, and finally decided that he should offer to paint Iberti's portrait, after he had completed the repairs. The Italian, plainly torn between a reluctance to be placated and a desire to be flattered, at last allowed himself to be persuaded to sit for this young Flemish master.

It was only after Pieter Paul finished a full-length portrait of Iberti in his grandest ambassadorial attire, a work accomplished with dizzying speed, that a thaw set in. Like the melting of the great glaciers, the process, once begun, was irreversible.

Delighted almost beyond words by Rubens' picture of him, Iberti now lavished praise on the artist for the miraculous work he had done on the damaged paintings, and reserved particular accolades for the two pictures of the ancient Greek philosophers Heraclitus and Democritus that he had created as replacements for those that were not salvageable. "No one would ever know, Maestro Rubens, that these things had come to any harm. And as for the two paintings from your own hand, they're finer than all the rest."

Pieter Paul let well enough alone; having made his point, he could see no virtue in reminding Iberti that he was today not a bit wiser about painting than he had been a few weeks before. Tranquillity had been established between them just before the king and his first minister led the court back to Valladolid. That was all that mattered. The representatives of Mantua made elaborate arrangements for the formal presentation of Vincenzo Gonzaga's gifts to Philip III, a ceremony which the

100

two men would perform side by side. Rubens was excited by the knowledge that he was soon to come face to face with the author of the continuing war in the Low Countries.

Or so he imagined. When the great moment arrived, the artist found himself isolated from the young monarch by a double row of royal bodyguards; he was given no choice but to stand by and watch as Annibale Iberti turned over the coach and horses, the magnificent pair of vases, and the lesser presents which, by rights, *he* should be offering in the name of Mantua to the Most Catholic King. After the court had risen, Iberti protested, with a disingenuousness that redoubled all the distaste Pieter Paul had originally cherished for him, complete innocence of any intention to keep the painter from sharing the instant of glory. "I can't imagine what went wrong," he repeated owlishly.

Pieter Paul would have been even angrier were he not by now aware that of the two presentations, the one to the Duke of Lerma was by far the more important. Not only from Iberti, but from other foreign diplomats in Valladolid, had he heard the phrase, "Philip reigns, but Lerma rules." Rubens made absolutely certain that it was he alone who transferred ownership of the collection of paintings from the Duke of Mantua to the Spanish king's first minister. And he decided he should inform Lerma that he had created the paintings of Heraclitus and Democritus.

The Duke of Lerma was the prototype and archetype of the kind of public servant who would govern the country until the last Iberian Habsburg perished, early in the following century, without having sired a son. He was everything the principal figure of a crippled nation ought not to be—greedy, shallow, bigoted, arrogant, and imbued with a stupidity that was but slightly mitigated by a certain shrewdness which prevented his major defects from being detected during twenty years of office. The advantage he enjoyed over his king was, incredibly, that he was fractionally the brighter of the two. But behind the powerful duke was the irksome person of Don Pedro Franqueza, an opportunist who, only four years later, would be found to have

101

embezzled more than two million precious ducats from the Spanish treasury. When Franqueza's crimes were discovered, he was replaced by a more proficient thief. Thus was a pattern set. *Desengaño* was the only political wisdom.

Lerma expressed himself as delighted with the gifts of painting. Unlike Iberti, he made no pretensions to knowledge or even taste. What he worshiped was novelty. Incapable of diverting or entertaining himself, he appreciated anything that could hold his interest for ten minutes or so—the average length of his attention span. Aside from pretty women, he enjoyed the company of a man who could pique his curiosity without taxing his limited intellect.

Rubens eagerly accepted Lerma's proposal for a portrait. Even Iberti was happy about this suggestion, though he cautioned the artist to keep constantly at the back of his mind in whose behalf he was acting. "You're not here as a representative of Prince Mauritz or his people. The Duke of Mantua isn't one whit concerned about the cause of peace in your country. He wants Andrea Doria's post as admiral. You're to refer to nothing else of a political nature."

The painter felt intuitively that in his interviews with the most powerful man in Spain, he should let his subject indicate the direction of their conversation. At the beginning of their initial encounter, the duke manifested an interest in the occurrence that was currently on the lips of most of Europe's courtiers and princes—the recent death of Britain's redoubtable Queen Elizabeth and the accession to that nation's throne of James I Stuart, son of the ill-starred Mary of Scotland. It was Lerma's opinion that the Jacobean age aborning would see the heretic islands brought to their knees before the bar of Catholic Europe's justice. At the very least, he hoped for an end to the piracy that was depriving Spain not only of the desperately needed gold and silver bullion brought out from the New World, but of the ships that carried it. "My ambassador in London tells me," he said with relish, "that the king isn't half the man the queen was."

Rubens chuckled with proper appreciation, and wondered

102

who had originated the *mot*. "But if he has good ministers, highness, does it make any difference?"

Lerma considered this question for a moment before perceiving the apparently pleasant allusion to his princely self. He smiled benignly. "None, of course. However, I'm happy to say that King James' years as King of Scotland have been very poor preparation for his new role. Now he has a curious institution called a Parliament to contend with. What folly, to give the people a voice in government." The duke resisted the urge to rub his hands together in glee. "He'll have much trouble before he's done."

"And that will be good for Spain?"

"Oh, yes," said Lerma affably. "What's bad for Britain is bound to be good for the rest of Europe. Now," he added with a nasty, vengeful glint in his eye, "we shall be able to finish off the Protestants in *your* country. James won't be able to help you. Parliament won't give him the funds for the ships and men to help Prince Mauritz."

"I hope that won't involve a great cost in lives, Highness."

The duke shrugged. "What does it matter? It's not as if heretics were people, is it?"

Rubens contained himself, but not easily. "I think," he finally observed with caution, "that you'll make no friends among the Catholics of my country by killing Protestants, highness. They're mostly related to each other, you know."

Lerma seemed surprised to learn this. "Is that so?" He laughed joylessly. "A pity. Perhaps we shall have to kill everyone, then."

In spite of the growing exasperation he felt for the fatuous first minister, Pieter Paul Rubens painted a masterful portrait of him. That he was able to do this seemed evidence of something Caravaggio had said of a Rubens picture he had been shown by mutual acquaintances: "He paints surfaces as if he were God." The duke was pleased with the portrait, and was doubly so when he learned that it was one of the first equestrian portraits ever made of a subject who was not a reigning monarch.

He gave expression to his satisfaction and gratitude in a tangible way. He paid Rubens a handsome fee for the canvas, and commissioned him to portray other members of his numerous family and household, including his current mistress, and ordered as well paintings of the Christ and the twelve Apostles—an *apostolado,* as this popular kind of series was called in Spain. In order to complete the portrait assignments given him by Lerma, Pieter Paul became an appendage of the peripatetic court—to his delight and Iberti's patent displeasure. He traveled during the months of summer and autumn to several of the palaces on the annual royal itinerary, notably to Aranjuez, Madrid, and the forbidding Escorial.

Rubens, who had remained in constant and intimate communication with Annibale Chieppio thoughout his Spanish stay, wrote him in October that he had had opportunities to see the important pictures in the numerous and scattered royal collections—most of them acquisitions of Philip II, whose admiration particularly of Raphael and Titian could be attested to by the extraordinary numbers of paintings by these two great masters to be found in Spain. There was, however, he informed the Mantuan secretary of state, no contemporary painter working in this dour country whose art was worthy of a second serious glance—a statement that was substantially correct.

He could, had he cared to qualify that generalization, have added that there *was* one eccentric painter living in Toledo whose work he had seen at the Escorial and in a convent church in Madrid. This man was a Cretan called El Greco, and though he had only briefly enjoyed the patronage of Philip II, he was regarded by the most important hierarchs of the Spanish church as the greatest painter of Europe. Rubens knew little more than that about El Greco, except that he had been for a decade a pupil of Titian's. This experience with the glorious Venetian seemed belied or rejected in the examples of his craft that the Fleming had an opportunity to study. He thought El Greco's canvases so willfully distorted and peculiar as to represent a total denial of all that had been so slowly and painfully absorbed and passed on over three centuries of artistic development in Italy. The man was surely no primitive; he handled color with immense skill and absolutely breathtaking audacity.

The fact was that El Greco's painting shocked Rubens. It even frightened him a little. Where else but in hermetic, God-stricken Spain could a man commit such frenzies of mad spirituality to canvas and be acclaimed a sort of lay hero by the princes of the Church? Pieter Paul despised El Greco's conception because it was incomprehensible to him, a private, personal vision wholly outside the scope of a worldly, hard-headed Erasmian's experience or inclination. He had no hesitancy about condemning the Cretan's style—but he could never forget it. To have seen it was like being accorded a sudden, brief glimpse of the true apocalypse; he refused to believe his eyes, but the image was engraved forever upon his totally retentive visual memory.

To leave Spain caused Rubens not a single tremor of regret. He returned to Mantua in the spring of 1604 with the conviction that although the Duke of Lerma might, as he swore, pursue the war against the United Provinces, the attempt would finally fail because his will and that of the malleable king were not nearly so strong as their words, and because Spain simply couldn't afford the continued cost of a major military effort which, even if successful, must be followed by a perpetual occupation in force. Sooner or later, there had to be surcease.

On his arrival in Gonzaga's city, a letter from his mother informed him that the Genoese banker-turned-general, Ambrogio di Spinola, had arrived in Flanders with a well-equipped army of 8,000 mercenaries; Ostend had at last been induced to surrender. "But that, alas, is not the end of it, my son. The supporters of Prince Mauritz in the United Provinces, especially the bankers of Amsterdam, have provided funds for him to raise yet another army and to purchase more vessels. Our harbor here in Antwerp is still blockaded. The war continues. You and Philip should stay on in Italy. There is nothing for you here."

It was only when Maria Piepelinx wrote so darkly of conditions at home that Pieter Paul felt the slightest nostalgia. It was perverse. He dismissed the thought from his mind. After a year in Spain, the good temper and the soft climate of Italy were welcome. He had no intention of going back to Antwerp; there was no sense in it. He replied to her letter by proposing that she join him or Philip, an idea she rejected summarily. Who would oversee her property? She was too old for travel. Besides, there must eventually be peace and an ensuing burst of prosperity. Then her beloved sons could reasonably return, and she would be on hand to find brides for them. They couldn't remain bachelors forever.

A year and a half in the constant company of Vincenzo Gonzaga was intermittently entertaining. The duke respected Pieter Paul—though he lost few occasions to remind him of the failure of the mission he had led to Spain; he had not acceded to Andrea Doria's post as admiral. Gonzaga admired Rubens' painting sufficiently to commission him to make a triptych of the Holy Trinity for the high altar of the newly completed Jesuit church of Mantua, a work in which he and Eleonora de' Medici appeared as worshippers of the crucified Christ—roles characteristically assigned to the wealthy donors of religious pictures. With his master, Pieter Paul made several short excursions around northern Italy—to Venice, to Verona, to Milan, and a long visit to Genoa, where the artist portrayed the beautiful Brigida di Spinola Doria and her husband, close relatives of the Spinola general who had succeeded in causing the resistants of Ostend to yield after three terrible years of siege.

But at the back of Rubens' mind was a plan to escape, as soon as he was able, to Rome. Mantua was, for him, a back water. Vincenzo Gonzaga had no intention of offering his painter opportunities to create wonders on a scale comparable to those afforded Andrea Mantegna or Giulio Romano. His available funds were to serve more earthy and more earthly desires. Oh, now and then, Pieter Paul would be ordered to paint a portrait or a triptych or even, in time, something a little more ambitious. But a project that could consume his boundless energy was not a likelihood. As for Chieppio's scheme to groom him as his successor, of which by now Rubens was well aware, while not devoid of interest, it seemed too remote an eventuality. "Dear old Annibale," the artist wrote to his brother, "takes such care of himself these days that I am certain he will outlive me."

Consequently, Rubens nibbled away at Gonzaga whenever the chance presented itself, demeaning himself by offering to make copies of pictures in Rome, using any pretext that had even a minute hope of success. The duke was not deceived. "You want the best of both worlds, Rubens. You want my patronage, but you want it in Rome, not in Mantua. Don't you think that just a little crass?"

"I want merely to improve myself in order to be of greater service to you, excellency."

"Then go," said Gonzaga, one day, with angry impatience. "But don't forget that I shall feel free to summon you back whenever I require you."

Pieter Paul promised absolute fidelity. He even meant it— though he made the single mental reservation to resist as conscientiously as he could any attempt to bring him back to Mantua. Rome, he knew, was where his future lay. Chieppio was equally aware of the painter's intention, but he evinced more perplexity than did Gonzaga. "There are many fine artists in Rome. Here there's only Pourbus, and he's scarcely your rival. Do you *want* rivalry?"

The Fleming hadn't considered this before. The notion that he might be competitive, that he enjoyed or needed the goad of others vying for the same commissions, had not occurred to him. It was a hypothetical question he thought impossible to answer, for he had never found himself in a competitive situation. So all he could say was what he did say. "I don't honestly know, *signore*. I *think* I'm called to Rome by its excitement, and of course by the presence of my brother there. But you may have discovered something about me I didn't know. I do perhaps feel the need for a little bit of rivalry."

"But what about all my plans for you?" said old Chieppio with histrionic wistfulness. "Are they to go for nothing?"

"It was part of my education, *signore*. Education is never for nothing. You've opened many doors for me, and I'll never allow them to close."

"Of what use will they be if all you do is paint pictures?"

"Nothing one learns is ever completely irrelevant." He smiled beguilingly. "Perhaps I wasn't intended for diplomacy or administration. I wasn't able to do in Spain what His Excellency wanted of me, after all. I'm sorry about that. But perhaps, some day, I'll find a way of putting all I've learned to good use . . ."

"For Mantua?"

Rubens shrugged. "Who can say? Perhaps for all of Christendom."

As had been the case in 1601, the permission in principle to leave Mantua was easier to come by than to put into effect. Once it had been granted, Vincenzo Gonzaga found reasons for postponing the actual moment of Pieter Paul's departure. He must make copies of two Mantuan masterpieces for the collection of the duke's direct liege lord, the Emperor Rudolf of Prague. There were several new additions to the already exaggerated number of lovely court ladies whose portraits he wanted Rubens to paint. The Trinity triptych for the Jesuit church didn't absolutely satisfy him, and he requested minor alterations. Rubens must accompany him on yet another visit to Genoa, for the Spinola family, who were the duke's main bankers, wanted more portraits from the artist's wonderful Flemish hand.

It was November of 1605 before Rubens was finally released from what had come to seem an unbearable servitude in Mantua. Yet it was a connection he couldn't bring himself to sever completely. The four hundred annual ducats could prove a lifesaver, helping to eke out the remains of the countess' dwindling legacy if he were unable to secure important com-

108

missions in Rome. Moreover, he couldn't afford to leave the duke with a poor impression of him, for reputation was of great moment to one who must earn his livelihood from those to whom repute mattered greatly. So however impatient he was to tear himself away from Gonzaga's hold, he kept his feelings to himself. By the time he actually managed his departure, he had all but renounced hope of ever being free of his dull and inconsequential obligations to the Mantuan court.

Philip Rubens, who had been kept apprised of his brother's constantly changing plans, felt much the same way. When Pieter Paul presented himself, unheralded, at the Roman palace of Ascanio Cardinal Colonna, whom Philip served as private secretary, there was a great commotion of incredulous delight. The prelate, to whom the artist was immediately presented, insisted that his valued assistant's brother take up residence under the palatial roof, "at least for the time being." The quarters put at Rubens' disposal were, by comparison with those offered him in the Palazzo Ducale of Mantua, nothing less than regal. "It's the kind of circumstance that I have no trouble getting used to," he happily told Philip, "but a lot of trouble leaving."

The older brother was full of Rome—but it was a different Rome from the one Pieter Paul had known during his previous visit. Philip's range of acquaintances included mainly scholars and divines, men whose principal concern was the literature, history, and culture of the ancient past, relics of which were constantly being exhumed as the richly endowed princes of the Church tore down old buildings to replace them with sumptuous palaces in the new quasi-classical mode called Jesuit, to honor Vignola's Chiesa de Gesu, the mother church of that religious order. One such discovery, made in the course of excavations on the Esquiline Hill, was a fresco of pre-Christian Rome, almost intact, depicting a festive wedding scene. By means of which no one in the city was quite certain, this antique masterpiece came into the hands of a papal nephew, Cardinal Aldobrandini, who had it installed in his palace and invited all of socially acceptable Rome to come to view it.

Conversation among Philip's friends tended to focus on

serious matters—though these subjects were not always treated very seriously. An inexhaustible topic was the sensational sequence of events that had followed the death, in the spring of 1605, of Pope Clement VIII. After a long conclave which rumor described as the most corrupt on record, a compromise candidate was elected, a cardinal of such frailty that he survived, as Pope Leo XI, for less than four weeks. So the struggle for the precious tiara had to be gone through all over again. The report was that some of the hardier collegiates had actually come to blows over the choice, and though it caused an eyebrow or two to rise a little higher than usual, no one familiar with clerical infighting thought improbable the allegation that some of the great ladies of Rome had offered their opulent charms to cardinals still young enough to appreciate them, in exchange for votes. Finally Camillo Borghese, a comparatively young candidate since he was but in his early fifties, was selected.

A Roman of the Romans, the new pope, as Paul V, vowed once and for all to assert the authority of the Holy See over the recalcitrant rulers of Venice, who dared to insist that clerics charged with civil offenses be tried by secular courts. It was precisely the same dispute that had brought about the split between Henry II of Britain and Thomas à Becket, and it had the same result. Venice held her ground, and the Vatican found itself powerless.

The new pope didn't confine his efforts at reform to Italy. He attempted to rescind the so-called Gallican liberties long treasured by the church in France, and was surprised to encounter resistance not only from Henri IV but from a majority of the French hierarchy. To find that religiously indifferent king and his cardinals and bishops on the same side of any issue was remarkable. The event may have been at least partially explained by a Spanish-inspired conspiracy, only recently uncovered, to name Henri's son by his mistress, Henriette d'Entragues, as rightful heir to the throne because, in a moment of passionate feeblemindedness, the monarch had proposed marriage to his lovely young courtesan—in writing.

110

Undismayed by his failures in Venice and Paris, Paul V turned his attention to London, demanding that James I abolish the oath of allegiance to himself, as head of the Church of England, which he extracted from all his subjects as a basic condition for life itself on his islands. The British monarch was enjoying a particularly stormy career in his relations with a Parliament which insisted on the right to ratify any royal tax measure—a pretension repugnant in its nature to any self-respecting absolutist. James I turned a deaf ear to the entreaties of the "Bishop of Rome," who presumed, in the king's view, when he called himself head of the entire "Holy Catholic Church." The near miss of the Gunpowder Plot, which took place while Pieter Paul was traveling to Rome, didn't shake King James' confidence in his capacity to reign *and* rule without the participation of the governed. He would soon order the translation of the Bible that was his only happy claim to immortality—conceived in part as a reply to Paul V's importunity.

Violence and conspiracy were somewhat greater novelties in foreign capitals than they were in Rome, where they were a commonplace. So much power and gold were concentrated in so few capricious hands that it was inevitable that they be contested for by foul means as well as fair. Indeed, it seemed to Pieter Paul, bemused by the internecine quarrels of the popes and cardinals and the relations and intimates, that there might even be a preference for foul play where fair play might have been at least equally effective.

A measure of the change his years here had wrought in Philip Rubens was his response to this suggestion. "I no longer believe there can be such a thing as heresy. I'm not even sure that I'm a Catholic." Pieter Paul was dumbfounded. Was this his brother speaking? It was, but a sadder and wiser man, one who warmed eagerly to the subject of clerical hypocrisy. He went so far as to pronounce the Counter Reformation a hoax, a gigantic plot intended only to recoup lost prestige, lost perquisites and prerogatives, not lost souls. "If I thought my immortal soul were in real danger, I think I'd revert to the paganism of

111

our Roman ancestors. But to tell you the most terrible truth of all, brother, I just don't care."

The younger Rubens thought this reaction a trifle excessive. "You needn't commit the generic fallacy, you know, simply because you're disillusioned. The hierarchy isn't the whole Church."

"Yes, yes, I understand. 'The Church is the body and blood of Christ,' and so forth. What an irony, Pieter Paul, that *you* should start arguing the point of view that I used to hold."

"No, Philip. My position is just the same as it was. I accept the faith with a whole heart, but I reject the cant." He shrugged. "I'm still a humanist."

"Humanism is dead."

"*I* accept it."

"You say that you reject the cant. That's very praiseworthy. But how do you *escape* it?"

"I pay it no heed."

"That's easy enough for you, perhaps. But *I* accept the Church's money."

Pieter Paul laughed lightly. "Better that it should come to you than to someone less worthy. That's my conviction, at any rate. I accept the Church's money too. I have no qualms about it."

"But you can *paint* with a free spirit. It's not the same thing as what I do. I'm an authority on canon law. Did you know that? I advise my cardinal on matters of orthodoxy. Can you imagine it?"

"Oh, very easily."

"You know me as I used to be, Pieter Paul, not as I am now. I tell you, the Romans were absolutely justified in torturing the Christians. The Romans believed in *their* gods. That's more than most Christians can say with honesty."

"Your explorations of the past have shattered your faith?"

"My exposure to the machinations of the present . . ."

"Ah well, Philip, you've started to look up, haven't you? You're finally seeing the world as it is."

112

"And I perceive that it's not perfectible."

"You're a very bundle of heresies, aren't you? Never mind. This is the safest place for heretics, right under the nose of the Grand Inquisitor. Read Erasmus again, brother. There's a sublimity even in the grossest folly."

Philip sighed sharply. "How *can* you be so calm? Do you have any idea what's happening all around us, all the time? This city is Sodom and Gomorrah rolled into one. Vice is everywhere. Virtue is unheard of . . ."

"And when someone spies it out, he suppresses it, for fear of its possible contagion."

"There's nothing to joke about."

"Oh, come, the cataclysm can't be all that imminent, Philip. The condition has been with us for centuries. You're surely not suggesting that Imperial Rome seems to you a Garden of Eden in retrospect."

"It seems more noble."

"Only because the ignoble is transitory. We forget it. Nobility survives."

"If I could only believe you . . ."

"You really don't have a choice, do you? It's either belief, or suicide?"

Presented with these alternatives, Philip Rubens allowed his younger brother to persuade him that though evil was undoubtedly invincible, it could be resisted effectively now and then by decent men. The reversal of positions was infinitely amusing to Pieter Paul, who found himself chuckling about it repeatedly for months; and he was unkind enough to tease Philip. " 'The last shall be first,' " he said. " 'A little child shall lead them.' "

Laughter still didn't come easily to the more somber Rubens, but he no longer reproached Pieter Paul for being frivolous, which he plainly remained. He would certainly not have agreed with the poet who described laughter as the one sure touch of genius in the universe; but he could now acknowledge it a place of importance in the emotional solar system—something

113

he would not, three years before, have considered remotely probable.

While Philip passed his many hours of leisure exploring the literature and philosophy of ancient Rome, his younger brother reacquainted himself with the contemporary artistic scene. The situation was, if anything, even more convulsive than it had been at the time of his first visit. The rivalry between the academicians, Zuccaro and the Carracci, and the admirers of Caravaggio had greatly intensified. Guido Reni, who had long cast his stultifying spell from distant Bologna, had been persuaded to come permanently to Rome, to reinforce the position of the Carracci who, if truth be told, were not altogether pleased with this development, for the Bolognese's vogue cut seriously into their flourishing trade.

Caravaggio continued to go his willful, violent way. With Cardinal Scipione Borghese, nephew of the new pope, as his most powerful patron and the French ambassador as an effective second, the "savage" received major commissions for religious painting. The resulting works were the objects of almost incendiary controversy—and always for identical reasons, that they were too "realistic" and insufficiently "respectful" of the holy scenes they depicted.

As was only to be anticipated, Caravaggio refused to confine his miscreant conduct to his art. On the night of July 20 of the present year, near the spectacular Fontana di Trevi in the Piazza Navona, the artist had quarreled with one Mariano Pasqualone, assistant to a prominent Roman notary. The dispute centered about the favors of a model known only as Lena. In the scuffle, the painter drew a knife and stabbed Pasqualone, injuring him severely, but not mortally—a fact of which he was unaware, for he left at once for Genoa. When he learned that his victim had survived the wound, Caravaggio returned to Rome and resumed his work for the most recently constructed and most fashionable of the city's churches, Santa Maria in Vallicella, always referred to as the Chiesa Nuova—the "new

114

church" of the Oratorian order, a dependency of Cardinal Borghese.

Pieter Paul didn't seek out the colorful, dangerous, opinionated Caravaggio. Yet so restricted was the society of artists in Rome that meetings were difficult to avoid, and he had no wish to make avoidance obvious, for he didn't want to offend Caravaggio—not only because he feared his wrath, but because he respected him. The peace-loving Fleming was mysteriously attracted to the belligerent Italian. And it was the *man* who attracted him at least as much as his art. Rubens didn't understand his feelings very clearly, and they alarmed him, made him wonder at times if he weren't, in reality, much more violent than he imagined or was willing to confess to himself. It was a thought he tried to dismiss—but the fascination with Caravaggio's personality and temperament was there as witness to the apparent contradiction.

To protect himself, or perhaps to protect his conception of himself, Rubens tried always to be in the company of some acquaintance when he entered an inn where he was likely to find Caravaggio. His companion might be young Deodat van der Mont, an *Anversois* who was studying art in Rome and who had introduced himself to Pieter Paul soon after the latter's arrival from Mantua. Deodat's credentials were impeccable; he bore letters from Adam van Noort and Octave van Veen. His nature was sweet, his talent negligible but polite—a matter of small importance, for his father was a prosperous goldsmith willing to support his son in any enterprise, so long as it was reasonably respectable.

The few encounters with Caravaggio were therefore tempered by the presence of at least one other person, and Rubens always contrived to escape the bibulous Italian's anger when the conversation took a direction that would cause him annoyance. He learned nothing new about the man, and even came to be bored by his drunken repetition of formulated phrases that were uttered more for effect than out of deep conviction.

In the end, Pieter Paul believed he had grasped the nature of

Caravaggio's strange power over him. It lay in the contrast between the reckless, garrulous, furious man and the scrupulously wrought paintings that came from his hand. He thought of what Jan Richardot had said to him years before: "There's only one Caravaggio . . . and more than one Rubens?"

The dichotomy he spotted in the Italian taught him much about his own self. Caravaggio was governed, allowed himself to be governed, by his passions of the moment. Pieter Paul Rubens compelled himself to be governed by reason. The reasonable man was just a little envious of the unreasonable one. Rubens saw in Caravaggio a distorted mirror image of himself. Caravaggio never allowed his grotesque emotions to disclose themselves in his work. *Only* in his painting did Pieter Paul Rubens disclose *his* great emotions.

Early in 1606, while London was being visited by a plague which the new pope solemnly declared to be a sign from heaven, Caravaggio delivered to the Chiesa Nuova the final painting for a chapel he was to decorate, a representation of the Virgin and Child with Saint Anne. The authorities of the Church, including Cardinal Borghese himself who could usually be depended on to defend the artist, rejected it as "lacking decorum," by which accusation they simply meant that it was offensive because it contained, as a portrait of the Mother of God, the features of the notorious Lena, for whose affections Caravaggio had very nearly killed a man.

Against his own better judgment and the entreaties of his brother, Pieter Paul intervened with the powerful primate, to whom he had been introduced on several occasions. The worldly Cardinal Borghese, whose collection of paintings and sculptures and Roman antiquities was one of the finest in the Eternal City, heard out the indignant visitor with exemplary patience. When Rubens had finished defending the rejected canvas as "a masterpiece, the finest thing that Caravaggio has ever done," the pope's nephew willingly acknowledged the justice of this description with an amused nod. "But do you really expect, Maestro Rubens, that we can hang the portrait of a common whore on the walls of the Chiesa Nuova?"

116

"The Saint Mary Magdalene . . ."

"That would have been admissible. But your friend and mine, Maestro Caravaggio, has given us this Lena of his as the Holy Virgin, not as the Magdalene." He rose from his seat in the magnificently ornate room that served as his official reception hall, and led Rubens through a door into a huge gallery. As they walked, the cardinal spoke amiably. "You mustn't think that Caravaggio and I have abandoned each other. Let me show you the painting he's just given me." They paused now before a picture of David posed with a sword in one hand and the severed head of Goliath in the other—a composition, as Borghese properly observed, more usual for the tale of Judith and Holofernes. "But look," he said, pointing to the head of the murdered giant, "it's Caravaggio. He's painted a self-portrait."

The expression on the dangling head was familiar to those who knew the artist—outraged, angered, frustrated. "You see no particular significance, no symbolism in this, excellency?" asked Pieter Paul.

The cardinal stared at his guest blandly. "Should I? Do you imagine Caravaggio is trying to tell me something special?" His smile was wry in its urbanity. "Am I to infer that he's accusing me of having severed his head?"

Pieter Paul shrugged. "I don't know. But I'm acquainted enough with him to believe that he never paints anything accidentally. It means *something*."

"And it worries you, obviously." Borghese patted Rubens' shoulder gently. "I find that charming, if a little quaint." He took two steps away from the artist, as if to suggest that the interview was terminated, then stopped and turned back. "I'm going to reward you for your Christianity, maestro. I wish *you* to contribute to the decoration of the Chiesa Nuova too. Goodness should occasionally be recompensed on this earth, though of course we know it will receive its suitable recognition in the bosom of Abraham. You're to paint a triptych for the high altar of my new church."

Pieter Paul grinned broadly despite his annoyance with the

117

cardinal's condescending tone. When a prince of the Church was so far removed in spirit from his see, it just had to be amusing. The alternative conclusion was too tragic to be considered. "I'm overwhelmed, excellency."

"I thought you might be."

If Caravaggio knew of Rubens' attempt to persuade Borghese to accept the painting, he made no point of expressing his gratitude. Nor did Pieter Paul ever learn precisely what construction should be placed on the remarkable painting of David and Goliath.

The months of winter and spring were devoted to sketches, and later to finished ink drawings to illustrate a volume of essays by Philip about the ruins of Imperial Rome, a task to which the artist brought most of his considerable powers of concentration—for it meant much to Philip, who wanted to see the work published by their great friends, Moretus *père et fils*, proprietors of the Plantin Press in Antwerp. Publication of a scholarly book could do much for Philip's reputation.

While Rubens made his illustrations for his brother's text, he also did the preliminary drawings for the important commission, the altarpiece for the Chiesa Nuova. Cardinal Borghese had followed up at once on his apparently impulsive and casual suggestion. It seemed possible that, willy nilly, Pieter Paul and Caravaggio might be doing work in the same church at the same time. The prospect was illusory. On the afternoon of May 29, Caravaggio brought his career in Rome to a sudden end by fatally stabbing Ranuccio Tomassini, during a dispute over the score of a court tennis match in which they were opposed. Tomassini, doubtless with some justice, accused his adversary of cheating. He never lived to apologize for what Caravaggio described as his damnable lie. The painter fled from the Eternal City, never to return. The scandal attending this tragic incident was disproportionately widespread because of the many powerful clerics and covetous artists who had for so long arrayed themselves against Caravaggio. At last they were done with him. Having committed a senseless murder, he couldn't possibly return to Rome.

118

Pieter Paul was stunned by the event and its consequences. He recognized, as did the few others who were sympathetic to Caravaggio, that something of the sort was bound to occur one day. But when it happened, its abruptness was too startling to be accepted readily. Cardinal Scipione Borghese summed it up: "Who else would have thrown away his life over such a trifle?"

"We don't think of Tomassini?" asked Rubens with some bitterness.

"You must try not to be so judicious, maestro," said the prelate. "There are hundreds, thousands of Tomassinis."

"And only two Caravaggios," murmured the painter, so softly that the cardinal failed to understand. He looked at him inquiringly. "Forgive me, excellency. I was just reminded of something that was said to me about him a long time ago."

"So now it's up to Rubens to carry on."

"I'm not a second Caravaggio, excellency. That's not what I meant. He and I just couldn't be more different from each other."

"You love him, though."

Rubens reflected a moment. "No, we were really quite repugnant to each other. There *may* have been some sort of sympathy, understanding. It's hard for me to explain."

"There was *some* kind of understanding between you. You recall what you said to me about that painting of David and Goliath?"

The artist nodded. "It did mean something, didn't it? But I wonder if Caravaggio himself knew its meaning then, or if he knows it now."

The cardinal stroked his beard. "You're suggesting that he portrayed his own murder?"

"Or his suicide. Anyone who lives as he does must have a kind of passion for his own death, even if he isn't aware of it, excellency. That's what he painted in that picture he gave you. That's what he meant."

"But he still lives."

"For how much longer, excellency? If he doesn't literally kill himself or drink himself to death, which comes to the same

119

thing, he'll one day put himself in a position where someone kills him. It doesn't matter which."

After four years of frenzied wandering and meticulous painting about the islands of Sicily and Malta, Caravaggio perished of delirium tremens on the strand of Porto Ercoli. But for Pieter Paul Rubens, he died on that day in May of 1606, when he departed from Rome.

The size of Cardinal Borghese's commission to make three paintings for the Chiesa Nuova created a problem of working space that could only be solved by Pieter Paul's removal from the palace of Cardinal Colonna, where he had resided with Philip since his arrival in Rome, to quarters where he was able to set up large canvases. The leasing of a house, however, required funds that neither he nor Philip, who proposed to move with him, had in hand.

Fortunately, the painter had the loyal Annibale Chieppio in Mantua to fall back on. Their correspondence had continued throughout the artist's absence from the city on the Mincio, much of it concerned with Vincenzo Gonzaga's desire that he return and resume his painting of court beauties. As usual, the duke was late in remitting the quarterly stipend he had undertaken to continue—accepting in exchange an occasional copy of a Raphael or a Michelangelo and the privilege of chastising Rubens for his reluctance to leave Rome. In the most recent of Chieppio's letters the tone had been a little more strident; if Pieter Paul didn't return soon, the payments would be cut off. The painter replied rather airily that he would willingly sever the connection, for he now enjoyed the patronage of the pope's nephew and he could, if he chose, find other sponsors of comparable magnitude. He counted on these casual references to stellar figures to invoke Gonzaga's pride in him, whom Gonzaga persisted in calling "my painter." The stratagem worked splendidly. The delinquent hundred ducats were delivered into the artist's hands in late July. He and Philip installed themselves a week or so afterward in a comfortable, half-furnished house in the Via della Croce, near the Piazza di Spagna.

It was the first time either of the Rubens brothers had ever occupied a dwelling of his own. They made the most of the resulting sense of freedom. The house became a gathering place for visitors from Antwerp, scholars and artists drawn to them by their growing renown. If it was Pieter Paul who now enjoyed the more celebrated name (because of his selection, over the heads of the illustrious native Italian competition, to adorn the high altar of the Chiesa Nuova), the erudition and brilliantly skeptical conversation of Philip made an interesting contrast to the younger brother's talk of the politics of art and the art of politics in Rome.

Some intrusions upon this amiable existence were not so welcome. In early December, a letter from Chieppio informed Pieter Paul in the most peremptory tones that the Duke of Mantua wanted him to return forthwith. Once again, Rubens turned away his master's wrath with a soft answer. He pleaded for another three months in which to complete the Chiesa Nuova triptych or, failing that, for permission to come back to Rome in the spring to finish the work. If the duke remained adamant, the painter added, he was certain that no less imposing a personality than Cardinal Borghese himself would intercede for him—since the commission, though nominally extended by the Oratorian fathers, had originated with the great prelate. And once again, Pieter Paul had his way. Indeed, he managed to stretch the requested three months into a delay of nearly eight.

But there could be no denying Gonzaga's demand the following June that Rubens accompany him to Flanders, where he planned to visit Ambrogio di Spinola, the Genoese general who had reduced Ostend's resistance. The idea of a journey to his homeland appealed to the artist, though he would have liked to complete the triptych before leaving; difficulties of an unforeseeable nature had arisen. This, said the duke, was out of the question; he must come to Mantua at once.

121

However, when Rubens reached the Palazzo Ducale of Gonzaga, it developed that there was, after all, to be no trip to Flanders, for Spinola had by then returned to *his* home on the Mediterranean. The duke and "his painter," with a large cortège, set out for Genoa in July. There, Pieter Paul made some additional portraits of members of the rich Spinola-Doria family, and complied with a request to paint an altarpiece. He even found time, while Gonzaga negotiated and ingratiated, to compose a number of architectural drawings of the handsome palaces, public buildings, and churches of the city, "just as a sort of journal," he explained to his master, who couldn't fail to observe that in less than two months Rubens had accomplished prodigies of work while, he added, "you've been more than a year at that thing for the Chiesa Nuova, and claim you're still not done with it."

"It presents problems of lighting, excellency," said the artist, feeling a slight twinge of guilt, for he well knew that he had given considerably less than his all to the completion of the commission in Rome, because there were so many other distractions and other projects—and because he wished to remain there. Yet what he told the duke was true. The light sources near the high altar of the Chiesa Nuova did cause problems, and though the triptych was nearly done, Pieter Paul felt certain that he was going to have to repaint it altogether, on a surface that would absorb some of the light's glaring intensity. *That,* however, he elected not to mention at the time.

Only at the beginning of 1608, after he had been back in Rome for almost four months, did Pieter Paul explain in a carefully phrased letter to Annibale Chieppio that he had to rework the three paintings on tablets of slate in order to resolve the difficulties posed by the windows of the Chiesa Nuova—this once more to postpone a summons to return again to Mantua.

By February, the altarpiece was completed and installed— and the artist was at work on yet another commission awarded him through the good offices of Cardinal Borghese, a painting for the high altar of the church of San Filippo Neri. Rubens was now so well established in Rome that there could be little doubt of his becoming, in relatively short order, the most prominent and most successful painter of the Eternal City—a goal he had set for himself. He had achieved this ascendancy over the native academicians by a combination of good manners, good connections, and the propensity of his painting to please almost everyone. He could imbue his canvases with a verve that communicated itself immediately to the beholder. This, he presumed, was what Caravaggio had really meant by his phrase about Rubens as a master of "surfaces." It wasn't that he was superficial; but it *was* that he could create a kind of beauty that was not disturbing or controversial even when it was novel. Where Caravaggio painted a reality that was often harsh, Pieter Paul Rubens celebrated life. His art was, as was the man himself, affirmative.

Yet he was not content. He was lonely, though hosts of acquaintances poured through the rooms of the house in the Via della Croce. Philip had returned to Antwerp the previous fall in order to present the finished manuscript of his book and Pieter Paul's illustrations for the consideration of Jan and Balthasar Moretus. He wrote in January that the work was in the process of being set in type, the drawings were being etched by skilled engravers, and he looked forward to seeing proofs of the Latin text within a month or two.

Philip's communications from the Low Countries were full of excitement. Things there had changed enormously, and for the better, during the eight years of his brother's absence. The talk was general and convincing that a truce with Spain must soon be arranged; and in any case, the war had all but ended, save for the presence of a few thousand drunken mercenaries billeted on the borders of the United Provinces. Even Maria Piepelinx, normally pessimistic, wrote hopefully of conditions at home. While neither she nor Philip urged Pieter Paul in so many words to return to Antwerp, he could easily read such a message into their letters. The decision must be left entirely to him. They would not reproach him for choosing the certainty of his now-established career in Rome instead of the admitted chanciness of starting from scratch in Antwerp.

He *was* tempted. He allowed his indecisiveness to intrude on his correspondence with Chieppio, who promptly and firmly replied that he must be mad. "How can you think of renouncing a commanding role in your elected field at the very center of the Christian universe?" It was a reasonable question to which there was only a single reasonable response: It was unthinkable. Yet he continued to consider it. In a way, the fact of having so easily triumphed in Rome against the entrenched opposition of the Italians (now that Caravaggio was no longer present) contributed heavily to his *malaise*. He required a new world to conquer.

And too, he was nostalgic for his mother and brother, for the coziness of Antwerp. He had certainly absorbed so much of Italian styles of painting that he had become, in effect, an Italian artist—but he had failed to become an Italian. He felt a need to go home. All that was required to commit him to such a course was a precise, convincing excuse that would make the decision easy. For, as Chieppio had written, a sensible man simply couldn't pack up and leave, renouncing without cause a life of comfort and security.

Not until late October of 1608 did such an occasion present itself—a letter of greatest urgency from Philip to say that Maria Piepelinx had taken suddenly ill and might very well be on her deathbed. There could no longer be any doubt. Pieter Paul wrote Chieppio that he must go at once to his mother's side in Antwerp. He wouldn't pause in Mantua on the way, but he assured the duke's secretary that he would return there as soon as ever he could.

He was, however, lying. He took with him, on his departure from Rome, everything he possessed. If he ever came back to Italy, it would be for a visit. Whatever the future held for him, it would occur in Antwerp, not in Mantua or Rome.

Four

"YOU'RE too late," said Philip, and embraced his brother. "Mama's dead."

Pieter Paul Rubens took a step backwards in the modest hallway of his mother's house, and peered into Philip's sad but tearless face which was only half illuminated by a single flickering candle, like a painting by Caravaggio. "When did it happen?"

The brother shrugged. "Six weeks ago. Possibly before you even received my letter. She went very quickly once she took to her bed."

The painter followed him into the small sitting room. "I left Rome as soon as I heard from you," he said apologetically. "I came as quickly as I could . . . Did she suffer a great deal?"

Philip nodded. "But in silence." He poured two glasses of *eau-de-vie* and handed one to Pieter Paul.

"That's remarkable. There weren't many things that mama accepted in silence."

The older brother smiled wryly. "She raised her voice only if she thought it would solve a problem. We would never have been born if mama hadn't raised her voice to save papa's life. But death is another thing. She knew her limitations."

*   *   *

The Rubens brothers went the next morning to visit their mother's tomb in the abbey church of Saint Michel. There was nothing to see other than an unmarked stone slab set into the wall of a plain chapel that had served the family for generations. Pieter Paul resolved to decorate it. He could hardly do less.

As they were returning to the house in Klosterstraat into which Maria Piepelinx had moved after selling the one in the Meir, Philip took his brother's arm. "What will you do now?"

"I've promised to go back to Mantua."

"Would you leave if some really fine commission came your way here?"

"It would certainly defer my departure."

The older Rubens smiled and drew his brother out toward the center of the Meir. "Well, I'll settle for a deferment. I want you to be here for my wedding."

Pieter Paul stopped dead. "Why in God's name didn't you mention that sooner?"

"It really didn't seem very propitious to talk about it last evening, did it? This was the first time . . ."

"It's wonderful news, Philip, but it's so sudden. You said nothing of it in your letters."

"Marriages may be made in heaven, but they're arranged on earth. The details require a great deal of time and talk and contract writing."

"So mama knew about it."

Philip gave a little nod as they moved on once more. "It was her idea, of course. The contract terms were agreed to just before she fell ill. We're to be married in February, the Saturday before *mardi gras*."

"February is a good month to have a woman in your bed."

"That doesn't sound like you, Pieter Paul. It sounds like papa."

"Oh, any month was good for papa." He paused, reflecting on the combination of half-truth and intuition that constituted his knowledge of his father. "I suppose I *do* have that of papa

126

in me. I love flesh, brother. I love young, firm, abundant flesh. *That* might keep me in Antwerp forever."

"That doesn't sound like you *either*. What's been happening to you since I left Rome?"

"Nothing. That's the trouble. I never found an Italian girl I really enjoyed."

"I'll see what I can do for you," said Philip, bemused.

The marriage of Maria de Moy and Philip Rubens took place on the designated day in the church of Saint Michel. Of the bridegroom's family, only his brother was in attendance. Blandine and Jan-Baptiste had predeceased their mother, carried off some years before by pestilence. But all of Philip's friends and professional associates were present, and they agreed that if the match wasn't brilliant, it was eminently satisfactory—since these things were measured in the practical Flemish terms of finance and social position, in that order. When flight could, at short notice, become a necessity, the amount of one's portable property (gold or credit) was of greater significance than the proximity of one's relations to greatness in the Church or the aristocracy. To be a banker's child, like Maria, would offset all sorts of other shortcomings.

In her early twenties on her wedding day, Maria de Moy had been the despair of her mother for the same reason that Maria Piepelinx had feared for Blandine; at such an advanced age, it was difficult to find a mate who was acceptable. Maria had the merit of intelligence which counterbalanced a certain plainness of appearance. This was a virtue more treasured by her new husband than the bride's parents felt they had a right to expect. "It's comforting to know," said Philip to his brother, "that the woman with whom one proposes to spend the rest of one's life is capable of exchanging coherent sentences with one."

"One sounds frightfully detached about it all, doesn't one?" replied Pieter Paul with mingled amusement and annoyance. "Doesn't one propose to sleep with one's wife, too, and have children by her?"

Philip refused to rise to this goad. "Oh, yes," he said casually.

127

"One wants children, right enough, and one should be gratified to know that their mother isn't a halfwit."

Pieter Paul readily detected their mother's firm hand in the arrangement of this match, and suspected that Philip had agreed to consummate it more out of respect for Maria Piepelinx's dying wish than from a genuine desire to wed. "One is told in Scripture," he observed wickedly, "that it's better to marry than burn. But when one listens to you speak of it, one wonders if you wholly agree with that precept."

"No, no," Philip responded, abruptly dropping the impersonal affectation of speech that was something of a rage among contemporary classicists. "I *want* to marry. I want children. Maria's a good, fine woman."

And so she was. To celebrate the occasion, Pieter Paul composed a portrait of the couple, an intimate, sensitive work that expressed feelings of tenderness and affection for his brother and his bride. He posed them informally, seated side by side in a room of the house in the Klosterstraat where the artist was still residing. Though posed, in the technical sense, the painting had none of the stiffness that marked contemporary portraiture. It conveyed what the painter intended—the sentiments of a man and a woman who were only recently married, who wondered without great apprehension about what might lie ahead for them, who were well pleased with the present.

Anxious that his younger brother's thoughts might turn again toward Italy, Philip had begun even before his wedding to forage for commissions that would delay his departure. He also allowed it to be known, as discreetly as might be, that Pieter Paul was looking for a bride. In the older Rubens' mind, based on what the younger one had said (in jest? he couldn't be certain), the two searches were of equal importance. But he was compelled to respect the artist's common sense in stating flatly that he was unwilling to accept a financially precarious living anywhere. If Philip turned up for him the most glorious bride in Antwerp, but failed to help him find the prospect of continuous and gainful employment, Pieter Paul would return without hesitation to Italy where, he knew, he could count on

128

the support of Vincenzo Gonzaga and Cardinal Scipione Borghese.

There were two immeasurable factors operating in favor of Philip's desire to keep his brother in the Low Countries. One was that, since his return, Pieter Paul had rediscovered a love for his homeland that didn't disappoint the nostalgia he had enjoyed toward the end of his long stay abroad. This affection was surely blighted by the continuing state of hostilities between the United Provinces and Spain, and by its corollary of a continuing but diminishing poverty in Flanders. But there *was* a coziness. There *was* the odd, guttural homeliness of the sound of the Flemish tongue. There was the gruff heartiness of the Flemings themselves; their odd, awkward gait; their love of primary colors. He simply felt at home, and recognized that most of the nostalgia he had submitted to while away had been purely geographical. The painter in Rubens found the North Sea light, which he had disparaged on his arrival in Venice, to be harsh but honest. It possessed none of the flattering gold afforded by the Mediterranean sun. What he had taken for granted as a young man he now appreciated.

The resumption of his precious friendship with the brave, crippled Balthasar Moretus proved a second link in the chain that Philip hoped would be strong enough to hold Pieter Paul in Antwerp. The two men had corresponded sporadically during the painter's absence, so there were no great voids to be filled. There was, indeed, a new bond—the illustrations for Philip's recently published book about Roman antiquities, which bore the impressive title, *Electorum Libri II*. Balthasar was so pleased with Pieter Paul's drawings that he proposed that he design the title pages and frontispieces for other volumes to be issued by the Plantin Press. The interest in printing, which he could trace to his days as a pupil of Maître Rombaut Verdonck, was thus revived.

The first quarter of 1609 passed swiftly. Though Antwerp had not been the center of Flemish society since the removal of the administrative apparatus to Brussels, the city remained in closest possible touch with the rest of the world. Everyone

hoped to hear, from one day to the next, that the long anticipated truce had been achieved. Instead, the word was of lesser
events. A group of English Puritan extremists had left Britain
to find refuge in Amsterdam, principal town of the United
Provinces and the focal point of a new struggle for power between men who had long been allies—Prince Mauritz and Jan
van Oldenbarneveldt. The immediate issue was political supremacy—that of Prince Mauritz's Holland over the lesser
provinces of the Protestant Low Countries. But it was complicated by a religious conflict between the "libertine" followers
of the temperate Jacobus Arminius, who was dying, and the
advocates of John Calvin's much more rigorous theology. What
prevented an outbreak of violence was the menace still posed
by the Spanish troops encamped at points along the border.

The New World, long considered by Spain to be her exclusive domain, was being explored and even settled by the British
and the French. The colony of Jamestown had been established
two years earlier. Henry Hudson, a Hollander in the employ of
Britain, was sailing up the river to which he would give his
name. In London, James I again informed members of an
unruly Parliament that the royal powers of taxation were derived not from man, not from the people, but from God. His
pronouncement was not very warmly received.

The Spanish rarely trailed the other European powers in the
pursuit of vain policy. This year proved no exception, for it saw
the announcement of the decision to evict from the country
some 400,000 "Moriscos," Christianized descendants of the
eighth-century Moorish invaders of Iberia. Arguing that their
nominal adherence to the faith of Rome was spurious, Philip
III and Lerma overrode the protests of the great landowners of
Valencia (where most of the Moriscos were settled as farm
workers and tradespeople) that the economic effect of the expulsion would be disastrous for the province and, therefore, for
Spain. It would be nearly five years before the last of the Moriscos left the land of their birth, most of them seeking asylum in
North Africa where great numbers of them were slaughtered by
Moslems who rightly considered them Christians. Lerma and

130

his relatives were virtually alone in profiting from this enterprise; they pocketed fortunes from the confiscation of Morisco property. But Spain, as the Valencian aristocrats had predicted, suffered incalculable losses.

Philip III had thought his people would consider the "purification" of Spain a laudable measure. It was publicized to coincide with a development which was a sharp blow to Spanish pride—the necessity of agreeing to a truce with the United Provinces after more than forty years of attrition. On April 9, an armistice was concluded, to endure for a period of twelve years. Its promulgation later in the month was the occasion for universal relief and celebration throughout the Netherlands, north and south, so long ravaged by war and pillage in the name of faith and power.

Europe was not, however, to know a time of total tranquillity. Only a short while before the Twelve-Year Truce was officially agreed to, Duke John William, ruler of the German provinces of Julich, Cleves, and Berg, had the misfortune to lose his life. The vacancy of his throne created the occasion for a dispute and provided the spark which ignited a small fire that eventually grew into a general Continental conflagration—the Thirty Years' War. The Emperor Rudolf, as suzerain of the late duke's estates, claimed the right to appoint his successor who would be, naturally, of the Catholic faith.

Henri IV denied the emperor's assertion—not so much over the matter of the successor's religion, but because the subjugation of these Germanic lands by the Habsburgs constituted a menace to the frontiers of France. The French king promptly allied himself with the Protestant rulers of Brandenburg, the Palatinate, and the United Provinces in a joint demand that Duke John William be succeeded by a Protestant. The emperor immediately responded by sending his son and heir, the Archduke Leopold, into Julich at the head of an army. Henri IV proposed to answer force with force.

This apparently minor international squabble, typical of the disputes that gave mediocre rulers a feeling of importance, was exacerbated by a purely personal and human complication that

131

was at once ridiculous and grotesquely amusing, another of Henri IV's grand passions. At the age of fifty-six, this greatest of all of history's royal rakes had fallen in love with Charlotte de Montmorency, a delicious child of sixteen. Charlotte resolutely rejected her monarch's advances; she wanted a husband, not a lover. To accommodate this desire for propriety, the king arranged for her to marry the Prince de Condé, scion of France's greatest noble house. As Condé's wife she need evince no further scruple about becoming a royal mistress—a formula Henri had employed more than once before. To the astonishment of a French court that fancied itself beyond surprise, the Prince de Condé, deeply enamored of his beautiful and desirable young bride, fled with her to Brussels where they sought and were given the protection of the regents. So annoyed was Henri IV that he proposed to pursue the elusive little Charlotte with an army, if that proved necessary.

Villeroi, the French king's foreign minister, understood his master well enough to know that there really was no length, no matter how absurd it appeared, to which he would not go in the interest of venery. Had such idiocy not already produced the plot to set a royal bastard on the throne? In the name of peace and common sense, Villeroi implored the Archduke Albrecht to allow the extradition of the Prince and Princesse de Condé and thus avoid a pointless war which, he was sure, might rapidly spread to every corner of Christendom.

On the specific instructions of *his* suzerain, Philip III of Spain, the regent of the Netherlands refused the French demand. Everyone held his breath. Would there be war? There would not, or not just yet. Henri IV was furious, but he wasn't mad. He now conceived a plan which he believed would solve several of his problems simultaneously. A concerted drive of his troops and those of his allies would break the Spanish hold over the Low Countries, regain for him the precious little person of Charlotte de Montmorency, and thwart the emperor's scheme to put his own man on the throne of Julich, Cleves, and Berg. Then Henri would turn against Spain directly, and eliminate her menace to his borders on the Pyrenees. He arranged for the

132

hiring of several regiments of Swiss mercenaries and secured the promise of 4,000 British troops from James I, whose interest was mainly the permanent suppression of Spain as a major factor in European affairs. Henri IV himself would raise a force of 30,000 men.

Insofar as the project was political in its intent, there was sense in it. But Henri made the egregious error of allowing the inference, among his own people, that the projected war was of at least equal importance to his heart as to his country—that he was willing to send many men off to death because of his passion for an adolescent girl. The taint could not be erased. Henri IV was the most competent and most popular monarch France had known since Saint Louis, five centuries earlier. In a little more than a month, he destroyed the basis of his power and esteem, made himself seem at once a fool and a knave in the public eye—the public, in the case of his country, being the Church (appalled that he should ally himself with heretics), the nobility (who thought him crazy to risk his nation's safety for a slip of a girl), and the Third Estate, the merchants, bankers, and peasants (the only taxpayers of the land, who were reluctant to sacrifice their gold to assuage a case of royal *ennui*). The king persisted, and the rancor his plan inspired created an atmosphere most hospitable to internal disorder.

The excitement induced by these events caught Pieter Paul Rubens between comparably conflicting emotions about his personal future. Though Philip had so far failed to secure a commission of such magnitude that it would make a return to Italy appear foolish, the artist had received several formal but amiable communications from the Archduke Albrecht's secretary, all expressing the "profound hope" that he would remain in the Low Countries and officially associate himself with the court in Brussels. His replies were evasive, for he had no inclination to become a courtier; the experience in Mantua had satisfied him on that score. To the last of the queries from the regent's secretary, Pieter Paul replied that he would endeavor to visit Brussels as soon as his affairs in Antwerp were settled—by which he simply meant that he wanted irrefutable reasons for

133

resisting the archduke's charm and remaining in Antwerp, where, if he stayed in the Low Countries, he meant to live rather than in Brussels.

Whenever Philip managed to tear himself away from the unexpected pleasures he found in matrimony, he made advances on the two fronts of his own campaign to prevent Pieter Paul from leaving. His success began to be most wonderfully apparent. Its first manifestation was a commission of the highest importance. Nicolas Rockox, Burgomaster of Antwerp and a close friend of Philip's, agreed to request from the artist a large painting of the Adoration of the Magi to adorn the place of honor in the refurbished Room of State in the Town Hall. So grandiose a work would require time, the older brother well knew, and time was what he needed for the realization of his second aim—to find a bride for Pieter Paul.

At the end of August, 1609, Isabella Brandt was formally betrothed to Pieter Paul Rubens. They had been introduced by Philip's wife, Maria de Moy, who was a remote connection of the Brandts. The presentation and ensuing meetings were discreetly supervised, according to the custom. After Pieter Paul and Isabella had agreed to the principle of marriage, they were permitted not a moment alone together. Such conversational exchanges as they had before the wedding were perfunctory and only superficially informative. Both were inhibited by the watchful presence of a duenna. All that Rubens knew about the person who was to be his wife was what he could see and what he was told by his sister-in-law.

Isabella was eighteen, slight and slender by the standards of beauty currently in fashion, with a small, rather angular face and large brown eyes that looked at him with a degree of candor that was just a bit unnerving; it seemed not at all virginal, though he wasn't worried on that account, since a bride's virginity was a staple guarantee of the usual marriage contract. The edges of her little mouth turned up easily to form a smile which was faintly sardonic—but at such an inclination of temperament the suitor could only guess, for nothing the girl uttered suggested it. She had beautiful hands; his eyes were drawn to them almost as often as to her interesting features. She had chestnut hair. That was the extent of Pieter Paul's inventory of knowledge about his prospective bride. The only logical response he could make to Philip's inquiry was that she didn't displease him.

As far as Isabella was concerned, Pieter Paul was a god. She knew much more about him than he knew of her simply because he was a man, because he was in the way of being a minor public figure in Antwerp, where the society of the prosperous, the intellectuals, the higher clerics, and the artists was extremely small. She found him very handsome. His eyes were gentle, his expression a little sad and remote when he was neither speaking nor listening. He was well groomed and fastidious. To a girl who had been raised in a house where it was as safe to eat from the floors as from the tables, fastidiousness was a solid virtue.

Of his mind, of his work, she knew little and at this point cared not at all; these were of no concern to a wife. Of his ambition at some time to be of service to the state, to be a successful painter in comfortable financial circumstances, he spoke to her in only the vaguest terms. Even if he had filled her with information, she wouldn't have been much the wiser, for these were contexts beyond her present scope and interest. He seemed sincere when he said that he would care for her; it was impossible for her to measure the degree to which these words were heartfelt. Her intuition, in conjunction with the assurances of Maria de Moy, suggested that he should be accorded full credence.

He impressed her as the sort of man who would never deliberately injure her physically, and in an epoch when wifebeating was common and proper practice, this was a much more important consideration than whether or not he "loved" her. How *could* he love her? He knew nothing about her. But Isabella could love Pieter Paul—for the qualities she knew he

135

possessed, for those she merely guessed at, and for the best of all irrationalities—because he wanted her. She wanted to be wanted, in every way.

Between Isabella's father, Jan Brandt, and Pieter Paul there developed at once a friendship of exceptional warmth. Barely ten years older than the painter, Brandt was a flourishing lawyer and, like the man soon to be his son-in-law, a conscientious humanist—a serious student of the poets and historians of ancient Greece and Rome, a disciple of Erasmus. A survivor, as a child, of the Spanish Fury, he had lost half his relatives, the Protestants, who had either perished at the hands of the Duke of Alba's bloodthirsty troops or fled to the north. Now, in the early months of the truce, he glowed with pleasure over the promise of a new era of religious tolerance. He was attempting to resume contacts with some of his connections in Holland, "just to learn which of them are still alive, you know," he explained to Rubens. "How we have allowed life to be squandered in Christ's name. I wonder if He had it to do over again today, whether He'd die for our sins a second time."

When discussion of finances came up in the first of their conversations, Jan Brandt dismissed as quite unimportant Pieter Paul's confession that he had no tangible assets, not even a house. "You have your future *ahead* of you, not behind you. This city abounds in men who *used* to be important or who *might* have been important if things had only gone differently. What is a house, when you think of it? If it's small, it's a kind of coffin for the living, and if it's large, it's a mausoleum."

"Coffin or mausoleum, *mijnheer*, I have neither. I live under my brother Philip's roof, as you probably know. He inherited everything from our mother . . ."

"I *know* the law," said Brandt wearily.

"And all the houses he owns, which he'd give me my choice of, are occupied. I couldn't evict a tenant at a time when there aren't enough houses to go around."

"Of course you couldn't. And you don't need to. You and Isabella can stay with Anna and me until you're able to find what you want. You can even do your painting here. Have you seen my attic? It should make a good studio for you."

He hustled the artist up three flights of stairs to an enormously lofty room at the top of his spacious house. "You see? It even has a north light. I'm told a north light is important for a painter's studio."

After their bargain had been struck, Pieter Paul was unable to tell his brother whether he was marrying Isabella for herself, since he scarcely knew her, or for her father, of whom he had so quickly become fond.

"I suppose," said Philip with a sigh of resignation, "that that means you weren't very exigent about her dowry."

The artist laughed, but didn't offer a direct response. "We discussed it."

"Of course you did. That's what you were there for. But what conclusion did you reach?"

"It was very embarrassing, Philip. Jan Brandt asked me which *I* thought a suitable settlement. I didn't know what to tell him. We're going to live in his house, after all. I'm going to do my work in his attic. God in heaven, it was a terrible moment. It was very embarrassing."

"You said that twice, brother. What figure did you name?"

"A thousand florins."

Philip was openmouthed. "You could have got more than a thousand florins from a well-off peasant. You're mad. I don't understand you. Wasn't it you who said you'd abide any anguish except poverty?"

"Jan Brandt insisted on ten thousand," said Pieter Paul softly, and waited for his brother's reaction.

"He offered ten when you asked him for one?" Philip was impelled to a gesture of utter renunciation, in the grand Italian manner. "Then both of you are mad."

"We like each other."

"What has that to do with making a marriage contract?"

"Nothing. I realize that. I daresay it *is* mad, Philip. If *you'd* done such a thing in my place, I'd have had the same response.

137

But it's of no moment, is it? The arrangement is generous, much more than I could reasonably have hoped, and we arrived at it . . ." He grinned. "We arrived at it backwards, didn't we?"

"The luck of fools," said Philip brusquely. "A brilliant fellow like you doesn't deserve such good fortune as a reward for stupidity."

The date for the wedding was set for early October. By this time, Pieter Paul estimated, his large painting of the Adoration of the Magi for the Town Hall of Antwerp would be well advanced, if not completed. Philip was delighted with himself, certain that he had created a set of circumstances that would make it very unlikely for his brother to return to Italy, or that he would want to. The only element still unsettled was the artist's status with the court. It was, as Philip tirelessly and tiresomely reiterated, a matter that could only be resolved by a visit to Brussels. He must seek an audience with the archduke and come to some agreement, face to face, about his appointment to the post of court painter.

Pieter Paul was of the same opinion, but it was an expedition for which he had, in a manner of speaking, to steel himself. He knew very well how much more difficult it would be to refuse in person a demand that he remove himself to Brussels, which he had successfully parried in the exchanges of letters over the spring and summer. It didn't seem politic to put the case baldly, to tell the regent that he desired the appointment but preferred to remain a resident of Antwerp, an arrangement which would make him unique—the only court painter so indulged. Nor could he very well add that this disposition of his case would enhance his reputation, draw to him a clientele of importance that was not attracted to most other artists of Antwerp. What he wanted, as the Duke of Mantua had said to him, was the best of both worlds. The appointment seemed important, but more crucial was his freedom to live in Antwerp. He

138

wouldn't like to refuse the regent's request—but if the offer of the designation as court painter were tied to the stipulation that he must reside in Brussels, he felt he would have no other choice.

Philip had no advice, for once. He accepted the desirability of his brother's aim, but thought it virtually impossible of realization. "Why should the archduke agree to such a request? Of what use can you be to him here, when he needs you there?"

Balthasar Moretus took more or less the identical lines. "Unless you have some hidden virtue, Pieter Paul, a talent His Highness can't do without, I see no likelihood of his assent. He wanted papa to move the Plantin Press to Brussels a few years ago. Can you imagine it? We finally convinced him that it was out of the question by inviting him to visit the plant and see for himself just what would be involved in moving all our facilities. After that, for a time, he threatened to sponsor a printer in Brussels, but the cost of it and the difficulty of finding a qualified man proved too much for him."

It was Jan Brandt who, as was his particular gift, synthesized all the arguments so far advanced and produced what appeared the most convincing possible case. "You have to persuade the archduke that it's in *his* interest to *keep* you in Antwerp. If you can just find the right key to the right lock, you might even enjoy the luxury of expressing regret over *having* to stay here. Balthasar touched on the central point—a hidden virtue. What is it that you and only you can do for him in Antwerp?"

Pieter Paul consulted the coffered wooden ceiling of his future father-in-law's study. *"Only* I? Nothing I can think of."

"Well, then, what is it that you can do *better* than anyone else?"

The artist smiled. "Paint."

Jan Brandt mulled over this reply for quite a while. "Precisely, precisely," he muttered. "Now that we have a truce, there's going to be much redecoration of the churches. If all the fine painters are attached to the court in Brussels, who will be free to devote his time to these other important tasks?"

139

Pieter Paul acknowledged this with a brisk nod. "But why, if that's so, should His Highness bother to make me a court painter at all? Why shouldn't he leave things as they are?"

"Because he'd want the best artist, no matter where he lives and works, to have an official connection with the court. It would reflect happily on him."

"It might work," said Rubens admiringly. "We'll soon know."

An audience with the archduke was arranged for the first week in September. The regent and the painter who had so impressed and pleased him more than a decade before greeted each other with a cordiality that transcended the cool decorum that protocol prescribed. For the first quarter hour, they spoke of Pieter Paul's experiences in Italy and Spain, about which the archduke was flatteringly well informed. "You made a splendid impression on the Duke of Lerma, Maître Rubens."

"I meant to, Highness," the artist answered candidly.

"And he was delighted with the pictures you made for him . . . In fact, *everyone* who speaks of you observes how well considered your work is, both in Spain and Italy. The Duke of Mantua wasn't at all happy about your leaving Italy so suddenly. Why *did* you come back?"

Pieter Paul described his mother's illness and death. "But I was prepared to return to Mantua, Highness, as I promised the duke," he concluded.

"You wanted to go?"

"I was uncertain. Practicality dictated that I should go. Personal considerations held me."

"Well, we're heartily glad to have you in Flanders permanently. But you don't like the idea of settling in Brussels."

The painter took a deep breath and launched himself into a polished rendition of Jan Brandt's argument. The archduke listened with courteous interest, his expression perplexed at first, then admiring. Pieter Paul ended with a thought entirely his own: "There's really very little, Highness, that I can do for you by living at court that I can't do as well while I'm residing in Antwerp."

140

"You could be a considerable ornament," said the regent reproachfully. "You're probably the most cultivated man in the country. No courtier here can rival you, let alone any painter."

The painter's smile was deprecatory. "Dare I say that it's precisely my familiarity with court life that makes me want to avoid it, Highness?"

A cloud of displeasure crossed the usually serene features of the archduke. "You're not suggesting that there are improprieties here. This isn't Mantua, you know, or Madrid, or Rome."

"Oh no, Highness. Oh, you misunderstand me. I speak simply of the distractions. If I'm to devote myself to painting, I have to have the time for it."

"Yet Vincenzo Gonzaga writes me that you can work at double the speed of any other painter he's ever heard of or known . . ."

"The duke exaggerates, Highness . . . The Italians, you know, do that."

The regent sighed regretfully. "Well, well, what shall we do? I want you near me to be amusing and instructive. You want to be in Antwerp so you can work. Whom shall we please, ourselves or you?"

Rubens looked boldly at his gentle master. "I take the question to be rhetorical, Highness."

"That's presumptuous of you."

"Forgive me for presuming, then. I do, as I said, believe we'd both be better served, and the country too, by my residing in Antwerp."

"Yes, I can see your point. A court painter living there would have a virtual monopoly on commissions for public and religious art. The advantage to *you* is perfectly evident, and so is the advantage to the country, since it would enjoy your services. But what's the advantage to *me?*"

"When I *do* appear at court, Highness, by your invitation, I'll have something to tell you."

The archduke's little smile was surprisingly bitter. "Everyone has something to tell me, *maître.*"

141

"*I'll* bring you word of Antwerp, of the provinces, not the stale gossip that circulates and recirculates in court. And of course, I'll paint for you, whatever and wherever and whenever you like."

"I'd rather hoped, I confess, to put your talents to quite different use . . . perhaps to send you to Madrid."

Pieter Paul recognized instinctively that this was perhaps the turning point of his entire career. Would he renounce art in favor of diplomacy? He must make that basic decision here and now. He temporized.

"Is there a purpose that I especially could serve, Highness? The truce . . ."

"We require a condition that's definite, permanent, *maître*."

"I understand. But surely that's something that has to be arranged between King Philip and Prince Mauritz. It's out of our hands, isn't it?"

"I'm not so sure. The problem isn't very clearly grasped in Spain, you know." He smiled wryly. "I'm *sure* you know. It never has been. They see all questions related to the Netherlands in terms of black and white. Lerma deplores the truce. So do the king and the pope. It's an economic necessity. If funds are available at the end of twelve years, the war will resume. In fact, I can tell you, in absolute confidence, that under certain circumstances the truce would be violated if Lerma had his way . . ."

"You're speaking of the asylum you've given to the Prince and Princess de Condé, and what France might do?"

The regent paled. "Is it so well known?"

"I'm afraid that secrets are treated as coin, Highness. They're useless unless you exchange them. Besides, so many people are privy to them."

"Be specific. Do you object to telling me where you heard that Lerma wanted me to break the truce?"

"From a Frenchman who became a friend while I was in Rome—Claude Nicolas Fabri de Peiresc. We correspond quite often."

"Ah, so it wasn't from a member of this court." The arch-

142

duke was relieved. "Well, it's true, as you guessed. The trouble is that Lerma thinks the truce a mere indulgence of the Protestants. He has no idea of the pain, the rage, the pathos. He imagines that armies can suppress ideas. The notion of tolerance is unthinkable to him. See what he and King Philip are doing to the Moriscos in their own country. You know of that?"

"I do, Highness."

"But *you*, Maître Rubens, because you're a Fleming, because you're intelligent and express yourself clearly . . . *you* might be able to persuade Lerma that he should negotiate a permanent peace treaty—or at least that he must abide by the terms of the truce."

Pieter Paul shook his head. "I fear not, Highness. If I thought it even remotely possible, I'd agree to go without a word of reservation. But I'm familiar with the duke. I've spent many hours with him. He's not to be persuaded by words, by reason. What he understands is coercion."

The archduke acknowledged this with a little nod and an appreciative smile. "Yes, that's so. And the United Provinces are hardly in a position to coerce Spain . . . I can hardly coerce my own suzerain. I have difficulty enough resisting his attempts to coerce *me*. The means of coercion are in the hands of the British and French, our enemies. What a pitiful thing it is, that only one's enemies have the power to make one's friends do the sensible thing."

"But how fortunate for us, Highness, that *you* know what the sensible thing is. Some of your predecessors . . ."

"Some of my predecessors regarded this little office as a step toward something loftier, and they found it a stumbling block, or a gravestone. I'm perfectly content." He interrupted himself. "No, I'm not *perfectly* content, of course. But I'm satisfied that what I want is right for my people, all of them. There's contentment in believing that. I'd be happier to have you closer at hand. Antwerp seems a long way off." He brightened abruptly. "What a pleasure it is to talk with an intelligent man who isn't greedy, Rubens. I remembered that you'd impressed me, but I'd forgotten how much I liked you, how you charmed me."

"You honor me too much, Highness."

"You know better than that, but we'll let it pass. To keep you, I shall let you go, give you your way." Before Pieter Paul could express his gratitude, the archduke raised a silencing hand. "*But* I put you on notice that I reserve the right, when the time comes, to place greater and more important demands on you. You'll have noted that I said 'when,' not 'if.' For the time *will* come, *maître*—perhaps not until the end of the period of truce, but it will come, soon or late. Who knows? You might prove the most useful weapon I have in my little arsenal. But in the meantime, do as you please. My only request right now is that you paint new portraits of my infanta and me."

On September 9, Pieter Paul Rubens was officially designated painter to the court of the regency, with the provision, in writing, that he might continue to reside in Antwerp. Philip was ravished. "His Highness has bound you to Flanders with chains of gold," he cried. This seemed something of an exaggeration, for the artist's annual stipend was only 500 florins. But the brother's enthusiasm was pardonable, for commissions of all sorts were awarded to Rubens as a direct result of his appointment—just as Philip had predicted. Nine months after his return from Italy, Pieter Paul was the painter most in demand in Flanders, and was well on his way to repeating the success he had made for himself in Rome.

The wedding of Isabella and Pieter Paul took place on October 3, in the church of Saint Michel. For Jan Brandt, it was an occasion for unrestrained rejoicing, so eagerly did he look forward to Rubens' joining his household. "One would think," said his wife Anna with feigned reproach, "that this was *your* day, not little Isabella's."

"But the day belongs to both of us, my love," said the jubilant lawyer. "I'll have Pieter Paul in the evenings. Isabella will have him in the nights."

Isabella Brandt had been well prepared for marriage by a sensible, forthright Flemish mother who had explained to her, without a shade of prurience, just what the act of bodily union consisted of. "It is," she had told her beloved older child again and again, "the one ecstasy we can count on in this life. It's God's way of making us want to go forth and multiply according to his holy ordinances."

"Will Pieter Paul know what to do?" the girl inquired in utter innocence. "His father died when he was so young. Who could tell him?"

Anna Brandt burst out laughing. "He'll know," she answered when she had collected herself.

"How?"

"What do you think men learn in brothels?"

"They learn from *whores?*" Isabella was more surprised than shocked.

"They do."

"And in the beginning, mama, who was the teacher? Eve or Adam?"

"God, I suppose. Love comes to us from God, doesn't it? All kinds of love."

Isabella, who had adored Pieter Paul from the beginning of their courtship, learned to love him in a new way on their wedding night—which they spent under her father's roof. Her husband was as gentle with her as she had imagined he would be, as tender, as solicitous of her feelings, as concerned for her pleasure, and very eager for his own. She startled him agreeably by assenting, with no evidence of false pride or shame, to his request that she stand before him naked in the candlelight. "You must please him," Anna Brandt had told her daughter. "He's your master, in all things. To submit is your solemn duty. And it's by submission that woman ultimately triumphs in this world."

"You're lovely," said Rubens.

"I'm a fence post."

"If you offend my wife, you offend *me*."

She offered him a small, grateful smile. "I shall try never to offend you again."

"I'll say it once more, then. You're lovely."

145

"I'm lovely," she murmured happily, "because my husband tells me so."

The next day, Pieter Paul made some sketches for a wedding portrait of himself and Isabella which he worked on intermittently over the next four months. It was a painting of sublime tact and tenderness. Isabella called it a portrait of love. It became the first treasure of her life as a bride.

The six months that followed the wedding were a period of domestic calm for the Catholic Low Countries—of work and pleasure and mutual discovery for Pieter Paul and his little Isabella. He thrived in her company, in the sense of her presence, in his feeling of new responsibility, of absolute stewardship over another human life. Unobtrusive, undemanding, she was always near, always alert to his needs as she became familiar with them, deferential without being obsequious, without losing her dignity or identity. Indeed, she seemed to *gain* identity through association with her husband. She had attained womanhood by marriage, had become an adult, a peer of her parents because she was now a wife. Her attentive intelligence helped her easily to accomplish the rest.

She learned osmotically—simply by listening to her father and Pieter Paul as they conversed about all sorts of things at table during and after the evening meal. She became aware of the universe that lay beyond the walls of Antwerp, of whose existence she had theretofore known little, cared little. Now it mattered to her because it mattered to her husband. This transition was achieved by small, almost imperceptible strides, from the cloister of a circumscribed, almost conventual life, to a knowledge of the strangely contorted social, political, and economic strife of Europe. That great creation, international society, was the work of men, and it was sustained by them. And that it was the deportment of men, as distinguished from that of women, that kept upsetting the balance of nature, she hadn't the least doubt. Had she not her father's and her husband's word for it? Though she declined to intrude in the exchanges between these two most hallowed figures of her existence. Isabella eagerly put the question to her mother: "If men are such fools and bigots, why is it that women do nothing to make the world a happier place?"

"We do more to improve things than most men are willing to admit, and possibly we do more to make them worse, too. But *whatever* we do, my sweet child, we do it without letting men know what it is we're doing, or why. Though as Pieter Paul says about the Italian women, some don't mind being found out." Anna Brandt smiled complacently. "And just think what some men are willing to do for some women."

"Like Henri IV wanting to go to war for the love of the Princesse de Condé?"

It was natural that Isabella should cite this example just now, for the French king was gathering an army at Châlons-sur-Marne during the first months of 1610. There was little question in the minds of Flemish Catholics that his intention, aside from wresting the little princess from her refuge near Brussels, was to join forces with the British, the Protestant German princes, and the United Provinces to eject the mercenaries of Spain from all the Netherlands.

If young Isabella Brandt was bewildered by the apparent paradox of a French Catholic king coming to the assistance of Dutch Protestants, she was in good company. There was comparable perplexity and considerable anger in the king's own country, where the Edict of Nantes still rankled among Catholics who belitved it heresy to tolerate heresy, even in the interest of civil order. They were particularly embittered by the prosperity enjoyed in the several Huguenot enclaves scattered about the land. If there wasn't room in heaven for two faiths, there surely wasn't room under the soft skies of France.

While Henri IV was preparing to join his army at Châlons, the Protestants of the United Provinces, taking advantage of the respite afforded by the truce with Spain, allowed themselves the luxury of bringing their internal differences, religious and political, into the open. The laxer Arminians, led now by van Oldenbarneveldt and the celebrated philosopher-jurist, Hugo Grotius, published an inflammatory document, the *"Remonstrantie,"* protesting the harsh austerity of the Calvinist

147

"Precisians." Reaction to this attack was almost immediate. The sterner-hearted Calvinists, who had long disapproved of the charity shown by the Arminians toward the Catholics who had dared to remain in their midst, issued an even more violent reply, a *"Contra-Remonstrantie."*

Words were quickly followed by deeds. The United Provinces were plunged into a full-scale civil war. The Duke of Lerma again attempted to persuade the Archduke Albrecht to abrogate the truce and march against the major Dutch towns, thus to end the division between north and south. The regent stood firm against the Spanish minister, claiming his right under the terms of Philip II's will to exercise sovereignty in the Low Countries as he and his infanta saw fit. The only purpose to be served by a military intervention against the United Provinces, he told Lerma, would be to reunite them. Like his first refusal, his second was no secret. His refusal to go to war made him a hero even to the leaders of the Protestant factions in the north, nominally his enemies.

As rumors and factual reports of troop movements all about Europe increased in frequency and degree of alarm, Pieter Paul Rubens was at last completing the great painting of the Adoration of the Magi. In the middle of April, he supervised its installation in the great Room of State, where it was juxtaposed with pictures by other, slightly older contemporaries—notably Frans Snyders and Jan Bruegel, who had been regarded until now, by most authorities, as Flanders' most proficient painters. Their work suffered embarrassingly when they had to be compared with this festive, brilliantly colorful celebration of Epiphany.

As Nicolas Rockox, a discerning collector of art and antiquities, gratefully remarked when he handed over to the artist the final payment for the painting, "This single thing sets you far above everyone else in Flanders. It makes me want to weep with happiness." The burgomaster added that Rubens could expect, in the relatively near future, a commission of even greater moment. "You'll never be sorry you decided to stay with us, *maître.*" Quite unconsciously, Pieter Paul parroted Isabella when he reported Rockox's remark to his father-in-law. "Is there anything nicer than to be wanted?"

However, before any word was forthcoming about the further major work, to which the burgomaster had alluded so tantalizingly, the attention of everyone was drawn to Paris, where an event of enormous but uncertain portent had taken place. On May 14, as he was leaving the Louvre to join his army at Châlons, Henri IV had been stabbed to death by François Ravaillac, a Catholic fanatic. The Huguenots were convinced that the assassination had been inspired and perhaps even managed by the Jesuits. Whatever Ravaillac's motivation or sponsorship, the death of the king would alter the complexion of Continental politics—though no one could yet say how.

All that was currently known was that Maria de' Medici had assumed the regency of France in the name of her nine-year-old son, Louis XIII. This boded ill for the Huguenots, for the queen mother was the darling of the very Jesuits who had purportedly ordered Henri IV's murder. The rest of Catholic Europe breathed more easily, however, for the day after the king's death, his widow renounced the plan to march against the forces of the Emperor Rudolf in Julich. Only James I was disappointed to learn that peace, for the time being, was secure—at least between nation and nation. It was safe for the Protestants of the United Provinces to continue their civil war.

This growing sense of stability and security had an effect on Rubens' career. In June, he received from Cornelis van der Geest, a prominent *Anversois* merchant, the order for a great triptych devoted to the Raising of the Cross for the high altar of the fine new church of Saint Walburga, the first to be built in the city in more than fifty years. Though it was to be a very substantial piece of work, this was not the commission to which Nicolas Rockox had referred. It could not have been more welcome nor more opportune, because within days of receiving this request, Pieter Paul was told by a stammering, excited Isabella that she was pregnant.

Her girlish pleasure was more touching to her husband than the occasion for it—though God knew he was happy to know

149

that he was going to be a father. But Isabella's joy was so softly ecstatic that he found himself, at moments, weeping quietly at the recollection of her expression when she whispered to him, "I'm going to have a child. Isn't that glorious?" It *was* glorious.

It was also a problem, because he was still unable to provide a suitable dwelling for his wife—a circumstance which, whenever Pieter Paul brought it up, his father-in-law turned aside with the caution that if he had *his* way, the couple would never leave his house. "You've become the son I never had. I hope you'll always stay with us."

Shades of Annibale Chieppio . . . But Jan Brandt was no Polonius. Fond though he was of his father-in-law, Rubens had reason not related to pride for wanting an establishment of his own. Brandt's commodious attic was proving too small for the artist's burgeoning enterprise. In addition to the triptych commission he had just been awarded, there were numerous smaller religious paintings and portraits to be completed; and, most crowding of all, he had to accommodate a number of pupils. A half-dozen youths of varying endowments were the fortunate few of many who constantly sought the tutelage of the artist now acknowledged to be the Flemish master. There just wasn't enough space on the top floor of Jan Brandt's house for so much activity. But until Pieter Paul had accumulated more savings and located a house of sufficient size in a suitable location, he must content himself with the confusion that reigned in his present studio.

How he managed to accomplish anything of value in the atmosphere of chaos over which he presided so casually and amiably, no other artist of Antwerp could understand. His powers of concentration were certainly singular, as was his speed. He constantly surprised the older painters, particularly Snyders and Jan Bruegel who were frequent callers. The latter had been for the past eight years dean of the Guild of Saint Luke, successor to Rubens' former master, Adam van Noort. Ten years older than Pieter Paul and himself a veteran of the Italian experience, Bruegel confined his work mainly to landscapes and still lifes, so that he and Rubens were hardly competitive. Even if they

150

had been serious rivals, the two men would have become friends: Pieter Paul was incapable of loftiness; Bruegel was incapable of envy.

Yet there was more than generosity of spirit in Jan Bruegel's frequent proclamation of Rubens' flamboyant genius; there was awe. It wasn't simply the younger painter's shattering swiftness with pen or brush, or his capacity to isolate himself absolutely from all that was going on about him that impressed Bruegel and others who could boast a special knowledge, it was the vividness of his work, his power to conceive and create, within the confines of principles acceptable to clerics and connoisseurs of Antwerp, pictures of amazing originality. That was to say, Pieter Paul had a style that was uniquely his.

Jan Bruegel, son of Pieter Bruegel the elder, had been born only a year before his father's death. When he was old enough to be entitled to opinions about painting, he came to share the common Flemish view that old Pieter's work was too brutally rustic and crude to be hung on the walls of churches or prosperous drawing rooms—and perhaps just a little bit mad. For the elder Bruegel had been much influenced by the maddest artist Europe would produce until the twentieth century, Hieronymous Bosch, the long-dead monk of the northern Netherlands so perversely admired by Philip II. Jan Bruegel rejected his paternal heritage in favor of an Italianate style so cool and lucid that one of his admirers described his work as "velvet." The adjective immediately adhered to the painter as well as to his art. In Rubens, Bruegel discerned a craftsman whose brilliance eclipsed all the masters he was familiar with, and he had seen enough of the paintings of the great Renaissance Italians to know whereof he spoke. Pieter Paul had the attributes that were indispensable to greatness—power, voluptuousness, majesty, audacity. He had another quality too. Caravaggio had mentioned his handling of surfaces; Bruegel talked in terms of "geniality." He saw the younger Fleming as doubly phenomenal because of his emergence in a period of general artistic and intellectual timidity.

"How do you *dare* so easily?" he asked Rubens one summer

afternoon as he watched him at work on the triptych for Saint Walburga. "If any other painter here made such a celebration of the flesh for a high altar, he'd be put in irons. Is it your connections, your friendship with the archduke?"

"You don't understand about the Jesuits," said Pieter Paul, not pausing in his labors. "I daresay much of the fault is *theirs*, not yours. Some idiot attached to them the name of 'soldier of Christ,' and ever since then people have jumped to the conclusion that they're militant, that their outlook is bleak, that their message is basically a threat: 'Believe, or go to the devil.' Nothing could be further from the truth. Their message is joy, a perpetual '*Gloria, in excelsis Deo.*' You know, Jan, I had much more trouble with the Oratorians over my altarpiece for the Chiesa Nuova than I did with the Jesuits in Mantua. Everyone has forgotten what the Jesuits were organized to do . . ."

"To suppress the Reformation," said Bruegel without hesitation. "To persecute the Protestants."

"Not to persecute them, to *persuade* them of their error. And what better way to persuade than by making the churches beautiful, joyous, colorful?"

The older artist was skeptical. "You certainly exceed the normal bounds. Your figures seem to me very nearly pagan."

Pieter Paul nodded happily, and continued to paint. "As nearly so as I think admissible. That's the object. It's a sort of bacchanale."

"I'd be interested in seeing your canonical evidence for the Raising of the Cross as a bacchanale," said Bruegel sarcastically.

Rubens laughed. "You sound like my brother. But it was *he* who gave me the original thought—unwittingly, of course. His studies of antiquity, you know. To the ancients, Greek *and* Roman, an orgy was a religious rite. I'm trying to bring the pagan orgy into church art."

As the panels for Saint Walburga neared their final state, Pieter Paul realized that it would be impossible for him to finish the central portion, which was painted on two wide planks of oak, in Jan Brandt's attic; when assembled, they were too large to be taken down the stairs. After consultation with

152

the donor, Cornelis van der Geest, and members of Saint Walburga's parish council, the artist arranged to have the panels transferred to the wall above the high altar that they were to occupy. In order not to interfere with the celebrations of the masses that were offered in one of the chapels of the new church, the artist and his young assistants surrounded the central altar with a great curtain of sail cloth. For the next fortnight, Rubens spent all his daylight hours putting the last touches on the painting. When the protective cloth and the scaffolding had been removed, this great triptych of the Raising of the Cross was described as the finest and most dramatic ever seen in the Low Countries. Jan Bruegel thought the word "theatrical" more apposite than "dramatic."

It was the theatricality that appealed to the Jesuits, as Rubens had known it would. There was talk of yet another church to be built by this order in Antwerp, to commemorate the most recent Jesuit saint, Charles Borromeo. Though no plans had been drawn nor even a site selected, it was tacitly understood that its entire interior decoration would be assigned to the one painter in the land who perfectly comprehended the mission of the Jesuits—to demonstrate by works and instruction that faith could be joyful.

The altarpiece for Saint Walburga opened up for Rubens a market for religious painting much more extensive than any ever before enjoyed by any other single Flemish master. The demand was especially great because new churches were being constructed with funds made available to various orders by the Flemish hierarchy which found itself enriched by the gradual economic recovery. Old churches, devastated during the religious wars, were being restored. Though some paintings and sculpture had escaped pillage, a large proportion was lost forever and must be replaced. In this era of better feeling occasioned by the truce, the presence in Antwerp of Pieter Paul Rubens, court painter and master of the new spirit of religion in art, was a godsend for the clergy—and for the rich who sought salvation through conspicuous good works. It seemed only proper that a Rubens should benefit from the righting of

153

wrongs that had brought about the downfall of another Rubens.

In harmony with the temper of the times, and in keeping with the vow he had made the day after his return from Rome, Pieter Paul asked Philip to join him in purchasing the right to decorate the bare little Rubens chapel in the church of Saint Michel, where all their relations were interred. The artist designed its furnishings, and adorned the altar with the painting of the Adoration of the Virgin which he had originally made for the Chiesa Nuova in Rome—the one he had had to replace with a replica painted on slate.

By the end of the year 1610, it was plain that he could put off the purchase of a house no longer. He had enough money put aside, and from his instruction alone he was now earning as much every month as he received annually from the regency in Brussels. He had every reason for pride and pleasure. "I'm becoming as prosperous as some of my patrons," he told Philip. "No anguish now, by God, and no poverty."

The prospects had never seemed so luminous. With the advice of Jan Brandt, who reluctantly agreed that the painter had to have larger accommodations, Pieter Paul decided to buy a house in the Wapperstraat, a structure that could be altered and enlarged to suit his purposes. On January 4, 1611, he purchased the house and an adjoining plot of land. He proceeded without delay to contract for the improvements. Isabella, well into her seventh month of pregnancy, occupied herself during the granite-gray days of the Flemish winter planning the details of changes she wanted to effect in the portions of their new house that were to be her responsibility—every room, that is, except for Pieter Paul's studio. He agreed unreservedly to all her suggestions. "You're to have anything you like," he said with an indulgent smile, and patted her ample belly. "So is my son."

"And if it's a girl?" she inquired.

"But I *love* girls, my dearest. Fathers always imagine their first-born will be sons. I suppose that's what they hope. Philip's child is a boy. Why not mine? But it doesn't matter."

154

He was as good as his word. Isabella produced a daughter for him on March 11. He was truly delighted—and greatly relieved to know that his wife had survived the ordeal, for maternity claimed the lives of an appalling number of women. The child was christened Clara Serena ten days later. Her uncle Philip was her godfather, as Pieter Paul had stood for his brother's son and namesake the previous year.

The family celebration that followed the baptism was the last happy meeting of the brothers Rubens. A few days afterward, Philip caught a chill while taking one of his "philosophic walks" along the Antwerp quaysides. He was ill for a month, during which time he suffered every conceivable pain that the incompetent "physicians" who attended him could devise as "cures." "Black magicians, they are," Pieter Paul mumbled bitterly to Isabella after each visit to his moribund brother's bedside. "They make death seem a boon."

Philip Rubens died at the age of thirty-eight, leaving a widow and son to the protection of his beloved younger brother. Thanks to the inheritance from Maria Piepelinx, the survivors were comfortably provided for financially. It was Pieter Paul's only consolation. He made all the funeral arrangements for the grieving Maria de Moy. He knelt and prayed through the high requiem mass. He watched in tearless, expressionless silence as his brother's coffin took its place in the wall of the chapel they had so recently decorated. The widow departed from the church with her parents. Rubens sent Isabella home with the Brandts. He remained alone in the chapel, the last of his generation.

He felt a tide of futility and apathy sweep toward him, slow but ineluctable, a kind of depression more hopeless than the despair he had witnessed while traveling through rural Spain years before. What did the Spanish call that? *Desengaño*. During the week that followed Philip's funeral, Pieter Paul accomplished nothing. It wasn't for want of trying. He mounted the stairs to the studio each morning at the accustomed hour. He looked at the painting he had been working on. He prepared his palette and brushes. But the torpor that enveloped him would not be dispelled. He said little to his intimates, to his pupils, to anyone; and the little he said was mere politeness—the habitual salutations, thanks, apologies, all conditioned responses. He was hardly aware that he spoke at all.

"He doesn't weep," said Isabella to her father. "Why doesn't he weep?"

Deeply though he loved his son-in-law, Jan Brandt felt he didn't know him well enough to intrude on Pieter Paul's sorrow. He consulted Balthasar Moretus, himself only recently bereaved by the loss of his father. "He doesn't weep," said Brandt to the new proprietor of the Plantin Press. "We don't know what to do for him."

Moretus painfully climbed to the attic studio. The pupils and apprentices stared in touched astonishment as he made his appearance; they recognized this great labor of love. The bent little man offered a regretful smile as he asked them to leave him alone with their master. If Rubens heard any of this, seated on a stool before the painting he hadn't touched since his brother's death, he gave no sign of it.

When the studio was cleared of people, Balthasar stumped slowly over to the side of the man who was now his dearest and oldest friend. Only then did Pieter Paul raise his eyes. He boggled. "What do you think you're doing here? You might have killed yourself." He leaped from the stool and brought a paint-stained chair to Moretus, then helped to place him in it—as he had done so many times before.

"And if I *had* killed myself, would you behave as you're behaving now?" Before Rubens could find a reply, Balthasar pressed on. "You're not God. You're not even *a* god. You're no Olympian who can look down on us mere mortals and say, 'Ah well, that's how it is. You humans can weep, you can purge your sorrow with tears, but not me, not Rubens. I don't have to weep.' "

"I haven't time for tears," said the painter softly, annoyed with his friend for this intrusion, yet moved by the gallantry of the gesture. "I'm not trying to be Olympian, for God's sake."

"You have no time for grief?"

156

"No time for wishing to undo what's not to be undone."

"You lie. You lie to yourself, Pieter Paul. You're trying to bury the pain."

"If only I *could* bury it. If only I could forget."

"Forget Philip?"

"Forget the loss of Philip."

Balthasar's smile was grim. "To undo what's not to be undone?"

Rubens acknowledged this with a slight nod. "Yes. Exactly. It's a circle, isn't it?"

"You'll not weep?"

"Is that what this heroic climb was in aid of, a display of emotion? You think that would be good for me?"

"It would do you no harm. It would be human."

"You think me inhuman?"

"I think you're trying to be superhuman."

Jan Brandt appeared rather timidly at the head of the staircase. He was carrying a bottle of *eau-de-vie* and three glasses. "Do I interrupt?"

The painter sighed and wearily shook his head. "Are you here to help exorcise poor Philip's ghost too, dear Jan?"

The lawyer approached gingerly, wearing his compassion as if it were a shroud. "You could say that. I'm here in the higher interest of life, as distinguished from death."

Pieter Paul watched as his father-in-law poured the colorless liquid into the stubby, thick little glasses. "Balthasar wants tears, Jan. He thinks I defy humanity by my inability to cry."

"By your *refusal* to cry," said Moretus. "You wept for your mama."

Rubens remembered the scene with Philip in the house in the Klosterstraat, just after his return from Rome. *Had* he wept? He couldn't recall. "Is that how it strikes *you?*" he asked Brandt.

"I can only guess, you understand. It seems to me that you're allowing your remorse to devour you. That's very destructive. It's inhuman. In a strange way, it's even remorseless."

Rubens studied his father-in-law's face with curiosity.

"Truly, Jan? Do I seem remorseless? What a terrible thing if it were so."

Moretus lost his patience. "Stop trying to play a role, Pieter Paul. That's what Jan means. We're not meant to carry such burdens without lashing out, without crying out."

" 'In the midst of life, there is death.' I know the formula, you see. I know that it must be accepted. It's not that I'm Olympian, Balthasar. If I *am* playing a role, that's not the one. I just haven't the passion. I haven't the energy left for the agony I feel. Don't you see? I miss Philip. I'll always miss him. I'll always remember him. He was my brother, my other soul. You want tears? I can find none. Besides, what are tears? They're only an outward manifestation. What could be easier than tears? What could be harder?"

"They cleanse the heart," said Brandt, without much conviction.

Moretus cleared his throat nervously. "So there it is. No tears for Philip."

"If I weep," said Rubens with sudden warmth, "it will be for the living, not the dead."

"Oh my God, Pieter Paul, no mewling, I beg of you, no self-pity. You'll not ruin our friendship by making believe you're sorry for yourself." Brandt's voice was strangled. "I thought you were the indomitable optimist. No one I know has greater reason for optimism."

"I *was* an optimist." The painter stared bleakly at the splotched planking of the attic floor for a moment. "I suppose, when this passes, I'll be an optimist again."

"There," said Brandt triumphantly. "We're making progress, Balthasar. He admits that his depression will pass." He handed glasses to his companions. "Tears for the living should be tears of joy. You're quite right, Pieter Paul. Philip is dead, but we're still here. Survival isn't everything, I know, but it comes first, doesn't it? There's nothing without survival. There's only death."

Rubens contemplated the glass. "I've been indulging myself, haven't I? You've shamed me."

158

"I don't think either of us wanted to do that."

"And touched me too, that you cared so much." He gave them a wan smile. "Philip would understand. I can't weep for him because he wouldn't want me to."

Jan Brandt raised his glass. "Then we shall drink to dear Philip's memory, dry-eyed, because he wouldn't want tears."

"No," said Pieter Paul, "let's drink to the living." But as he lifted the glass to his lips, his broken heart betrayed him. He sobbed helplessly.

Five

I surprised no one familiar with Pieter Paul that once he had managed to come to terms with the death of his brother, to recognize that he must turn a corner, he rarely looked back. There was too much to look forward to, too much involvement with the present, to allow him to dally for very long over an event, no matter how distressing, which couldn't be altered by his unhappiness. He continued to mourn Philip and to miss him. His brother's resolute, calm features often visited the painter's vivid recollection.

But the fact of Philip's death had finally been accepted. Rubens could say, "Philip was . . ." or "Philip used to be . . ." without finding himself at a sudden loss for breath, or on the verge of tears. It wasn't necessary for him to become an Italian man of his time, one who sought to dissipate personal grief by generalizing it, universalizing it in the way that was to become the literary rage of the court of Louis XIV. In 1611, death was a constant companion. It took very little to kill a human being; any illness could prove fatal, any infected wound, any childbirth, any "chill." He had to look no farther than to his friend

160

Balthasar Moretus, who had lost his father, to see that life did continue—sometimes in spite of one's wishes.

And for Rubens, life was extremely and increasingly active. There was an abundance of work, an abundance of teaching. He was dismayed to feel compelled to turn away a protégé of Jacques de Brie, an engraver who often made reproductions of Pieter Paul's paintings for the Plantin Press. The studio in Jan Brandt's attic was just too small to allow even one additional pupil; he had had, he explained to de Brie, to reject similar requests from almost a hundred other applicants. This exaggeration was intended to soften the blow to his acquaintance, but there was enough truth in it to carry conviction. Rubens was *the* artist of fashion in Flanders, and in these years when painters were in ever greater demand, it was logical that his tutelage should be solicited by many more prospective pupils than he could possibly cope with.

Another preoccupation was the house in the Wapperstraat, still in the process of renovation, to which he gave daily attention. It was a cause of much frustration, for he had hoped to install himself within a year of his acquisition of the property. With every passing month, it became evident that this aspiration was not to be realized. "It's your own fault," said his father-in-law, who was delighted by the delays, for they kept the little Rubens family beneath *his* roof. "You insist on making changes and additions to the plan." The accusation was too just. "You're building a mausoleum for the living," Brandt said. That *might* be true. He was certainly building something of a palace—though he referred to it more austerely as a "town house." What he had in his imagination was an adaptation of a middle-sized Genoese *palazzo* for his residence, the principal structure connected by a covered colonnade to a separate building which would be large enough to house two workshops—a spacious one to which his pupils would be restricted, and a somewhat smaller room where he could paint and receive callers.

The question wasn't one simply of confining a certain vol-

161

ume of space within walls and floors and roofs. Rubens' plans were elaborate in their detail. The masonry he called for was complicated; only a few artisans of Antwerp were proficient enough to produce it and *they* must divide their limited working time among a number of projects that included repairs to damaged churches and ecclesiastical residences. No matter how important a figure the artist had become, he ranked lower than the clergy in the estimation of workmen, for the priests held the keys to the gates of Saint Peter. By the end of the year, Pieter Paul appreciated that it would be a very long time indeed before he and his wife and daughter were able to move into the house in the Wapperstraat—perhaps even years. There was nothing to do but accept the reality—and be touched by Jan Brandt's happiness over the postponement of their departure.

The nature of little Clara Serena Rubens gave the lie to the implication of her second name; she was demanding and attractively temperamental. She was spoiled. Only Anna Brandt attempted to resist the appeal of the plump blond infant. She did so as a matter of principle. "If you pay so much attention to her now," she protested to the other three adults of the household, "you'll ruin her for the harshness she'll have to face in later life." But she too yielded often to the pretty blandishments of the child, consoled her when she cried for an absent parent, nourished her with sweetened water and soft biscuits, or tranquillized her with a fine linen sugar-teat. For Anna Brandt was really no less susceptible than anyone else to the custom of the prosperous to indulge very young children. No one could be certain how long they would live. Infant mortality exceeded fifty percent in the first year of existence. Life seemed all the more precious because it might be so brief.

To these constant and welcome calls on his time was added that comparably pleasant company of a growing number of acquaintances—mainly men of some importance in Antwerp who were introduced to him by his intimates, Moretus and Brandt, and by the admiring Nicolas Rockox, all of them eager to present the artist to any rich or noble gentleman who might provide him with a commission. The burgomaster, still promising an order that would exceed in magnitude and importance the "Adoration of the Magi" for the Town Hall, arranged for Pieter Paul gradually to meet all the members of Antwerp's most exclusive society—the Corporation of Arquebusiers, an assembly of merchants, bankers, and nobles who were the self-appointed but officially recognized keepers of the peace. The name of the group derived from the *arquebuses* which they carried, or had carried for them by servants. The *arquebuse* was a muzzle-loading blunderbuss so heavy and unwieldy that it could only be fired when resting on a stout cane, so inaccurate that its value was far greater for its alarming sound than for the likelihood of injuring anyone it was aimed at, and very nearly as dangerous for its operator as for the intended victim—for it had a nasty way of exploding or misfiring.

Because of the distinction of its membership, it wasn't astonishing that Rockox should be the principal officer of the Arquebusiers. So diligent was he in seeing to it that the painter receive in his studio most of the others of the corporation, where each could speak with him and have the opportunity of viewing studies of his previous paintings and major work in progress, that Pieter Paul could have no doubt of Rockox's intention. In early September of 1611, all became clear. As a mark of their gratitude for the truce and the prosperity that had resulted from it, the Arquebusiers had decided to redecorate the chapel in the Cathedral of Notre-Dame of Antwerp of which they were the patrons. The whole cathedral had been sacked by the Protestants half a century before and remained denuded. Only now were the funds available for refurbishing. What was required was a fine triptych altarpiece whose theme would be the Descent from the Cross. And who but Pieter Paul Rubens, whose "Adoration of the Magi" in the Town Hall and the "Raising of the Cross" in Saint Walburga were the splendors of contemporary *Anversois* painting, could be invited to compose so important a work?

This was the most auspicious commission Rubens had so far been awarded, and he was the more satisfied with it because it was also the first he had been asked to do for the cathedral. The

163

subject had a special appeal for him during this period when he was still in mourning for his brother. He conceived the central panel as a tribute to Philip, though naturally conforming to the Arquebusiers' request that the canvas pay particular homage to their holy protector, Saint Christopher, the bearer of Christ. To this personage the artist gave the clean-shaven face of Philip Rubens as a young man, clothed in red, his expression one of torment; he dominated the lower right-hand portion of the picture. What gave the work its enormous dramatic power, its "theatricality," as Jan Bruegel would say, was the brilliance of the illumination cast on the figure of the dead Christ as His body was being folded into winding sheets—a broad, diagonal band of light which thrust downward to the center. By the year's end, Rubens had completed studies for the panels, which were enthusiastically approved by Rockox.

But more than two years would elapse before all three elements of the triptych were installed in the cathedral, so many projects was the artist already committed to, so confined was he in Jan Brandt's attic, so concerned was he to make as broad as possible, as rapidly as possible, the scope of his market. There were numerous portraits to be done, and though he could accomplish these quickly, the sheer volume of the demand cut severely into the time he could allocate to larger commissions. For portraits were the bread-and-butter trade of all artists because they could not only be swiftly made but were immediately paid for.

Another kind of painting was become modish, its popularity among the rich and noble Flemings inspired by the taste of Italian magnates, wealthy clerics, and potentates—pictures based on incidents described in classical literature, all themes lending themselves ideally to Rubens' talent and affection for the voluptuous: Hero and Leander, Juno and Argus, Jupiter and Callisto, Cupid sharpening his Bow. This was a style of art that appealed directly and exclusively to the physical senses—a manner that only a decade ago would certainly have been condemned in Flanders as degradingly profane, even obscene. But now, with the Jesuit theologians enjoying a cultural ascendancy over all other orders, it was acceptable fare for anyone who could find the price.

A narrow-minded bishop, unwilling to accept the new wave of joy and beauty that was, as Pieter Paul had so correctly pointed out to Jan Bruegel, the essence of the Jesuit message, might occasionally lash out at the undisguised sensuality of such a Rubens painting. These objections were ignored despite the fact that the affluent Flemings who purchased them were excellent and dutiful followers of the True Church. So powerful were the Jesuits, so compelling and appealing was the force of the style that would ultimately be called Baroque, that all quibbles about glorifying the sins of the flesh were dismissed.

Could pleasure, especially the pleasures of the body, exist at all without the approval of God? So went the defense. The occasional reproof leveled against a Rubens mythological scene was parried with the excuse that it was "allegorical"—though few of the artist's patrons were very clear about the symbolism to be deduced from the pictures they so eagerly purchased. Nor did they take the trouble to find out. It was sufficient to know that what Pieter Paul painted enjoyed the tacit approval of the omnipotent Jesuits. The bonds of prudery, which most Erasmian Flemings had always found rather irksome, were broken, never to be restored.

Not that the Jesuits had decreed the human form to be the object of worship; but in propitiating the body's urgencies, there was a spiritual as well as a physical renewal. Rubens summed up this new outlook for a Jan Brandt who clung, in his lawyerly way, to the precedents established in his youth by the Edicts of Trent. He took them seriously and literally, and thus was not a little shocked by his son-in-law's renditions of ancient scandals. "Physical love is just as important a part of the beautiful life for men and women as spiritual love, as their mutual love of the Trinity. Without physical love, what you insist on describing as 'obscenity,' there could *be* no spiritual love, no love at all, because there'd be no human on the earth to adore the Father and the Son and the Holy Ghost. Amen."

"So you'd have me believe that Jupiter and Callisto were man and wife?" Brandt inquired sardonically.

Pieter Paul grinned. "The gods didn't need to marry, Jan. They enjoyed *le droit de seigneur* with every goddess and every mortal woman."

"So you're just pandering to the tastes of the debauched. You should hang your head in shame."

The painter shrugged. "It's not as if I were the author of the myths."

"You don't have to paint them. It's corrupting. Don't you see that? I wouldn't want your little Clara to live in a house with such pictures."

"The corruption, dear Jan, is in your *eyes,* not in the paintings."

"I know a dirty picture when I see one. No one has to explain the principles of fornication to *me*. You corrupt, I tell you, because you make fornication seem attractive and pleasurable."

"But it *is* attractive and pleasurable."

"And it's sinful in the bargain."

"It's *life*, Jan. It *happens*. Who am I to set myself up as a judge of the conduct of others, so long as it doesn't hurt anyone else? Who are you, if it comes to that?"

"It's just not permissible," said Brandt doggedly.

"It was permitted to Henri IV. You certainly don't imagine that poor Vincenzo Gonzaga was denied absolution on his deathbed last month because he'd been a fornicator and an adulterer all his life."

"That's all very fine for kings and dukes . . ."

"And for bishops and archbishops and popes . . . for men like my father?"

Jan Brandt flushed. "If you insist on itemizing in that way . . . Yes. Such things *are* permitted men like that."

"The privilege of rank?"

"Something of the sort."

"But not for the people. These pictures would be acceptable

to you if they were hung in places where they couldn't be seen by the servants and tradesmen?"

"They give them ideas they shouldn't have."

Pieter Paul was incredulous in the face of his father-in-law's obtuseness. "You really imagine they don't have such ideas already? Have you never been to a *kermesse* at *mardi gras,* at Easter time, on midsummer's night, or after the harvest, Jan? What the devil do you think those couples are doing in the mounds of straw?"

"The beer and the *eau-de-vie* release their inhibitions. They can't help themselves."

"But is the idea different from the one in the head of Jupiter —*or* Callisto?"

"For the people, it's not an idea at all. They're simply drunk. They don't know what they're doing."

"And you're telling me that my pictures have the same effect on them as drink? I only wish it were so. Imagine it, a painting as powerful as a jug of *eau-de-vie* . . . But I've never heard you cursing the taverners or the brewers or the distillers. Surely they're more guilty of leading the innocent to sin than I am, than any painter, if sin is simply the breaking down of inhibitions."

Jan Brandt became reflective. "I'd never thought of that . . . Not, you understand, that I'm *agreeing* with you, or even excusing you, but I'd never thought of that."

There was one source of revenue for which Rubens was obliged to expend no effort whatever—the sale of engravings of his paintings to collectors unable to afford originals. At first, the income was a mere trickle remitted occasionally by Balthasar Moretus, who saw to the printing and distribution of the etchings. But as Pieter Paul's reputation grew, so did the demand for reproductions of his work. By the onset of 1612, the copyist Jacques de Brie, of the Plantin Press, was a familiar figure in the artist's crowded studio. Every major canvas was thus

167

recorded, and many portraits of illustrious personages who sat for the master.

In order to protect his rights to the exclusive sale of the engravings, Rubens had to obtain a patent from the regent in Brussels—a matter that presented no difficulties. The Archduke Albrecht, however, had no jurisdiction over prints to be sold in other countries. And securing copyrights from the rulers of the United Provinces, the Empire, France, Italy, Spain, and Britain was complicated by the necessity of having agents who could be trusted to offer suitable bribes to the proper officials. For some years, neither Moretus nor the artist was successful in finding reliable representatives abroad. During this period, inept forgeries of the Plantin engravings enjoyed complete impunity and considerable success, since they were offered at prices much lower than those asked for the ones produced in Antwerp. In spite of this contraband, the market flourished and increased. Pieter Paul was grateful to his friend.

Rubens painted a triptych of the Resurrection, to adorn the altar of the Plantin chapel in the cathedral, a work that Moretus had requested as a memorial to his late father. When the panels were completed, at the end of April, Balthasar insisted on paying the fair market price for them. Pieter Paul wouldn't hear of it. "How could I take your money?"

The crippled printer was adamant. "For a Fleming, you're not much of a merchant. I don't give you books, do I?"

"I was fond of your father. You're my friend," responded Rubens with equal obduracy.

But Balthasar persisted. "How much do you earn in a day?"

"It depends."

"Of course it depends. But what is the average? Don't you have any idea?"

"I suppose I could calculate it from what I earned last year."

"Do that." Moretus stood at the painter's shoulder and watched as he scribbled numbers on a sheet of drawing paper. "A hundred florins?" He asked, as he saw his friend underline that figure.

Pieter Paul nodded. "That doesn't include what I receive

from teaching, you understand, or from you. It's what I earn just from painting. About a hundred florins a day."

"It seems modest enough."

"Oh, it will increase. But I have no desire to price myself out of the market."

"And how long did it take you to paint that triptych of mine?"

"About a fortnight, I should think . . . including Sundays . . . say twelve actual working days."

"So twelve hundred florins is what you'd charge someone else."

"Six hundred. There are so many interruptions, you know, like printers who ask me how much I earn. Six hundred."

Balthasar sighed. "I'm glad you don't represent *me*. You'll take no more?"

"I'm agreeing to take as much as that only because I know you'll hound me until I do."

"I shall have my revenge," said Moretus.

"I'm sure it will be sweet."

"It will be secret. You'll never know," was the printer's parting comment. And he was right. He simply inflated the accounts of Rubens' engravings sold, until he had made up the 600 florins Pieter Paul had refused.

In June, when the weather in the Low Countries was its finest, when the impudent tulips succeeded the brave daffodils and jonquils, Britons of note and wealth crossed the Channel from Folkestone to Ostend and proceeded to the inland watering place of Spa, there to purge their internal organs and sweat away their winter's itch. Among the midsummer voyagers of 1612 was Thomas Howard, fourteenth Earl of Arundel, heir to the dukedom of Norfolk, grandson of the faithful servant whom Queen Elizabeth had designated "first subject of the realm." Like his forebears, the earl was an unreconstructed Catholic who managed to cling at once to his titles and his faith by dint of important services rendered to his Anglican king.

His mission to the Low Countries was not altogether personal. James I had requested that he convey the royal respects to the Archduke Albrecht and, as discreetly as possible, learn what he could of Spain's intentions with regard to the rebellious United Provinces, where religious and political strife was mounting. The British king's main concern was that the Dutch fleet continue its patrol of North Sea waters; he wanted no worrisome Spanish vessels menacing his ports or shipping.

Howard came away from his audience with the charming regent with two pieces of intelligence, only one of them interesting to his monarch: Spain was so embroiled in the domestic difficulties resulting from the expulsion of the Moriscos, and so short of funds, that a revival of the war was unlikely, the more so because the archduke and the infanta were so firmly disposed against it. The second revelation was more personal. The earl expressed great admiration for the portraits of his host and hostess that hung in the room where they received him. He was told that these pictures were the work of Pieter Paul Rubens, court painter and favorite, who lived in Antwerp. The archduke would be enchanted, if Howard desired it, to pen a note to the artist suggesting that he find time to paint the Englishman's portrait. The earl replied that he could imagine nothing that would give his wife greater pleasure than a portrait by so skilled a master.

As soon as he was lodged in Antwerp, Arundel sent a servant around to Jan Brandt's house with the archduke's letter and a request for an appointment at Rubens' convenience. An hour was immediately set, and Thomas Howard arrived on the dot. Remarkably, for so great a nobleman, he was accompanied by neither a courtier nor even a page. At twenty-seven, he was without a hint of affectation, of the self-important pomposity or grandeur that afflicted so many of the notables and titled figures whom the artist had portrayed.

Pieter Paul felt oddly uncertain about the meeting, for he didn't know whether or not the man spoke any language except that strange one of his native land that the painter had, on one or two occasions, heard in Brussels and Rome, and which he thought more to resemble the baying of hounds than a

170

means of communication between animals of a higher species. Moreover, he had been informed more than once that the English prided themselves on their ignorance of foreign tongues.

As the young man made his appearance at the top of the stairs, Rubens bowed in his most courtly manner, and said not a word. The earl's bright eyes were filled with mild amusement, but he too kept silent. "You're welcome to my studio, *mijnheer*," the painter finally muttered in Flemish. Arundel looked at him in perplexity. Pieter Paul repeated the phrase in German, in Italian, in Spanish, and as a last desperate resort, in Latin. To the last language, there was a faint flicker of recognition.

The peer raised one eyebrow and stammered, "You have French, perhaps?"

Rubens nodded and offered his guest a grateful smile. "I do, *monsieur*."

"Thank God," said the earl, in a French that was fluent enough but seriously flawed. "We might have been able to struggle through in Latin, but the best I can manage is very poor, I'm afraid. I had ten years of it at Eton and Cambridge, and I've nothing to show for it but '*amo, amas*,' and the rest of it. But French is a bit easier, what?"

"I regret that I have no English," said Rubens as he arranged his subject in a chair and showed him how to hold his head. He prepared the materials with which to make a preliminary sketch. "I've never before had the pleasure of meeting an English gentleman, though I've heard much about your country."

The portrait was accomplished after a week of sittings, each of which lasted about an hour. Conversations between painter and nobleman took several turns, most of them having to do with art. The earl, it proved, was an educated and eager collector, not only of paintings, but of Roman antiquities. When he left Antwerp, he was to proceed directly to southern Italy where one of his agents had discovered what he called an important number of marble statues which probably dated to the epoch of ancient Rome. The theme of classical art provided ample fodder for a satisfactory exchange of opinions—the earl's views much more rigid than Rubens'; the ancients couldn't possibly be improved on, and to *attempt* improvement was heresy.

On the state of the arts in his own country, Arundel was infinitely scornful. "We have a few good journeyman builders. But in the whole kingdom there's only one man who bears comparison with the master architects of France or Italy." This figure, it seemed, was Inigo Jones, a Welshman who had traveled to Venice and there been stunned into total submission by the style of Palladio. Now, returned to London, he was beginning to enjoy a modest success. "But that's only to be expected. We English have always taken our best artistic ideas from the Continent—except for our poets, of course. But you know nothing of our poets, do you?"

"Poetry, I should think, translates badly," said Pieter Paul apologetically.

"Our language may be clumsy, but it's rich."

"I don't doubt it for a moment, *monsieur*."

"You ought to come to London, Maître Rubens."

The painter demurred politely. "I have more to do right here than I can deal with, *monsieur*."

The earl pointed to the pupils who were pretending to be at work at their easels or drawing papers—though in fact all were listening and watching as their master portrayed this exotic creature from across the sea. "You could teach. I don't believe we have even one competent teacher."

"But I have my lads here." Pieter Paul suddenly lowered his voice, knowing perfectly well that they were eavesdropping. "I have one pupil who may perhaps one day be a very great painter." He inclined his head slightly toward a pale boy of thirteen with curly, ash-blond hair and delicate, almost beautiful features. "Van Dyck, he's called. Anton van Dyck. He's a wonder. He may eclipse me. I know he'll try." Then the artist's voice resumed its normal volume. "Should I leave fellows like that behind, *monsieur*? Besides, I'm very happy in Antwerp."

"No urge to travel?"

"I *have* traveled, *monsieur*. I'd like to visit Paris, of course."

172

He paused; then, embarrassed, he added hastily, "and London too, naturally, though I know very little about it."

"It's very unlovely, is London. The weather is notorious. It requires the beauty that such a man as you could bring to it."

"That's kind of you to say, *monsieur*, but I can imagine nothing at this moment that would bring me to London. And after all, I could do nothing to improve the climate."

The earl laughed. "That, God knows, is so. But if I can't lure you to London, then I shall simply have to send London to you. When this portrait is seen there, my friends will be beating down your door."

"But there's no need, *monsieur*. My door is always open to your friends."

Arundel kept his word. Almost every English nobleman who passed through Antwerp thereafter sought a Rubens portrait; and most of these men and their ladies urged Pieter Paul to establish himself in London—or at the very least, to make an extended visit there. The city, they assured him, was starving for genius in the graphic arts. To all, he gave the reply he had offered Thomas Howard: "I'm very happy in Antwerp."

He spoke only the truth. There were so many tranquil delights—and an occasional cause for great excitement, like the appearance of young Anton van Dyck. He had come to Pieter Paul after two years in the studio of a good teacher, Hendrick van Balen. There had been, in van Balen's recommendation of the youth to Antwerp's greatest master, something of the same quality of bitter remorse that Adam van Noort had expressed when passing the young Rubens on to Octave van Veen. "He's learned all I can teach him. Soon he'll be a better painter than I. I don't think I could abide that," said van Balen. For that reason alone, Pieter Paul had made room in his studio for one more pupil than he could comfortably accommodate.

Anton van Dyck was not merely gifted; he was outrageously charming. He was able to ingratiate himself with everyone he encountered; his fellow-pupils, who recognized his talents; his master, who almost immediately came to dote on him as if he were a son; and the other members of the Brandt-Rubens household—especially Anna and Isabella, who showered him with little favors, sweetmeats (because he looked so frail and undernourished), and affection (because he seemed so lonely and helpless when in their company). It was nearly miraculous that Anton failed to incur the envy or anger of pupils who had been members of Rubens' entourage longer than he without ever enjoying the privileged position he had assumed from the outset of his stay. His impudence and willing self-mockery may have been responsible. Among boys, he could be simply a boy. If he had a single quality that alarmed Pieter Paul at this early stage of his career, it was his apparent *insouciance* with respect to craft. Everything came so readily to Anton that nothing seemed crucially important to him. He painted brilliantly for one of his few years, but he was not particularly impressed with his own endowments. It was, perhaps, merely a defect of youth. Rubens had quite forgotten how very similar his own outlook had been at Anton's age, and there was no one to remind him. In any case, the young van Dyck's presence in his life was a blessing unmitigated.

Of a different order of pleasure was the compliment (or flattery) implied in the master painter's regular inclusion among the select of the city invited to receptions offered by the *échevins* to honor distinguished guests—like Don Rodrigo Calderón, Count of Oliva, Philip III's special ambassador to the court in Brussels, who paid a brief official visit to Antwerp in September. A sly, greedy-eyed predator of a sort in which the Spanish court had abounded during Pieter Paul's stay there nearly a decade earlier, Calderón thought himself subtle, a connoisseur of beauty, a creature of ineffable cultivation. The fact, as Rubens divined when their eyes first met, was that the count enjoyed over his master, Lerma, the same advantage the doltish duke commanded over the king—a slightly greater intelligence; thus was the Spanish pecking order disarranged.

The Spaniard was introduced to Rubens by Nicholas Rockox as a longtime admirer, a statement which Calderón at once supported. "Your portrait of the Duke of Lerma and your *Aposto-lado* are true masterpieces, *maître*," he said in French.

Pieter Paul had great difficulty being correct with this thief who had taken the place of Don Pedro Franqueza as Lerma's most trusted henchman. It was even more difficult when he realized that he was being wooed. He was expected to offer, humbly, to paint Calderón's portrait, *gratis,* of course. Well, by God, he would do no such thing. He wouldn't give an inch. "I was but a young man, *señor,* when I painted those things. I do much better work than that today." He spoke in Spanish.

"Ah, and you have our tongue. Is there no limit to your cleverness?" Calderón made a half turn and indicated Rubens' "Adoration of the Magi," the principal ornament of the Town Hall's Room of State. "And that magnificent painting is from your hand as well, I believe. What I wouldn't give to be able to bring that back with me to Spain for the pleasure of His Majesty." The ambassador reverted to French—thinking, Rubens reasoned, that in French, the language of diplomacy, his avarice would be less detectable.

"For His *Majesty?*" Rockox inquired. His tone alerted Rubens to the realities; whatever his personal feelings, there was afoot a game the burgomaster deemed to be of some importance.

"But of *course,* for His Majesty," protested Calderón, though no one had accused him of any wrongdoing.

"I could make a copy," ventured Pieter Paul.

"That's so thoughtful of you, Maître Rubens, but I fear I shall be leaving your charming country before you could finish a copy." His eyes glided to Rockox's face. "But what an impression it would have made on the ruler we all revere and rejoice in serving."

"A copy could be sent to you," the artist stubbornly pursued. "I've had much experience with the packing and shipping of paintings."

"Ah yes, but it wouldn't have quite the same effect then, would it?" The Spaniard inquired of the lofty spaces of the

175

Room of State. "I mean, if I were to return to the court with such messages of goodwill as Monsieur Rockox and the other gentlemen of Antwerp have asked me to convey . . . *and* that painting . . ."

"I'm certain," said the burgomaster in a very small, unsteady voice, "that something can be arranged."

"I do hope so," was Calderón's bland reply.

The next day, a bitter, resigned Pieter Paul Rubens reluctantly supervised the delicate operation of unstretching the painting of the Adoration of the Magi. The workmen laid the canvas on the floor and gently covered it with waxed cloth, then slowly rolled it up and placed it inside a wide zinc tube. After the canvas had been inserted, the ends of the tube were covered and sealed. The final maneuver was to place the tube in a wooden packing case stout enough to sustain the hazards of distant travel.

Nicolas Rockox, well aware of the artist's view of this transaction, thought it wise to wait until the onerous task was finished before making an appearance in the Room of State. Pieter Paul, when he saw his friend and patron, made not the slightest effort to conceal his unhappiness. "This is just blackmail, *monsieur.* You know as well as I that the king will never see this picture, or if he does, he'll be told it was a present to Don Rodrigo from the *échevins* of Antwerp."

The burgomaster could only nod sadly in agreement. "But what were the alternatives, *maître. We* know the truth. Calderón *knows* that we know. By wittingly submitting to his blackmail, we may be able to use a little blackmail of our own against him. We've asked him to perform some services for us, very important ones that would bring more commerce back to Antwerp. If he accomplishes a quarter of what he promises to do, we can panel this entire room with paintings by Rubens."

"At Rubens' new prices?" The painter's smile was not in harmony with his tone.

"At ten times his new prices," Rockox replied very seriously. "And we shall, I promise you. After all, Calderón gets just one painting by Rubens. We have *Rubens* the man. It seems a rather

176

little sacrifice, if you think of it that way. And you mustn't forget," he concluded with soft remonstrance, "that it *is* our painting to dispose of as we see fit."

"No, no, *monsieur.* You misunderstand me. It's not the painting but the principle that disturbs me. Men like that ought to be racked."

"That man runs Lerma. Lerma runs Spain. And you've told me you were a diplomat," said Rockox with a sniff of disdain. "You astonish me, *maître.* If men like Calderón weren't open to a little bribery, there'd be nothing done, no progress."

Rubens shook his head. "That's not the role of diplomacy, *monsieur.* That's for the Calderóns."

"*And* for the burgomasters. It's for the man on the spot, whoever he happens to be."

"I see that you've not made a study of the book by Bernard du Rosier."

"What would I have learned?"

"That diplomacy is more than simply the exchange of compliments or favors . . . of bribes. The object, the *only* object of diplomacy in its highest, noblest sense, is peace."

Rockox offered the artist a weary, worldly sigh. "Oh, indeed? Well, we *have* peace, *maître.* And Antwerp has less than half the trade it had before the Spanish Fury."

"*Not* peace, *monsieur.* We have a truce. And for how long? For nine more years, unless His Most Catholic Majesty stumbles over a fortune. Then what?"

"But *exactly.* We have to stay on good terms with Spain, so the British don't gobble us up."

"And we have to stay on good terms with the British so the French don't gobble us up," said Pieter Paul with some heat. "We seem to be very appetizing."

The burgomaster gave a little grunt that abruptly evoked in his listener a recollection of Vincenzo Gonzaga, so recently gone to his reward in hell. "That's the penalty we suffer for living on a piece of territory that has no natural frontiers. Since we're unable to defend ourselves, we must seek powerful friends who are willing to do the job for us."

177

"Calderón is powerful, I grant you, *monsieur*. But he's no friend."

"And Philip III? He's not our friend?"

"I wonder, *monsieur*," mused Rubens, who, when it came to that, might equally well have wondered about any of the major European nations. The years since the promulgation of the Twelve Years' Truce had passed with much uneasiness. The "four corners of Christendom" were alive with accounts of plots and counterplots, abortive and successful. The balance of power, as the year 1612 drew to a close, was precariously maintained, because power balances within individual nation states were delicate.

James I's older son and heir presumptive, Henry, died in November, bequeathing to his brother Charles the title of Prince of Wales and eventual succession to the throne of Britain. For the first time since the revolt of the nobles that had culminated in the concession by Bad King John of the right of the barons to a voice in government, the authority of the British crown was being hotly contested—and not only by the nobles, this time, but by the Commons. The more resolutely the king attempted to affirm and exercise his power to rule without let or hindrance, the more Parliament resisted him—with the only means at its disposal, a refusal to grant tax increases.

Good friend to the Netherlands or no, Spain was spent and very nearly ruined. There was a sublime justice in the knowledge that Philip III had agreed to the truce of 1609 in considerable measure because of his heavy indebtedness to the very people his country had for so long been at war with—the Protestant Flemish bankers who had been forced to flee to Amsterdam. Approximately one-third of all Spanish revenues had to be paid out as interest on current loans, so poor was the nation's credit in the wake of three bankruptcies induced by naval and military adventures that had come to absolutely nothing.

Nominally ruled by the boy-king, Louis XIII, France floundered beneath the heavy, clumsy, alien hand of the queen mother, Maria de' Medici. Her advisers, the most trusted of

178

whom were ravenous Italians, counseled caution in foreign affairs until disparate factions within the realm could be fused —a prospect so remote that no rational man would predict the decade, let quite alone the year of its advent. Some Frenchmen openly questioned the legitimacy of young Louis' claim to the throne, holding that the pope had erred in his annulment of Henri IV's marriage with Marguerite de Valois. There was a willing alternate pretender whose supporters would not hesitate to kill if assassination would advance his cause. And too, the issue of the Huguenots remained unresolved, though under the terms of the Edict of Nantes it was not supposed to be any longer an issue at all. Snug and fat in their citadels, these Protestants were anathema to the pope and to Spain, as well as to the Jesuits who stood at the queen mother's corpulent side.

Even closer at hand, the evidences of domestic untidiness were manifest. As they continued their blockade of the mouth of the River Scheldt, denying Antwerp access to the North Sea, the Protestants of the United Provinces were still having at each other, Arminians against Calvinists, advocates of Prince Mauritz against those of van Oldenbarneveldt, provoking a revolution within the Reformation whose outcome, regardless of which side emerged victorious, could not produce unity.

Antwerp failed to profit from the gift her *échevins* made to Don Rodrigo Calderón of Rubens' wonderful painting. Their requests to ease taxation and restrictions on commerce were summarily rejected by the Duke of Lerma. If any presents had been sent to *him,* he didn't receive them, and as Pieter Paul had predicted, the "Adoration of the Magi" was hung in the house of Don Rodrigo, to remain there until the count's goods were confiscated and his life forfeited a few years later. Neither Lerma nor Philip III had any interest in reducing Spanish revenues or in encouraging efficient competition with national manufactures already suffering from the deportation of the Moriscos who had provided the best labor, from the want of indigenous raw materials and competent management. To that degree, then, the artist's objection to the handing over of his picture seemed amply justified by the outcome.

But his skepticism was dealt a modest blow in 1613. Through the good offices of Calderón, he was awarded a commission to paint a second *Apostolado* series for the court of Spain. He never learned the circumstances that led up to this command, but the irony of it escaped no one's attention, least of all Pieter Paul's. Nicolas Rockox seemed philosophical. "Antwerp's loss is Rubens' gain." With that single utterance did he spurn the painter's expression of regret. Yet the burgomaster and his colleagues were unhappy. The failure of their entreaties to be hospitably received in Spain meant that they were unable to afford a replacement for the "Adoration of the Magi" with which they had so casually parted.

There was no recession in Pieter Paul's economy, however. He was continuing to enjoy a brisk trade in the mythological paintings that Jan Brandt had so deplored, but which he was coming to find more acceptable "through exposure," he supposed. The artist completed the central panel of the triptych of the Descent from the Cross for the Arquebusiers' chapel, and saw to its installation in the cathedral. And as if to compensate him for the inability of the *échevins* to finance a duplicate of the "Adoration of the Magi" for the Town Hall, Nicolas Rockox himself commissioned for his family chapel a triptych altarpiece depicting the skeptical Saint Thomas; the donor and his Spanish wife were to appear in the flanking panels as worshippers. So great were the demands on Rubens' time that he didn't complete this work until more than two years had elapsed.

To round off the impressive number of successes he had earned since his return from Rome, Pieter Paul was named to preside for the next two years over the Antwerp Guild of Romanists, an offshoot of the Guild of Saint Luke whose membership was limited to artists who had studied in Italy and adopted the styles of painting and sculpture and architecture made popular there by the Renaissance masters and their descendants.

Rubens accepted the designation with gratitude and misgiving; for less and less, as he told the men who had selected him, was he truly a "Romanist," more and more simply himself, although certainly much influenced by what he had seen and learned in Italy. His fellows ignored the *caveat*. He deserved an honor, and this was the only one in their power to give him. There was, as Rubens well knew, a motive that might be called ulterior; by naming him their leader, the Romanists were hopeful that some of his success would accrue to them. He begrudged them none of it.

But the finest news of the year was Isabella's revelation, in the autumn, that she would be bearing Pieter Paul a second child, which she expected to be delivered of in late May or early June. As he had done in the course of her initial pregnancy, he showered her with attention and concern. Isabella accepted her husband's affectionate interest with wry amusement. "I should keep myself with child all the time," she said to her mother. "It's the only time he notices me."

"Not quite," Anna Brandt retorted. "You *are* pregnant, after all."

"Oh, he notices me in *bed*, all right. He knows I'm *there*."

"Then you've nothing to complain of, my girl. I *told* you it was the only ecstasy . . ."

"But the rest of the day I might as well be off the earth."

"You expect too much. You're too demanding."

"I demand nothing. I'm just telling you what the facts are."

"Has he a mistress?"

Isabella snorted. "He doesn't have time for a mistress. He has time for nothing but his work."

"If a man wants a mistress, he manages to find the time for her, believe me."

The painter's wife sighed. "So I'm to count my blessings, am I? I'm to say nothing."

"You say you're getting a great deal of attention now. Take the present. Don't worry about the future. There's nothing to be said."

That seemed irreproachable counsel. Isabella accepted it,

181

and basked happily in the sunlight of Pieter Paul's love—
though she felt it was not love for *her,* as a person, but for her
as the mother of his second infant. He hoped, she doubted not,
that his love would communicate itself to the embryo and cause
a son to be born.

Such was just what the painter hoped. But he didn't devote
himself exclusively to his wife. In January of 1614, he completed the first of the lateral panels for the Arquebusiers' triptych; in March, the second was finished and mounted above the
altar. Months would pass, however, before the redecorated
chapel of the cathedral was formally consecrated—not through
the fault either of the canons or the members of the corporation. Pieter Paul found himself embroiled in a dispute with the
clergy—something he had never before experienced.

Since 1612, he had been under contract to produce for the superb cathedral of Ghent an altarpiece of a grandeur that would
match the splendor of that great church which, like so many
others of the Low Countries, had been sacked during the Spanish Fury. In the interim, the death had occurred of the bishop
who had assented to the studies for this triptych which the
painter had submitted. Without having taken the trouble of
asking to see these designs, the successor to the episcopal throne
of Ghent had decided to entrust the work to another artist—a
determination made all the more galling by the fact that Pieter
Paul learned of it at second hand.

Fearful that he might be allowing pride to becloud his judgment, he consulted Balthasar Moretus and Jan Brandt before
taking responsive action. They agreed with him emphatically
that there was an important matter of principle involved—the
sanctity of contracts. The knowledge that the present bishop
hadn't looked at the preliminary studies merely fortified the
fundamental argument that a solemn, written agreement had
been unilaterally abrogated without prior discussion. But how
to proceed?

"You're a lawyer," said Rubens to his father-in-law. "What
can I do?"

Jan Brandt stroked his gentlemanly beard and shrugged. "You *could* offer to sue."

"You don't sound very hopeful."

"Bringing an action, even a civil action, against the clergy is never easy. The Bishop of Ghent, like all our clerics, is beyond the jurisdiction of the secular courts." He grinned. "This isn't Venice, you see, *or* Britain. That means that you'd have to seek a judgment against him in the clerical court of his diocese. I don't have the statistics at hand, but I'd guess that your chances were one in ten of winning. Churchmen aren't fond of finding their fellows in the wrong. In my opinion, a lawsuit would be a waste of time. You'd gain nothing, and you'd lose a lot of friends in the Church. I don't think you can afford to do that, even *you*."

"So what am I to do? Just beat the air with my tongue?"

"You might try to bring some pressure on the bishop. Ask the archduke to intercede for you."

It was a suggestion that Pieter Paul greeted with some hesitation. He wanted the regent to stand as godfather to his second child, if the issue proved to be a boy, and would ask the Infanta Isabel to perform a similar role if the baby were a girl. The regents might frown on this request, which meant much more to the artist than the breach of one contract, if they were doubly imposed upon in the same season.

Balthasar thought his friend much too cautious. "Don't you have right on your side? Isn't the archduke your patron? Doesn't he claim to be your protector? Write him about this Ghent matter, then go to see him after the child is born. This really is a vital question, Pieter Paul, because it entails more than merely the shabby treatment of an individual artist. A precedent is involved. If the Church can break a contract with you, it can break contracts with anyone. You have an obligation to do something for the very reason that of all the painters in Flanders, you can describe yourself as the most disinterested. Your position is the most unassailable. You don't need the money, and you can demonstrate that. But suppose such a thing

183

happened to some poor devil who needed the money desperately . . ."

"You've convinced me, Balthasar," moaned Rubens. "For God's sake, tell me no more. I'm weeping already."

He composed a long, carefully phrased letter to the Archduke Albrecht in the middle of March, setting forth the sequence of events to date, reminding the regent that he himself had seen the studies for the Ghent altarpiece and had expressed extravagant admiration for them. He requested that the court intervene informally in the dispute, with a demand, at the very least, that the Bishop of Ghent look at the designs before rejecting them, and that he have the courtesy to deal directly with the painter instead of allowing word to leak out, as had been the case so far. His conclusion was a model of seventeenth-century diplomatic rhetoric: "I should be most obliged to Your Highness if you would support me . . . with a note to the Bishop of Ghent, assuring him that I have not any profit in view . . . (indeed, I have at present more commissions for large work than ever before, and some of them I shall bring to Brussels for Your Highness to see . . .), but only because I can affirm upon my conscience as a Christian that this design for Ghent is the finest thing I have done in all my life. For this reason I am so anxious to bring it to completion that this request is perhaps couched in more importunate terms than is proper . . ."

As he wrote, his conception for the altarpiece was certainly a very admirable thing, but he had to confess to himself that it was not the finest he had ever done—if only because he hadn't done it yet. By early April, he had a cautious reply from the hand of the archduke's private secretary. His Highness would be pleased to look into the matter, but could promise nothing until he had heard from the Bishop of Ghent. There was no doubt, said the regent, that the facts were as Rubens had stated them, but there might be another interpretation of them; it might be a simple case of misunderstanding.

The painter was less put out by this equivocal reaction from Brussels than were Brandt and Moretus, who cast doubt on the

184

archduke's good faith and value as a patron if he were so reluctant to take decisive action in an affair whose terms were so categorically clear, just as Rubens had characterized them. "At this rate," said the painter's father-in-law, "the thing will be dragging on into the next generation. By then, it won't matter one way or the other."

"If I can prevent the bishop from signing a contract with another artist," replied Pieter Paul, "I'll have accomplished something."

"You'll have accomplished a stalemate."

"Well, I've no intention of trying to press the archduke any further. I don't think anything is to be gained by it. I'm sure he'll do everything he can."

There the tortured question was allowed to rest. At the end of May, as she had forecast, Isabella gave birth—to a son. Pieter Paul's joy knew no rational bounds. He realized how silly he was to want a male heir. It wasn't as if the name of Rubens would die out if Isabella had no sons, for there was his nephew Philip to carry it at least into the next generation. And it wasn't, either, that he wanted a son to follow in his footsteps. He recalled too vividly his mother's resistance to the idea of his becoming an artist; he resolved to let any son of his determine his own career. Besides, there was the brilliant young Anton van Dyck to carry on the Rubens tradition; better by far to be succeeded by a gifted pupil than an unwilling son.

When he was certain that his darling, silent, dutiful wife was well and that the child was as likely to survive as could be assured by the most careful nurturing, Pieter Paul made a hurried journey to Brussels for an audience with the archduke. As he had promised in his letter of March, the artist brought along with him a set of grisaille studies of major works that had either been completed or were sufficiently far advanced to make these little prototypes superfluous. He grandly presented them to his amiable, intelligent patron.

The regent, gratified by these tokens of Rubens' affection and loyalty, apologized at some length for being unable to do as his painter had requested with respect to the delinquent behavior of the Bishop of Ghent. "He writes me that he was *told* your studies for the altarpiece were inappropriate. I'm sure that's nonsense, *maître,* and I replied to him in just that vein. Of one thing I'm fairly certain. He'll make no other arrangement, at any rate for the time being. I have no power to prevent him from doing as he pleases, so long as the security of the state isn't involved . . . I fear we can't make out much of a case for *that,* can we? I allowed the bishop to know, nevertheless, that he would incur our profound displeasure if he proceeded as he'd originally planned." The regent gave Rubens an apologetic smile. "Our profound displeasure . . . What a pitiful thing it is, when all is said. He won't be *much* alarmed, you understand, but I may have shaken him a *bit.* That's the best I can do for the moment."

"I'm grateful to you, Highness, for doing so much, and I'm embarrassed to tell you that I have a further request."

The archduke described himself as "touched" by Pieter Paul's desire that he become the godfather to his first-born son. He only regretted that the demands of state would make it impossible for him to attend the ceremony in person on June 5. He hoped that an illustrious proxy would be satisfactory. Rubens was naturally disappointed, but realized that the notice had been very short. He was pleased beyond words, he concluded, that the regent was willing for a Rubens to carry the archducal name.

"I could only be happier if the son were my own, *maître,* but I'm afraid such an event will never occur. When the infanta and I are gone, Spain will again rule in the Netherlands."

There seemed nothing Pieter Paul could say in response to this. He said nothing. The silence was very disturbing and embarrassingly long, each man contemplating his private vision of that moment in the indeterminable future—and not liking the prospect at all. "Well, it's no good brooding about it, is it?" the regent murmured. "We must hope for wisdom when the time does come." His tone became more matter-of-fact. "If *my* time should come before the infanta's, which seems likely in view of

186

the difference in our ages, I shall expect you to make yourself available for any mission she proposes for you."

Rubens bowed his head. "I'd prefer not to dwell on such an eventuality, Highness."

"We needn't *dwell* on it, *maître*. I simply want an understanding."

"You know you can count on me, Highness, to do anything you or Her Highness think I'm able to do."

"Can we, indeed?" The regent became thoughtful. "You're on friendly terms with the English, I believe?"

The artist was puzzled. "I've painted some portraits of the English, Highness. It was *you* who recommended me to the Earl of Arundel. And he's given my name to some of his friends."

"Have you learned from them anything about their country? Have you heard from the earl?"

"Nothing of moment, Highness. Perhaps, if you have something specific in mind, I could ask it of the next Englishman who comes to me."

"We're not brilliantly represented in London. I can't understand exactly what's happening there. The king has summoned another Parliament. He wants war, of course, against Spain— which means against us as well, but he can do nothing without funds. The last Parliament refused them, so he dissolved it. He apparently doesn't know quite what to expect of this new Parliament. The reports I receive are fragmentary and confusing. If the king has his way, he'd hire the Swiss to fight for him on the Continent, but they'll only fight for payment in advance . . . One can hardly blame him . . . No, I don't know what to think about events in Britain."

"I'm sorry that I have no information, Highness. You know much more than I. But to judge from what I hear from friends in France, we have no reason to worry about war from that quarter."

"Because young Louis is to marry Princess Anne of Austria? Yes, that's the popular viewpoint. I don't necessarily share it."

187

"But surely it will bring a permanent peace between France and the Empire."

"Do you think so? French policy isn't likely to change. A strong Empire and a greedy Spain on her borders are always going to be treated as immediate threats."

"But the marriage should soothe relations with the Empire, Highness, and Maria de' Medici's support of the Jesuits ought to placate the Spanish."

"I know that's the usual argument. But our good Maria relies too heavily on her Italian friends. That alienates the French, and just at the time when she's decided to convoke the Estates-General to ask for new kinds of taxation."

"Everyone thinks of taxation, Highness. Where will it end?"

"For France? For Britain? For Spain? In bloodshed. Especially in France, I think."

"The Estates-General won't thwart the royal will, surely. It's not like the British Parliament."

"Because it never has before?" The archduke frowned. "I wonder. I think it a very dangerous practice to allow the people to imagine they have a role to play in government. Just see what that policy has led to in the United Provinces . . ." He broke off, his tone becoming brisk again. "But Britain is the riddle I'm trying to solve at the moment. I have good people in France and Spain."

"I'm sorry, Highness, that I have no answers to offer you."

"A pity you don't speak the language. I had rather hoped . . ."

The interview ended on this faintly plaintive note. Rubens returned to Antwerp in a somewhat bemused state of mind, realizing that the archduke had wanted to send him on an important mission to London. Jan Brandt told his son-in-law that he ought to be relieved that he spoke no English. This was no time to be an ambassador, even to the Vatican. The constantly shifting patterns of power that deranged Europe seemed especially unstable just now. "Keep your head. Bide your time. Accumulate your resources. Make yourself better known. Keep yourself informed. Your time will come."

188

"With the archduke's death?"

"Why, I do believe you'd welcome a chance to lay that fine head of yours on the block. Are you bored with what you're doing?"

"No, Jan. But it's all so locked in. One feels so helpless here, when the *important* things are happening somewhere else. I'm not bored, but I *am* restless now and then."

"Thank God the archduke is a healthy man. If you're needed no sooner than the time of his death, you should count yourself fortunate, restless or not. There's madness afoot. No right-minded man would want any part of it. And you're a right-minded man . . . restless or not."

Jan Brandt may have exaggerated a little in describing Europe's condition as one of madness. There had been many periods of greater general insanity. But certainly, events were taking an unusually chaotic and unpredictable course because of the introduction of an unfamiliar element—the people, whether in the form of Parliament or Estates-General. The exasperated James I dissolved his second Parliament just two days after the baptism of Albrecht Rubens. History would call this Parliament "addled," but in fact it was addling; its members had denied the king's demands for funds. What sort of absolutism was it when a monarch was held accountable by a legislature?

In France, matters were scarcely happier for Maria de' Medici. She had rejected the sage counsel of Henri IV's great and impeccable minister, Sully, to surround herself with a crowd of shrieking Italian scoundrels—the most notorious being Concino Concini, who was seriously thought to have the queen mother in his thrall. Concini and his frivolous cronies had mulcted the French treasury of the ten million gold francs on hand at the time of Henri IV's assassination only four years before. To Maria's peremptory demand for more money with which to finance her court of venal foreigners, the nobles of France, whose acceptance of monarchical authority had rarely been enthusiastic, responded with what they considered cunning. There could, by long-accepted custom, be no alteration of

189

the basic tax structure without the consent of the Estates-General, a body not very often consulted.

There was no wise French adviser at the queen mother's side to tell her how hazardous an undertaking this might be. Without a second thought, she assented to the suggestion—in the belief, which was shared in drastically differing ways by the nobility and the clergy who constituted two of the three estates to be summoned, that the question of who ruled France would be settled once and for all. What neither faction was prepared for was the forceful presentation of the case for the Third Estate, the one that represented everyone else in the land. In the long years since the previous convocation of the Estates-General, the Third Estate had found leaders, had evolved alarmingly, become aware of its power, and was more than willing to express demands that despots could only regard as outrageous. The most scandalous idea advanced by the representatives of the Third Estate, when sessions began in October of 1614, was that the Church and the aristocracy pay taxes. Alongside this truly atrocious notion, all other grievances seemed insignificant. The very thought that the First and Second Estates, which collectively owned practically all the land of France, might reasonably be expected to help defray the cost of government was so frightening, so revolutionary in its implications, that the queen mother hastily dissolved the Estates-General the following March. It would not be summoned again until 1789.

Did anyone, anywhere, detect a trend? It was easy enough to observe that conditions were anarchic, by which was meant that a moneyed class without rank or station had begun to sense its potential might and had even attempted, so far without success, to exercise it. Not a soul imagined that one day a French abbot would truthfully state, "What is the Third Estate? Nothing. What can it be? Everything."

That Abbé Sieyès might issue this cry in print a full century after the British House of Commons had been "gloriously" enfranchised, no one alive in 1615 would have the temerity to think possible. Another prediction of interest had been made the year before in London, by Sir John Napier, father of logarithms, who gave it as his opinion that the whole world would come to an end in 1688. In 1688, the world of the Stuarts did come to an end, and, with its passing, monarchy made its first obeisance to oligarchy.

But in 1615, such a sensational end couldn't be seen because the beginning was cloaked in confusion. It was the same for the Archduke Albrecht in Brussels as for Pieter Paul Rubens in Antwerp. Isolated incidents occurred, personalities made their presence felt, but it took time and perhaps clairvoyance for meaning, even immediate meaning, to be evident. If the painter's main concern was the fate of the Spanish Netherlands, he must nonetheless try to understand what happened elsewhere in Europe, because what happened elsewhere might easily have a bearing on the security of his own country. The only comfort came from the shaky assumption that as long as foreign nations suffered from internal dissensions, it would be hard for them to cause trouble for their neighbors.

Rubens mainly followed his father-in-law's conservative pre-Panglossian advice. He cultivated his own garden. But he had no illusion that he was doing so in the best of all possible worlds. The painter's garden flourished marvelously in spite of the occasional altercation—like his difference with the Bishop of Ghent, which showed no signs of resolution. His prosperity increased. Consequently, he made more modifications to the plans for the renovation of his house in the Wapperstraat, thus postponing for at least another year the date when it would be ready for occupancy. "It's going to be your mausoleum, for a fact," Jan Brandt warned him, but without complaint; he was just as pleased as ever to have the Rubens family live with him.

The presence on this earth of a son was the central circumstance for Pieter Paul in 1615. He had vast love for his four-year-old daughter, but in a society owned and operated by men, a father was more drawn to sons. The reserved Isabella was pleased as well, though more for her husband than for herself. Their little Clara Serena was *her* delight—blond, cherubic, like

191

the *putti* that proliferated in her father's paintings, with a pale complexion that flushed brightly with emotion, to which she remained as susceptible today as in her first year of life.

Isabella took another and rather more secret pleasure from the inadvertent privilege afforded her by Clara's occasional escape from feminine custody; the child would invariably dash up the stairs and enter the forbidden territory of the artist's studio. This was a realm where a well-tutored wife ventured, as a rule, only upon specific invitation. But little "Clarissima," as Pieter Paul called his daughter, was welcomed for the very reason that she was trespassing, a feeling she naturally sensed. At such moments, Isabella, in hot pursuit, had a legitimate excuse for climbing to the bustling workshop. If this were possible, she found it even more enchanting than did Clara, and for the same reason; she was entering a forbidden kingdom.

This idea that she was intruding was a creation entirely of her imagination and rearing. She was never permitted to enter Jan Brandt's study; he demanded and was accorded total privacy and maximum silence. Such, of course, had never been a requirement of Pieter Paul's. He could work serenely through every sort of din. Isabella, however, couldn't bring herself to think that what was true for her father wasn't equally true for her husband. And the artist, seeming to understand as he intuitively understood so many things about her, invited his wife to his studio only when there was reason for celebration—like the completion of a major work that had been an inordinately long time in the accomplishment. Thus he never tried to rob her of the pleasure such visits gave by adorning them with the drab of routine.

During the first year of their marriage, she had occasionally wondered why Pieter Paul never asked her to pose for him. She would never have had the courage to query him directly. The answer to her question was to be found in his paintings. Her features, her body, in no way resembled those great, full mounds of flesh he so loved to paint—and that his patrons so loved to acquire. His models were mostly the whores of

Antwerp—splendid, lusty girls who quite frightened gentle Isabella when she saw them enter and leave her father's house, or when, from the foot of the stairs that led to Pieter Paul's studio, she heard their raucous laughter as the artist or one of the older pupils slapped a capacious bottom. But these girls saddened her too, for as she came to recognize them in their comings and goings, she could trace, from week to week, the withering of their bloom, see them live a whole lifetime in two years or three, waste themselves in drink and disease, then perish at the age of twenty-two or twenty-three.

It would never have crossed Isabella's mind to be critical of Pieter Paul for employing these buxom, brawling bawds. As Anna Brandt had put it to her early in her marriage, "It's the only honest money the poor things will ever earn." Nor would it have crossed her mind to wonder if her husband had any sexual contact with them, for she well knew that no gentleman would ever lie with a woman whose clients were drunken mercenaries on leave and sailors home from the sea. Indeed, the entire question of Pieter Paul's marital fidelity, or want of it, rarely occurred to her. Again Anna Brandt was her guide. "A man will do as he likes, because that's the way he's arranged the world. If he comes home to you before morning, if he takes good care of you, if he loves you, ask no questions." Maria Piepelinx had very likely given similar counsel to her daughter Blandine, before *her* marriage. Taking into account as fundamental fact the rumors still circulating lethargically in Antwerp of the wide swath Jan Rubens had once cut through the matronly bedchambers of the city, Isabella reckoned she had nothing to complain of. If Pieter Paul had lapses now and then, he had them most discreetly.

In fact, the painter had yet to stray. As his wife had once observed to her mother, he hadn't time for a mistress. Nor had he the inclination—for which, as Anna Brandt had shrewdly replied, he would have *found* the time. He took very much to heart the instructive, if not very clear example set by his father. He was human enough to enjoy, now and again, a pang of quickening desire when confronted with the luxuriant contours of a toothsome country wench, all breasts and hams, come to Antwerp out of the desperate need simply to survive, no matter how terrible the final price of brief survival was. But the whores he splashed so copiously across the generous expanses of his canvases were untouchables.

If Isabella wasn't his ideal woman, or rather Woman as he had idealized her in his paintings, she possessed certain qualities that attracted his pens and brushes. He sketched her features for his pleasure, and for hers—though sometimes to her mild annoyance, for he insisted on catching her at moments when she was least prepared, when her hair was untidy or her clothing slightly awry. "You'd never *allow* a great lady to pose for you so," she complained.

"Life on the wing, just like a bird," he said to her. "That's what you and the children are for me—life on the wing. I sketch you into my memory." He tapped his balding head with a finger. "I put you there and I keep you there, for future use in a picture. You've no idea how often some gesture of yours, some expression, finds its way into a painting."

On the sixth anniversary of their marriage, Pieter Paul presented Isabella with a portrait of herself—a work much more tender and understanding than the comparatively stiff painting he had composed of the two of them just after their wedding. To a woman like Isabella, who consulted the looking-glass only briefly each morning, who was without great vanity, the little picture was almost overpowering—not for itself, for she made no pretense of understanding or appreciating "art," even Pieter Paul's. This portrait moved her because of what he had made of her in it, what he had seen in her. He had perceived and captured her love for him, her gently acerb wit, her maternal warmth; and miraculously, it seemed to Isabella, he had added to these truths something of himself—*his* love and compassion.

She gasped. She was speechless, awed. He was dismayed, fearing that she was offended by the candor, however brilliant. He thought this picture the finest portrait he had ever made, because it was at once the most faithful and the most deeply felt.

194

He believed she didn't recognize herself. "But it's there," he protested, touching her closed eyes. "It's right there."

Through her tears of happiness, which caught her by surprise, Isabella stammered, "I didn't know. I had no idea. You see what I *feel*. How can you do that?"

Six

THE next few years, in retrospect, seemed a blur of minor events and major labors. As 1618 reached its midpoint, Pieter Paul was bewildered by the rapidity with which the time had appeared to pass. He had unconsciously allowed himself to be inundated by a flood of commissions, great and small, any that came his way—only occasionally pausing to look up and behold the mortal universe that lay beyond the ramparts of Antwerp's parochial little world.

It was a period of spectacular productivity, when religious paintings and mythological scenes and portraits were accomplished, as it were, overnight. In his peculiar case, speed was an ally, not an enemy, of quality. His most satisfying work, he believed, was swiftly done; for it was imbued with a spontaneity not to be discerned in painting to which he gave greater care or longer hours. It was this talent for invention in great haste that made his larger altarpieces and extravagant interpretations of the classics of ancient literature and myth more laudable than many of his portraits.

The important personages who sat for him insisted that the minutest details of their costumes be depicted; in their opinion, absolute fidelity in the rendering of their dress was at least as significant as the accurate delineation of their features. And since Rubens always aimed to please his clientele, and nearly always succeeded, he reluctantly complied with such demands. The results were usually stiff, formal likenesses, wooden in feeling and without much distinction—quite like the people he was asked to paint. Nevertheless, the portraits he gave himself the luxury of painting for his own pleasure during these years —of Isabella and their two children—were indelible evidence that when permitted to work as he chose, swiftly and impulsively, he could give life and tenderness and understanding to portraiture.

The rhythm of his accelerating professional life didn't wholly obscure its delights for the painter. Pupils came and went, all of them considerably enlightened and improved for their exposure to Pieter Paul's instruction and to his gentle, sunny nature. Of those who had been with him in 1612, only Anton van Dyck remained. He was no longer a pupil, but rather his most proficient assistant, the only one in the studio to be trusted to furnish the numerous canvases turned out in these years with more than background details—like clouds, scenery, incidental figures in the middle distance. Van Dyck, in his nineteenth year, was so sure a master of his master's style that sometimes only he and Rubens could be certain which of them had painted what portion of a particular work.

It was judged uncanny by other artists how similar were the manners of Rubens and his brilliant young disciple. Even that astute and friendly admirer, Jan Bruegel, was often unable to distinguish between the brushstrokes of the two painters, and when asked to make such a judgment by a Pieter Paul paternally proud of van Dyck, he erred as frequently as not. There was, Rubens told his friend, only one real difference between them, but it was crucial. Van Dyck's technique, though just as rapid and dazzling as his master's, was not informed by much imagination. "He can't create," said Pieter Paul sadly. "Isn't that curious? He can imitate, but he's unable to produce something that's entirely his own. He tries now and then, but he fails. Inventiveness doesn't seem to interest him. All his attempts come out as virtual duplicates of pictures I've already made. Oh, the details may be different, but the composition, the spirit, even the coloring are mine. I don't know how to help him."

So the *insouciance* he had detected very early in his tutelage of van Dyck was proving a persistent quality. The young man, who would soon be ready to be received as a master in his own right and be admitted to membership in the Guild of Saint Luke, didn't really care about creativity, and perhaps didn't really care about art either. His mastery was not an end in itself, but rather a means by which he would attain ends that were as yet imprecisely defined in his mind. The lissome, personable Anton knew very well that his talent and charm could take him anywhere. He had only to determine the goal; he couldn't, or wouldn't do that—not yet. Unlike his great teacher, he found little joy in the practice of his profession. It was simply a rope that the good God had seen fit to throw to him. He was pleased enough with his accomplishment, but as Rubens suspected, he lacked artistic commitment. If he had a genuine passion, it was for pleasure; he already drank much more than was good for him, gambled away most of the generous allowance his successful merchant father provided, and spent the remainder on gifts for the fine women of Antwerp who seemed to find his attentions irresistible.

Exasperating as he could certainly be to Rubens, who cherished such hopes for him as an artist, van Dyck invariably could disarm his master with his candor. He never pretended to be a bit better a fellow than he was. "We love life differently, *maître*," he said. "I think that if you'd grown up in easier times, you might have been very much like me." There was just enough probability in the suggestion to stop many of Pieter Paul's protests before he uttered them. Van Dyck remained the darling of the household. Even the cautious Jan Brandt found him beguiling, and he sometimes chided his son-in-law for taking too stern or gloomy a view of the youth's prospects. "When he gets some age on him, he'll find himself. You'll see. When

198

he's had a chance to live in the world and study the arts, as you have, he'll come to his senses. In the meantime, let him please *you* as he pleases the rest of us. We need that sunshine. Let be, Pieter Paul. Let be."

Of European events that occurred in that period, none very long deterred Rubens from his compulsive devotion to work. Even so important a passing as that of Claudio Aquaviva, who had presided over the Jesuit order for almost thirty-five years, failed to stir him greatly. The most effective general of Christ's soldiers since Ignatius Loyola, founder of the Society, Aquaviva had understood from the outset of his stewardship that the secret of saving souls, and retrieving those in peril of darkness, lay in education. The Jesuits traveled and taught. By the time of his death in 1615, there were more than 350 Jesuit *collegia*, where clerks and scribes were trained for lay and religious tasks and shown the single path to salvation, which led (as had all roads in ancient days) to Rome. There were now twenty-four Jesuit universities in all western Continental countries, where the most promising graduates of the colleges were offered more luminous opportunities for serving the best interests of man and the Church—these, in the Jesuit view, being identical. During his lengthy rule, Aquaviva trebled the numbers of the order.

His successor, Mutio Vitelleschi, was an admirer of Aquaviva's energetic propagation of the faith and of the Society's hegemony, but he felt constrained to admonish its growing membership that the very success enjoyed by the Jesuits carried with it, in the eyes of many in high places, the implication of inherent menace. Important people, cleric and layman, were suspicious of a movement that had gained such credence and authority among the common people—the masses of illiterates who were enchanted by this new gospel of joy and beauty and love and exuberance that was spread not only by evangelistic words but by works—in the ornate churches that sprang up all over Europe, even in the Spanish and Portuguese colonies of the New World, and in the gorgeous decoration of them that was a feast for eyes too bitterly accustomed to visions of squalor and depravity. A Rubens painting of the possible joys of paradise, a picture by Rubens and Jan Bruegel of the lost joys of Eden could rescue more strays than a Bosch fantasy of perdition; for the poor needed no Bosch to inform them about perdition. Perdition was their home address.

There was nothing astonishing in the fear and revulsion of the Anglicans, separated for more than half a century from the pope and all his works, at the brave persistence of the Jesuit missionaries secreting themselves all over Britain. There were many ostensible converts to the new Church of England who quietly adhered to the faith of their ancestors and who found great solace in stolen confessions offered to hardy brothers who lived in constant danger in order to prevent the British from losing the sight and word of God.

But the Archbishop of Canterbury and James I were not the only prelate or monarch to raise a hand against the "threat" of the Jesuits. The members of the order were responsible only to their Vicar-General and to the pope. This independence of state hierarchies provoked much jealousy, for Jesuit power was tangible. Though it was not the order's stated policy, many of the brothers gave at least the appearance of advocating or condoning popular revolt and, if the rumors attending the death of Henri IV were true, even regicide. Vitelleschi counseled his increasing flock to tread lightly, to be prudent, to avoid displays of excessive wealth or pomp, and above all, to function strictly within the framework of existing public order—except, of course, where Protestants attempted to suppress the faith and practice of their Catholic brethren.

Britain remained the principal field of religious combat in Europe. By a blending of main force and judicious bribery, James I maintained on the principal British island the ascendancy of the Church of England in the face of opposition from astringent Puritans and recidivist Catholics. But in Ireland, his ploys were regarded with stubborn hostility. The Catholic Irish treated the British creed with the same unrelenting hatred that they cherished for those who attempted to impose it on them; it was a heresy made all the more distasteful by its being the product of a culture they viewed as alien.

Given the king's obdurate resolve to Anglicanize his entire domain, his subjects were befuddled by his equal determination to marry off the Prince of Wales to a Catholic princess. James I replied to those who dared to criticize his autocratic decision by pointing out that reasons of state always enjoyed priority over reasons of faith. It was essential to keep both France and Spain at bay, and if this could be accomplished in the Habsburg manner, by marriage, the Anglican God would just have to look the other way.

The first expedition in quest of marriageable ladies took place in Spain. The king's current favorite, George Villiers journeyed to Madrid, there to exchange magnificent gifts with Philip III and to survey the field. The mission was fruitless—except for Villiers, who was already a viscount and would, in dazzling sequence, become Earl, Marquis, and ultimately Duke of Buckingham. The heir to the throne of Westminster wanted none of the accessible infantas. Moreover, Villiers perceived from his discussions with the Duke of Lerma and Don Rodrigo Calderón that Spain would never again be a presence of much consequence on the European stage. It seemed preferable to improve relations with France, whose likeliest princess, Henriette Marie, was yet to know puberty.

Friendship with France seemed all the more relevant because two of that nation's royal children were already affiliated by infant marriage to the offspring of Philip III. The French Princess Elisabeth was the bride of the Spanish Prince of the Asturias, heir to the Most Catholic throne. Philip III's daughter, Anne of Austria, was the childless wife of Louis XIII, France's juvenile king. Her treasury looted by foreign courtiers, her subjects divided over matters of faith and the administration of power, France nonetheless represented a formidable potential threat to James I's plan to keep the Continental states off balance and dependent on Britain to provide the critical alliance that would make the difference between peace and war.

The British king had good reason for alarm over developments in France. So did Maria de' Medici. The docile Louis, her first-born and so long the dutiful son, suddenly turned against his mother and her entourage in his seventeenth year. He summarily ordered the assassination of Concini, the queen mother's closest friend. His motivation was mainly one of sheer petulance; the Italian had made sport of him since childhood, had teased him mercilessly about his traumatic wedding night with his little Spanish bride when, both of them fourteen, they had been compelled by tradition to make love under the watchful eyes of the leering Florentines and Genovese of the court. When the princess miscarried, the king, scalding beneath Concini's scorn, refused to enter her bed again —and continued to refuse until 1637, twenty-three years after their wedding. Concini had made the mistake of forgetting that, youth or not, Louis XIII was King of France. Maria de' Medici was horrified that her son should have selected so conclusive a way of recalling it to the man's attention. She protested. She threatened, forgetting *herself* with whom she was speaking. Her vociferations resulted in her banishment to Blois' comfortable château on the gracious river Loire.

Disappearing with her were all the foreign advisers who were the bane of the king, and most of the Frenchmen who had chosen to associate themselves with the queen mother's cause. Among the exiles at Blois was Armand Jean du Plessis de Richelieu, Bishop of Luçon, not really a major figure in Maria's court. He soon became one by assisting in an abortive conspiracy to effect the queen mother's escape. When the plot was revealed to the king, the bishop had to find refuge in distant Avignon. His career was apparently in ruins. But he was to prove astonishingly resilient. Within a very few years, the name of Richelieu would be synonymous with that of the king who had so recently banished him—a name Pieter Paul Rubens would have cause to conjure with.

While the greater countries of the Continent were grappling with internal and external problems, the United Provinces followed suit, after their fashion. In August of 1617, after eight of the twelve promised years of truce with Spain had passed, they were still cultivating religious disorder, a crop that thrived mightily. To the outrage of Prince Mauritz, his erstwhile ally van Oldenbarneveldt induced the Council of Holland to pass a resolution asserting its sole authority in matters relating to faith and education, and ordering all the towns of the province to arm themselves against the probability of attack by Calvinist factions. Less than a year later, van Oldenbarneveldt used his great influence with members of the Council of Utrecht to take similar action.

Prince Mauritz's patience was at an end. He entered the city of Utrecht at the head of a Calvinist army, just as van Oldenbarneveldt had predicted, and commanded its garrison to surrender. In August, the Estates-General of all the provinces, a gathering dominated by the prince's supporters, decreed as outlaws all the Arminian leaders, signers of the *Remonstrantie* uttered years before. Van Oldenbarneveldt and Hugo Grotius were condemned as heretics at a drumhead trial held in Dordrecht later in 1618. Their adherents were placed under the same kind of formal interdict hitherto reserved for Catholics of the region, were deprived of their clerical and teaching posts and were forbidden to hold religious services or public assemblies. Many Arminians fled to Britain, where they received a cordial welcome from the Anglicans and were spurned by Puritans, who thought their outlook far too soft.

The civil war in the United Provinces could not have taken place had Spain, at more or less the same time, not been suffering comparably momentous upheavals. After twenty years of feckless service, the Duke of Lerma was finally found out by Philip III to have been a thief, a knave, and a fool. His dismissal was not exactly rude. He was given a cardinal's hat, and was replaced in the king's favor by his son, the Duke of Uceda, who had learned everything his father had to teach him, and not a bit more. The only man to suffer more than mere dislocation from this transaction was Don Rodrigo Calderón, who fell from grace and, three years later, was put to death by Philip IV, who confiscated Calderón's possessions and thus acquired Rubens' "Adoration of the Magi" that had been intended for his royal father.

Pieter Paul paid only casual attention to these tremors abroad because he was wrapped up in his own private affairs. Isabella was about to produce a third child. After seven full years of renovation and new construction, the house in the Wapperstraat was on the verge of completion. And he was profoundly involved in a prolonged haggle with Sir Dudley Carleton, British ambassador to the United Provinces at The Hague, over an exchange that would bring him more than a hundred pieces of antique Roman statuary and give Carleton a number of Rubens paintings, some Brussels tapestries, and a little ready money. Jan Brandt and Balthasar Moretus were half amused, half exasperated by the amount of time Pieter Paul devoted to the lengthy correspondence with Carleton that preceded the striking of the bargain. "For once," said the proprietor of the Plantin Press, "you're behaving like a Flemish merchant. But I can't see the purpose of it."

The purpose wouldn't be evident until the new residence was ready to be viewed by Rubens' friends and patrons. Even Jan Brandt remained in the dark. Only Isabella, who had followed the tortuous evolution of the plans over the years since Pieter Paul had purchased the house and land in 1611, was aware of why her husband so eagerly pursued Carleton's collection of marble relics. The Rubenses had built a formal, elaborate town house which some would call a palace. It had to be decorated in a fashion that harmonized with its architecture whose style was Italian, a marked departure from that selected by other *Anversois* of property and position. Its many arched niches and the spaces between ranks of stone columns were designed to be filled with pieces of sculpture.

From the opposite side of the Wapper, the sluggish canal that bordered the entrance and main façade of the mansion, the appearance was one of surprising severity. Like some of the more austere fortified churches built in France and the Low Countries during the recent wars of religion, Rubens' house presented the casual pedestrian or boatman with an impression of

204

grimness which was only to be dispelled, almost shockingly, by passing through the central doorway. The interiors were the more stunning for their contrast with the harsh, rusticated stonework of the canalside elevation.

The atmosphere inside was bright, warm, welcoming. The reception rooms were perfectly Flemish in their immaculate coziness, with furnishings especially designed by the artist in oak and fruitwoods to fill particular areas. White walls and dark-stained woodwork suggested a certain starkness that was offset by tapestries and rugs and by the colorful paintings by the master-in-residence and his friends—brilliant still lifes and landscapes by Frans Snyders and Jan Bruegel, and the portraits Pieter Paul had made of the children and Isabella that were so precious to her.

The larger works from Sir Dudley Carleton's collection of antiquities were housed in the most eccentric of the buildings that made up the complex on Rubens' property—a sort of miniature rotunda, modeled after the Pantheon in Rome and illuminated in the same way as its prototype, by windows in the dome. It was a curious folly, this circular structure in the garden, the single room serving as the setting for such large formal receptions as the painter felt called upon to offer now and then.

His studio was spacious without being immense, a main-floor room that measured about forty feet by twenty-five, with a very high ceiling and a windowless attic for the storage of canvases and surplus objects from the Carleton collection for which there was insufficient display space in the dwelling or the rotunda.

A stone-columned summerhouse at the bottom of the garden completed the architecture of the domain. There, on the earliest Sunday of the summer of 1618, the artist sat in some splendor, surrounded by his family, including the newborn Nicolas who was still at his mother's breast. To help him contemplate the achievement of seven years of the most strenuous labor were the senior Brandts and their younger daughter Clara with her husband, Charles Fourment, an efficient assistant to his father Daniel, the most successful merchant of Brussels tapestries in Flanders.

A picnic was arranged and presented by the servants, an admirable *collation froide* to be washed down with wine from the Moselle and concluded with a selection of the most succulent fruits and ripest cheeses to be found in the markets of Antwerp. "It looks like one of Jan Bruegel's paintings," said Pieter Paul as he considered the baskets of fruit and the garlanded columns of the summerhouse. But if anyone heard him, he couldn't tell; all seemed immersed in a post-prandial torpor.

After a silence, Jan Brandt observed languidly, "Well, Pieter Paul, you really must feel yourself arrived, even past arrival. You've made the handsomest mausoleum for the living in Antwerp. If you're not careful, the governor or the archbishop will try to take it away from you."

"They can't afford it. It's hard for me to believe that *I* can afford it. I certainly couldn't have when I bought it."

"You've set a new standard," said young Charles Fourment, who had supplied the tapestries for the house as well as those that had been shipped to Sir Dudley Carleton at The Hague. "But I confess that I don't understand the use of all those busts and statues."

Jan Brandt grinned. "Why, my dear Charles, Pieter Paul has brought Rome to Antwerp." He looked to his son-in-law. "That *is* the intention, isn't it?"

Rubens responded with a shrug. "As former dean of our Romanists, I thought I should pay tribute to the source of all our wisdom."

The aging lawyer sighed. "But what will you do next to impress us?"

"Try to find repose in a dazzling humility, I should think. I'm going to slow my pace a little."

"Ah? Enough of money? Enough of esteem? You're going to live the life of a gentleman?"

"I said I was going to *slow* my pace, Jan, not stop altogether. No, what I plan is to stop teaching."

Brandt nodded. "Find that you're repeating yourself?"

206

"And weary of the sound of my own voice, too. I'm going to hire a student from the *collège* to read to me. While I paint, I shall improve my mind."

"Very commendable."

Isabella flashed her husband an expression of unwonted anxiety. "*All* your pupils going?"

"All."

"Even Anton?"

"Oh no, my love, but Anton is hardly a pupil. No, no, he's my right arm. He'll certainly stay."

His wife was relieved. "I can't imagine the household without him. He's lived with us that long."

"What do you suppose your daughter can mean, Jan?" asked Rubens good-humoredly.

Isabella flushed furiously and hurled a bunch of grapes at him. "Monster. What a thing to say."

He laughed, and once again addressed himself to his father-in-law. "You see, Jan? After nine years of marriage, she finally throws something at me. Would you call that the reflex action of a guilty conscience?" He detached a single grape from the stem and threw it gently at Isabella. She winced as it struck her; it might have been a ball fired by an *arquebuse*.

Jan Brandt was rather more flustered than his bland countenance suggested. Was Pieter Paul joking or was there more to it than he knew? He reserved judgment and comment, merely shaking his graying head slowly as if to suggest that the ways of women were an absolute mystery to him. Charles Fourment was not so wise. He chose this moment to leap into the silence with both feet. "My sister Suzanne, the one just widowed, you know, says that a woman in love doesn't know the meaning of the word 'conscience.'"

The stillness grew deeper, the gulf of perplexity wider. Pieter Paul, who had in fact been bantering, just now appreciated that he had opened Pandora's box and had better close it as quickly and securely as he could. "Your sister," he said, rather more sharply than seemed called for, "talks too much."

Charles Fourment was not to be repressed. "How can you say that, Pieter Paul? You don't even know her."

The painter snorted contemptuously. "I know *you.*"

Jan Brandt put a hand to his face and averted his glance. Isabella touched her younger sister's hand. "Pay no attention, Clara. Pieter Paul means no harm."

Anna Brandt sought to redirect the conversation. "You can handle so much work by yourself, Pieter Paul, you and Anton?"

"By not having to teach, he and I and perhaps one or two other fellows ought to be able to accomplish more than I'm doing now."

The conversation trailed off again, but the mood in its aftermath was altogether different from the euphoria that had preceded it. Now everyone, except for the obtuse Charles Fourment, was a prey to some sort of mild anxiety or apprehension, a perturbation to which no precise label could be attached. What had happened? What was happening?

By December of 1618, barely six months after the Rubens family had moved into the new quarters, the painter had divested himself of all his pupils. It was the sensible thing to do, but until he had done it, he hadn't fully realized how sensible. The drain on his energies demanded by the daily obligation to teach and to guide a half-dozen youths of indifferent talent had been far greater than he knew. Only now did he grasp what an immense relief it was to be free of instructional duties, with Anton van Dyck and two less-gifted assistants to aid him when required. Only now did he appreciate the luxury of complete independence, whose purchase had required ten good years of his life. He was as happy and as carefree as any reasonable man could be in a land, in a world, where strife was increasingly the order of things abroad, with Europe just dipping her toes into the moiling waters of a conflict that was to last for thirty years.

It was afternoon, perhaps a half hour before the winter's early darkness would end his day's work. He was painting, only half-listening to the pleasant voice of the young seminarian

208

who read to him from Seneca, the poet of stoicism. His thoughts were of contentment. No, they were of rejuvenation, of renewal, of rediscovered and refocused energies. If he had accomplished prodigies of art in the past, despite the encumbrance of a studio full of brawling boys, he would now perform wonders, even miracles.

The first indication of intrusion was a hesitation in the voice of the collegian. Pieter Paul looked away from the canvas he had been finishing to see his wife standing in the doorway, her face gray, her eyes tearful. But it wasn't grief that he read in Isabella's expression; it wasn't death or desperate illness. The young reader fell silent. Rubens dismissed him with an amiable smile and gesture of his head. The black-gowned student glided silently across the studio, made a curt bow to Isabella, and sidled past her into the fading light of the courtyard.

When he had gone, Pieter Paul rose from his painting stool and walked quickly to the trembling woman who seemed incapable of leaving the opened door. The painter pushed it shut, then turned to her. "What is it?" he asked, steadying his voice.

She staggered. He took her arm and led her to the chair where his subjects usually sat for their portraits. He stood back and studied her. "What in God's name *is* it? What's happened?"

Isabella placed her head against the high back of the chair and stared up at her husband, her mouth open. She seemed short of breath. "Anton," she gasped in a rasping whisper. "I was dressing after my nap."

In the utter stillness that followed her words, Pieter Paul had little difficulty in imagining a scene that suited. He wasn't surprised. Or rather, what surprised him was his reaction of no surprise. He felt neither anger nor outrage. He leaned over and gave his wife a gentle embrace. "Calm yourself." His tone betrayed so much less emotion than had his earlier question that she was startled.

She jerked herself free of him. "Calm myself? I've just been raped."

"Raped?" His voice conveyed only mildest wonder. "By a boy you've known for such a long time?"

"He's no boy. He's a man." There was a good deal more than flat assertion in this statement; there was defiance, even pride.

"Oh?"

She glared at him angrily, as if he were the culprit, not Anton. "Well, what are you going to do about it?"

"What do you propose that I do?"

"You'll certainly have to bring a charge against him. It's a question of honor."

His eyes widened. "You're willing to testify, in open court, that you were ravished by Anton van Dyck?"

Isabella allowed her head to fall for a moment, then lifted it, her expression sullen. "You're not being very sympathetic. I thought you'd understand."

"I think I *do* understand, my love. It's just that I'm not convinced that it's a case of rape."

She was unable to believe her ears. "You think I *allowed* him to . . . ?"

He reached for her hand. She rejected his offer. He sighed. "I suspect that you didn't offer very strenuous resistance."

She started to whimper. "Oh, how can you, Pieter Paul? How *can* you?"

He straightened himself and put his hands on his hips, assuming a posture he had seen Jan Brandt affect when interrogating a witness in a court chamber. "Did you scream when he attacked you?"

"He covered my mouth with his hand."

Rubens sneered. "And raped you that way, single-handed? It can't be done." He smiled sorrowfully. "Oh, I daresay a great, strong sailor could do such a thing, but Anton van Dyck? Never."

"What am I to do if you don't believe me?" she wailed.

"You might try telling me something I *can* believe. You might try to tell me what really happened. Did Elsa or one of

210

the other servants discover you? Is that why you're telling me, so I hear it from you, not from someone else?"

Again there was silence. He held her eyes, his smile still doleful but tinged increasingly with real amusement. Isabella was at first incredulous, then relieved, then infuriated—and finally, as if the burden she bore had broken her will, she nodded and looked away from him. "But I didn't invite him, Pieter Paul. I swear it. Nothing I've ever said or done or intimated should have given him the idea . . ."

He chuckled. "But *everything* you've ever said and done where he's concerned *would* have given him the idea. I half sensed it myself, that afternoon in the garden last summer, but of course I didn't understand what it was I sensed."

She was indignant. "What kind of a woman do you take me for?"

"What kind of a question is that for a woman to ask her husband?"

"The implication . . ."

"The implication isn't wicked, Isabella. I take you for a woman. What else do you imagine Anton saw in you, sees in you? You may not have *thought* you were encouraging him. I'm sure you imagined nothing of the sort. But you *were* encouraging him, all the same."

A look of horror spread across her gentle, anguished, tear-stained features. "You believe that?"

"It's not a thing a husband says lightly. And I'll say something that will scandalize you even more. I think you wanted this to happen, not consciously, perhaps, but profoundly."

"Never," she cried, but she was wringing her hands nervously.

"Oh, I'm sure it was a fantasy."

"Never."

"You never imagined Anton in your bed, in your arms?"

She started to speak, to offer a categorical denial of so heinous an accusation, but she couldn't make the words utter themselves. She flushed, and cast her eyes toward the floor. "In

211

dreams, I admit, he sometimes appeared." She looked up at him, pleadingly. "But I always confessed, Pieter Paul. Whenever I had such a dream, I asked for absolution at mass the next morning."

"And had the same kind of dream all over again?" He didn't wait for an answer. "Of course."

Isabella stamped her little foot. "How can you be so abominable? You could *kill* me. You could kill *Anton*. The law would excuse you. I've heard papa say so."

Rubens' expression suddenly became anxious. "Good God, woman, you've not mentioned this to your father, have you?"

"How could I? It just happened."

He relaxed. "Well, in heaven's name, say nothing to him. He wouldn't understand."

Her anger returned, but with less vigor. "How can *you* understand? How can you be so understanding about it? What right . . . ?"

"What do you expect? You want punishment? Is that it? You want me to hurt you, to kill you, to have Anton whipped in the center of the Meir?"

She wept again, softly. "I want . . . expiation. *Mea maxima culpa.*"

He solemnly made a sign of the cross on her smooth white forehead. "You are forgiven, my daughter. Go forth and sin no more."

Isabella howled in her outrage. "Oh, blasphemy." Abruptly, her manner changed, became composed. Her features stiffened. "I believe you're enjoying this. You like seeing me squirm. You want to *make* me squirm. That's it, isn't it?"

Pieter Paul drew up his painting stool and sat down before his wife. "No, no," he replied very slowly. "I don't think so. What I feel is that I'm as much to blame for this as you. I should have seen. I *did* see. I simply didn't appreciate, didn't recognize what it was I was seeing."

She eyed him cautiously. "Are you saying that to make me feel better or worse?"

212

"I'm just telling you the truth, my dearest. Why don't you tell *me* the truth? Tell me exactly what happened, what really happened, I mean, without any of the frills. No hand over your mouth. No rape. Just the facts."

She blushed once more. "Yes, that *was* a lie. I'm sorry. I didn't know what to say, how to tell you. He came into our room . . ."

"Without knocking?"

"No, he did knock, only I thought it was Elsa come to help me dress after my nap."

"You were in the bed?"

"I was up, just taking off my gown."

"Oh, I see. The propitious moment. He must have been watching at the keyhole." Rubens' little chortle gave her the notion he was savoring van Dyck's cleverness.

She pursed her lips in stern disapproval. "You *are* enjoying this."

He shrugged. "Well, you'll have to admit that it's not every day a man hears how his wife was raped."

Her mouth remained tensed. "This is not *une conte galante,* you know. I'm not *la reine Margot.* You ought to be ashamed of yourself." But as soon as she had spoken, Isabella realized the ludicrousness of it, and started to laugh.

"There now," Pieter Paul murmured happily. "Now you've begun to see how funny it is."

"If it's so funny, why do men kill over it?"

"*Some* men."

"You're not jealous?" The thought that he mightn't be plainly annoyed her.

"Have I something to be jealous about?"

"Men have killed for furtive glances."

"*Some* men, as I said." He paused and looked at her earnestly. "Do you love him?"

"Certainly not."

"Do you want him for your lover? Do you want him for your husband?"

213

"*No*, Pieter Paul. You know very well that I don't."

"Just so, my love. I know very well that you don't. So what have I to be jealous of? You yielded to an impulse."

"It was an accident . . . For *me*, it was an accident. But Anton had been planning it for months. He told me so."

"So I should punish him?"

Isabella boggled, shaking her head and beginning to sob again. "I don't know. I don't *know*. You've got me so confused that I don't know what to think any longer, what to do, or even what to want from you."

"Well, let's see," he drawled. "You don't seem to want my sympathy. You don't seem to want my laughter. What you apparently want is my blind anger. You want me to shriek in rage or pain. You want me to utter a vow of vengeance for the lost virtue of a sweet, gentle woman who, in a moment of vulnerability, gave herself up to a dream, to the realization of a wishful thought. You want vengeance against an impetuous, sensual boy who had in his eager head a vision of your affection for him and thought it meant something it really didn't . . . or something it really *did* mean, or almost meant, until it happened. That's what you want. Or that's what you imagine you want." Rubens stood up and once again took his wife in his arms. "No, my heart's own, I can't give you that. I can't invent out of thin air feelings of jealousy or anger or hatred or a desire for revenge. I don't feel anything of the sort. What I feel is regret for your regret. I'm sorry for you that the dream wasn't matched by the reality . . ."

Isabella freed herself from his embrace and looked up at him, utterly amazed. "Now how did you know *that*?"

"If you'd really enjoyed yourself with Anton, you'd have done the intelligent thing. You'd have bribed Elsa to keep silent . . . I assume she burst in on you, that Anton in his fever of lust forgot to close the door behind him, or that you didn't hear her knock . . ."

She turned crimson yet again. "I don't see why you bother to ask me what happened when you seem to know as well as I."

"I was just guessing. I know *you*."

"So well?" Her tone was plaintive, as if to suggest that he had no right to such astute intuitions about her. She gave a vast sigh. "Yes, you're quite right. Elsa did come in. I don't know whether she knocked or not. I certainly didn't hear her. But there we were."

Rubens burst out laughing. "By God, it certainly is *une conte galante*. Brantôme never wrote a more amusing one . . ."

"But this isn't fiction."

"It started out as fiction, didn't it?"

"My lies?"

"Your dreams."

"They seemed very real."

He pointed to a painting of Hero and Leander propped against a wall. "Where is the line drawn, my darling, between the dream and the reality? It's simply a question of credulity, isn't it? It's what we're *willing* to believe—and we're unwilling to believe. . . . So go on. There you were. Elsa entered the room and found you, *en flagrant délit*. Oh, it's too delicious. You looked up and saw her standing there. You screamed to her, 'He's raping me. He's raping me.' "

"No," replied Isabella with some complacency, "I maintained my composure. I simply said to Anton, 'Sir, you forget yourself.' "

"You didn't say that, did you? Oh, love, you've hidden such aplomb from me all these years. Did you really say that?"

She was bewildered by his surprise. "It was only a servant, after all. It was only Elsa."

"But if it had been *I*?"

Isabella thought for a moment. "If it had been you, I *might* have screamed."

"And what would I have done?"

She had to giggle. "I did think about *that*, you know. I was sure you'd go for a knife."

"Why? When have you ever seen me angry?"

"I haven't."

215

"You really thought I'd kill him?"

"Oh," she said blandly, "I rather imagined you'd kill both of us. It's what we deserve."

"And that's what you wanted."

"Yes," she murmured.

"And Anton? Did he want me to murder him too?"

"We didn't discuss it." Her tone was almost demure.

"What perverse creatures we are, to wish death as the penalty for stealing a little pleasure."

"The only pleasure of it was in the stealing. Anton . . ." She interrupted herself and gazed at the floor, unable to complete the sentence decently.

"He's not all you hoped he'd be, not all you dreamed?" asked Pieter Paul with some grim satisfaction. "Maybe *that's* why he goes from woman to woman as a dog goes from tree to tree. Not one of them wants him for very long."

"Perhaps," she whispered, and stood up, allowing herself to be embraced. "I was so foolish, Pieter Paul. I don't deserve your tenderness."

He took a half-step back from her and looked with some severity into her eyes. "I wouldn't be tender if it happened again."

She didn't flinch. "I wouldn't have told you about it if there were a chance of its happening again."

"I'm sure that's so," he said. "The subject, as far as I'm concerned, is closed."

"But what will you say to Anton?"

Rubens laughed sarcastically. "What do you think Anton will say to *me*?"

The scene between Pieter Paul Rubens and Anton van Dyck was imbued with neither the melodrama nor the humor of the artist's confrontation with his wife. For once, van Dyck seemed unable to muster much self-confidence, and when made to deal with his master's invincible equanimity, he was further muted. He spoke in mumbled monosyllables of crawling apology and abject humiliation. It was altogether possible, Pieter Paul

216

reflected, that Anton would thereafter despise him for the forbearance he had shown. Like Isabella, though for rather different reasons, the young painter wanted chastisement, required it as a means of catharsis—to clear the air between the two men as much as to cleanse his own spirit. "But it's not the sin you regret, my boy," Rubens admonished. "It's having been discovered in it. I can scarcely flog *you* and spare Isabella. We must all simply try to put this thing behind us."

This was more easily said than done for the two culprits. Van Dyck did move out of the Rubens house, but chance encounters were inevitable; and it was pitiable to Pieter Paul to see how they avoided each other's presence and, when this was impossible, how they averted their gaze. "Shame is simply the shattered image of vanity," the artist told his assistant. "You have to learn to live with it. *You*, especially, Anton, for this is certainly not the last time you'll be found in bed with another man's wife."

Van Dyck could never bring himself to despise the great Fleming, because Rubens must be the least despicable man God had ever created. He *wanted* to despise him, for this would have rationalized the injury he had done him. Instead, he found the artist's clearheadedness unnerving. How could one live in such evident comfort without illusion? This trait, like Pieter Paul's inexhaustible inventiveness, was a puzzle that the younger painter would never solve, though he kept trying during the next two years of his intermittent employment in Rubens' studio.

Fortunately for both of them, perhaps, this period was one of such a frenzy of activity that van Dyck was not often free to speculate about his master's equable disposition or about much else of so abstract a nature. Since 1615, when ground had at last been broken for the magnificent new Jesuit church of Saint Charles Borromeo in Antwerp, Rubens had been frequently consulted by the order's local rector and by the architect about the decoration of the ornate, Baroque façade as well as about the paintings from his workshop that would eventually adorn the high altar and the body of the church.

217

By the end of 1618, Pieter Paul had contributed two enormous paintings devoted to the miraculous works of Saints Francis Xavier and Ignatius Loyola. These were to be hung during alternating months behind the high altar. Thereafter, he and van Dyck and other aides were primarily absorbed with the completion of thirty-nine large pictures which were to be installed in the ceiling of each of the chapels of the ground floor and the bays of the gallery on the upper level.

Pieter Paul had many excellent reasons for wanting this immense commission, the largest by far that he had ever received, to be a work of absolutely surpassing splendor. Recalling the achievements of Romano and Mantegna in Mantua, of Raphael and Michelangelo in Rome, and of Tintoretto's Scuola di San Rocco in Venice, he completely understood the signal opportunity afforded him in his home city, unique in the history of church decoration in the Low Countries and possibly anywhere outside of Italy—a church whose interior decor was left entirely to the taste and skill of a single craftsman. More than that, this was the first major Baroque basilica to be constructed in the Netherlands. Even before its completion, it had gained a renown that spread as far as London, where Inigo Jones demanded to be kept fully informed about its architecture and its manner of construction; for it was widely reputed to be, and so it was, the most ambitious undertaking ventured in the Netherlands since the building of the Gothic cathedral centuries before. Its very modernity made Rubens' close association with it a matter of much importance to his career and his own widening reputation.

What this huge commission for the ceilings of Saint Charles Borromeo lacked in opportunities for decorating great individual expanses of space, it made up in possibilities for invention and variety. So numerous were the pictures to be created, and so quickly were they required, that he did only the sketchiest of penciled outlines for each, proceeding directly to a set of grisaille studies on which he based a series of small *modelli*, miniatures of the final canvases, which were submitted to the church authorities for approval of general thematic material and arrangement. What particularly dazzled the older established artists of Antwerp who visited Rubens occasionally in the course of his performance of this mammoth project was his capacity to convey such an impression of freedom and spaciousness in these little pictures—that he was able, on so reduced a scale, to suggest the generous flow that typified his larger work. If Anton van Dyck was not so struck by his master's lightning genius, it was because, Jan Bruegel told him reprovingly, he had no basis for comparison. "There's not another living artist who can manage it. And the greatest of the dead ones, Titian or Michelangelo or Tintoretto, would never promise to deliver so many paintings in so short a time." He grinned wryly. "Or if they promised, they'd not keep their promise. Pieter Paul will," he concluded without envy.

The ceiling pictures for the chapels on the lower floor depicted scenes from the Old and New Testaments. The ones to be placed in the gallery above were devoted to the lives and accomplishments of the major saints. They were put into place as soon as the paint was dry; so it was possible, over the period of nearly three years that Rubens gave to the monumental task, only gradually to comprehend the true awesomeness of his conception.

In early December, 1620, when the work for Saint Charles Borromeo was within a few months of completion, one of Inigo Jones' informants visited Antwerp—the very beautiful young Countess of Arundel, wife of Thomas Howard, whose portrait Pieter Paul had painted a number of years before. It was the most natural of occurrences that the countess, an admirer of the picture Rubens had made of her husband, should ask that he do the same for her. Indeed, her request had novelty, for she wanted the painting to include her children, her absent lord, and a grotesque dwarf who was her constant companion. Though still pressed by the church authorities, the artist willingly complied with the lady's wishes, and happily managed to locate the sketches he had made for his portrait of the earl on which to base his re-creation in this new work.

The lovely countess was a more accomplished linguist than her husband, and much more conscious of the greatness of her position in British society. Yet as she and Rubens chatted, now in French, now in Italian, the tenor of their conversation was quite similar to the exchanges he had had with the earl—turning frequently to the paucity of competent arsists in London and, consequently, the desirability, "nay, *maître*, the utter necessity of your coming to us as soon as you're able." Pieter Paul expressed pleasure at his beautiful sitter's insistence, but replied as he had done to Thomas Howard. He was happy in Antwerp. He had many more commissions than he could comfortably manage, and he was therefore not really interested in seeking greener fields when the grazing at home was more than adequate.

"However, *madame*," he added, more by way of keeping her features animated than in great earnest, "there is Maître van Dyck, here. He's young and unfettered and a splendid portraitist."

The eyes of the countess fell upon the trim figure and pale, fragile face of Anton, who was at work on one of the paintings for the ceilings of Saint Charles Borromeo. "Unfettered?" she inquired archly.

"Unmarried, *madame*," Rubens responded with a little laugh. "No responsibilities. Nothing to hold him in Antwerp."

He perceived without difficulty that the lady's interest in van Dyck was prompted by more than a desire to raise the level of art in Britain. Pieter Paul summoned Anton from his labors and briefly summarized Lady Arundel's suggestion. The young man's eyes grew bright. Then he frowned. "But I must help Maître Rubens complete the work for the church."

"Nonsense," responded his master scornfully. "If the countess thinks you might be able to carve a place for yourself in London, you ought to go without delay. We haven't so much more to do here that we can't manage without you."

The matter was not settled there and then, but it *was* settled soon. Anton had learned a modicum of discretion as the result of his shattering experience with Isabella, but he disclosed to Rubens, merely by the way he spoke of her, by his expressions and gestures, that he had made an easy conquest of the Countess of Arundel and that his conquest of London would follow as a matter of course. "She's promised me an introduction to the king himself," he told Pieter Paul excitedly. "If the king approves of me, my future in England is assured."

Van Dyck departed with his protectress and her strange little companion at the end of December, leaving behind him in Rubens' fine house and studio some very mixed emotions. "I'm not sure whether I should feel sorry for London or for van Dyck," said the artist to his wife.

"What," she replied, with a bitter little smile, "no tears for the countess?"

"Ah no, she's much too familiar with the path she's leading him down. That's the pathetic charm of it all. Each has the idea that he's fooling the other, and both are merely deceiving themselves. But of the two, Anton has so much more to lose than the countess."

"In London, what can he lose?"

"Time. At the moment, for him, that's everything. The Arundels are Catholics. I don't believe her presentation of Anton to the king will prove much of a help to him." The painter sighed. "But at least he'll learn some English."

By the end of the following June, all of Rubens' paintings for Saint Charles Borromeo had been installed. Soon the church would be ready for consecration. Preparations for this ceremony, the most auspicious religious occasion Antwerp had known for well over a century, were elaborate. The mass was to be celebrated by the primate of the Netherlands, by the Papal Nuncio, and perhaps even by Mutio Vitelleschi, Vicar-General of the Society of Jesus. Every dignitary of the Church, the state, the aristocracy, and the diplomatic corps was invited. The most honored guests, it went without saying, were to be the Archduke Albrecht and the Infanta Isabel, so well and properly beloved by all their subjects.

But hardly had invitations for the September consecration of the great new house of God been dispatched than word was received in Antwerp that the Archduke Albrecht, who had been enjoying ill health for some months, had succumbed in late July. Thus in a trice, the prospects for the Low Countries, only yesterday so bright, had been transfigured by sorrow. An occasion for joy was abruptly transformed into one for mourning. And mourning there was, even in the United Provinces. A disciple of moderation was dead.

For Rubens, who vividly recalled the archduke's demand, seven years before, that he hold himself in readiness for any call the Infanta Isabel might place upon him, the news of the regent's death caused an involuntary shudder of anticipation. He would, of course, honor the pledge he had so willingly given, not merely in remembrance of the long years of cordiality and patronage and friendship with the archduke, but because it very well might be that there was something of value he could do for his country in this summer of 1621—the year when the truce between the United Provinces and Spain was terminated.

Rubens was not immediately importuned by the Infanta Isabel. Yet there was ample cause for any well-informed Fleming to be alarmed by the shocks that Europe was being called upon to absorb. The end of the Twelve-Year Truce had come in April, only a month after the death of Philip III. The successor to the throne of Spain, Philip IV, was no wizard—but he had no need to be in order to shine most brightly when compared with his dull-witted father. The new Spanish king made a few things clear at once. The most startling was that he meant seriously to take up the cudgel that had fallen soon after the death of his grandfather, Philip II; he planned to restore the Catholic integrity of Christendom and, in the process, to regalvanize the economy of Spain, so long pillaged by his father's advisers and their hangers-on.

As his first minister, the young ruler selected the aged, wise Don Baltasar de Zúñiga, theretofore ambassador to the Holy Roman Emperor at Prague. However, the power behind Zúñiga was his nephew, Don Gaspar de Guzmán, Count of Olivares, who would before long be directing Spanish affairs in his own right, after his uncle's timely death. Olivares infused his eager master with the stirring concept of Spain's manifest destiny to dominate both hemispheres. And the first step in the direction of fulfilling this dream must be taken against the United Provinces whose merchants and bankers and shipowners had grown fatter every year on the profits from legitimate trade and even more lucrative piracy—mostly at the expense of Spanish and Portuguese vessels carrying treasure from the New World.

The resumption of the war against the Dutch Protestants had been strenuously opposed by the Archduke Albrecht. His demise eliminated the only obstacle to this renewal of violence. For Philip IV's aunt, the Infanta Isabel, was less persuaded than her late husband that the United Provinces should be granted the independence they demanded—and even if she had shared the archduke's conviction absolutely, her powerlessness and her bereavement conspired to incapacitate her at this critical time.

Ambrogio di Spinola, who had successfully concluded the siege of Ostend almost fifteen years before, appeared in the Netherlands little more than a week after the regent's death to mount a concerted assault against the rebellious Dutch from every major border town. The troops of Prince Mauritz, fresh from their labors of suppressing the Arminian heresy, had much more to lose than did Spinola's Spaniards and Italian mercenaries. They offered savage resistance wherever battle was joined. It was not quite a repetition of the Duke of Alba's Spanish Fury and its corresponding Protestant retaliation—but many with long memories feared that this would be a natural evolution. For unless the Spanish scored a swift and definitive victory, the struggle would drag on for years, creating poverty and acrimony on an unlimited scale. Spinola obtained no quick military decisions. In sporadic fashion, the war would continue as a feature of Netherlands life until 1648.

But the little war in the Netherlands was only one phase of a conflict that was becoming increasingly general. James I's hand-picked Swiss soldiers were also embattled, fighting the army of the emperor for political and religious control of the Palatinate—the issue almost identical to the cause of the succession to the crown of Julich which Henri IV had been preparing to contest at the time of his murder in 1610.

In France, where Louis XIII had grudgingly permitted himself to be reconciled with his mother, largely through the good offices of Richelieu, the state was campaigning against the eight Huguenot strongholds within her frontiers. This civil war, which sadly resembled the terrible Albigensian Crusade of the twelfth century, was not soon to be conclusively settled. After eighteen months of bumbling generalship and halfhearted fighting on the part of the royal troops, six of the Protestant enclaves were brought to their knees. However, La Rochelle and Montauban succeeded in withstanding siege and were allowed to survive. In the judgment of Richelieu, by then the young king's most trusted counselor, the more serious threat to the crown's prerogatives came not from the Huguenots, but from good Catholics, *la noblesse d'épée,* the hereditary nobility who resented the royal insistence on appointing to major administrative and judicial posts ennobled commoners, *la noblesse de robe,* whose loyalty was not to be questioned. Thus did Richelieu begin the majestic work of enforced unification that was to make him France's greatest and most detested first minister of the monarchy.

Pieter Paul Rubens followed these hectic events of August and early September from the tranquillity of a house at Eeckeren, a few miles outside of Antwerp, which he had leased for a holiday. With the paintings already completely installed in the church of Saint Charles Borromeo, awaiting only the consecration which would take place without the presence of the widowed infanta, he had a little time to rest, to contemplate the gentle, intensely cultivated Flemish countryside, and even to paint a few landscapes—subjects to which he had hitherto only casually lent his hand. There were many visitors, for the artist loved company. Bruegel, the crippled Balthasar Moretus, and merry Frans Snyders passed some days beneath his roof. Jan and Anna Brandt came to stay, to take in the bucolic scenery and be amused by their grandchildren. Isabella's sister, Clara, and her husband, Charles Fourment, arrived, bringing along with them Charles' young and beautiful sister, the widowed Suzanne, a sumptuous contrivance of Flemish flesh, ripe and rich as a seckel pear.

To the artist, this brief period of *détente*, after so many years of assiduous attention to his work, was an occasion for unbridling. He didn't think of it just that way. Until Suzanne Fourment appeared before him in the garden at the house in the country, he felt only that at the age of forty-four, a great deal of his life had slipped away from him, its passing remarkable for nothing more than heroic effort—without heroic joy. He was not so much disturbed by this realization as remotely saddened. He suffered from a sense of slightest waste and loss.

By any standard one chose to employ, he was a great man, certainly a great artist and a great *Anversois*. The only honor that had so far escaped him was ennoblement, and he had no special reason to desire such a final accolade. He was too sensible for that; success depended not on titles, but on the systematic accumulation of wealth. *His* accumulation was more than ample to his needs. But what were his needs? To what end had he made this accumulation? He had spent so much time, invested so much money in the creation of the stately dwelling on the Wapper, because that was good for commerce—a house that anyone, no matter how illustrious, would think it a privilege to enter. Even the regents had found it so.

Very well. But what now? What more was possible? Certainly, nothing more was necessary. This was the thought that caught up with Rubens in the summer of 1621. All sorts of commissions were coming his way, so many that he rejected the ones that seemed inconsequential. His condition had greatly changed since his return to Antwerp from Rome thirteen years before—but in the main, Rubens himself hadn't changed very much. It was this faintly nagging feeling of personal incompleteness, with its context of financial and popular success, that made the introduction of Suzanne Fourment into his life at once happy and hazardous.

For Suzanne Fourment, with her dark hair, her sharp features, and her bright, popped eyes, the encounter with the great

Rubens was filled with tantalizing possibilities. But of one matter she was certain: She was looking for a husband, not for a middle-aged lover. She was dressed in a manner that she hoped would attract the former, and easily ensnared the latter. Her low-cut bodice nicely proclaimed a full bosom. Her black, broad-brimmed velvet hat, with its rakish feather, contrasted brilliantly with her pale skin. She was still nominally in mourning, a condition she honored only by her attire.

Suzanne Fourment was, as a poet put it, a flame sent to nest in Rubens' flax. She didn't deliberately arouse his passion. Her presence, her arrogant but charming indifference, her cruel wit accomplished this. His readiness was the essential, and it was all. He offered to paint her portrait. She accepted. He offered to make love to her. She politely declined, but took no offense.

Instead she merely asked, "Why is it that men seem to imagine widows more susceptible to such blandishments than maidens, *maître*? Are we supposed to have buried our virtues in our husbands' tombs?"

"You're not being very friendly," he protested mildly.

"Perhaps I'm just trying to counteract your overfriendliness."

The painter gave a little sigh. "Can you blame me?"

"Obviously."

"Look at yourself in the glass, *madame*. What can you expect from a man who looks at you?"

"Discretion, *maître*."

"I'm not unsympathetic to discretion."

"Your sympathy seems rather flawed. To trumpet your lust is neither sympathetic nor discreet."

"*Have* I been trumpeting it?"

"Your eyes."

"*Your* metaphor is flawed, *madame*. I'm sure it's your only defect."

She scoffed. "You're not to get around me with flattery, *maître*. We were speaking of discretion."

"Do you think I'd parade it all over Antwerp on a pennant

226

that you'd become my mistress? I have as much at stake as you. Some would say I had more."

"*You* would say more, I'm sure. But not I. Let me assure you that the next man to bed me will be a husband."

"Oh, enviable man."

And so it went with them, day after day, during the week she had originally planned to stay at Eeckeren. She agreed to remain a bit longer when Pieter Paul complained that in order to do the promised portrait properly, he required more time—a lie that the artist and his wife alone were in a position to disabuse her of. Isabella chose to say nothing, though she knew instinctively what was in her husband's mind. She saw in the beautiful young woman not a rival for Pieter Paul's affection, but a means of expiation. If Rubens seduced Suzanne, the sin Isabella and Anton van Dyck had committed would be atoned for. If this reasoning ran against the teachings of the Church, it sufficed for a wife who suffered frightfully from feelings of remorse and guilt. So she tacitly conspired with Pieter Paul, but only to the extent of joining him in urging the widow to stay on a bit longer at Eeckeren.

Pieter Paul ruefully understood his wife's motives. The rue, however, was occasioned by his apprehension that she might imagine his passion for Suzanne to be inspired by a desire for retribution. He hoped not. He didn't, in any case, allow this fear to dampen his ardor. Once the question of the young woman's departure had been resolved in his favor, he altered his tactics. Instead of pressing his suit, he became aloof—a posture he assumed with some discomfort, for it was unfamiliar. If he couldn't seduce her by being simply himself, he would try to overawe her, impress her with his importance. Did she, he inquired, fully understand with whom she was dealing? Had she seen his work? It was in every major church in Flanders. "Soon it will be in the cathedral of Ghent," he concluded. For after years of annoying negotiations, a compromise had finally been reached with the tiresome bishop over the long-disputed altarpiece.

Suzanne *was* impressed. For this was the man she had expected all along to meet, the best-connected commoner of the
Low Countries. It wasn't his paintings nor where they were displayed that intrigued her; it was his influential acquaintances.
She would parry without a qualm the advances of a lustful
man, because she had everything to lose by yielding. But to one
who might find her an eminently suitable male, the balance of
advantage shifted sharply in his favor.

She immediately recognized his game, and respected him for
choosing to play it as he did. Suzanne Fourment was, after all,
playing a game herself, and she enjoyed a contest with an opponent who could put her to the test. To be the prize as well as a
participant in such a match made the game that much more
amusing. She was touched by Pieter Paul's finesse. He never
tried physically to corner her, never offered her drink to break
down her resistance. This was a duel purely of wits and wills.

When, a couple of days into the second week of her visit, she
abruptly said, "Very well, *maître*," it was from a sense of compassion and admiration blended with a most hardheaded ambition. It wouldn't do to exhaust his patience; she must now try
to turn his desire for her to ends that would serve her.

Pieter Paul was at first puzzled by her remark. "Very well,
what?" he responded, for he had said nothing to her to which
this seemed a rational assent. And then, suddenly, it came to
him. He beamed. He laughed. He embraced Suzanne Fourment. "Very *well*," he said, and laughed again.

They did not, in the way that was usual for these affairs in
the great cities of Europe, become lover and mistress. After a
feverish first meeting of bodies came a meeting of true minds.
They became friends, sometimes rather embattled ones, for
they were able to agree on almost nothing. Suzanne appealed to
Pieter Paul, once the hottest flame of his desire for her had
been dampened by their commingled juices, because she was almost everything Isabella was not—hot-tempered, demanding,
not in the least acquiescent or submissive.

The game that had led to her seduction continued afterward,
with neither deception nor disappointment. He found in her

for a time a companion of the late afternoons, when his day's work was done, one who could divert him by disputing him, by arguing with him—not about the great events of the world, nor even the lesser concerns of Antwerp or Flanders, but about such trivialities as taste in clothes and decoration of a room, about manners, about morals, about people. Suzanne mistrusted everyone, even Pieter Paul Rubens, "because everybody wants something. And he who wants something of mine depletes me when he takes it."

When he replied by inquiring what *she* wanted, he recognized the question to be rhetorical; he knew the answer before she gave it. This was part of the game they played. "I want a rich husband." By the year's end, Rubens found her one, Arnold Luden, an affably nondescript scion of a banking family who was willing to marry the unruly and amoral Suzanne for her important dowry and her beauty. She accepted Luden's proposal with poor grace—though in reality she was delighted with him. "He'll do," she told Pieter Paul, "if he understands that I'm not going to be transformed." It was, as her lover remarked, a gratuitous protest. No one could change Suzanne. "No one would want to. Only a fool would try."

Luden and his bride exchanged marriage vows just before the beginning of Lent in 1622. But Pieter Paul was not in attendance for this ceremony. He was in Paris, summoned there suddenly the previous December by the Netherlands ambassador, Baron de Vicq, "to look into a project that is so grandiose that I dare not attempt to describe it for you."

Seven

IT was saddening for a reasonably conscientious and dutiful family man to be away from his wife and children at Christmastide. Even to find himself at this season in a great European capital, one that he hadn't previously visited, was only a partial mitigation. Yet the very fact that he was lonely for his loved ones left behind in Antwerp had its instructive side; this was, after all, the first journey of consequence Rubens had undertaken since his return from Rome in the autumn of 1608.

He remonstrated with himself for having so long treated so much of his domestic happiness as a matter of course. For all his material prosperity, it occurred to Pieter Paul as he went off to sleep in his chamber of the Netherlands embassy in Paris, his first night there, that his greater endowments by far were his simple contentment, his family, his friends, and his cheerful, healthy skepticism about most other people and the little puddles of misery and confusion they seemed to rejoice in creating. *These* riches he rarely gave much thought to, so were they taken for granted. Having to tear himself away, and especially at joyful Christmas time, he was able to measure the value of those half-remembered assets. He had to smile. The image

230

of Suzanne, recently so brilliant that it threatened to obscure all else, faded like a patch of dyed linen in the sunshine of his thoughts of Isabella.

This was, of course, as it should be. By the next morning, extroverted Rubens had easily dismissed these pillow thoughts. Introspection came to him no more readily in middle age than it had in his youth. There was work to be sought here, and there was Paris to be seen.

The Paris of late 1621 was a place that the twentieth-century visitor would find it difficult to get his bearings in. Few of the treasures and horrors of architecture that now endear this world's most graciously made city had yet been built. None of the shambling brick or half-timbered houses had yet been razed to make room for the broad avenues and *grands boulevards*. The Place des Vosges (then Place Royale) was in the process of completion. Of the monuments occupying the edge of the right bank of the Seine today only the Louvre and the church of Saint-Germain-l'Auxerrois stood in Rubens' day, both somewhat different and reduced in aspect by comparison with their present form. The Palais des Tuileries, quite new, was essentially a part of the Louvre's complex, but would be burned to the ground two and a half centuries later. Near Les Halles was Saint-Eustache, that extraordinary marriage of the Gothic and more modern styles, dwarfed in all Paris (as today) only by the cathedral of Notre-Dame on the Ile de la Cité. The Bastille formed part of the city's fortifications. Beyond these walls, Montmartre was a village committed to the memory of Saint-Denis, not yet scarred by the Sacré Coeur.

La Sainte-Chapelle, Saint Louis' dazzling little wonder of stained glass and delicate stonework, could easily be seen from Notre-Dame, its narrow *flèche* piercing the turbulent Parisian skies. The imposing turrets of the Conciergerie were much more numerous than now, this building only recently abandoned as the royal palace. The familiar landmarks of the left bank were fewer still—no Beaux-Arts, no Institut, no Invalides. No domed Sorbonne adorned the little rise of Montparnasse, though not so far away from the site it fills was the fine church of Saint-Etienne-du-Mont which, like Saint-Eustache across the river, was a transitional work. Its rood loft was perhaps the most glorious example of Renaissance masonry in Paris. Smaller Gothic and Romanesque churches dotted the close-packed parishes. Saint-Julien-le-Pauvre kept watch on Notre-Dame. The tower of Saint-Germain-des-Prés guided drunken whores and scholars and clerics home through unlit streets whose surfaces were not invariably paved.

The Paris of Louis XIII was only a slight modification of the city whose character was first altered, after the ruinous plagues and sieges and battles of the Hundred Years' War, by François I. He had died in the middle of the previous century. The medieval ramparts and gateways still separated the *cité* from the *faubourgs* and adjacent countryside of the Ile-de-France. Little of the new construction was noteworthy. Apart from the harmonious Place Royale, only the Louvre and the Tuileries commended themselves, the former rising on ground once occupied by the massive fortress-castle where Philippe-Auguste had lived and planned campaigns that gave France hope of attaining her modern boundaries.

On the opposite side of the Seine, approximately midway between Saint-Germain-des-Prés and the river, was the Palais du Luxembourg. It had been planned during the regency of Maria de' Medici and its actual construction begun before her banishment to Blois. Now that she had been allowed to return to Paris, this splendid new stately house, designed by Salomon de Brosse, the queen mother's favorite architect whom she quarreled with regularly, was arising with exceptional rapidity. The Medicis hated to be kept waiting. An additional reason for urgency was Maria's well-grounded apprehension that she might be exiled once again and therefore never see the building finished. For her banishment had taught her absolutely nothing; to France, Louis XIII might be the king, but to his mother he was a callow youth who had to be enlightened, whether he wanted to be or not.

Though most of the exterior construction of the palace was accomplished, there remained the important question of interior decoration. It was this task for which Pieter Paul Rubens had been summoned from Antwerp to discuss. The Netherlands ambassador, the old aristocrat Baron de Vicq, had refused to give the artist any details prior to his arrival in Paris. But he had been forewarned by his friend and frequent correspondent, Nicolas-Claude de Fabri de Peiresc, a Provençal resident of the capital whom many regarded as the foremost humanist of his country, perhaps of all Europe. Fabri had visited Rubens several times in Antwerp and had always urged him to come to Paris—using arguments identical to those of the Earl and Countess of Arundel in their efforts to persuade him to voyage to London: There were few good painters at the French court, certainly none of Pieter Paul's rank. Fabri's brother, Palamède, took a similar line.

In truth, by 1621, there wasn't an artist in the known world whose name could reasonably be uttered in the same breath with Pieter Paul's, so prominently was he established as the *ne plus ultra* of modern painting—a reputation for greatness that was reinforced by the claim of such men as the Fabris that Rubens possessed other attractive virtues, such as intellectuality and close relations with the court of Brussels—not that his brilliance of mind or his political influence were much of a recommendation to anyone requiring the services of a painter.

It was to Fabri's house, in the parish of Saint-Germain-des-Prés, that Pieter Paul hied himself the morning after reaching the French capital. And it was with Fabri that he walked through the cruel December winds, through narrow, crooked, half-cobbled streets to the queen mother's new palace. The wide central portion of the building was flanked by elegant pavilions which projected forward, the whole overlooking a considerable expanse of scrupulously landscaped park that had been the private garden of the Duke of Luxembourg—from whom derived the name of the building.

Fabri was very excited. He assured Pieter Paul that the occasion for this initial sortie to Paris couldn't possibly be more auspicious. He predicted that it was the first of many visits, that having once set foot here, he would never again be content with the life of a provincial city in the Low Countries. Politeness prevented the artist from demurring. *His* world, his life, his vision were all in his mind, in his imagination. Had he not gone so great a distance figuratively by staying in one place, literally? To his French friend, however, he merely said evasively, "Perhaps. We shall see."

The painter's formal presentation to the queen mother was a matter for the Netherlands ambassador to arrange. The old man fussed over it, wondering aloud if Pieter Paul had brought along suitable dress, if he knew the rules of protocol, understood that he mustn't speak until spoken to. Rubens accepted these admonitions with good nature. "I shall try not to disgrace you, *monsieur le Baron*. But I don't think you need to be too worried."

"The woman is a tigress, *maître*, a tigress," the diplomat muttered between toothless gums.

"I'll try to keep clear of her claws."

The claws of Maria de' Medici were not entirely her own. Indeed, the most dangerous were thought to be those of her closest adviser, Richelieu, yet to achieve his absolute preeminence in the councils of the king, and who was accurately suspected of playing a double game which, despite allegations to the contrary, was neither wholly nor even mainly in his personal interest. He meant to save France, an end he believed attainable only by keeping the impulsive queen mother under reasonable control while he simultaneously mollified her royal son. The difficulties of France's internal affairs were infinitely complicated by clerics, aristocrats, and rich members of the Third Estate who appeared willing to sacrifice the well-being of the nation to their selfish advantage. Though Richelieu himself was endlessly accused of similar aims, the evidence was slight.

The quintessence of the domestic problem was that France was not yet France, but rather a collection of provincial dukedoms, counties, enclaves, and principalities that had been the prizes won in earlier conflicts. One was, as Fabri explained to Rubens, first of all a Provençal, a Breton, an Auvergnat, a Bourguignon, a Normand—in just the way the artist called himself first of all a Fleming. Each locality had its arms, its ancestral traditions, its ancient rights and privileges, its economy, its individual identity and a consequent sense of separateness.

In these earliest days of 1622, shortly after Rubens came to Paris, the spirit of factionalism, religious as well as political, economic, and geographic, governed the atmosphere. Motivations of various "parties" were inspired quite as often from abroad as from the provinces. Politic marriages from generation to generation made strange bedfellows. And as the Thirty Years' War intensified, these ancient and recent affiliations would cause more and more curious turns of history's wheel of fortune. *Everyone* was playing at the least a double game; some played five or six. It was a wise king who could coherently describe his own policies, domestic or foreign, except in terms of keeping his crown and his head attached at the same time to the same body.

Beyond this simple statement of the instinct for self-preservation, only the pope could be said to know more or less precisely what he wanted, the restoration of things as they had been before the upsetting advent of Martin Luther. Even Philip IV, convinced though he was of the desirability of such a reactionary movement, understood the goal to be chimerical—and the Most Catholic King wasn't above giving comfort to French Huguenots by failing to give promised aid to French Catholics, or failing to give it when it was most required.

The young King of France sympathized with papal aims, but found it hard to determine from month to month which of his many enemies was most likely to bring him low—the Huguenots, the Habsburgs of Spain and the Empire, the British, his own dear mother, his younger brother Gaston, or his half-brothers—the Duke of Vendôme and the Prior of the Knights of Malta, bastards of Henri IV by the magnificent Gabrielle d'Estrées. With so many determinedly against him, he saw his first obligation as the discovery of a single faithful ally. It would be almost three years before his search ended with Richelieu.

In the meantime, this bishop from Luçon moved restlessly in the background, mistakenly distrusted by Louis XIII, mistakenly trusted by Maria de' Medici. Already becoming a figure of legend, Richelieu operated most effectively in the shadows, manipulating his betters rather than taking action himself. He was "a brilliant second," as Charles de Gaulle would say of General Maxime Weygand. For a man reputedly so ruthless, he was uncommonly shy—and uncommonly religious, though terribly torn between his intellectual accord with the principles of the Counter Reformation and his instinctive sympathy for the practices long cherished by the Church in France. Come to that, he was wracked by doubts about almost everything except the ineluctable necessity of making *"une seule France"* governable by *"un seul roi."*

Fabri was convinced that the choice of Rubens to make the paintings that should decorate the new Palais du Luxembourg had originated with Richelieu, not with the queen mother. *"She* would have preferred Guido Reni or some other Italian." No French artist now working seemed consequential enough for the assignment. Louis Le Nain painted pretty little genre and religious pictures and occasional portraits. Nicolas Poussin, though destined for acclaim in France after his death, was too young, too difficult, and concerned in any case mainly with managing the finances of a trip to Rome. It was doubtful if Richelieu knew more of Poussin at this point than the fact of his existence.

In the first week of January, Baron de Vicq announced to Pieter Paul that he had been accorded an audience with the queen mother—and again admonished him about dress and deportment. The presentation went off well. It took place in the unfurnished, dusty entrance hall of the palace Maria de' Medici hoped one day to occupy. All of her attendants, save one, fairly danced in their agitation—a condition induced by her mercurial temperament. The exception was the trim, fastidious Bishop of Luçon, whose eyes never left Rubens except when Rubens' eyes sought his. Of the dozen or so in the queen mother's entourage, the beautiful little teen-aged Duchesse de

Luynes, just widowed by an elderly general who had fallen to typhoid in the royal service, stood out as somebody—though as somebody it was probably dangerous to know. Pieter Paul saw in Maria's court all the trappings to which his years with Vincenzo Gonzaga at Mantua had made him accustomed—a little cluster of sycophants, cherishing preferment or seeking it in the protection of the corpulent, stubborn, stupid, flighty, imperiously regal Florentine. If the Duchesse de Luynes and Richelieu singled themselves out, it was for different reasons—she for her loveliness and for her certainty of where this beauty, harnessed to a fitful intelligence, might take her; he for a brilliant humility, a patient watchfulness.

Maria de' Medici ordered the painter and old de Vicq to rise from their kneeling postures, and with a peremptory gesture indicated to the baron that he should stand aside, leaving Rubens alone before her. She addressed him in French, saying how highly he had been recommended to her by those in a position to know the problems posed by a project as ambitious as the one she was about to propose to him. He replied in Italian, for the queen mother's mastery of the tongue of her adopted country was imperfect. De Vicq was horrified by the artist's presumption, but his qualms gave way at once when he looked at Maria's flushed plump features; she was smiling as she inquired where Pieter Paul had learned her native language so fluently. He explained, finding it meet to add that he had been present at her wedding, twenty-two years before, as an attendant of her brother-in-law of Mantua.

"God rest his soul," said the queen mother, crossing herself. "Such a son he left behind him. But then, such a dreadful example he set the poor boy. I only hope this young Vincenzo makes an heir before his debauchery carries him off." Her hope was vain. Before long, succession to the throne of Mantua would pose another dilemma for Europe's embattled rulers.

The Bishop of Luçon advanced a deferential step, bowed to his portly mistress, then to the painter. "I think," he said in French, "that it would be useful for us to show Maître Rubens just what this decoration is to consist of, *madame*. Time presses

237

us a bit. There's a meeting of the Royal Council this afternoon." His voice was like his person, thin but with an element of steeliness.

She nodded and made to rise, causing a little flurry among her people who rushed forward to help her stand. "You," she said to Richelieu, "will explain to the *maître* what's expected."

The entourage proceeded from the hall to make a tour of the spacious public rooms in both wings of the palace's ground floor. The bishop meticulously described the themes proposed for the great *salles*. There were to be, in fact, two commissions, the second to depend on the satisfactory completion of the first. The initial project called for a series of twenty-one great canvases devoted to the whole career to date of Maria de' Medici, from the time of her marriage to Henri IV to her recent reconciliation with her son. "You must, *maître*, treat some of these important events with considerable tact," said Richelieu with a touch of irony but none of humor. "We want above all not to offend His Majesty. That won't be easy."

"I quite understand the problem, *monseigneur*," Rubens replied. "I shall just have to make abundant use of allegory."

"Precisely, and make your symbolism as obscure as you can."

This first group of paintings was to adorn one complete wing of the palace. The second, intended to be a parallel in dimension and spirit, would be dedicated to the seemlier aspects of the life of Henri IV—for which, as Richelieu softly noted, "your tact will have to exceed itself."

The bishop and the artist had, by this time, trailed well behind the cortège of the queen mother. Standing alone in an empty hall, their voices resonating, though they spoke mutedly, the two men faced each other. Richelieu, eight years younger than Rubens, seemed a decade older because of his fragile health and his tendency to worry. "Tell me," he murmured, looking about him to be certain they were unobserved, "where do you stand?"

The painter raised an eyebrow. "With respect to what, *monseigneur?*"

238

"Come, come, you're a political person. I know that about you. But are you Spain's man?"

Rubens shrugged. "I'm a Netherlander, a Fleming. So most of all, that makes me a man of peace."

"Ah, but peace on whose terms, *maître?* That's the question I'm asking you."

Pieter Paul gave the illustrious bishop a small, sad smile. "You know very well, *monseigneur,* that the Flemish peace, if it comes, will be based on someone else's terms. Like the states of Germany and Italy, we're simply one more pawn in the games that are played by France and Spain and Britain."

"But if you had your *choice* . . . ?"

"Forgive me, but I can see no sense in trying to respond to a question whose hypothesis is preposterous. I shall never have such a choice. . . . May I ask what you're trying to make out from such questions, *monseigneur?*"

"Just what I put to you at the beginning, *maître.* Where do you stand?"

The artist considered Richelieu for some time, and wondered where *he* stood. "With Her Highness, the Infanta Isabel. Where else should I stand?"

The bishop gave a little nod. "And Her Highness? Will she support Spinola in his war against the United Provinces?"

"With half a heart."

"The half that sees her Flemish bankers growing richer at the expense of the Dutch?"

The waters were getting too muddy. Rubens sought to extricate himself. "I'm not Her Highness' confidant, *monseigneur.* I'm not on the Privy Council. My opinion about such a matter would be merest conjecture."

"*My* information is that you're soon to become a member of the Privy Council."

It was, Pieter Paul knew, quite wrong for him to show amazement, but he couldn't help himself. His jaw fell. He grinned disarmingly. "Then you're better informed than anyone *I* know, *monseigneur,* or badly misinformed."

239

"I'm *better* informed, *maître*, I can promise you. It's how I stay alive."

The bishop and the painter strode off briskly in the wake of the queen mother and her attendants, who had by this time returned to the central hall. Richelieu approached her, knelt humbly, and rose only at her signal. "Maître Rubens appears to understand perfectly the nature of the task, *madame*."

"The money," said Maria de' Medici. "Have you discussed the question of the money?" She addressed herself now to the artist, who duly genuflected. "How much is the first series going to cost me, *maître*?"

"It's an enormous undertaking, *signora*," he replied defensively, still on his knees.

"I didn't select you because I imagined you'd do the work cheaply." She still refused to allow him to get to his feet.

"I could only give you an approximation of the figure, *signora*. There are many measurements to be made, you understand."

"Well, well, then give me an estimate."

"Twenty thousand *écus*."

The queen mother gasped, and this expression found numerous echoes among her entourage. "Twenty . . . thousand . . . *écus*? Why, in God's name, I could equip a regiment of cavalry and keep it in the field for six months with twenty thousand *écus*."

Pieter Paul, still kneeling, could only bow his head. "I can explain the high cost, *signora*, in terms of time and labor and materials and transport between Antwerp and Paris and the immensity of the paintings you require and the speed with which you ask them of me . . ."

She finally waved him to his feet with an angry, impatient sweep of her chubby hand. "Is there no way of reducing your fee?"

"None, *signora*, except by having to paint fewer pictures."

She shook her large head sharply, causing her jowls to flop recklessly, like a bloodhound's ears. "No, no, I can't have the place looking stark naked. That wouldn't do at all. I'm a

240

Medici." When Rubens allowed an interval to pass without further comment, she said rather gruffly, "How do I know I'll be pleased with the pictures you give me for my twenty thousand *écus?*"

"You can of course reject them if you don't like them, *signora*. I'll make two sets of studies of all of them, so you'll know exactly what to expect."

She studied him for a moment before replying. Rubens knew she was seeking some way of getting a little advantage. "Would you paint my portrait, in addition?"

Pieter Paul bowed. "But gladly, *signora*."

"And would you also paint the portrait of His Majesty and the queen?"

"No painter could ask a greater honor, *signora*."

"All to be included in your price of twenty thousand *écus?*"

Repressing a smile, Rubens bowed again, allowing himself just the intimation of an audible sigh, so she would think she had got the better of him but not that he was protesting. "Yes, *signora*."

"Very well, then," she said with finality. "The Abbé de Saint-Ambroise, my secretary, will arrange the terms of the contract. You will come to me next week and make my portrait. In the meantime, I shall tell His Majesty of your willingness to paint his portrait and the queen's." She dismissed him and Baron de Vicq with a characteristically abrupt gesture of head and hand. They bowed and backed their way out of the great presence.

As they emerged from the Palais du Luxembourg into the watery, wintry light of noon, the ambassador clutched Pieter Paul's arm. "Twenty thousand *écus, maître?* You've asked the earth of her. How did you ever arrive at such a figure? Did you just pull it out of the air?"

"Not at all, *monsieur le Baron*. I was paid ten thousand for my work in Saint Charles Borromeo in Antwerp. My rough guess is that there'll be about twice as much canvas to be covered here, so twice as much ought to be charged for it."

"I had no idea," said the old man with a tremulous shaking

241

of his head. "I'm sure no one had any idea you'd ask so much. I only hope they pay you when it's all done."

Rubens smiled. "I always make an allowance in my price for large commissions, *monsieur le Baron.* I doubt that the queen mother will prove any slower to pay me than the Church."

Though naturally he expressed his gratitude to de Vicq for helping to put this gargantuan commission in his way, only to Nicolas de Fabri did Rubens confess a purely aesthetic delight in the project. "You'll just have to come with me to see," he said. "All that light. All those walls. It must be the finest thing that's ever happened to me."

When asked by his friend for his impression of the Bishop of Luçon, the artist sought a suitable adjective, and ultimately settled for "elusive," which was only partly satisfactory. He was constrained to add, "I suppose that's how I struck *him* too. We were like a pair of wary dogs, sniffing at each other, our ruffs bristling, our ears flared—suspicious, cautious, ready to be hostile but unwilling to be at the same time, not wanting to fight but prepared for it. I don't believe I'd enjoy having him as an adversary."

Richelieu did feel about him as Rubens suspected, and so informed the king when he advised him of Maria de' Medici's plan to have the great Flemish master paint portraits of him and his queen, Anne of Austria. The sickly Louis XIII was bemused by the bishop's troubling to tell him his opinion. Of what possible concern could be the political connections or outlook of a mere artist? Richelieu reminded the monarch, who thought the highly strung cleric overfine in his judgments, that when sitting for a portrait, he just might let slip some observation that could be useful to an enemy. France, as embodied in himself the king, need give her enemies no advantages; they enjoyed too many as things stood.

Louis was not much impressed. He found Rubens charming, which he certainly was, and not at all the devious character depicted by the fretful bishop. As he sketched the features of the frail young king, Pieter Paul pondered without envy the frightening burden that was borne by one whose authority could

242

be as great or as modest as his nature and circumstances allowed, an obligation made particularly onerous because so many of the circumstances were beyond French control.

When compared with the fierce, arrogant Vincenzo Gonzaga, or the gently firm Archduke Albrecht, or even the foolish but physically regal Philip III, Louis XIII seemed not to possess the attributes of kingliness. He was said to be, like the last of the Valois monarchs, a homosexual, and the artist acknowledged to himself that the repugnance this inspired in him may have distorted his appraisal of the man. As Fabri put it, "Sexual promiscuity is hardly more of a sin between people of the same gender than between men and women. I don't think His Majesty will menace us with war over his love for a *man*. That's more than can be said for his father, whom we're pleased to describe as 'normal.'" There seemed no answer to this but silent agreement.

Pieter Paul found it, all the same, difficult to infuse his painting with an aura of royalty, of power. Clothes might make the man, but they didn't make a monarch. He knew his subject was not prepared to relax in his presence. What Louis wanted was an "official" portrait, one in which as much attention was given to the details of the royal robes as to the narrow, anguished features of an infirm young man in his twenty-first year. It was an admirable likeness, the sallow face made luminous, as was Rubens' custom; but like all his formal portraiture, it gave its author no pleasure. Nevertheless, Louis himself was so pleased with this painting and the companion piece of his rather withdrawn little Spanish queen that before Pieter Paul returned to Antwerp, he received a second commission, to paint a series of cartoons of scenes from the life of the great Roman emperor Constantine to serve as models for Gobelin tapestries eventually to be presented to the pope.

The six weeks of Rubens' first visit to Paris were from every professional standpoint a total success. The portraits he so deplored were universally acclaimed. Maria de' Medici was even delighted by a little painting of dancing shepherds and shepherdesses that Pieter Paul made for her amusement in half an

243

hour, after one of her sittings with him. "It's a wonder," she said again and again, amazed by his celerity and skill. "In only thirty minutes, he makes before my eyes a little masterpiece." This trivial picture did much more for Rubens' reputation in Paris than his portraits—for it smacked of prodigy, and thus was fodder for the kind of gossip on which *le tout Paris* nourished itself.

He was glad to be back in Antwerp, despite the vile, icy winds of late February that blew in over the city from the estuary of the still-blockaded Scheldt. Everyone welcomed him. Everyone sought news of Paris. Isabella wanted to know how greatly Maria de' Medici had changed since Pieter Paul's preview sight of her in 1600—for she had always enjoyed her husband's vividly embellished account of the Florentine wedding. Jan Brandt and Nicolas Rockox were eager for information about Richelieu in particular and, more generally, about the internal political struggles of France whose ferocity made them a topic of interest all over Europe. Suzanne Fourment, to whom he made cautious afternoon visits, always with her new husband present, inquired about the fashions now being worn by the great ladies of the French capital—for Paris had by now come into its own as the fountainhead of that particular luxury. Only the painter's three children expressed no special fascination for what their father had seen or accomplished in Paris; they were simply enchanted to have him home again. The warmth of their greeting touched him most of all.

Balthasar Moretus had news of his own to convey. In the artist's absence, he had received from Italy the text of a book dealing with the contemporary architecture of Genoa, a manuscript he had long awaited. His plan to print it, along with illustrations based on Pieter Paul's drawings of the palaces and churches of that city made more than a decade before, would soon be realized. However, work he had done so long ago stirred Rubens very little now. He was utterly involved in the production of twenty-one grisaille studies, with which he would return to Paris in the spring, to present for the approval of Maria de' Medici. And while time was of the essence in this most ambitious commission he had ever received, so too was quality. This was precisely the kind of painting he had long known he did best—canvases on the largest possible scale, permitting him a range and scope not accorded him even in Saint Charles Borromeo. For in the Luxembourg, he could deploy his fertile imagination to the fullest degree, following most liberally Richelieu's enigmatic injunction that he make his allegories as obscure as possible. Nor was this the only current urgency. The order from Louis XIII for tapestry cartoons would also occupy the back of his mind—though he planned to make no immediate effort even to sketch this lesser project until he had completed the studies for the Luxembourg.

There were more than the usual interruptions in these spring months of 1622. Anton van Dyck had returned from London during his former master's visit abroad. The young painter was full of bitterest disillusionment. Pieter Paul's surmise about his fate in the British capital had been correct—but for the wrong reasons. Contrary to what he had imagined, it wasn't the Catholic connection of the Earl and Countess of Arundel that had prevented van Dyck from establishing himself at the court of James I—for the Howards had seen the political error of their ways and been converted to Anglicanism. Rather was it the presence in London of an inferior Flemish painter, Daniel Mytens, who feared the intrusion of one so sprightly, young, and comely, one so swift and skilled, upon a preserve so long exclusively his own. Mytens poisoned van Dyck's name at court before his presentation to the gouty king, with the result that James I was so ill-disposed to Anton that their single meeting was icy, and without happy issue.

It was van Dyck's plan to set himself up in Antwerp. He solicited, with an arrogance Rubens found amusing (and Isabella thought scandalous), any portrait commission that his former teacher was unable or unwilling to undertake. Pieter Paul believed the young man's project a mistake. "You're young, Anton. Go to Italy before you find yourself encumbered by a wife and children. It will help your reputation if you decide eventually to come back to Flanders, and in any case it will give you a chance to *see*. It will broaden you, stimulate you, and perhaps even give you a bit of inspiration. You need that."

Van Dyck misconstrued the motives of Pieter Paul's counsel, taking it to be based on apprehension or jealousy. "He doesn't want me here competing with him," he told his contemporaries. But his accusations wholly missed their mark, because even had they been founded, Rubens was impervious to them, and almost everyone in Antwerp knew them to be false. Only Lucas Vorsterman, an engraver whose relations with the master had been made stormy by Vorsterman's derangement, shared van Dyck's conviction. To discover as one's solitary ally a man generally conceded to be mad wasn't very encouraging. Finally, van Dyck reluctantly agreed to set out for Italy. He departed from Antwerp in April, but initially got no farther than a provincial Flemish town where, quite in character, he became intricately involved with a pretty young matron whose attractions delayed his progress south by several months.

The defection of Lucas Vorsterman, who had for four years been Balthasar Moretus' principal etcher and a frequent visitor to Rubens' studio, complicated the already difficult problem of obtaining patents for engravings sent to foreign cities. While trying to complete the studies for the Luxembourg, Pieter Paul had as well to communicate with his and Balthasar's agents abroad about the question of submitting proofs, which alone could be the basis for securing copyrights. Among these representatives was Pieter van Veen, a lawyer at The Hague and the younger brother of the painter's second *Anversois* master, the pompous Octave.

Most momentous of the interruptions was a summons received in early May from the Infanta Isabel. He was to come at once to Brussels. Rubens had told Jan Brandt and his other close friends of Richelieu's prediction that he was soon to be made a privy councillor; all were intrigued, but none had heard a word of such a designation. It seemed to them as extraordinary as it did to Pieter Paul himself that a Frenchman

246

should possess such an intelligence system in a land where the interests of France appeared minimal. This appraisal was, of course, to underestimate the cardinal's acumen and his breadth of concern. For the Flemish counties of Artois and Picardie were just as susceptible of attachment to France, because of their ancient affiliation with the French duchy of Burgundy, as to the Netherlands.

When Pieter Paul flung himself at the feet of the widowed regent, she urged him to rise at once and take a chair beside her. "We've known each other too long and too happily, Maître Rubens, to abide more than the appearance of ceremony. I need your help. You must go to The Hague and do your best to persuade Prince Mauritz to give up his futile struggle for independence."

It was a matter of some delicacy for the artist to assent to the principle of the infanta's request and, at the same time, to decline this specific assignment. In consonance with his habit and temperament, he attacked the problem affirmatively. "I should be delighted, Highness, to do as you ask, and will of course go where you think it wisest. But I wonder if I can't be of greater service to you in France at this time. I have important connections there. At The Hague, I know only Pieter van Veen, who isn't the most significant figure."

The regent appreciated Rubens' finesse, but she was not deceived. "You mean that you have obligations which would take you to Paris in the normal course of things, and nothing that would otherwise prompt you to make a visit to The Hague."

"That, certainly, Highness. I'm to be in Paris in a fortnight's time."

The infanta sighed. "Well, I shan't stand in your way. But as you know, Baron de Vicq already represents us perfectly well in Paris. I shall have to find someone else to go to the United Provinces . . . Would you, however, when you return to Flanders, consider joining my Privy Council? My late husband spoke well of your wisdom in worldly matters. I confess to you, *maître,* that I sometimes feel very helpless in the face of all the stresses that are being placed on me."

Rubens could only acknowledge that the world was in a more than usually parlous condition. "But if you think my advice would be of the least assistance to you, Highness, I should be honored to serve." He frowned as he continued. "I do think I should tell you that the Bishop of Luçon, Monsieur de Richelieu, seems inordinately well advised about your intentions, Highness. He told me in January that you were planning to ask me to become a member of the Council."

The great lady clasped her hands together and rocked back and forth uneasily. "Yes, yes, I know. There are spies everywhere, everywhere. I don't know what to do about it. Have you any suggestions?"

"Could you guess who might be interested in giving such information to the bishop's agents?"

"Anyone, anyone, for a handful of gold or a promise of betterment. You know what people are like, *maître,* better than I do. How can I tell?"

"Who knew of your plan, Highness?"

"It was discussed at some length during a meeting of the Council a week or so before Christmas, as I recall."

"And approved?"

She nodded. "Yes, pending your agreement, of course . . . You're surely not suggesting that one of my present councillors is in the pay of Richelieu?"

"Ah no, Highness . . . But naturally there could have been an indiscreet remark made in the presence of a servant, or something of the sort. Who can say? There are wheels within wheels."

"Are there *not?*" was the lady's rhetorical reply. "I find that my poor head spins with them."

Rubens took leave of the infanta with the understanding that he would be named to the Privy Council as soon as permission for his appointment, together with a patent raising him to the nobility, were received from Madrid. There was a certain giddiness among family and friends in Antwerp when they learned of Pieter Paul's impending elevation. He, however, kept his head. "It hasn't happened yet," he told his father-in-law. But he couldn't help agreeing that there seemed no reason to suppose anything would occur to prevent it.

"And you told me," said Jan Brandt, "that you didn't care about becoming a member of the nobility."

"I don't," protested Rubens. "But it appears that one must be, by definition, a 'gentleman,' in order to be a member of the Council. And I presume that this rule applies to being an official emissary."

"It's fine, all the same," said Brandt. "You mustn't think I disapprove. I'm delighted."

"All the same," the artist parried, "I'd prefer to be ennobled for my art than for my political wisdom, if I have any."

"Who ever heard of such a thing?"

No one had.

A hurried trip to Paris at the end of May produced a response of almost embarrassing enthusiasm for the grisaille studies of the projected Luxembourg canvases—and a staggering demand that the finished works must be in place by May of 1625, only three years from now. Pieter Paul returned to the French capital once more in this year, at the end of November, to submit for the king's pleasure the tapestry cartoons he had commissioned. These too were well received, as were some full-color *modelli* of the Luxembourg paintings.

Baron de Vicq had died the previous September, and for a time the Infanta Isabel trifled with the idea of naming Rubens to replace him, a notion in which she was much encouraged by the reports of Maria de' Medici's reaction to the painter as well as to his work. The queen mother had twice suggested that Pieter Paul become chief painter to her little court—an invitation which he had politely but firmly rejected. When he was informed by Fabri (who professed to have heard it directly from the lips of Richelieu) of the infanta's proposal, Rubens hastily returned to the Low Countries, pausing in Antwerp only long enough to exchange embraces with his loved ones and discard dispensable baggage before proceeding immediately to Brussels

249

where, once again, he knelt before the regent and implored her not to designate him as de Vicq's successor.

"It seems to me, *maître*, that only a few months ago you were telling me how useful you thought you could be to me in Paris. Now, when I think of offering you the opportunity of proving it, you ask me yet again to spare you. Are you truly interested in serving me or not?"

"I think I can be of greater utility to you, Highness, as a sort of rover than as one attached permanently to one spot."

"You're too attached to one spot already, to your fine house in Antwerp."

"And to my wife and children and my friends. Yes, Highness, perhaps."

"To one who has never been blessed with children, *maître*, that argument strikes me as indelicate, if not underhanded."

"I promise you I didn't so intend it, Highness. I was simply confessing to a certain selfishness."

"These aren't times for selfishness, *maître*. We must do everything in our power to prevent this ghastly war from going on."

Nevertheless, the infanta relented one more time. She wouldn't press him into her service against his will. Moreover, the letters patent for his ennoblement had yet to arrive from Spain. She agreed with Pieter Paul that his father-in-law, who had eminent friendships among the Protestants of the United Provinces, would be an excellent substitute in any negotiations that might be arranged at The Hague in the immediate future.

Jan Brandt was angry over this proposal. "You presumed," he warmly informed Pieter Paul, his asperity remarkable. "You had no right to do that. You imagine yourself the only one with important things to do?"

"Forgive me, Jan. I thought you'd be proud."

"Of course I'm proud. But it gives me a little pause to think of myself as merely a replacement for my son-in-law."

"But that's not the way it's been put at all. I didn't propose your name as someone who was second-best. I said you were more qualified than I by far."

"That was presumptuous of you too. I admit your credentials

250

as an artist, but I certainly don't think you the greatest living authority on our relations with the United Provinces."

Rubens stared at his beloved father-in-law with consternation. "What have I done to make you so furious with me, Jan?" he asked plaintively. "How have I injured you?" There were tears in his eyes—something so rare that Brandt was incredulous.

"You're asking me to act as bargaining agent on behalf of the Netherlands with my own relations on the opposite side. Don't you see? You've put me in the middle of a dispute I want no part of." He suddenly gave way to tears himself. "Oh, I know you meant well, Pieter Paul. Forgive me for allowing you to imagine I thought anything else. But you'll just have to get me out of this. The position is impossible."

Rubens made a quick return to Brussels and managed, with difficulty, to explain Jan Brandt's dilemma. Before he could do anything else, however, he was flattened. On January 23, 1623, Clara Serena Rubens, still in her twelfth year, succumbed to the winter's chill. It was not to be credited. Her slim little body had been unable to resist the attack of infection. Her brave spirit had prevented her from telling anyone of her illness until she was beyond earthly salvation. Stunned, Pieter Paul stood for hours after the funeral in the room of his commodious house where his most recent portrait of his dead daughter was hung. He studied it fixedly, as if by this contemplation he could restore the sweet creature to this life.

Isabella, equally devastated, reacted differently. "She'll always live there," she told her husband softly. "And we can't stop living."

"Why not?" he asked. "Where are we going that's so very important?"

She embraced him gently, startled that so worldly, so easygoing a nature as Pieter Paul's should prove so vulnerable to such a commonplace occurrence as death—albeit of his cherished Clarissima. "Clara is with Our Lord. We're still here, still together."

He responded to her embrace with unexpected ardor. "Just

so. Just so. And we have to stay together from now on. I shall go nowhere."

She pushed him a little away from her. "No, I think that would be a mistake for you. I think you *should* go away. You have those paintings for Paris. Travel will be good for you, will change your ideas."

"And you?"

Isabella shrugged. "I'll be all right . . . You think me heartless for saying that?"

"I know better. But I hate to leave you at a time like this."

"I'll miss you. I've missed you every moment you've been away. But somehow, I can't say why, a woman deals more rationally with matters like agony and death than a man does. Perhaps it's just that we're always a little closer to them. Men flirt with these things, I suppose, when they're in battle. It's a game, a terrible kind of game. But women are married to death —just as they're married to birth."

For his own sake, but even more for the sake of Isabella and their two sons, Rubens compelled himself to work once again on the great Luxembourg paintings and found solace in the total absorption and concentration demanded by this immense creation. His intimates marveled that none of his anguish over the death of his daughter showed itself in these vast canvases which evoked feelings of bursting joy.

By the beginning of May he had completed nine of the final paintings. So great were their dimensions that there was no alternative to taking them to Paris; he had no room to store them in his studio. This fourth journey to the French capital was more doleful than the earlier ones. But as Isabella had foreseen so wisely, it proved diverting.

All Paris was laughing over the misguided exploit of George Villiers, Duke of Buckingham, and the young Prince Charles of Wales who had made a visit in fantastic and easily detected disguise to Madrid, once again to consider a marriageable infanta. In the absence of evidence to the contrary, it was assumed in France that the King of England had taken leave of his senses in allowing such a madcap adventure, whose discovery made

252

both the duke and the prince the objects of all Europe's derision. The idea of this extraordinary mission had originated with Buckingham, who had convinced the blindly adoring king of its brilliance. In the outcome, the duke evinced not a hint of bitterness over the laughter he and the heir to the throne of Westminster had provoked.

No one, with the possible exception of Richelieu, properly grasped the profundity of Buckingham's vain stupidity. James I considered the duke to embody all virtues except virtue itself—the personification of wily intelligence, mistaking an invincible self-esteem for wisdom. But as the former Bishop of Luçon, now cardinal, said to Rubens as he had studied with satisfaction the nine enormous paintings that hung in their proper setting in the Palais du Luxembourg, "There is probably not a lesser wit in a greater head than Buckingham's. That's my opinion, *maître*, but I understand why others find it difficult to believe. I find it difficult to believe myself."

Rubens spent only a fortnight in Paris. Soon after his return to the Low Countries, he was summoned yet again to Brussels, and this time he could find no reasonable excuse for declining the regent's demand that he represent her on a mission to The Hague. His appointment to the Privy Council had been ratified by the Duke of Olivares, and the letters patent raising him to the nobility would be confirmed by Philip IV, he was informed, in due course.

He set out on this vital embassy with no light heart. Far more talented and experienced diplomats than he had brushed rudely against the obduracy of Prince Mauritz. When he reached the capital of the United Provinces, he at once sought out Pieter van Veen and solicited his advice. It was not encouraging; the Calvinists were convinced that even a resumption of the truce would be in the interests more of Spain than of the Dutch. Rubens, therefore, had no reason to think he could succeed where his predecessors had failed. However, as the infanta had told him as she sent him on his way, "As long as we keep talking to each other, open warfare is less likely."

In fact, there *was* open warfare, but in the spring and summer months of 1623 it consisted mainly of skirmishes near the unrecognized but well-protected borders between the Spanish Netherlands and the United Provinces. The Dutch were just as unwilling as the Spanish to engage in a full-scale siege or battle. Dutch ships, in the service of Britain or acting in the interests of the United Provinces, were constantly harassing those of Spain and occasionally France. What caused confusion among most Continentals at this time was the problem of who, exactly, was at war with whom, and over what cause—so complex was the system of rivalries, so incredible the multiplicity of issues, most of them appearing insignificant except to those who thought them vital.

Rubens, armed with his diplomatic passport and letters of credence, proceeded in late summer to the handsome, modestly proportioned palace at The Hague where, three-quarters of a century before, the great Emperor Charles V had made a present of all the Netherlands to his dour son, Philip II. Opposite this splendid medieval structure with its Gothic modifications was the smaller and more elegant residence, the Mauritshuis, which Prince Mauritz had caused to be erected for himself within the moats and ramparts of the palace compound. There the special emissary from Brussels first encountered the stalwart who had so long and so successfully pulled the Spanish lion's tail.

Prince Mauritz of Orange and Nassau was not much like the image Rubens had of him in his mind. There were, understandably, no portraits of the man on public display in the Netherlands, where he was officially classified as comparable in malevolence only to Lucifer and his agents, Martin Luther and John Calvin. He was short, inclining to fat, certainly neither the white nor the black knight of chivalric legend. He looked, Pieter Paul later said to his father-in-law, like a jumped-up Dutch or Flemish burgher—all bluff and hearty, "but with a nasty tongue in his head."

To the nastiness of the princely tongue Rubens made no reference in his official reports to the Privy Council at Brussels. Having accepted Rubens' credentials, Prince Mauritz studied

254

them with much more than casual interest. Then, as he looked down upon the kneeling ambassador, he mumbled in a deep register, "Rubens? Rubens?" He ordered his visitor to rise, then repeated his name several more times, musingly. "That means *something* to me. I can't make it out."

"You may have seen a painting from my hand, Highness. There are some in your country, I believe, and engravings of them are quite common."

The prince dismissed such an idea with an expression that required no accompanying words to demonstrate how implausible it was. He twisted his luxuriant gray mustachios, still murmuring the artist's name. Then his eyes brightened, his face cleared—and as abruptly darkened. "By God, I *knew* that I knew your name. It was your *father* who fucked my *mother,* wasn't it, in Westphalia years ago?" He broke into a great thunder of laughter. "Is that the piece they sent you here to discuss with me?" His jest reduced the great soldier of Calvinism to a paroxysm of hilarity. When he finally recovered, he seemed surprised that Pieter Paul's features had registered no change. "Well, what do you have to say for yourself?"

"About my father, Highness, or about the peace we seek?"

The stadholder's puffy face turned dour. "You don't think it's funny, Rubens, our meeting in this way? Give it a little more consideration. But for the grace of God, you and I could be related."

"Just rumors, Highness."

"*Rumors?*" Had the wooden coffers of the fine ceiling been less securely fixed, they would have collapsed at the roar of the prince's voice. "Rumors? Why, Rubens, I've known about your father and my mother since the moment they were found out." He contemplated the artist with interest. "Do I understand you to suggest that you've never heard the true story?"

Somewhat falteringly, Pieter Paul had to confess that he had never been told of the exact circumstances of his father's disgrace—though of course, from Maria Piepelinx's countless allusions, he had recognized them to be much more serious than she had admitted. Prince Mauritz recounted the events in great and relished detail. He concluded, "Your papa was a very naughty *échevin.*"

The artist grinned, and wasn't altogether certain whether he was moved more by pride or by chagrin—though the former emotion seemed to predominate. In any event, the prince appeared to bear him no grudge for Jan Rubens' peccadillo. "But as to this peace," he resumed, "we really have nothing of importance to say to each other. We must be realistic, Rubens. I respect your lady, the Infanta Isabel. If she had her way, I know she'd be content with at least a truce. But her hands are tied. If I thought she could do anything to ease the terms Spain wants to impose on us, I'd be only too happy to discuss the question with her—with you. But *you* know and *I* know that the issues between us are going to be decided either in Madrid or on a field of battle. There can be no middle ground because Olivares and His Most Catholic Majesty won't allow it."

Pieter Paul Rubens' first diplomatic mission was a total failure. He could see no useful purpose to be served by debating with a man whose viewpoint he essentially shared. The only success he enjoyed during his visit to The Hague was personal—a commission, conveyed to him by Sir Dudley Carleton, to paint a self-portrait for the Prince of Wales, a request that touched him, for the British ambassador said that the future King of England was a great admirer of Rubens' work, adding correctly that he was as well Europe's most discerning royal collector of art.

From the moment of his departure for The Hague, Rubens found himself harried as never before. Like the Infanta Isabel, to whom he had become principal adviser and chief of her Privy Council, his head spun with matters to which he had previously paid little or no attention. To the perpetual abrasions between and among foreign powers that he *had* paid some attention to were added questions of a purely domestic nature—trade, taxes, transport, and the querulous demands of special interests. Though the day-to-day functioning of government was

256

left to the hands of a chancellor in Brussels, Pieter Paul was repeatedly beset by petitioners even in Antwerp, men and women whom he had never met or heard of, seeking favors and indulgences largely beyond his competence or desire to grant. Soon after his appointment to the council was made public, he abandoned his practice of going for a walk or a ride on horseback each afternoon when his day's work in the studio was done. Too many people chose this time to importune him. "My privacy is ruined," he complained to Jan Brandt.

"But you're no longer entitled to privacy," his father-in-law replied. "You're not a private person anymore."

He was officially raised to the nobility in June, 1624, with heraldic ceremony at the regency palace in Brussels. The infanta ascribed to him, in addition to the title given him by Philip IV, the office of "Gentleman of the Household." Barely two months later, in Paris, Louis XIII at last offered Richelieu the recognition he had so long merited; he became the king's first minister in fact—a post to which, in short order, that name was given. Though Pieter Paul had yet to appreciate the thrust of the cardinal's policy, which was primarily aimed at containing and, if possible, reducing the Habsburg hegemony, the painter's growing intimacy with the Habsburg infanta made him suspect in the French capital. Richelieu required no spies to keep him apprised of the closeness of artist and regent; the French ambassador wrote his eminence in August that Pieter Paul Rubens was her most trusted servant.

The new presiding officer of the Netherlands' Privy Council was more interested in Richelieu, however, than Richelieu was in him. Rubens tried to understand the paradox of a Catholic first minister's support for the Protestant cause of the United Provinces. He took it to suggest that, so far as the cardinal was concerned, the enemy of France's enemy was France's friend. This evident indifference to the religious issue made Richelieu's relations at home increasingly difficult, a quite gratuitous development. He needed no exacerbation of problems to make his days pass more rapidly.

He had come to power not because the king loved him; the

king found him loathsome, but saw in the cardinal a superb administrator for a nation where dissidence of every sort prevailed at every level. He saw in him a disinterested politician among throngs intent solely on attaining personal ends, an advocate of *"la seule France"* among nobles who could see no farther than their own property lines.

Rubens, trying to bring some order to his own chaotic thoughts (let quite alone chaotic conditions at home and abroad), was hard put not to conclude that almost every man of authority in Europe, save perhaps Richelieu, was a little bit out of his head. He made an exception of the cardinal because he felt it an obligation to believe that such apparent deviousness could only be the product of a kind of genius. How else to explain France's war against the Habsburgs of the Empire and Spain over the right of access to a mountain pass in Switzerland, a war in which the cardinal set his country against the will of the pope? How else to explain Richelieu's support for the United Provinces who were, as best they could, giving comfort and succor to his enemies, the Huguenots of France? How else to explain French willingness to discuss a marriage between the Princess Henriette Marie and the Prince of Wales, while opposing Britain's European aims in general and especially her desire to put a Protestant on the throne of the Palatinate? How else, finally, to explain Richelieu's simultaneous toleration of the Huguenot faith in his own land and his resolve to repress the Huguenots' political influence? If the cardinal were not a genius, then he must be the most dangerous of all the madmen at large in Europe's courts.

There were many in France, though they were fortunately unable to harmonize their views about anything else, who were united in the belief that Richelieu was dangerously mad. Only the cardinal's intimate friend and confessor, Père Joseph du Tremblay, and the king himself were sure of his sanity and probity. He needed no other props; but he would have lost his soul without the one, his life without the other.

The contradictions of Richelieu's policies were brought home to Rubens very soon after the cardinal's rise to the office of first minister. At the suggestion of Jan Brandt, and strongly seconded by his son-in-law, the Infanta Isabel proposed to the Count-Duke of Olivares a conference of peace between the Netherlands and the United Provinces. The painter-politician was surprised to learn that Prince Mauritz, who only a year before considered such a meeting purposeless, would be willing to attend if the King of Spain had no objection. His amazement was redoubled when approval in principle was forwarded from Madrid. Though it was couched in the most cautious terms, Olivares' letter indicated that he, for the moment at any rate, shared the regent's view that talk was preferable to war.

This did not suggest, however, that war would cease. Ambrogio di Spinola undertook a siege of the border town of Breda, an action designed to make Prince Mauritz's attitudes at the conference table a little more pliable. In Paris Richelieu lodged a strenuous protest with the United Provinces' ambassador, for the possibility of peace in the Low Countries, remote though it certainly was, would strengthen Spanish hands elsewhere. Thus it was clear that the cardinal would do all he could to thwart or delay the peace conference. He was successful in seeing talks postponed at least until the spring of 1625. By that time, a major portion of Europe was on the brink of staggering change.

In January, before leaving for Paris with the remaining dozen canvases for the Luxembourg, Pieter Paul dispatched to London the self-portrait ordered by the Prince of Wales. It seemed peculiarly fitting that this work, in which the artist depicted himself exactly as he was—a gentleman of advancing middle age, saddened but not disheartened by his growing burden of labor and wisdom, should go to Prince Charles at this season. For when Rubens reached Paris with his cargo of huge paintings, the great news was that the Princess Henriette Marie and the Prince of Wales were to be wed in the spring. To make this information the more titillating, it was believed that the prince's father, James I, was near death and that he would not live to meet his daughter-in-law.

Only Richelieu might have offered a satisfactory explanation of the fantastic circumstances leading to this betrothal, predi-

259

cated as it was on lies, deceptions, and a misunderstanding on the part of the British so basic that it would contribute heavily to the future king's fall and execution. But not even Richelieu could have explained the reasoning of Buckingham, who had negotiated this transaction through the Earl of Holland. For Buckingham, so far as could be determined, was not motivated by reason.

The French cardinal, who was rarely baffled by those with whom he dealt and who had already given Pieter Paul his poor view of Buckingham's intelligence, simply couldn't believe the British duke to be even more abysmally endowed than he had imagined. Nor could he comprehend, assuming Buckingham's total fatuity, James I's limitless confidence in this vacuous, arrogant peacock of a man who was fit for work no more taxing than the draining of the Tower's moats.

Richelieu urged Louis XIII to consent to the match between his younger sister and the British prince only on terms that, it seemed to the minister, no sensible King of England could agree to. He was correct. Had James I, who was indeed suffering from an illness that would shortly terminate his life, been fully aware of the conditions set by France he would have refused his assent. What the abjectly trusted Buckingham didn't gloss over hastily, he simply lied about. The marriage contract provided, among other things, the promise that the children of this royal marriage would be raised in the Catholic faith, and, more unthinkable still, there was a secret promise that British Catholics would be allowed to practice their faith without legal hindrance. This clause had been inserted at the instigation of the pope, without whose permission this wedding between Roman and Anglican could not take place at all. In exchange, James I was given by Buckingham to understand, quite erroneously, that France would support a Protestant candidate for the throne of the Palatinate.

When he learned in December of 1624 that the ailing British king had affixed his signature and seal to this document, Richelieu was transfixed with wonder, and certainly suspected that

260

there would be difficulties attendant on the enforcement of all the provisions. In the event, even he did not prove sufficiently skeptical.

The painter from Antwerp, prompted by numerous letters from Maria de' Medici's secretary and from his friend Nicolas de Fabri, arrived in Paris late in February to see to the installation of the remaining pictures in the wing of the Palais du Luxembourg which would, he was promised, be one of the main centers for festivities to mark the royal nuptials. While he was seeing to the framing and hanging of the paintings, Rubens learned that James I had died. The Prince of Wales was king, to be styled Charles I.

It was one of the more memorable springs of the seventeenth century. To spend it in Paris, which was the cockpit (some said the bear pit) of Europe, gave Rubens a further opportunity to improve his imperfect understanding of the Continent's dizzying affairs. When he was attending to his professional business in the Palais du Luxembourg, he could bask in the sunshine of his growing fame as an artist, painting occasional portraits of residents and visitors, meeting the acquaintances he had made, with nothing more serious to mar the pleasant passage of the weeks than the queen mother's complaint that in one of the mammoth paintings he had brought from Antwerp he had illustrated the great lady's departure into exile from the French capital—an event which, however elliptically alluded to, she had no desire to see commemorated in so permanent a fashion.

The artist promptly dazzled his admirers and awed other painters in Paris by producing, in less than a week, a brand new work of identical magnitude devoted to the accomplishments of the epoch when Maria de' Medici had been France's regent. In a letter to Fabri, who was taking his ease on his estate in Provence, Rubens expressed minor annoyance over the necessity of making this alteration. The subject of the original picture had "nothing to do with reasons of state, nor does it apply to any

261

particular person . . . I feel that were I to be looked to and trusted, none of the subjects would have aroused the least scandal or censure."

He *was* looked to, but he wasn't trusted. That did concern him—not as a painter, for his career was in no jeopardy, but as a diplomat. As he well knew, he was attempting to live rather dangerously in his dual role here. The test of his artistic success was not of great interest; but if one career became confused with the other, he might well impair his usefulness to the Netherlands. The approval of Maria de' Medici of his breathtaking paintings in the Luxembourg was less important than that of her son, Louis XIII, who asked for a private viewing prior to the gala opening in May, for which he requested the company of the artist, of Richelieu, and of the queen mother's secretary, Claude Maugin, Abbé de Saint Ambroise.

Rubens decided it would be wise to plead a diplomatic illness. For he was sure that if the king, as seemed inevitable, should ask for explanations of the elaborate allegorical symbolism he had made so free use of in the pictures, he could hardly avoid offending him—for the monarch and his mother, though officially reconciled, were actually leaders, along with the king's bride, Anne of Austria, of camps at bitter political odds with each other. He didn't see that there might be an even greater risk in allowing Richelieu to interpret the works, for, after all, the treatment of the queen mother's career in allegorical terms had been the cardinal's idea in the first place.

The purported ailment which prevented Rubens from joining Louis XIII on his tour of the Luxembourg galleries was gout, an illness that in fact he suffered slightly from. He composed a carefully phrased note to the cardinal, apologizing effusively for the necessity of his absence and swearing solemnly that if he were able to walk even with the aid of canes, his physician would not have prevented him from attending His Majesty.

Some days after the royal tour of the new palace, Pieter Paul received from Richelieu a courteous but terse response, inquiring with measured anxiety after the painter's health and expressing a desire to meet with him when he was sufficiently recovered to call upon him at his cabinet in the Hôtel de Bourbon, just across from the Louvre, where the king resided. An apprehensive Rubens replied at once that he could see His Eminence at any hour convenient to him. He was relieved to learn by return messenger that he might wait on the French first minister the following morning.

"You have created an indubitable masterpiece, Maître Rubens," Richelieu told him as soon as the formal amenities of greeting had been got through.

"I'm overwhelmed with gratitude, Eminence, that you find it so."

"*I* find it so, *maître,* but I fear His Majesty has taken some degree of umbrage." Before Pieter Paul could express his dismay, the cardinal went on, his features bland, his tone slightly placating. "His Majesty doesn't, of course, question your genius. Not even a king seeks to fly in the face of the obvious. It's rather the subject matter that distresses him."

"Ah," said Rubens. "But that could scarcely have come as a surprise to *you,* Eminence. You and I discussed it at some length, if you'll recall."

"Quite, *maître,*" the cardinal said dryly, and appeared inclined, for the moment anyhow, to add nothing to this curt observation.

Pieter Paul had no trouble inferring what he might have said, what he meant to say—that four years before, when the two of them had talked about the theme of the series of pictures, Richelieu had been ostensibly the queen mother's man. Now he was the king's man, to the exclusion of the queen mother. "I'm sorry, Eminence, if the work displeases His Majesty."

As if stirred by some faint flicker of compassion, the austere cardinal allowed an expression of sorrow very briefly to inform his almond-shaped eyes. "It would have been little short of miraculous if His Majesty had been satisfied, *maître.* The subject . . ." The reedy voice trailed off.

"Do I understand that this means His Majesty would not

favor my completion of the work, the paintings for the second wing devoted to the life of his late father?"

Richelieu's reply was so menacingly slow in coming that it was almost not required. "I would not have put it so succinctly, *maître*. He *has* evinced a certain question . . . not, let me tell you again, about your competence. That's not the issue. He asked me, I'm compelled to tell you, whether I could think of some other painter more . . . suitable."

Rubens waited for the minister to drop the second shoe, but prodding was plainly in order, for he failed to continue. "And your reply, Eminence?"

"That as an artist, there was no one in Christendom who could possibly be more suitable than Rubens."

The painter found it a great strain to maintain his equanimity. "That was good of you, Eminence. But . . . ?" he inquired, governing his intonation as best he could.

The thin mouth of the cardinal broadened for a fraction of an instant. It was hardly a smile, but the merest suggestion of one. "*But*, as you say, I agreed that your official ties with the Privy Council of the Netherlands and your affiliation with the queen mother . . ."

It was in this moment that Rubens understood why Richelieu was described as satanic by his plethora of enemies. There was no use in pointing out that until only a few months ago the cardinal himself had been much more closely affiliated with Maria de' Medici and for a far longer period than Pieter Paul Rubens. To quarrel with the cardinal was to quarrel, by extension, with the King of France. The matter of whether or not Rubens would be invited to complete the Luxembourg commission was secondary to the maintenance of more or less tidy relations between France and the Netherlands. A less devoted patriot or a painter in less prosperous circumstances would have remonstrated with Richelieu. Pieter Paul Rubens just smiled. "I see," he said, very quietly.

His mild reaction appeared to discomfit the cardinal, who raised his high, arched brows in tentative wonder. "I have somehow amused you, *maître*? I have said something funny?"

"The smile, Eminence, was simply one of admiration. You've succeeded in telling me absolutely everything without telling me anything."

"May I then correctly infer that you bear us no ill will—as an artist and as, so to speak, an official representative of your government?"

"I should far prefer, Eminence, that you and I not confuse my two careers. What we're speaking of at the moment has solely to do with me personally, as an artist. And as an artist, I don't feel I have the *right* to any ill will. His Majesty is free to select any master he wishes. That seems to me to go without saying . . . I confess, however, to a faint curiosity about the master he eventually chooses."

"The name of Cesari, Giuseppe Cesari, did come up," Richelieu responded with some diffidence, for he recognized that he was now on ground that was treacherous for *him*.

"*Cesari?*" murmured Rubens, who believed he knew by name every Italian painter of repute. "Cesari?" he repeated. "*Il Cavaliere d'Arpino?*" he exclaimed.

The cardinal gave him a little nod of affirmation. "I think he's also known by that title. You're familiar with him, then, *maître?*"

Pieter Paul grinned. "We met in Rome, Eminence, many years ago. He's a lot older than I. I'm glad to hear he's still among us. He has the distinction of being one of the few men to survive unscathed a duel with Caravaggio."

"I hope," said Richelieu with some acerbity, "that you don't find that to be his only distinction."

"I confess, Eminence, that I've forgotten how his work appeared to me. It was so long ago that I saw it. I *can* tell you that the occasion for his quarrel with Caravaggio was his painting. Caravaggio made his disdain for it very clear."

"You hold Caravaggio's work in esteem, then?"

"The noblest Roman, Eminence, and perhaps the last of great quality. Rome can no longer compete with Paris and London and Madrid for great painters."

"And Antwerp?"

Rubens smiled sadly. "I am *from* Antwerp, Eminence. I merely returned home. I do not compete. If my services are required, I furnish them, but I stopped *seeking* commissions years ago. I stopped seeking anything but tranquillity for myself and peace for my country."

"Those desires may be mutually exclusive, *maître.*"

"They may *be*, Eminence. I hope not. But to the question at hand, let me advise His Majesty, through you, not to employ a man too old to finish the task in the Luxembourg. Homogeneity of style as well as theme is essential."

"I've no doubt, *maître*, that His Majesty will do what he thinks proper."

"No doubt, Eminence." Pieter Paul started to rise; there appeared nothing more to be said. That anyone, even a king and cardinal who professed to know nothing about art, should dream of d'Arpino as the man to complete a work Rubens had so superbly begun was more than a supremely gifted artist, however diplomatic his turn of mind, could abide. But Richelieu indicated with a sudden, darting gesture of his index finger that there was more to be said.

"I wouldn't want you to leave, *maître*, without my congratulations on your appointment to the Privy Council. That is an honor."

"It is, Eminence," Rubens replied, and tried to make an abrupt shift in outlook, to become an ambassador instead of a painter.

"I'm sure the confidence in your second talent is as merited as confidence in your first."

"I hope so, Eminence."

"And the plans for the conference of peace go forward unabated?"

"One hopes, Eminence, that nothing or no one will impede them. Our little country has had almost sixty years of war."

"But war, *maître*, is man's natural condition, don't you think? Why else should we breed mindless noblemen and such an abundance of peasant babies?"

Pieter Paul studied the cardinal with great attention. Could

266

he possibly mean that? "I have a quite different view, Eminence . . . I'm disappointed to hear a man of God exalting violence."

"Did I exalt it? I merely called it man's natural condition. And surely I'm not alone in my opinion. Doesn't your lady sovereign endorse the siege of Breda?" There was a glint of malice in the canny eyes of Richelieu. "Does she oppose her nephew Philip or her cousin the emperor in this endeavor?"

The painter gave a little shrug of helplessness. "With what force is she to oppose them, Eminence? She's not France, not England. As you well know, Her Highness is a sovereign without real sovereignty. The Netherlands, if I may make so bold, is not unlike the Palatinate. Her Highness, moreover, has no children to serve as hostages to fortune."

"If I interpret your meaning correctly, you're suggesting that this impending marriage between France and Britain has brought with it a compromise over the throne of the Palatinate. You're quite mistaken."

"If *I'm* mistaken, Eminence, so too is most of Europe."

"Most of Europe comprehends many mortals, *maître*. I shall seek only to enlighten *you*. You are mistaken."

The highly unsatisfactory interview terminated thus. Rubens regretted with some bitterness the apparent loss of the opportunity to complete the decorations for the Luxembourg so brilliantly commenced, and he resolved not to allow the matter simply to drop—though he recognized the futility of pursuing it. On principle, he would persist in reminding the court of France of its promise that the entire undertaking should come from his hand. If he achieved nothing more than the occasional disturbance of the consciences of the king and his first minister, it was a purpose well meriting service.

On April 30, 1625, the day before the fateful wedding of France and Britain, Pieter Paul Rubens learned, in a letter from his father-in-law, of Prince Mauritz's death a week earlier. He darkly recalled his exchange with Richelieu about the progress of plans for a conference of peace. The prospects were not a bit improved by the succession to leadership in the United Provinces of Mauritz's younger brother, Prince Frederick Henry of Orange and Nassau, a young man who had a reputation, a talent, and a taste for violence just as strong as his brother's—and who hadn't almost forty years of it behind him to give him much of an appreciation for the virtues of peace.

It was with a sense of mourning and foreboding that the painter took his appointed place outside the west transept portal of Notre-Dame to watch the dark, diminutive Henriette Marie stand on a specially erected platform to take as her husband Charles I, for whom the French Duke de Chevreuse stood as proxy. The wedding could not be solemnized before the high altar of the cathedral because of its mixed nature; the pope refused to allow a Protestant to partake of a Catholic celebration within the confines of a church. Pieter Paul had as well a sense of repetition, remembering his attendance, a quarter of a century before, at a similar ceremony in Florence, when Maria de' Medici had married Henri IV. It was impossible not to wonder how this ill-assorted union would turn out, and equally difficult not to think it a portent of great disaster.

A full month of celebration followed the event. Balls, galas, morning and afternoon receptions, and nocturnal routs succeeded one another endlessly. Only the most resolutely convivial of residents and visitors had the stamina to stay the whole course. Remarkable for his absence, apart from the bridegroom himself, was the principal author of this ill-starred match, George Villiers, Duke of Buckingham. His duties as first minister to his young master in London were said to have detained him. The duke made up for the time and festivities lost. He appeared in Paris at the beginning of the final week of May to bring the adolescent bride back with him to the British capital. He made every effort to dazzle the French court with a display of finery improbably gaudy in its splendor and variety. In the brief period of his visit, he was seen by the public that counted to have made no fewer than twenty-seven changes of clothes, some of the fantasies he affected so ludicrous that only the most

268

disciplined of Parisian fops resisted the temptation to snicker when he made his spectacular entrances.

Slowly and incredulously, the laughter turned to amazement, then to consternation, when it was reliably reported that whatever the impression made by Buckingham on the other members of the court, he had certainly not tickled the risibilities of the queen—or, if he had, she was laughing at him in utter secrecy. From his first presentation to the lonely, neglected Anne of Austria, the duke made no attempt to conceal the fact that he had conceived for her a passion that was boundless. More earthshaking still, this handsome, compact little woman of twenty-four did not overtly reject his ardent pursuit—or not at first.

Whenever Buckingham and the Queen of France found themselves in the same room, he managed to stand or sit at her side—or, even more egregiously, to kneel at her feet. It was a performance that left *le tout Paris* literally reeling. If Buckingham were genuinely enamored of the queen, a notion that *had* to be accepted, since to do anything else was to take him for a lunatic, the queen, though properly raised a Spaniard and a Catholic, appeared to reciprocate demurely, rejecting the grasp of his hands but not his looks of love. Those in her closest confidence knew her to be playing a wicked and perhaps dangerous game. She found the duke repulsive, but this granddaughter of Philip II saw no good reason not to use Buckingham's folly to annoy her husband. She feigned an interest, thus adding fuel to a flame that might one day ravage all of western Europe.

The baffled Rubens, watching this remarkable spectacle from an extremely peripheral position, was suddenly drawn perilously near its vortex. Balthasar Gerbier was a Flemish painter who had spent a year or so as a pupil in Pieter Paul's studio, from which he had departed not a bit improved by the experience. He was now a skulking, furtive, obsequious man in his early thirties, in the service of Buckingham as artist and agent, for both of which tasks he impressed Rubens as without great talent. Gerbier, almost as fanciful in his attire as his bizarre master, called on his former instructor three days after Buckingham's arrival in Paris.

The artist was surprised by Gerbier's appearance and his manner, both so markedly different from those of his student days in Antwerp. They exchanged some pleasant and inconsequential phrases about that portion of the past which they shared. Then the visitor came with some brusqueness to the point. His grace, the duke, required a Rubens portrait. Would the *maître* be good enough to present himself at the residence of the British ambassador the next morning? It was a question in the form of a command, which irritated Pieter Paul, who condescended to no one and didn't at all relish being condescended to. Had Gerbier represented any less lofty or less intriguing a personage, he would have found himself escorted unceremoniously to the door without so much as a word of reply. But he did represent the Duke of Buckingham, and Pieter Paul would never have forgiven himself had he passed up a chance to spend a few hours in the company of this eccentric peer who, according to some of his compatriots, gave evidence of having modeled his dress and his deportment on the collective peculiarities of several extravagant characters created by the late William Shakespeare, a folio edition of whose collected plays and poems had first been published in London two years before.

Since Rubens had no English, and since Shakespeare had yet to be translated into any foreign tongue, he was unable to judge the accuracy of this analysis. But his meeting with Buckingham inclined him to the view that no poet, however audacious, would have dared to imagine a character so richly odd. Yet was the duke truly mad? The answer demanded knowledge that a handful of hours' contact could scarcely offer him. He didn't *seem* mad, if madness connoted aberrations of gesture or conduct, or sentences that refused to cohere.

After the artist and his notorious subject had exhausted the possibilities of casual chatter about acquaintances they shared, which were numerous, and the obvious topic of the recent wedding, described by Buckingham as the most brilliant of

270

modern history, they turned to art. The duke knew from his friendship with Sir Dudley Carleton of Pieter Paul's fine collection of antiquities, and frankly told the artist that he coveted such precious objects. He was knowledgeable, even to the point of volunteering the opinion that if Balthasar Gerbier were merely a painter, he would starve to death. "Fortunately for him, and for *me,* he has greater and more useful attributes." These he chose not to enumerate; Pieter Paul deemed it improper to inquire.

The royal favorite spoke then of a matter close indeed to the painter's heart—the Banqueting House in London's Whitehall which the late James I had ordered Inigo Jones to build for him and which Rubens had often told his English portrait subjects he would be honored to decorate. "After having seen your marvelous work in the Palais du Luxembourg," the duke assured him, "I'm more than ever convinced that no other artist should even be considered for the commission. If you'll allow me, I shall say as much to His Majesty on my return to London."

Mad or not, Buckingham certainly knew how to find and prompt a friendly nerve. Rubens could only respond in kind—the more so since he believed it to be in the interest of the Netherlands. "I think, Your Grace, you should know that France's intentions with respect to the Palatinate may not be all you've been led to hope."

The duke reacted sharply, as if he had been slapped. Then he resumed his pose, and inquired calmly, "Is it impolitic to ask you how you come by such astonishing information, *maître?*"

Rubens recounted the relevant portion of his conversation the month before with Richelieu. "I rather fear," he concluded, "that your king has married the wrong enemy. I hope you'll forgive my putting it so bluntly."

Buckingham seemed not to have heard these final phrases, so absorbed was he with the import of what the cardinal had said to Pieter Paul about the Palatinate. But the moment he spoke, it was plain that he had taken in everything, and without offense. "Which enemy would *you* have proposed for us, *maître?* We have so many to choose from."

"Spain, Your Grace."

"But surely Spain is even more hostile to our policies than France."

"And yet much less powerful, therefore easier to woo, however wild the Spanish rhetoric."

"You say this for a fact?"

"All I can say for a *fact*, Your Grace, is what I told you of my conversation with the cardinal. The rest is simply conjecture, but quite in the logic of the circumstances. If France seeks to use your country against Spain and the Empire, as I'm sure she will, then Spain might be hospitable to the suggestion of a tacit alliance with Britain against France."

"But the question of religion, *maître,* always comes up in our talks with the Spanish. The French are so much more pliable on the subject."

Rubens gave the duke a wry smile. "They *seem* more pliable, Your Grace."

"Why are you telling me these things? Are you not in France's service as an artist?"

"I *was*, Your Grace, but even if I still *were,* as a privy councillor of the Netherlands, I serve a higher interest than my own. It's not necessary to agree with every viewpoint of Spain in order to think the viewpoints of France more dangerous for my little country."

"*That* much I can easily believe." The sitting ended. Buckingham gave the painter a familiar pat on the shoulder. "I shall bear in mind what you said to me, *maître,* and I have ways of demonstrating my gratitude—just as *you* have ways of showing your disillusionment."

The portrait was completed, but the paint was too wet to be varnished, when its subject departed in the direction of Calais with Britain's new queen. Rubens remained in Paris until the picture could be safely rolled and transported to London. During his last days in the French capital came word of low comedy with possible consequences of disaster. On his trip to the Channel, Buckingham had taken a detour to Amiens, where Queen Anne of France was reposing after the vigorous month of festivities in Paris. There he had contrived to elude the watchful eyes of his *inamorata*'s attendants and, in a bedchamber, spent an unspecified length of time alone with her. The reaction inspired at court by this ultimate assault upon the virtue of the sullen Habsburg queen, whose cries had finally summoned help, was of a scandal so beside itself that for all the outraged words spewed forth, none could accommodate the volume or intensity of passionate anger. So even before little Henriette Marie had been joined with her mate, and before Charles I had dissolved Parliament to prevent the impeachment of Buckingham for his hand in the drafting of the detestable marriage contract, France had an emotional *casus belli* which Richelieu would husband jealously and find it useful, before very long, to exploit.

A second catastrophe occurred while Rubens was traveling back to Antwerp. The Dutch border town of Breda, for months beseiged by the obstinate Spinola, finally surrendered to the troops of Spain and, having already suffered all the horrors of privation normal to so prolonged an investment, the citizens of Breda submitted to the appalling indignities of defeat—rapine and pillage on a scale not seen in the Low Countries since the days of the Duke of Alba. Prince Frederick Henry, if he had ever been inclined to discuss peace, abandoned such intentions completely, vowing an equally hideous revenge. The sporadic little war of the past four years might now become another holocaust.

Eight

The fall of Breda, which Rubens learned of as soon as he reached Antwerp, was the occasion for more rejoicing in the Spanish Netherlands than the painter thought either seemly or justified. He spent only a day at home before going to Brussels to report to the Infanta Isabel and the other members of the Privy Council on his conversations with Richelieu and the Duke of Buckingham, and also to express his severe misgivings over what he considered the ill-advised celebrations of the Breda surrender; they were premature, he said. The regent listened attentively to the account of his impressions about French and British foreign policy, instructing him to pass these on at once to the Count-Duke of Olivares in Madrid.

She was particularly distressed by Rubens' prediction that the effect of Breda's fall would be to stiffen the resistance of the United Provinces. It didn't seem sensible to her that so great a defeat should have such a result. He explained, as coherently as he was able, his view that by opening the way to Amsterdam, which was the major military implication of the successful siege, the Spanish troops of Spinola had placed the Dutch in the kind of jeopardy that would cause the French as well as the

British to intercede openly in their behalf. It could, he argued, readily be the case that the United Provinces might turn this disaster more completely to their advantage than a stalemated siege would have made possible. Both the French and the British had a vital interest in maintaining a Dutch fleet on the seas to maraud the shipping of Spain. To that end, they might well subsidize Prince Frederick Henry's army. They would certainly oppose by every means available the conclusion of a peace that brought the United Provinces back into the Habsburg hegemony and would try to abort any conference with that purpose in view.

The poor infanta could only mourn the loss of her husband and, figuratively, throw herself on Rubens' tender ministrations. What, poor woman, was she to do? Pieter Paul acknowledged himself to be as bewildered by events as she. The Netherlands *must* have peace. Spain would have war until her goal of reuniting the Netherlands had been achieved. Policies so inimical were not easily to be reconciled, if reconciliation was feasible. Yet it must be attempted, for the alternative of more desperate battles and protracted sieges on the territory of the Low Countries was intolerable—though he warned his mistress that they might have to be tolerated.

Was he, she asked, for peace at the price of Dutch independence? He was. Did it not seem to him too high a cost? It did not; merely the reopening of Antwerp's harbor to foreign vessels would more than offset the permanent loss of the Dutch ports of whose use the Netherlands had been deprived since the onset of the Spanish Fury almost sixty years before. The Dutch were prospering from the war, from piracy, from colonial expansion in the New World. The Netherlands' economy was merely surviving. What about the religious issue? As to that, the painter-politician replied, it was now so beclouded by even papal cynicism that it made little sense to anyone. He had only to cite the recent marriage between Henriette Marie of France and Charles I of Britain as evidence of the Vatican's willingness to temporize when the pope thought it suited his purpose. The policy of the Netherlands, therefore, should be to seek peace, a general European peace; for only in such conditions was a settlement of the Dutch question likely or even possible. To such a cause he promised to give his full support and his whole heart.

The infanta wavered. A sister of Philip II, that truly Most Catholic King, widow of a man who had not been merely a cardinal but a cardinal with great and abiding faith, she had herself donned the simple garb of the Poor Clares on the death of the Archduke Albrecht and vowed never again to wear any other. In the teeth of advice as cogent as that of Rubens, she held in her soul to the conception of Christendom as it had existed more than a century earlier. She *must* publicly honor Ambrogio di Spinola's victory at Breda in the same festive way it was being commemorated in Spain. She *must* believe in the fundamental wisdom of Olivares' policy, for to believe anything else was implicitly to comfort heresy. The economics, the politics, the military aspects of the *imbroglio* of her country must all be subservient to the crucial and anguishing battle to save men's souls. She consoled herself as best she could with this conviction—that the deaths occasioned by a renewal of active and perpetual hostilities in the Netherlands (if Pieter Paul Rubens' judgment was exact) would be virtuous deaths, provided naturally that those who fell had espoused the True Faith. No medieval crusader was more dedicated than the Infanta Isabel.

Yet the lady wavered. Her heart and her spirit were committed to a continuation of the war. Her mind, which functioned more intermittently than did her emotions, informed her of Rubens' sagacity. She dared not, on impulse, prevent him from seeking peace, even on terms she felt to be theologically irresponsible because she knew her late husband would have shared the painter's opinion. The whole of the Netherlands, north and south, must become a good place in which to live as well as die. Thus divided within herself, the infanta personified the genuinely pious Catholics and Protestants of all Europe. It was hateful and sinful to express a willingness to sup at the same table with the Protestant (or Catholic) devil, especially if one seemed to have him at a disadvantage. But if one used a long spoon . . . ?

This interview was the most trying Rubens had ever had with the regent, and its inconclusive termination left him most disturbed. He was to return to Antwerp. She would consider all he told her and would, she promised, give him her final decision within the next month or so. Dutifully but sorrowfully, Pieter Paul knelt before the lady and, in silence, took his leave of her —all admonitions spent. A very discouraged public figure, he traveled by official coach that late June day to his home and his loved ones.

Yet when he was once again seated with his wife and children, conversing with them about the extravaganzas he had witnessed in Paris, his ministerial worries were rapidly dissipated by the private pleasures of being with family and friends and assistants, of contemplating the accumulation of commissions for pictures that increased in volume each year, reminding him that, though he was a man of state, no one had forgotten that he was a man of art as well. Indeed, his second career added luster to his first. To own a Rubens painting today connoted something more than it had prior to his joining the Privy Council. Orders were now received from the patrons who had learned of Rubens the artist by encountering the name of Rubens the politician.

Jan Brandt, a keen student of such phenomena, thought that his brilliant son-in-law was very probably the richest man in the Low Countries. Certainly, he said by way of qualification, his liquid or immediately liquidable assets were the largest. Brandt's estimate was very near the mark. Never again, until the fame of Pablo Picasso began to approach its apogee on the eve of World War II, would an artist achieve such enormous wealth solely through the sale of his own pictures.

Yet as soon as he had, so to speak, bathed and changed his clothes, Pieter Paul returned to his work as if the past eight weeks of intimate contact with nobility and royalty and heads of governments had never occurred—as if there had been no interruption at all. He took a clean palette, mixed a few colors, and resumed his labors to complete a painting of the Assumption for the high altar of Antwerp's cathedral, a canvas commissioned six years before and allowed to languish, half-finished, while he took up the enormous Luxembourg assignment. So far as anyone, himself included, was able to determine, his energies and powers of total concentration had not been appreciably diminished by the years or been diluted by the new diversity of his occupations. He was, Jan Bruegel said with no less awe today than he had felt on first meeting Rubens, a true wonder of the world, "a man without shadows." That, Bruegel believed, accounted for his capacity to give himself so absolutely to everything he touched.

This might be the case of Pieter Paul the person, even of Pieter Paul the artist. But of Pieter Paul, privy councillor, it was not so. Yet he chose not to disturb the impression that the description could be applied to his entire self. It could enhance his possible usefulness to the state, as he conceived it, for others to imagine him "without shadows" as a negotiator, as a diplomat, as a politician. His contacts, particularly with Richelieu, had richly influenced his notions of statecraft. He thought it excessive to suggest that he had become as devious a character as the cardinal, but he would certainly like to emulate him in this.

Unhappily, as Rubens saw it, such a wish was irrelevant. To be cunning was all very well, provided one also had the means, the instruments of political pressure and physical force to implement one's most cunning schemes. Whatever others perceived in him as a public person, he perceived in himself something remarkably different: a beautiful woman with a speech impediment, a magnificent warhorse with a broken leg, a sublime poet perishing of consumption. The defect, for Rubens the statesman, was his nation's poverty and weakness. He would do all he could to overcome this handicap, assume any posture, travel any distance, use any ruse; but the defect could not be wished away. These shadowy thoughts did not, however, obscure the sunshine that bathed the life of Rubens the husband, the father, the friend, the artist—because he refused to allow it. There was a secret pleasure in this knowledge of himself that he proposed to share with no one. Such was *his* deviousness.

His wife and friends were of course aware that he possessed information that he wasn't at liberty to disclose. With Jan Brandt alone did he feel free to discuss the terrible problems of his country that so disarranged his inner life. His father-in-law's advice was as precious to Pieter Paul as was Pieter Paul's to the infanta. Brandt, moreover, was a useful foil in the debate that Rubens more and more often carried on within his own mind, for Jan had many close relations in the United Provinces, understood far better than he the temper of the people in the north, and offered his opinion of their possible reaction to various ploys that the artist propounded. Both Brandt and Rubens appreciated to what degree they were conversing in a vacuum. Not before the regent made up her mind would the head of her Privy Council know precisely what official line he was to take.

A week after his return from Brussels, Rubens learned that the Infanta Isabel had come to a decision of sorts, whether she fully understood it or not, by her announced intention of paying a state visit to Antwerp in the company of Ambrogio di Spinola, "hero of Breda," on July 10. The *échevins* of the city, all of whom were more or less active proponents of peace with the United Provinces at any price, sadly instructed the military governor of the town to see that the dress uniforms of the local garrison were ready for the occasion, and ordered that the principal streets be appropriately decorated.

The citizens put as brave a face on their indifference to this procession and its occasion as they could manage. Their cheerless expressions and halfhearted cheers didn't deceive the regent. It was not important, however, that *she* be deceived; what mattered was that Spinola be accorded the honors she thought he merited. The major tangible evidence of this modest outpouring of public sentiment was to be a portrait by Pieter Paul Rubens of the man who had driven the devil's agents out of Breda—a commission of which the artist himself was informed only when he offered his official respects to the regent and her general at the Town Hall reception which followed their triumphal entry into Antwerp.

Though he made not the least show of his annoyance as he begged permission to leave the infanta's presence and go to prepare his studio to receive his illustrious and unexpected guests, Rubens was furious—or as furious as he found it easy to be. He deplored the regent's display of approval for Spinola; but that, after all, was ultimately her affair. To implicate *him,* by ordering him to portray the Italian soldier, was quite another matter. He felt his position as potential honest broker between the Netherlands and the United Provinces to have been hopelessly compromised; for every detail of the state visit to Antwerp would be known in The Hague by the next morning.

He bowed gracefully to the inevitable, presented Isabella and his two sons to the infanta and to the Genovese captor of Breda, and engaged his subject's interest by presenting him with a copy of the Plantin Press' edition of the book on the architecture of Genoa which he had illustrated. The two men spoke nostalgically of the general's native city and of the members of his family whom Pieter Paul had portrayed twenty years before. In addition to a number of hasty sketches of Spinola's strong features, the artist made some studies of the regent in her somber conventual robes, and produced, as a result of this little hour's visit, his finest portrait of the Infanta Isabel.

He completed these two pictures with the greatest possible dispatch, for their delivery would give him a legitimate reason to wait on Her Highness and to tell her discreetly that he thought her apparently complete espousal of the Spanish cause a dreadful mistake. He was in Brussels within a week of the state visit to Antwerp. After allowing the infanta to expatiate for several minutes on the splendor of his portrait of Spinola and the dark tenderness with which he had imbued his picture of herself, Rubens came obliquely to the question that was the main object of his journey to the capital.

The lady listened carefully, nodding periodically to indicate

280

that even if she wasn't agreeing with him, she was following his line of argument. When he concluded, she surprised him by reaching for his hand. "You *are* my most faithful servant, *maître*. Dear Albrecht was quite right. When I saw the faces of the people as we rode through Antwerp last week, I realized that no matter what my religious scruples, I must pursue the policy you propose." She was therefore all the more shocked by Rubens' bald assertion that the brief visit of Spinola to his studio had destroyed his usefulness as an emissary to Prince Frederick Henry, at least for the moment. "Whom can I possibly send in your place?" she asked querulously—more angry with herself than with Rubens for telling her an unlikable truth.

"Jan Brandt, Highness. I've discussed it with him. He's the only man I know who's in all ways qualified."

"He must be sent for directly. No more time should be wasted."

Pieter Paul could scarcely have agreed more with his desire for haste. He immediately wrote his father-in-law a note requesting that he come to Brussels to receive his credentials and whatever formal instructions the regent had to give him. In total contrast to his anger with Rubens of an earlier year, Brandt was elated to have this command—for, as the painter had indicated to the infanta, the two men had considered at some length the possibility of the mission, and they had jointly concluded that if any solution short of a resumption of the war was to be achieved, it must be sought now, before Prince Frederick Henry had a chance to gather funds and arms and forces to respond to the Spanish threat to the very heart of the United Provinces—Amsterdam. After cordial but hurried consultations with Rubens and the Infanta Isabel, Jan Brandt set out for The Hague in the last week of July. Pieter Paul accompanied his father-in-law as far as Antwerp, and saw him on his way.

It was just in this most hectic time that nature saw fit to intervene. Hardly had Brandt reached the Dutch capital than he received word from Rubens that regardless of the prognosis or

281

outcome of his talks, he should remain there until further notice. The day after his departure, Antwerp had been visited by
the plague.

The plague that invaded the coastal and harbor towns of the
Low Countries during the late summer of 1625 did not consti-
tute a major epidemic, but no one could know this *a priori*. Im-
bedded profoundly in the folk memory were horrific tales of the
pandemic of the final three-quarters of the fourteenth century
—the Black Death which had carried away as many as
25,000,000 souls, one-fourth of the Continent's population, before it had run its full, terrible course. Every subsequent outbreak, which seemed spontaneous because nobody then
understood from whence it had come, prompted hysterical reaction, especially among the urban poor, who existed in crowded
hovels and thus were easier prey to the agents of this horrible
disease—the rat and the flea.

Of the three varieties of the pestilence to manifest themselves
sporadically, bubonic, pneumonic, and septicemic, the last was
the most to be feared because its victim was usually dead within
three or four days of having been infected, before revealing the
obvious symptoms that typified the two other species—swelling
of the lymph glands or congestion of the lungs. An epidemic of
the plague was more frightening to the *Anversois* by far than
either war or famine; for the enemy couldn't be seen, and it
was not in the least selective. There was no certain defense
against it—though the instinct to flee, to which Pieter Paul Rubens responded without hesitation, was as sound a method as
any.

Immediately after sending word to his father-in-law to stay at
The Hague, Rubens made arrangements to evacuate his family,
his assistants, and his entire household staff to a country house
at Laeken, not far from Brussels, where they resided for seven
months, all their days particularly prayerful—since God was
thought to be the author of this appalling threat to their lives.
The proximity to the capital was no accident. However appre-

282

hensive for the safety of his loved ones, the artist wanted to remain in close touch with the regent, to keep her resolute in her determination to solicit peace. At the end of August, he was able to write Jan Brandt that she appeared as firm as ever in her desire to follow the course they had set for her.

Time was a factor operating powerfully against the interests of the Netherlands. Brandt replied to his son-in-law by return that he had just learned of France's decision to come to the aid of the United Provinces with the promise of an annual subvention of a million florins, a sum that would arm and maintain a substantial number of troops and/or ships. Richelieu's subsidy was meant to be a secret, because at the very moment when he was offering it to Prince Frederick Henry, he was beginning negotiations for a treaty of peace with Spain.

Pieter Paul imagined that he could see in this apparent contradiction a treachery which might be put to his own country's use. He advised the Infanta Isabel to go to Dunkerque with him to confer with Balthasar Gerbier, Buckingham's agent, over the possibility of preventing British assistance from reaching the United Provinces. What he hoped to prove to his former pupil was the folly of a plan which would, because of this new French intervention and the cardinal's simultaneous treatment with Spain, have the effect of giving aid to a Spanish ally.

The meeting with Gerbier on the Channel coast was unavailing. Buckingham's Flemish aide was friendliness itself, but he told the infanta and her councillor that for Charles I to withhold support from the Dutch would imperil his domestic position beyond a tolerable point. Already his Parliament was in an uproar over the French marriage and all that this implied by way of accommodation to the despised native Catholics and to the Catholic French. To compound a felony by defecting from the cause of the Protestants of the United Provinces would certainly seal Buckingham's fate and perhaps the king's as well. The situation was just that serious, he swore—and truly. This dismal assurance did not, however, preclude the possibility of further discussion. The Duke of Buckingham was contemplating a visit to The Hague in November and might hospitably entertain the idea of a pause in the Netherlands on the way. With no more hopeful option at hand, Rubens urged Gerbier to extend an invitation to His Grace to be his guest should he decide to come to Antwerp.

The duke arrived with his Flemish accomplice to find the great Rubens establishment all but deserted. Only the master was present. For though it appeared that the pestilence had subsided, Pieter Paul, with the death of his little Clara still vivid in his recollection, would allow no unnecessary risk. Buckingham declared that he understood perfectly, but evinced polite regret at not having an opportunity to meet the wife and sons of the artist he so admired.

It was a considerably subdued George Villiers whom Rubens showed through his house and rotunda and studio. The duke, evidently deeming it advisable to dress himself in the black which was affected by the men of the Low Countries, presented an appearance of uncommon sobriety. An alternative explanation may have been the calamitous failure of a British naval assault against the Spanish port of Cádiz the month before, a humiliation that threatened the British first minister's career and perhaps even his life. Cádiz was not discussed.

The artist repeatedly attempted to draw Villiers out on the subject of British relations with the United Provinces, but his guest refused to permit it, each time cleverly turning the conversation back to Pieter Paul's magnificent collection of antiquities, or to the paintings, finished and unfinished, that hung in the studio. The duke averred that he had spoken with Charles I "at length" about the possibility of Rubens' being invited to London to view Inigo Jones' Banqueting House and to offer his opinions about its interior decoration.

Buckingham came back, again and again, during the hours he spent with the painter, to the marble sculptures which Rubens had acquired from Sir Dudley Carleton. "I want them," he said. "I'll pay any price to have them." As politely as he was able, his host expressed himself as vastly flattered that the duke

284

so admired his treasures, but there could be no question whatever of his parting with them.

"The house would be stark naked without them, Your Grace," he protested.

"We'll see," said Villiers as he made ready to leave for the United Provinces.

Jan Brandt informed the painter that the British first minister was not in The Hague more than two days before he signed a protocol in which he committed Charles I to aid the Dutch very materially and to allow their ships free access to all British Channel and North Sea ports, There was also a secret provision (to which Brandt was not privy, but one he easily and accurately surmised) promising naval action against certain Spanish harbors, attacks that would, both the duke and the Dutch hoped, be more effective than the recent *débâcle* at Cádiz.

Far from heeding Pieter Paul's advice of the previous spring, Buckingham was determined on a plan which must lead him into direct conflict not only with Spain, but with France. Further to complicate the prospects, France and Spain would, by April of the following year, become allies—at least on paper. Britain had chosen, Rubens told his father-in-law on the latter's return from The Hague, a collision course.

The Rubens family moved back to Antwerp at the end of February, 1626, certain now that there was no further menace from the plague. As winter turned to spring, the artist devoted himself to his painting, disgusted and disappointed by the insistence of the great powers, and particularly Britain, to do the wrong things for the wrong reasons. He presumed that France was wise and Britain foolish because, while Charles I was summoning and dismissing surly and unruly Parliaments in his efforts at once to raise money and prevent Buckingham's impeachment, Richelieu was pursuing a policy that became more and more intelligible to him. By ordering the destruction of all private family fortresses in France, the cardinal was significantly reducing the capacity of the rebellious aristocrats to resist the authority of the king. If, with this edict, Richelieu failed to destroy the pervasive remnants of feudal political philosophy, its rigorous and impartial enforcement at least made that philosophy ineffectual. With no redoubts to hide behind, provincial nobles were left with two possibilities—obedience or exile. The Huguenots of La Rochelle resisted the cardinal's demand, for they believed that they had everything to lose by accession to it. Richelieu urged them to change their minds, and waited patiently for sweet reason to do its work. He waited in vain.

Rubens, intent solely on keeping all possible avenues to peace open, maintained regular correspondence with friends in France, in the United Provinces, and with Balthasar Gerbier in London. His singlemindedness was touching to those he was in communication with, and to men like Prince Frederick Henry, Richelieu, Olivares, and Buckingham, who were regularly informed of the artist's semi-official viewpoints. But he recognized that there was little hope of his will prevailing against the currents of war which daily grew stronger. It was tragic for one of Europe's sanest and wisest and most sanguine men to stand helplessly by and watch others, presumably as sane as he, commit their manpower, their armaments, and their treasure to war and the danger and horror of reprisal.

Then, with a suddenness that briefly felled his wonderful spirit, none of these great affairs mattered to him in the least. Isabella was dead.

The date was June 20, 1626—Midsummer's Day, a week before Pieter Paul turned forty-nine. The air in the formal garden was trim, sweet with the aroma of lilacs; the borders of tulips and irises and flowering shrubs were in their most brilliant bloom. A few casual clusters of lazy clouds drifted across the tranquil light blue of the Flemish sky. It was a flawless day, the sort of day when Isabella might come to the door of his studio and implore him to step out, for just a little while, to savor the gentleness, the temperateness, the hint of soft voluptuousness in the air. But Isabella was dead.

286

The cause of death was not determined. A physician was summoned when Elsa, Isabella's most devoted servant, reported tearfully to her master that his wife was stretched, inert, across the matrimonial bed. The doctor probed the limp, ashen flesh; he put an ear to the cold bosom, and reported with a seriousness so solemn that it seemed to Rubens all the more fatuous, "Her heart has stopped beating. She is dead." There was no evidence of disease. She had done or been doing nothing particularly strenuous. She had just died.

Sudden death, especially when it is supported by no ready explanation, is like a phrase broken off at midpoint, before its predicate has been stated. One may guess at its meaning, but in itself it lacks comprehensibility. The minds of those bereft may accept the fact, but like an amputee who for a time continues to imagine that the severed member is still attached to his body, their spirits are unable to deal with a reality that cannot be believed, for they are so totally unprepared for it.

It seemed bitterly odd to Pieter Paul that after the initial, stunning blow of this news, he should have rebounded so much more rapidly than he had been able to do after the deaths of Philip or Clara. This was not a matter he could tactfully discuss with anyone else, least of all Jan Brandt. Yet his father-in-law and his other friends couldn't help remarking on the extraordinarily calm purposefulness he displayed, and couldn't help contrasting it with his behavior on comparable previous occasions. The ones who knew him and loved him best were puzzled, for as they looked back on all the outward manifestations of this relationship that had endured for seventeen years, they could discern few troublesome moments, none nearly so deranging as those which had been successfully survived by most other couples of their station. Were there secrets? Were there shadows of which they had been kept in ignorance? It seemed unlikely, but they compelled themselves to stare with fresh eyes at this figure of Pieter Paul Rubens. Was he, then, the man they thought they had known, the man they loved and who, they believed, loved them? His appearance was unchanged. What, then . . . ?

The difference was one that Rubens himself was to decipher only weeks after the event that had shattered the gentle, easy tenor of his domestic life. When he did understand, he was startled by the simplicity of the explanation, and wondered at his own obtuseness. He reacted with such aplomb to Isabella's death because her sudden absence left him responsible for all the mundane tasks that she had charged herself with and accomplished with such serene competence. The head of the house had to become the head of the household. There were, as the most important obligations of all, Albrecht and Nicolas Rubens who must be consoled and cared for. The father must become a mother too.

The boys, at the ages of twelve and eight, tapped Pieter Paul's unsuspected reserves of strength, thereby disclosing to *him* how very strong he could be when the circumstance demanded. They were neither of them yet at the point in life when well-to-do sons normally made the transition of dependence from mother to father. Now there was no choice. Rubens had to become intimate with his children. He was embarrassed and chagrined, for he didn't know how to go about it. It wasn't exactly as strangers that he had hitherto regarded them, but as growing fixtures in his life, part of the furnishings of his house, functioning perfectly well under their mother's watchful eye—flourishing, happy, polite, decorous, dutiful. They were the kind of sons a much-preoccupied father wasn't required to think about very much or very often.

The painter searched for a key, for a method of approach to these boys he was suddenly full master of, and found it, surprisingly, in his own experience. He remembered the sense of uncomprehending bereavement he had felt when his mother told him of Jan Rubens' death. He and Philip had been of approximately the age of Albrecht and Nicolas. Pieter Paul's recollection was relevant because he had always felt much closer to his father than to his mother—just the reverse of his own sons' case. What he himself had wanted most of all in those sorry weeks of exile in 1587, after Jan's death, was tenderness—an embrace, a touch, a contact, a feeling of warmth, a shoulder on which to weep, a voice to say, "I understand . . ." even though such a loss was beyond all understanding. But Maria Piepelinx hadn't known the meaning or value of tenderness; the eternal, bitter anguish of the life she led had hardened her, given her a shell that couldn't be penetrated by such childish needs.

Pieter Paul Rubens brought Albrecht and Nicolas home in his own coach from the funeral of their beloved Isabella, a requiem mass in the Church of Saint Michel where all Rubenses were sent on their way to whatever reward the good God had in store for them. He took the boys to the large, bright chamber which he and their mother had shared. He removed his black felt hat and placed himself on the center of the bed, beckoning his sons to join him there, one on each side. Without a word, they obeyed his signal, and nestled their small faces at his breast. He encompassed them with his arms, stroked their curly heads, and waited patiently for their sobs to begin.

"I understand," he murmured, kissing them in turn, clutching them to him. "I *do* understand."

As word circulated abroad about Isabella's death, Rubens began to receive warm letters from friends and acquaintances, and from those highly placed in foreign governments who expressed their condolences in terms so starched by the usages of protocol that they were more an annoyance than a source of solace. An exception was the Infanta Isabel's sympathetic letter. "I know only too well how you must feel just now, *cher maître,*" she wrote. "I wish only that a word could heal as easily as it can wound. Please feel yourself free of all obligations to the court until your affairs are in order."

The most touching communication of all was a letter from Pierre Dupuy, librarian to Louis XIII, whom Pieter Paul didn't know very well. He was a great admirer of the painter's work, an intimate of the brothers Fabri whom he had replaced as Rubens' personal and professional representative in Paris; he watched over the sale of his engravings in France, prodded the queen mother and Richelieu about their moral and material

289

obligation to contract with Pieter Paul to complete the Luxembourg cycle of pictures, and periodically reminded the royal treasurer that the Flemish master had still not been paid in full for the tapestry cartoons depicting the life of the Emperor Constantine.

In the middle of July, the artist tried to summarize in a reply to Dupuy the quality of emotion he thought he could and ought to share with those outside his very small sphere of closest family and friends in Antwerp: ". . . I have lost a very pleasant companion, whom I could and must in reason love; for she had none of the faults of her sex. She was neither morose-tempered nor weak; but so kind, so good and so virtuous that everyone loved her during her life, and mourns her since her death. Such a loss touches my inmost being; and since the only cure for all our ills is forgetfulness, child of time, I must await from him my only comfort. But it will be hard for me to disentangle my sorrow from the memory I shall hold all my life of that dear and adored soul. I believe that travel would help, for it would tear me away from the sight of all that surrounds me, and at length relieve me of my misery . . ."

The notion of forgetfulness was his own. It was the advice he had given Isabella and Anton van Dyck. He meant to forget the pain of his loss, not the beauty of her presence. The idea of travel was, of course, Isabella's own prescription, offered after the death of their little Clara. It had been effective then; Pieter Paul saw no reason why it shouldn't be helpful now. But to go away implied the necessity of returning. He looked about his house, made a tour of the rotunda, forced himself to do alone the things he had so recently done so happily with his wife. If he were to leave Antwerp for a time, would this fine house and all its furnishings be bearable to his sight on his return? He thought not. It would redound with too many echoes of the lamented Isabella. Its character must be altered.

He remembered the Duke of Buckingham's assertion that he would have, at any price, the antiquities that Pieter Paul had acquired from Sir Dudley Carleton. He wrote a letter to His Grace saying that he would be willing to sell him the entire collection, and some Rubens paintings the duke had admired, for the colossal sum of 100,000 florins. Rubens didn't add that though he acknowledged the figure to be astronomical, it would cost him a substantial part of it to refurbish a house denuded of its principal treasures. In late September, Balthasar Gerbier responded that his master was delighted by the offer and requested only that Pieter Paul send along a detailed inventory of the items he proposed to sell him and an indication of how soon they could be packed and shipped to London.

On December 1, Rubens and his sons set out for Calais at the head of a caravan of ox-drawn carts containing his entire collection of ancient Roman sculpture and a number of mythological and allegorical paintings of the sort so popular for so long among rich connoisseurs of the feminine form in its unadorned splendor. The plan was to meet Gerbier at the Channel port and transfer the great number of packing cases to his custody. A second and more important purpose of this proposed encounter with the duke's representative was the discussion of a possible armistice between the United Provinces and Britain, on the one hand, and Spain and the Netherlands on the other. Gerbier was not to be found at Calais because Buckingham, smarting still from the disgraceful defeat suffered by the British fleet at Cádiz the year before and menaced by continuing Parliamentary efforts to condemn him for treason, required his agent's presence at his side.

Having deposited the huge cargo of art treasures in the care of the harbormaster of Calais, Rubens and his sons traveled to Paris, where they lodged in the comfortable right bank house of Pierre Dupuy. He asked the royal librarian to describe his visit, to anyone who thought it proper to inquire, as a "private" one. He was there to show Albrecht and Nicolas the charms of the city, not least his own contributions to them which hung in the Palais du Luxembourg. He had no official mission, nor even a semi-official one; it was strictly personal.

The lads were impressed—not only by the sights of the great French capital, but by the evidences of respect that were on all occasions shown to their father. Until this journey, his position, his role in the world, had been mysteries to them. Their mother had always described her husband as "a very important man and a very great painter." But her words had little impact on the sons because they were unable to appreciate her frame of reference. To them, "an important man" was their school-master. They knew Pieter Paul to be the main celebrity of Ant-werp, a close friend of all the *échevins*, an intimate and adviser of the regent, but that their father's reputation extended be-yond the confines of that city or even the Netherlands was un-imaginable simply because such were the confines of their world; they didn't know about the rest of Europe, and until now, they hadn't really cared to know. And to be "a very great painter" meant nothing either; they had often seen Pieter Paul at work, and there seemed no wonder in *that*. To find that his fame had spread to Paris, to see him treated deferentially by those who were confidants of the King of France . . .

They returned to Antwerp in such high spirits that Jan Brandt was offended. He felt left out, as if, with Isabella in her grave, there were no longer a close connection between himself and the surviving Rubenses. He reproached his son-in-law for having been away over the Christmas season. He was shocked that Pieter Paul had abandoned the wearing of mourning be-fore the expiration of the prescribed year. He taxed his grand-sons with having forgotten their mother barely six months after her death.

For once, Rubens made no attempt to mollify Jan Brandt. Instead, he chided him. "Do you remember what you said to me when Philip died? You said that there's nothing without survival, that if we must shed tears, the tears should be for the living, and they should be tears of joy."

"Then we were talking about your brother. Now we're talking about my daughter."

"What was good counsel then is bad counsel now?"

"You don't miss Isabella?"

"I won't indulge myself, Jan. That's what you accused me of doing when Philip died. You were right. Now you're doing it yourself."

292

"How can you be so hard, Pieter Paul?"

The son-in-law laughed with some bitterness. "No one ever called me hard before. You know better, Jan. You know very well that I loved Isabella, that I miss her terribly, that my house, my life, my thoughts, my emotions are all empty without her—that I run and I run because, when I stand still for more than a moment, I can hear her voice, or imagine that she'll soon be coming through a door. I'm sorry if I caused you pain by going to Paris for Christmas, but to have spent it here would have been agonizing not only for me, but for Albrecht and Nicolas. I don't know why it should be, but memories don't seem so poignant when one has them in unfamiliar surroundings."

Brandt nodded. "Perhaps I understand. I certainly forgive."

"I'm glad. I want not the smallest blemish to mar our friendship, Jan."

His father-in-law's expression was plaintive. "I was being selfish. I wanted to share my grief. Anna is like Isabella. She contains it. She finds it easier. I thought *you* would feel differently."

"I do," said the artist sorrowfully. "But I mustn't."

"And so you'll continue to run, to run away."

"To run, but not to run away. Yes, for a while I think I must."

The exigencies of his two demanding careers as painter and politician made it more difficult for Pieter Paul to get away from the Netherlands than he had originally hoped. There was a mountain of work to be done in his studio, and the calls of his time imposed by his position on the regent's Privy Council didn't diminish. Indeed, the Infanta Isabel added to his burdens as an artist in the early months of 1627 by commissioning a series of eighteen cartoons devoted to the Triumph of the Eucharist to be used as the basis for tapestries to be woven at the justly famous Brussels factory. And there was the further complication of a novel and purely domestic problem—finding a housekeeper who was capable of maintaining some control over a large staff of servants and, during his brief but frequent absences, of caring for his two motherless sons.

In February, Balthasar Gerbier appeared in the Low Countries with a proposal from Buckingham for an armistice and trade agreement which involved the Netherlands, the United Provinces, Denmark, Spain, and Britain. At Rubens' suggestion, the regent made a counterproposition which would restrict the arrangement to Spain and Britain alone, since it was their enmity that was at the heart of the larger difference which included the Netherlands, north and south. The Count-Duke of Olivares refused to believe that Charles I would find this modification acceptable and thus had no hesitation in agreeing to it for Spain. He was embarrassed when the British monarch, through Buckingham, gave his approval. Rubens was thereupon ordered to drag his feet in any negotiations that might ensue, for it was apparent to Olivares that the British interest in reducing tensions between Spain and Britain, so far as the Low Countries were concerned, was inspired by Buckingham's plan to come to the aid of the Huguenots of La Rochelle, where Richelieu was planning a siege.

In spite of mutual mistrust, appearances had to be kept up, though neither Gerbier nor Rubens had any illusions about the other's intentions. Together, they traveled to the principal towns of the United Provinces in the summer of 1627, including Breda, which Prince Frederick Henry had recaptured along with Maastricht and 's Hertogenbosch after the redoubtable Ambrogio di Spinola had returned to his native Italy to preside over Spanish troops warring against the French for control of the Duchy of Mantua.

This journey, which took him as well to Delft, Utrecht, Amsterdam, and Haarlem, afforded the Flemish artist his first opportunity to meet the painters who were flourishing in the earliest years of what would be called the Dutch Renaissance. To one like Rubens who was steeped in Romanism and who had evolved from that style a flamboyance that was peculiarly his own, the rather sober, literal genre painting that was the accepted mode of the United Provinces seemed a retrogression to the less fantastic panels of the elder Pieter Bruegel, dead these sixty years or so. Because the Calvinists were obdurate in their uncharitable view of religious art, painters of this region under Protestant domination confined their work to portraits, still lifes, landscapes, and scenes of innocuous domestic activity. Not until the middle of the century, after the formal termination of the Thirty Years' War, would there be a revival in the United Provinces of religious painting—and it was to be a far more somber evocation of faith than Rubens' ebullient proclamation of a joy in things spiritual that was less sacred than profane.

Of the many painters he met casually during this stay and a shorter visit he made the following October, only one seemed to him worthy of more than passing attention—Frans Hals of Haarlem. Their meeting was brief and not very satisfactory. The Dutch painter was drunk, a condition described by his acquaintances as common with him, and not at all interested in conferring with the greatest of Flemish masters about anything more serious than the relative virtues of ale and *eau-de-vie* in Haarlem and Antwerp. But the man's pictures spoke volumes for him. There could be no two artists who deployed the same kind of jubilant, impulsive energies more differently. Rubens created an immense world of fleshly fantasy; Hals captured exuberant life, especially in his portraits, in the most fleeting of facial expressions, in attitudes and gestures superbly observed and annotated. Hals' paintings were rooted utterly in this earth. Rubens transported the earth itself to a celestial realm of his own creation. Each could recognize the brilliance of the other's unique gifts. Hals was not inclined to be altered by this acknowledgment. Rubens, however, filed in his prehensile visual memory all of Hals' paintings that he saw. It seemed doubtful that these would ever be of use to him, but he was helpless. He remembered every striking object he had ever seen.

The diplomatic purposes of these trips through the United Provinces were, from Pieter Paul's viewpoint, wholly unserved. Prince Frederick Henry was more intransigent than his brother had been about a possible armistice. His recent victories against the poorly directed Spanish troops served to reinforce a convic-

295

tion already well established. If he couldn't win absolutely, he was surer of not losing than Prince Mauritz could reasonably have been. He felt he could blackmail Britain into furnishing him promised assistance. France had declared war against Charles I, an action provoked in part by Buckingham's offer of aid to the Huguenots of La Rochelle, in part by the bitter and vivid memory of his conduct with the French queen. If the British abandoned the Dutch, Prince Frederick Henry's navy and merchant vessels could more easily menace King Charles' shipping than that of France or Spain. This was a *rationale* that Rubens deplored as a Fleming, since it assured the continuation of a military struggle in his own land, but it was one he was unable to refute. The peacemaker was yet again caught in the middle. However desirable all sides professed to consider the idea of peace, none was willing to compromise in order to secure it; each faction labored under the illusion, or so it seemed to Rubens, that procrastination would operate in its favor.

He returned, much discouraged, to Antwerp late in the autumn, determined to apply himself for a time to his work. He had found in his pupil Willem Panneels, just admitted to the Guild of Saint Luke, a young master engraver who, with the cooperation of Balthasar Moretus, would see to the etching and distribution of prints based on Rubens' paintings. Panneels enjoyed the further attraction of being much admired and respected by the artist's growing sons. Pieter Paul felt confident, if he had to leave his home for a longer period than had so far been the case, in the knowledge that young Panneels would minister to Albrecht and Nicolas with a suitable mixture of kindliness and authority.

The prospect of a protracted absence loomed large in the early months of 1628. The Infanta Isabel, to whom Pieter Paul delivered the tapestry cartoons of the Eucharist in March, confided to him that she was giving serious thought to sending him on a mission to Madrid. She felt that he alone could explain coherently to Olivares and Philip IV precisely her own position with respect to the continuing war. She was convinced that he alone might succeed in persuading them that peace, more or less on Prince Frederick Henry's terms, was the only reasonable course. She said that she had just written her great-nephew, the King of Spain, of her proposal to give Rubens plenipotentiary powers. As soon as she had a reply, he must prepare himself for the journey.

The painter found himself torn by this news. To leave his young sons for a period that could hardly be less than a year seemed too cruel—for them as well as for him. Since the death of their mother, they had developed a closeness that was the most precious thing in his life. Nevertheless, he must, as he tried to explain to them, accept the infanta's embassy precisely *because* of his love for them. "If I can do anything to bring peace, it's for you that I shall do it. You'll be the ones who finally benefit from it." At fourteen, Albrecht Rubens was able to follow his father's argument. The younger Nicolas could think only of the separation. To him, separation and death were synonymous. He begged Pieter Paul to take them along with him. The father sadly refused. "Your education would suffer, and after a few weeks, you'd be bored to death by life at court." They dared not oppose him. He was, after all, their master, author of all wisdom, seat of all power.

In June, the Infanta Isabel summoned Rubens to Brussels to show him a communication she had just received from Madrid in which Olivares angrily demanded a full explanation of the painter-diplomat's independent determination to negotiate a peace with the Dutch in preference to the official Spanish policy of continuing a futile war. He must, said the regent, go to Spain as soon as possible, bringing along with him his entire correspondence with the various Dutch authorities he had been in touch with.

It was, however, well into August before Pieter Paul departed. The trip across France was not, perhaps, without the possibility of hazard, for the papers he carried might, if they fell into the hands of Richelieu, thwart his mission. In spite of this danger, he determined to pause along the way at La Rochelle—or as near to that beleaguered town as he could safely go, to see for himself what was transpiring there. The cardinal himself was in residence near the French encampment, and to Rubens' request that he be received, the first minister offered the dustiest answer consistent with propriety: He was, alas, too busy with military matters to see anyone.

There might be enough truth in this reply to prevent an ambassador from taking offense. La Rochelle was nearing the end of its agony. The cardinal had reason to concentrate his faltering energies on bringing the Huguenots to heel. And he certainly had reason to gloat. Just a little while before, a great British fleet, come to relieve the besieged *Rochelais*, had been humiliatingly turned away by land-based French artillery fire and by a bridge of ships. Thus faded the last possible hope of standing off the forces of Louis XIII.

Not until he crossed the Spanish border at Irún did Rubens learn that this disastrous British operation had been Buckingham's swan song. In June, Charles I's third Parliament had voted him a substantial sum with which to finance the wars against France and Spain—but only after extracting royal assent, in writing, to a Petition of Right, a statement clearly setting forth the distribution of powers between king and Commons. Having succeeded in this maneuver, the Commons demanded Buckingham's dismissal. Charles I refused and hastily prorogued the Parliament before further debate on this subject, about which he was absolutely adamant, could be pursued.

A week before Rubens had left for Spain, the question of Buckingham's retention of office had been definitely resolved by assassination. He had been stabbed to bloody death at Portsmouth by John Felton, a maddened, wounded ex-officer who held the foolish duke responsible for the failure of the crown to pay his arrears of pension. Not since the killing of Henri IV in 1610 had there occurred an event so full of portent for all of Europe. The balance of political and military power, precarious in the happiest of seasons, had been unpredictably altered for every nation and state, large and small. No one, in September of 1628, knew what future British foreign policy was to be —save that Charles I would ignore the passionate will of his

Parliament only at his direst peril, and that a second maritime adventure to rescue La Rochelle, planned by Buckingham, had been canceled.

What the new situation signified for the Low Countries Pieter Paul Rubens could only conjecture wildly as he journeyed in the last days of the summer across the desolate landscape of northwestern Spain toward Madrid. In the twenty-five years since he had seen this region last, nothing seemed to have changed; in the faces of Spanish peasant and townsman alike, he read the same fear and anguish he had detected so many years before. If possible, conditions were worse. How could Philip IV inflict on his pitiable people the burden of a war he couldn't hope to win?

After he reached the Spanish capital, he must remain for some weeks in this condition of perplexity. Though he met almost at once with the powerful Olivares, who impressed him as of mediocre intelligence, bigoted and cynical but with a measure of charm which he demonstrated to those of use to him, the Flemish emissary learned very little of Spanish intentions in the matters that concerned him directly. He was wryly amused to hear that Spain had dispatched a powerful fleet to aid the French in compelling the surrender of La Rochelle—its arrival nicely timed to coincide with the capitulation of the Huguenot garrison. Thus, Philip IV had demonstrated his good faith to Louis XIII without having lost a drop of Spanish blood. It was the only clever thing he ever learned of this monarch.

The King of Spain, to whom Pieter Paul was presented several weeks after his arrival from Brussels, was put off at first by the fact that his great-aunt had seen fit to send as her ambassador a painter, when what seemed required was a professional diplomat. He wrote her tartly to this effect, and for a month thereafter refused to have anything to do with Rubens. This period of enforced diplomatic inactivity was a boon. Pieter Paul put it to the best possible use by "going back to school," as he himself described it to Philip IV's favorite court painter, Diego Velázquez, whose pictures were of a technical brilliance matched only by Caravaggio at the height of his powers.

299

Velázquez and Rubens were bound to get along. Both were accomplished courtiers. But they were equally bound not to understand each other as artists. There was no element of fantasy in the Spaniard's soul, which was simply to say, as Rubens did, that there was none of the Fleming in him. Yet together they visited the magnificent royal collections of Madrid and other cities. Pieter Paul was struck in 1628 as he had been during his Italian days by the glory of Titian, whose works were to be seen in great numbers here. He copied more than twenty of the great Venetian's pictures during his stay in Spain. He even retouched his own painting of the Adoration of the Magi that Rodrigo Calderón had brought from Antwerp and which was now part of the royal collections. He painted portraits of important personages, including Olivares, and by the end of the autumn he was invited to portray the features of the Most Catholic Philip IV and other members of the royal family.

By this time, the king was prepared to change his opinion of Rubens. So many intelligent *madrileños* had sung his praises, commending not merely his art but his intellect, that Philip IV had to have another look at him and listen to him with ears more sympathetic than those he had lent on their previous meeting. And what he discovered was that he had allowed prejudice to obscure the truth—a discovery he might, had he been so disposed, have made almost daily about something. His great-aunt of the Netherlands was just in describing Rubens as the most gifted Fleming of his day, in every respect.

Pieter Paul was gratified to find acceptance in the eyes of the Spanish king, for gaining his confidence was essential to the success of his mission in Madrid. Though he had convinced Olivares of his integrity and skill, and though Olivares governed, Philip IV remained all-powerful in matters of protocol. If he refused to accept Rubens as a suitable representative, negotiations could not begin. Only now, having won Philip's favor as a person, could he undertake his real work—and not a soul in authority here was philosophically inclined to make his task easy for him. The death of Buckingham added to the difficulty. For it suggested to Olivares, and therefore to the king, that there was no advantage to be gained from a peace treaty with Britain. Pieter Paul learned, in fact, that the Spanish first minister had made a secret compact with Richelieu to mount a combined assault against the British shores with a view to enforcing the provision of the 1624 marriage contract according freedom of worship to the Catholics of that land.

To argue straightforwardly with Philip IV and Olivares that this scheme was evidence of insanity, as he believed it to be, would alienate these men he was seeking to convince of the wisdom of a negotiated settlement between the United Provinces and the Netherlands. To say nothing would be equally foolhardy, for if such a mad adventure were actually attempted, the Netherlands, so close and so accessible to British wrath, would be more likely to suffer the consequences than would Spain. Pieter Paul elected to follow a more circuitous path, one he thought Richelieu himself might admire in an abstract way. He agreed with his Spanish hosts that nothing would be more to his country's interest and wish than a holy crusade to release the Catholics of the British Isles from their Protestant bondage. What could the Netherlands do, he asked, to assist in the fruition of this noble endeavor?

As both Olivares and the king knew very well, the question had only one answer. There was nothing the poor deflowered Netherlands could do. Rubens went on in a slightly different vein. Did the Spanish really believe that Richelieu could be depended on? What ground had they for imagining that the French minister would suddenly depart from the single policy to which he had held so resolutely from the onset of his career in that office? Were the Habsburgs a bit less France's mortal enemies today than they had been only yesterday? Was it not at least possible that the cardinal had made peace with Spain merely to free his forces for an attack against the Empire? Rubens permitted himself to wonder aloud if the French position regarding the succession to the throne of Mantua wasn't, in its fashion, more anti-Catholic than Charles I's rather fitful repression of the faith—for in the case of Mantua, Richelieu was setting himself once more against the will and authority of the pope.

The painter posed for the Spanish courtiers other questions in the same spirit, all intended to evoke doubts in the minds of Olivares and Philip IV about the wisdom of an alliance with France. He followed his argument systematically for several more months, with increasing efficacy. He was determined to assist Olivares and the king to persuade themselves that however they might disapprove of Charles I's official outlook on the Catholic religion, he was a more logical and more trustworthy ally than Louis XIII. Britain had no territorial ambitions on the Continent. France obviously meant, sooner or later, to regain all Spanish-held lands north of the Pyrenees, as well as portions of the Spanish Netherlands and perhaps even Alsace, Lorraine, Franche-Comté, and Savoie, provinces and principalities all in some manner attached to one branch or another of the Habsburg family.

Richelieu unwittingly played into Rubens' hands by his lenient treatment of the surrendered citizens of La Rochelle. The Flemish diplomat lost not a moment in pointing, with a cynicism that chilled him, to the cardinal's charity in allowing Protestant practice to continue as evidence of his questionable honor in wishing, at the same time, to make war against the heretics in a foreign land. By Christmastide, the news was received in Madrid that, so far from intending to launch an attack against Charles I, Richelieu was secretly negotiating terms of a peace treaty. The death of Buckingham had eliminated one major obstacle to the reconciliation. The British king's newly discovered affection for his French wife had removed another. She was pregnant.

Abruptly, Pieter Paul Rubens, already accepted by the court of Spain as a master portraitist and man about the world, was pronounced a political oracle of boundless wisdom. Early in 1629, Philip IV conferred on him a title, a pension, and the promise of a mission to London as special ambassador. Spain would now seek to prevent the very development that Rubens foresaw—a military alliance of France and Britain against Spain and the Empire. If the terms proposed were not too exorbitant, a restoration of peace seemed the only possible solution to the immediate problems. Immediate problems were the only ones that heads of state had time to think about.

A formal treaty of peace was signed by representatives of Louis XIII and Charles I in April. Rubens left Madrid at the end of May, proceeding at maximum speed through France to Brussels. There he recounted to the Infanta Isabel the entire saga of his months as her delegate in the Spanish capital. She was as cheered as he by the success he had achieved—though she chided him amiably for his slyness in dealing with Olivares and Philip IV. On the basis of what he unfolded to her, however, she could only agree that no other method was likely to have been persuasive. She also conceded that in this case, Richelieu's dark dealings had been of inestimable value to the cause of the Netherlands. Rubens assured her that this was an accident. The cardinal couldn't be counted on always to come to the aid of his enemies.

After a painful few days in Antwerp, where he was able to do no more than embrace his sons and his friends and say farewell to them once again, Pieter Paul set out at once for Calais and Dover to try to realize a hope for peace that he had been nurturing for so many frustrating years. No consummation could have been more devoutly wished.

The land of strange language and even stranger customs for which Pieter Paul embarked from Calais in June of 1629 was not in the happiest condition it had ever known. "Steenie," as James I and Charles I had called their darling George Villiers, Duke of Buckingham, was dead. The young king had found no one to replace him as first minister or intimate friend. In different circumstances, this lacuna might not have been such a bad thing; if, for instance, Charles I had been able to give *himself* good counsel, or if he had been capable of enjoying solitude. Out of loneliness, he had turned most unexpectedly to his wife, and the resulting pregnancy and a consequent peace with France were blessings that few important Britons seemed interested in counting just then.

The House of Commons had once again been dissolved for the grievous offense of *lèse majesté*; its vigorous, outspoken leader, Sir John Eliot, was languishing in the Tower of London where, in a few years, he would be carried away by consumption. However, the spirit of *lèse majesté* which prevailed in Britain couldn't be dissolved by royal decree; nor, as it was to prove years later, could it be forcibly repressed.

The resentment was motivated in the main by money, the right of the crown to levy taxes and the limitations the Commons felt empowered to impose on that right. Charles I, in according his assent to the Petition of Right, had seemed to enshrine Parliament's authority over getting and spending—but by dissolving that body almost immediately after acknowledging its primacy, and by refusing to reconvene again until 1640, the king appeared guilty of *lèse peuple,* a crime he naturally refused to recognize. Like God, he gave and he took away in virtually the same instant.

Since monetary issues had only a limited political and emotional value, the advocates of greater Parliamentary control of government, most of whom happened to be Puritans, discovered in religious bigotry an issue that would burn a lot longer and with much more heat. They accused the established Anglican Church of acting merely as a shield for the twin heresies of popery and Arminianism—that is, as protection for religious tolerance. They regarded the achievements of the "tolerant" Anglicans in Ireland as of no significance. In Ireland, Catholicism was synonymous with anti-Britishism. Therefore, the Puritans argued, the Anglicans weren't really suppressing a feared and detested faith but rather a feared and detested people.

Pamphleteers found it useful, nevertheless, to exploit royal extravagance. And here they seemed on more reasonable political ground, though reason didn't figure more in the polemic literature of the seventeenth century than it did in that of succeeding eras. The royal household laid out approximately half of the crown's annual receipts for its own maintenance. Since these revenues were very large, this was not an easy accomplishment, but it was managed by clever and conscientious application. The queen, once she had reconciled herself with the king and resigned herself to the filthy British climate, offered the public a stunning adumbration of the tastes and attitudes of Marie-Antoinette. From the moment of her wedding, when a strong man had been summoned to assist three infant bearers to hoist her heavy, gold-embroidered train, Queen Henrietta Maria (as she was known to her subjects) had manifested an insatiable affection for expensive baubles and costly entertainments.

Ben Jonson and Inigo Jones combined their dazzling talents to produce lavishly designed masques for the amusement of the court. Jones, tame architect of James I, had become arbiter of official taste under Charles I. He was Master of the Royal Works as well, in which capacity he devoted much of his time and energies to the confection of palaces, ballrooms, chapels, and to the creation of the first of London's urban redevelopment schemes—Covent Garden. At the request of William Laud, Bishop of London, he added a new façade for Saint Paul's Cathedral. Laud, later Archbishop of Canterbury, would be beheaded for purported popery. The cathedral was burned in the great fire of 1666. Only Jones survived, through other works—of which one of the finest was the Banqueting House in Whitehall, intended to be part of a far greater undertaking that was never achieved.

The king's hobbies were even more extravagant than the queen's. He was a passionate and voracious consumer of art. After the death of Buckingham, he purchased the murdered duke's entire collection of antiquities—a considerable proportion of it acquired from Rubens. He bought all the detachable objects that had once been the pride of Vincenzo I Gonzaga, Duke of Mantua, on the demise of the duke's sonless heir. His only royal rival had been Philip II of Spain, who had had the advantage of being able to purchase most of the masterpieces in the collections of Madrid, Aranjuez, Valladolid, and the Escorial directly from the artists who created them—an economy measure not afforded Charles I.

Every royal British residence was crowded with paintings, sculptures, and *objets d'art* accumulated through the help of agents and ambassadors in every Continental capital and important town. The king's love of art was certainly quantitative, but he wasn't without some discernment. His acquisitive principle assured him of obtaining a number of genuinely wonderful pieces, just by the operation of the law of averages; but he could usually tell the difference between a good painting and an indifferent one—for of all the objects he gathered unto himself so indiscriminately, paintings were his particular favorites.

It wasn't merely the extravagance of the royal family that annoyed the pamphleteers and those who employed them, it was more especially the fact that so much of the money thus squandered was placed in the hands of foreigners. As the Earl and Countess of Arundel had said to Rubens so long before, graphic art in Britain, almost entirely the product of aliens, was not very healthy. Neither was music. Indeed, the only genius of which the British could unabashedly boast was literature, a form that traveled badly, like fine white wine, because few Continentals thought it worthwhile to learn the complicated structure and illogical pronunciation and syntax of a tongue spoken by fewer than 5,000,000 souls, the Britons who called themselves English, and read by a mere handful. Two diametrically opposed forces were at work—the congenital xenophobia that had blighted the land since the Norman Conquest by William the Bastard, and the passion for beauty to brighten an atmosphere better suited to seals than humans, a beauty that was not being produced by native craftsmen.

Pieter Paul Rubens was aware of some of these problems when he disembarked at Greenwich-on-Thames in the week of his fifty-second birthday. He still had no English, because every Britisher he had so far met spoke at least one of the languages he had mastered. Like every other European country, Britain exported only her best people and her worst—her statesmen and holiday-makers who were literate and worldly, and her warriors who were not. Rubens mingled happily with the elegant, and had devoted much of his recent life to preventing the circulation in his country of the soldierly rabble.

In the glowing midsummer's afternoon, as he walked with some gouty difficulty from the bank of the Thames up a broad avenue to the new, sober, brick building by Inigo Jones that was called the Queen's House, he needed the sound of no strange tongue to inform him that he was in a foreign land. The people who lined the walk demonstrated their difference from all the other Europeans he had ever seen. They were at once more animated and less deferential than their Continental brothers and sisters. Some men, it was true, tugged reverently at their forelocks as he followed the royal equerry up the walkway; some women curtsied awkwardly. But most just stared at him with unabashed and usually hostile curiosity. Here was yet another foreigner come to treat with a king who was married to a Frenchwoman. And even if Charles I had, in a rage, driven off to France all the servants his wife had brought to London with her, including the bishop who had been her confessor, there lurked in the public mind the black suspicion that because most visitors from abroad were Catholic, there was always a possibility of a popish plot afoot—a thing, the pamphleteers and Puritan demagogues told them, that was to be feared as much as an epidemic of the plague.

That Rubens, a Fleming, was here as official representative of the King of Spain was a fact that bewildered Charles I, who wondered even more than Philip IV had that a painter should have been selected to serve as a diplomat on a mission of such importance and delicacy. Like nearly everyone except Richelieu, Charles I was immediately charmed by the fastidious, worldly, well-spoken gentleman and knight from the moment of his first audience, which occurred the day after Rubens' arrival.

Pieter Paul had long pondered his opening speech to the British monarch, drawing on intelligence acquired from the now-dispossessed Balthasar Gerbier and from Lord Bristol, the

307

British ambassador to the Spanish court. After the king expressed, in halting French, his pleasure at meeting at last the artist whose renown was universal and whose self-portrait he owned and had long admired, Rubens replied in kind, adding, "I only regret, sire, that His Grace of Buckingham . . ."

The king, bursting into tears, held up a forfending hand and stammered, "No, no, I implore you, *maître*. You're never again to utter that name in my presence."

The startled ambassador gazed down at the fine carpet on which he most uncomfortably stood. No one except the queen was permitted to sit in the presence of the British ruler. "Forgive me, sire. I had no intention of distressing you."

Charles' congested, meager features cleared a little, and he shook his head. "No, of course you didn't. I'd quite forgotten that you and Steenie had been friendly. Your portrait of him is exquisite. He praised you to the skies, told me you were the only artist capable of decorating the Banqueting House. Well, well, we'll have to see about that . . . He's been gone almost a year. I can't believe it still. That monster Felton. You have no idea, *maître*, what a loss it was, what a loss it *is*. He was my brother, my spiritual brother."

"I too lost a brother, sire. I know what such a pain can be."

Charles demurred. "I lost my *true* brother as well, of course." He gave a shrill little giggle. "That's how I became Prince of Wales." He sighed. "I think, on the whole, I should be more content to be simply the Duke of York. Oh, the problems, the unhappiness, *maître*, of being ruler of a great and miserable country."

Rubens found no suitable comment. It never failed to surprise him when great men complained of the responsibilities of high office—which they rarely abdicated. He waited for the king to give direction to their talk. Charles appeared lost in a dream of how happy he would be if the problems of kingship had devolved on his dead brother Henry instead of on him. He twitched nervously and grasped the arms of his throne as if to prevent himself from toppling out of it. A courtier rushed to the royal side. The king, suddenly conscious of the servant's

308

presence, turned on him in a rage. "Go away. Get away from me." Then, observing Rubens' interested eyes but immobile features as he righted his narrow head, he gave him an embarrassed smile. "I'm sorry for that absurd outburst, *maître,* very unseemly, very unkingly. But I was thinking of my dearest Steenie . . . His Grace of Buckingham was . . ." He broke off. "What exactly is the nature of your mission? I've been told, of course, but I want to hear it from your lips. I'm surrounded by assassins and liars."

"I've come to London, sire, to discuss the possibility of a treaty of peace with Spain."

"I presume you've been given plenipotentiary powers."

"No, sire." Rubens smiled sadly. "I'm merely the first swallow of what I hope will prove to be a long and happy summer."

Charles stamped his little foot petulantly. "Why trouble yourself with such matters if you're not authorized to sign a treaty?"

"I'm empowered to *treat,* sire, to negotiate, to recommend. Perhaps mistakenly, His Most Catholic Majesty believes that my nationality and experience suit me to such a preliminary task, but it's only natural that the formal signature should be affixed by a Spaniard."

The king was not pleased. "I'd prefer to deal only with someone who has the authority to speak definitively for his goverment."

"I *have* such authority, sire. I'm simply not permitted to sign the resulting treaty."

"It's a problem, all the same, *maître.*"

"May I say, sire, that I dearly hope that to be the most serious problem we encounter."

Charles considered the fine figure of Pieter Paul Rubens for a moment before responding, his expression warm and even gentle, "Yes, *maître,* I hope so too."

While eager that there be no resumption of actual hostilities with Spain, the British appeared in no hurry to settle the terms of a peace—an opinion Rubens formed within the early weeks of his stay in London. He suspected that Châteauneuf, the newly arrived French ambassador, was doing Richelieu's work well, the plan being to prevent anything resembling a coalition of Britain and Spain that could threaten France. Yet whenever the opportunity presented itself during these summer months, the artist urged on his British counterparts the enormous benefits to be derived for both parties, indeed for all of Europe (not least the Netherlands), from the conclusion of a formal and stable agreement.

Such opportunities were not very frequent. For a time, Pieter Paul had to content himself with an acceptance at the British court more as painter than as ambassador. It wasn't the first time he had had to do this, and he did it with his customary grace and apparent ease. The favorable impression he had made first on the king radiated widely and quickly. Soon he was being invited to every important aristocratic house, was introduced to every major collector and scholar—except for those who, like John Selden, were imprisoned in the Tower for their conduct as members of the recently dissolved House of Commons. He particularly regretted the impossibility of becoming acquainted with Selden, who was author of a significant work on the celebrated Arundel Marbles, a book he read after viewing the collection as guest of the earl whose portrait he had painted in Antwerp. He made another in July.

Though King Charles was unwilling seriously to discuss peace, he was eager to discuss art with Rubens, and prided himself, as he took the Flemish artist through many a royal gallery, on his ability to identify the author of each work his guest singled out for admiration. The royal connoisseur commissioned two ambitious picutres, an allegory based on the themes of Peace and War, and a rendition of the legend long hallowed by Britons, Saint George slaying the Dragon, for that spurious holy man was patron of the British monarchy.

The king was immensely pleased with the finished canvases and, as a direct result, took Rubens one September afternoon to Whitehall for an inspection of Inigo Jones' superbly proportioned Banqueting House, whose vast ceiling he now proposed that the estimable Pieter Paul should decorate with paintings in the same genre as those he had made for the walls of the Palais du Luxembourg—these illustrations to evoke the highlights of the career of the king's now-venerated father, James I. The visit to London, even if it failed to produce the peace that the artist so longed for, was made worthwhile by this great assignment that he had coveted for almost a decade. He solemnly promised Charles I that he would never regret his decision to confide this task to him. He would create for him a ceiling as fine in its Baroque, Rubensesque fashion as the one by Michelangelo in the Sistine Chapel.

The king threw up his hands in horror. "My God, *maître,* no popery."

Pieter Paul laughed. "I used the Sistine only as an example. You need have no fear about its misinterpretation. My allegories confuse everyone."

"You'll attend to the installation of the panels yourself?"

"I shall indeed, sire. I'd want to see all of them in place in any event, and there'll undoubtedly be a few blemishes that I can repair at the same time."

The monarch raised an admonitory finger. "These are to be all by your own hand, *maître.* I'll not have any of your famous apprentices toying with them."

The artist frowned. "Sire, that rumor about my maintaining some kind of painting factory will never cease to haunt me. The fact is that I haven't allowed an assistant to do anything more than prepare the undercoating of a canvas of mine since I completed the work for Saint Charles Borromeo six years ago—and *that* work was done with the express approval of the church authorities. I swear to you that these paintings will be entirely from my own hand."

This reference to assistants served one useful purpose. It allowed Rubens to bring up and recommend to the king's kindness and possible patronage the young, talented Anton van Dyck, who had been floundering for the two years since his return to Antwerp from Italy. "He wants to come to London, sire."

"Then you can assure him on my part, *maître,* that he'll

receive a right royal welcome. If he's all you say, I ask nothing better than to help him establish himself here."

In the middle of September, the treaty between France and Britain, whose terms had been agreed to the previous spring, was formally ratified. This, Rubens believed, might clear the way for a similar arrangement with Spain. He reasoned that whatever Richelieu might wish to the contrary, a Britain anxious above all else to avoid war on any front would now logically turn a friendlier eye toward Madrid, having reached an accord with Paris. He started at once to press a little more impatiently for serious conversations—not entirely convinced that he would be successful, but as persuaded as ever that he must persevere.

To his astonishment, royal agreement to his ideas for a formal peace was reached by the middle of the next month. Britain would send Sir Francis Cottington, as talented a diplomat as she could boast, to Madrid with the draft treaty early in November. A minister plentipotentiary would come to London from the Spanish capital shortly after Cottington's arrival there. It was, it now marvelously appeared, only a matter of time.

That time was filled very flatteringly for Rubens. Soon after the preliminary terms were settled, he received an invitation to visit the medieval university town of Cambridge, where he was awarded an honorary degree of Master of Arts, an accolade never before bestowed on an artist of any nationality. He divided the twelve days of Christmas between the royal palace at Hampton Court, that richest of Tudor splendors, and the less awesome sumptuousness of the Earl of Arundel's London residence.

Two days after Epiphany, Don Carlos Coloma, the Spanish plenipotentiary, reached London to present his credentials to Charles I. He informed Pieter Paul of Olivares' specific request that the artist remain in the British capital until the final details of the peace treaty were set—a matter of a few more weeks at the most, for the Count-Duke was more than well pleased with the general terms that Rubens had proposed and sent on to Madrid.

Though he was by now anxious to return to Antwerp, the painter felt more than merely an official obligation to see the treaty in its final form. It represented, after all, the partial realization of a dream. Largely through his efforts, a peace between Spain and Britain that had theretofore seemed unthinkable was on the point of conclusion. There were still some unsettled issues, notably the question of the independence of the United Provinces, but with peace established among the great powers, however uncertain the prospects, this lesser problem might more readily be resolved.

The few nettles in the Anglo-Hispanic garden of peace were uprooted by the end of February, 1630. The treaty was ready for resubmission to Madrid. There was nothing more for Rubens to do in London. He promptly solicited a final audience with the king, to say farewell and to express his gratitude for the many signs of honor and confidence that had been shown him everywhere during his eight-month visit to Britain.

On March 3, he was summoned to Hampton Court Palace, expecting simply a brief, formal conversation with the fragile Charles I. Instead, he found himself ushered into the great Hall of State. The monarch was on his throne, adorned in exceptional finery, surrounded by a considerable group of courtiers and foreign diplomats. For an instant, the artist's equanimity deserted him. He felt certain that he had intruded on a ceremony to which he had not been invited. In his embarrassment, he began to bow himself apologetically out of the room. The king raised a hand and beckoned him to approach. Pieter Paul complied, and knelt before him. There was a hush occasioned by His Majesty's rising from the throne to take two steps down to the level of the painter, who was still kneeling, his head respectfully bowed. Only when, out of the corner of his eye, he saw a flash of steel and felt the blade of the royal sword lightly touch a shoulder did he look up in amazement. The smiling Charles murmured, "I knight you, Sir Peter Paul Rubens, for the selfless service you have rendered to the kingdoms of Great Britain and Spain in the blessed name of peace."

There was more. The king made him gifts of fine cloth, of

gold, and of a locket bearing a likeness of the royal features. The thanks so formally expressed was nonetheless genuine for its wording. Thomas Howard, Earl of Arundel, who saw the new-made knight off at Greenwich three days later, told him of Charles I's observation that Pieter Paul Rubens was the most disinterestedly good man, and perhaps the only such, he had ever met or was likely to meet. The artist had to deprecate himself. "I've only tried to do, *monsieur,* what any reasonable third party would have done under the circumstances."

Yet he had done much more, and he knew it perfectly well. He had contrived to create a degree of order where there had been total chaos. He had brought at least a hope of permanent general peace. He had, therefore, spared some human lives. He was, in a phrase, delighted with himself. If he had any complaint, it would be, as he said to dear Jan Brandt who greeted him when he reached Antwerp a week or so later, that again in London as in Madrid, he had been ennobled not for his painting but for his diplomacy. "I wonder," he said wearily as he walked with his father-in-law to the door of his fine house in the Wapperstraat, "which I shall be better remembered for."

Brandt chortled. "You *know* the answer to that, Pieter Paul. Can you cite the name of a single peacemaker?"

Nine

HAVING done his conscientious best to put Europe's house in some sort of order, Pieter Paul Rubens found on his return to Antwerp that his personal household required immediate attention. During his long absence, Willem Panneels had been taking advantage of the master's celebrated generosity and good nature to fabricate and sell replicas of his employer's most popular canvases. In itself, this enterprise might have been pardonable. What the artist thought deplorable was that Panneels had been successfully passing these copies off as Rubens' own handiwork. So great was the demand that many larcenous purchasers, imagining that they were securing incredible bargains, had been deceived by the forgeries, though the younger painter's technique, inhibited by the necessity of reproducing as exactly as possible Rubens' brushstrokes and his method of applying layer upon layer of semitransparent pigments, was cramped and awkward. To a practiced eye, the copies bore only superficial resemblance to the original works.

The scene that ensued was one of the most distasteful Pieter Paul had ever willingly subjected himself to. Instead of simply admitting to the crime, Panneels maintained that he had always told his clients that the pictures were replicas. If any of them claimed otherwise, it was surely no fault of his. They hadn't, after all, been required to pay Rubens' usual prices. The bargain hunters had been had. There was no more to it than that.

Pieter Paul felt that he had no choice but to dismiss Panneels. He was so angry with him that he threatened to bring a legal proceeding against him, but was ultimately dissuaded by his father-in-law. Jan Brandt agreed that the matter was probably actionable, but felt it would be wiser to reimburse any dissatisfied purchaser of a counterfeit painting than to celebrate the whole affair in open court. Rubens was, after all, a great public character. It just wouldn't do for a man of state, for a gentleman, for a knight, to parade so sordid a little business.

Panneels' unceremonious departure from the house in the Wapperstraat couldn't be the clean sort of break Pieter Paul would have desired. After four years as a member of his staff, he had created an important place for himself in the lives of the artist's two sons—a role, unfortunately, their father could scarcely claim. With their dear Willem gone, Albrecht and Nicolas, now sixteen and twelve, suddenly found themselves bereft—more painfully, in one sense, than had been the circumstance at the time of their mother's death. A second cleavage is harder to bear. Moreover, Panneels still lived, was still to be seen frequently on the streets of the small city of Antwerp. No matter what he might have done to offend Rubens, an association of such intimacy for so long a time formed a bond that couldn't neatly be severed. It left an ugly scar of which father and sons were miserably reminded each time they encountered the treacherous Willem. The scar, instead of growing smaller, became more pronounced with each meeting. Panneels was unable to find employment, and soon went through the profits of his forgery. He seemed more wasted, more desperate every day. Unwilling to feel responsible for the devastation of another soul, no matter how culpable he might be, the master finally relented —to the extent of composing for the young painter a letter of recommendation so glowing that within a week he was installed in the studio of an artist eager to know all of Rubens' secrets.

316

Jan Brandt called his son-in-law a sentimental fool. "You needn't have turned the other cheek."

Pieter Paul was rueful. "I couldn't do anything else. He was haunting me—and the boys were in an agony of divided loyalty."

Once again, the master painter had to become a responsible father. This wasn't so simple a thing as it had proved four years earlier. He was older and wearier. His sons were older too, and were developing identities of their own. This was particularly true of Albrecht. He was expressing, under the strong influence of his grandfather, a desire to travel to Louvain to begin his study of the law. Nicolas, if not dependent anymore on his father, did lean heavily on his older brother. Consequently, he viewed the idea of Albrecht's leaving with alarm. Rubens thought it wiser to postpone any decision about this until the following year. By that time, he hoped, he and Nicholas might have rediscovered a *rapport* that would make Albrecht's departure a little more bearable.

This untidiness of morale at home was especially dismaying to Pieter Paul because he had looked forward to the comfort of return. He had been away nearly two years, the most strenuous and demanding and fatiguing period of his life. He was approaching his fifty-third birthday, a ripe age for a man in that epoch. He felt he had earned the tranquillity he so wanted. On closer examination, however, he had to confess that there was more to his unhappiness than Panneels' treason and the uneasiness of his relations with Albrecht and Nicolas.

The plain truth, the one that overrode all others, was that he was lonely. He rattled around miserably in his studio, in the denuded rotunda, in the rooms of his house. He missed the objects he had so impulsively sold to the Duke of Buckingham, and set about filling the empty spaces with paintings, his own and others. But instead of giving him pleasure, these new decorations enhanced the atmosphere of unfamiliarity. He felt himself a stranger in his own abode. In spite of the long four years that had elapsed since the death of Isabella, her aura remained pervasive. Subconsciously, he kept seeking her, half-certain that at any moment she would make an appearance—that his shattered

317

life, of which he had been kept unaware during his absences, would be miraculously made whole once more. He admitted to Jan Brandt that the fantasy was idiotic, hardly the manifestation of a rational mind in good working order. "I *could* go on running," he said. "But I'm too tired, and it wouldn't be fair to the boys."

His father-in-law staggered him. "What you really ought to do, my dear Pieter Paul, is to find yourself a new wife."

"At my age?"

Brandt acknowledged this reality with a little shrug. "Call it a marriage of friendship, of companionship. It's not unheard of. I'm sure there are any number of fine widows of the nobility who'd be only too happy to share your declining years."

Rubens wasn't at all pleased to think of himself as in a state of decline. Depressed he was. But declining, no. He laughed sardonically. "A noblewoman? Oh no, Jan. Never that. You forget that I work with my hands. No matter how prosperous that work has made me, no noblewoman would ever honestly accept me as her equal."

"But you're several times a knight."

"A *made* one, not a born one. The difference is regarded as crucial. Those are titles, after all, that I can't pass on to my children."

Brandt was incredulous. "Why, by God, you're a damned snob."

"Am I?"

"Pretentious, then."

"Is it pretentious to want not to be condescended to? I don't understand."

"You wanted a peerage."

Rubens nodded. "I've earned it ten times over."

"You've not asked for one?"

"I'd never dream of it."

"I'll do it for you."

"My father-in-law? It would come to the same thing. Everyone would think I'd put you up to it."

"You're a coward, Pieter Paul. You want a peerage, but won't

318

ask for it. And you won't marry a peeress for fear that she'd scorn you."

"I am what I am. And I've no reason to be ashamed of it. I've no plan to try to make myself conform to any great lady's image of what I ought to be."

There the matter of Rubens' remarriage rested, as far as Jan Brandt was concerned. But the seed, once sown, germinated and took root as spring gave way to summer and summer to the first days of autumn. Perhaps it was the very sorrow that afflicted all the Flemish earth at this season which infused Rubens with a greater and greater longing for companionship. He visited Suzanne Fourment, not with any intention of attempting to revive their long-abandoned intimacy, but just to have the pleasure of a beautiful woman's company. They had no need any longer to be particularly discreet. Arnold Luden, her husband for almost a decade, was not a jealous man. And even if he were, there seemed little reason to become apprehensive about the friendship between his wife and an aging man. Besides, Luden stood in awe of Pieter Paul and was still grateful to him for his role in finding him Suzanne.

She had not mellowed noticeably. The difference in their years seemed less important to her now than it had at Eeckeren in the summer of 1621. The long period of separation, which had seen Suzanne become a prominent hostess of Antwerp's prosperous *bourgeoisie*, had furnished her quite gratuitously with more confidence in herself—in inverse proportion, it might have appeared, to the sapping of Pieter Paul's steadfastness by age and weariness. They met now as personalities of equal power, with the distinction that Suzanne was eager to test her new authority; his had already been often tried and not found wanting. He had nothing to prove to her, except that he was glad to see her. She meant to show him her new self, flaunt her new position. She called him Pieter Paul, something she had never dared to do even when she was in his naked embrace. She spoke to him in the diminutive *"tu"* form, an audacity that he found charming and novel. He had always so addressed her.

Pieter Paul couldn't be certain whether these liberties were meant to be signs of affection or of contempt. It was, as ever, this uncertainty about Suzanne's basic motivation that made her an amusing friend. She was a bitch. He was not the first man to find bitches more attractive than women who were demure and decorous. She was as tantalizing to his spirit as she had been years before. Her physical maturity had taken the edge off her allure as a woman. But of course, years before, *he* had been in the prime of life. Now, as he told her mournfully, he was catabolic.

She snorted. "All you have is a twinge of gout now and then, or so you claim. What well-fed gentleman doesn't suffer from that? It's just your reward for having led too good a life."

There was a perverse appeal to him in her scornful treatment. In his loneliness, he had imagined that what he required was sympathy. But when he discovered himself grinning as Suzanne slashed at him with her tongue, he realized that a more respectful companion would have bored him. Suzanne Fourment was incapable of boring him, though she could often annoy him—yet these annoyances were pleasurable.

She too suggested marriage. The alternative, she averred, was that he find himself *"une maîtresse en titre très raisonnable."*

To her second proposal he responded with an asperity that she laughed at. "I'd never do such a thing to my sons. The idea," he exclaimed. "You'd really have me move a whore into my bedroom?"

"You could keep her somewhere else. God knows, it's being done every day by countless 'fine gentlemen' of Antwerp. Would you like a list of their names?"

"No."

"Well, then, get yourself a wife."

"Whom?"

"How should *I* know? You're acquainted with every eligible lady in the town. There must be . . ."

"Yes, yes, I know," he broke in impatiently. "Jan Brandt, Moretus, everyone else says the same. There must be . . . who knows? . . . perhaps thousands of noble widows just praying for such an opportunity. I want no part of them, any of them."

320

Suzanne's fine, large eyes narrowed. "What exactly is it you want?"

"A companion, an amiable companion."

"Like me?" She gave a sharp little laugh, but the inquiry itself led him momentarily to wonder if she weren't, in fact, obliquely offering herself.

"For a wife, my little Suzanne, I'd want someone just a bit more manageable than you." His smile was remote, nostalgic. "But someone who could be just as tart as you now and then."

She gave him a rasping sigh of exasperation. "There isn't a sensible *bourgeoise* spinster in all of Flanders who wouldn't marry you."

"I don't want a sensible *bourgeoise*. I'm not sure I want a wife. I'm not sure I want anyone who's even terribly sensible. *I'm* sensible, after all. Besides, most sensible spinsters are plain as a stone wall."

"Ah," she whispered. "Now we're learning a few things. She mustn't be plain. She needn't be sensible. She can't be a widow, or at least not an old one or a peeress. What else? Education?"

"Cultivated, if possible," he replied, beginning to enjoy her game. "And compelling."

"Talkative or taciturn?"

"She needn't be as taciturn as Doctor Faustus' Helen."

Suzanne's rejoinder was of pure puzzlement. "Who is Doctor Faustus?"

"The principal character in a play I saw while I was in London."

"You learned English, then?"

"A few phrases. But Balthasar Gerbier took me to the theater several times. He translated the main points of the plot as we went along."

"And Helen? Who is she?"

"A creature of Faustus' dreams. She was Helen of Troy."

Suzanne made no immediate reply. She was lost in a tangential thought. Then, her eyes wide as if she was amazed by what had suddenly come into her head, she muttered, "*I* have a sister named Hélène."

321

Rubens recognized Hélène Fourment, who was seated across the table from him, but he couldn't associate her with the child he had seen only a few years before. She had been twelve or thirteen on that earlier occasion—awkward, stringy, retiring. The only resemblance between that insignificant child and the fulsome girl of sixteen he now beheld was the flaming hair. The rest represented revolution, transfiguration. No other words would serve. Though few men could have been more constantly alert to the development and decay of human flesh than Pieter Paul, it astounded him to realize that so relatively brief a period should have effected so stunning an alteration in the girl. Nothing of a comparable sort had happened to either Albrecht or Nicolas—or was it rather that the changes to which they had been subjected had no sexual connotations for their father?

Images cluttered his febrile brain—all of them related to fruit. Hélène Fourment was a peach, a pear, a plum, an apple. She was ripe. She was toothsome. But metaphors and adjectives were soon beggared by emotion. She was a creature out of one of his own paintings—the very incarnation of a Rubens woman. She could be the issue of the union of Zeus and Leda. Yet were there critics who presumed to suggest that only the peasant whores of Flanders conformed to the contours of the feminine prodigies he had for so long so warmly depicted.

"Hélène," he murmured fatuously, still stupefied by this apparition of flesh's fullest summer seated opposite him. "So you're Hélène." Was he capable of no comment more stimulating than that, of nothing likelier to provoke a reply that would tell him something helpful or interesting about her?

She nodded. Then she blushed. Such inconsequential words could cause her to blush? Oh, the marvelous power of age and position and wealth. Would she say not a thing? "I have a son who's just about your age," he ploughed on madly, driven by some terrible demon of self-destruction. "Do you know my Albrecht, or my younger son Nicolas?" Why in God's name should he mention his sons? What had *they* to do with it? To do with *what?*

322

Hélène Fourment just nodded once again, and smiled brilliantly; her mouth ajar was a perfect melon halved. She tittered. Rubens had forgotten that girls tittered. The memory of his little Clara pierced his consciousness with a stiletto wound and momentarily arrested his satyr's pursuit; it seemed a sacrilege to the specter of his dead daughter to evince the bashful laughter of this delicious child. But his enchantment with Hélène repressed all finer feelings—if that was what they were. A man of stone, which Pieter Paul thought years of diplomacy had turned him into, wouldn't for long have resisted the attraction of this girl's vivacity, so superbly contained as it was in a body designed by God in a moment of voluptuous whimsy.

"What do you like, Hélène?" he asked. But this was becoming more ludicrous every minute. If she refused to reply to *that* inane query, he might next hear himself asking her opinion of the weather they were having, or what season she preferred. And for a dreadful instant, it appeared that he might indeed have to seek some other topic. But just as he was on the point of exquisite desperation, Hélène glanced up from the plate in front of her, which had seemed a source of inordinate interest, and flashed him another brief, shattering smile, allowing her deep, Delft-blue eyes to be held for a fraction of a moment by the intensity of his quite alarming gaze. Then once more she dipped her fine auburn head. "I like clothes," she said so softly that the words were scarcely audible to him above the babble of the luncheon conversation. "I like clothes and flowers and jewelry."

Rubens chuckled gently, then began to laugh convulsively, raucous, hysterically, with all his aging, sentimental heart. It *was* funny, perhaps the single most amusing reply he had ever heard —a perfectly sensible answer to an asinine question. "Yes," he finally controlled his voice sufficiently to say. "Yes, of course you do."

His laughter drew the attention of the others at the table. Suzanne had been observing the one-sided exchange with undisguised attention. She perceived in the artist's creased, puffy, elegant features something of the rapt pleasure and eagerness he had shown *her* a decade earlier. The first phase of her plan had gone successfully into operation; she was not surprised. "What did Hélène say, Pieter Paul? *What* did she say she liked?"

"What lovely young girls ought to like. Things to enhance their beauty." His glance returned to Hélène very briefly, then back to Suzanne. "But of course in your sister's case, jewelry and clothes would be quite superfluous, quite unnecessary. She requires nothing to enhance *her* beauty."

"Do you mean," said Suzanne, obviously relishing her wickedness, "nothing at *all?*"

"Not a solitary stitch," Pieter Paul replied with enthusiasm.

Hélène's pale, full features turned crimson. She mumbled a hurried apology to the others at table and rushed from the room. Daniel Fourment, placed at the far end, at some distance from the painter and this youngest of his eleven children, had not paid any heed to their dialogue. But as the girl closed the door sharply behind her, he inquired of no one in particular what had happened.

Suzanne responded with sarcastic pleasure, "Your guest, papa, Maître Rubens here, has just frightened poor little Hélène into womanhood. He told her she didn't need a stitch of clothing on to make her beautiful."

The artist scowled furiously at his quondam mistress. "And what's wrong, dare I ask, with my saying that?"

"Nothing wrong in suggesting that you'd prefer to see her stark naked than clothed?"

"I meant no such thing, and you know it."

"That was my inference."

"You've become an evil woman, my dear Suzanne, to have imagined such a thing. I'm surprised at you." To all present save Suzanne, the master's innocence was without need for proof; but to her, he wore his hypocrisy at a very rakish angle indeed.

"You may not have said it in so many words," she persisted happily, "but Hélène understood your meaning, just as I did. *You've* become a lecherous old man, Pieter Paul. So I'm surprised at *you*, too."

Daniel Fourment was beside himself with distress. "Suzanne,

you must apologize at once. How dare you speak so to my honored guest? It's a scandal, a scandal. You're a disgrace."

Rubens came to her defense. "Suzanne and I are ancient adversaries, Daniel, ever since I painted her portrait. She's got nothing to apologize for."

The young woman was having none of his falsified compassion. "You're quite right," she retorted. "I have nothing to apologize for. I was telling the simple truth. Admit it."

The soft-spoken, easygoing Arnold Luden felt that he had to intervene. "I'm astonished that you show so little respect for Maître Rubens, Suzanne, when he deigns to join us for a meal."

"Well said, Arnold," approved Fourment.

Pieter Paul knew better than most how little Suzanne respected any man. Nevertheless, as she turned from father to husband to him, her expression mellowed from one of truculence to a sly ironic smile. "Oh, I think Maître Rubens and I understand each other very well. And in my own peculiar way, I respect him."

Addled by this turn of the conversation, his mind still trying to dwell intently on the image of the vanished Hélène, Pieter Paul replied with less caution than was his diplomatic wont. "Like everything else," he said offhandedly, "I take respect where I can find it."

Suzanne Fourment eyed him suspiciously. What could he mean? *Had* she offended him? That wouldn't do at all, not now, with the hook baited and the fish about to take it. She tried to cover herself. "I'm sorry, Pieter Paul. I was rude."

Brought suddenly back from absorbing thoughts about her delectable sister, he turned on Suzanne with more emotion than he intended. "You're almost always rude."

"I'm sorry," she repeated, the picture of utter contrition.

"I hope," he went on, "you'll not be disillusioned, though, if I tell you that rudeness suits you better than remorse. Remorse is a shade of feeling you should avoid wearing."

Daniel Fourment and Arnold Luden laughed heartily at this. Themselves rarely able to get the better of Suzanne's hot tongue, they were relieved to know that her match, if not her master, was abroad in the world. But she was endowed with that most redeeming of virtues, a sense of humor. She laughed at herself easily as she responded. "I'm glad the years seem to have sharpened your wit, Pieter Paul."

"Have they?" He sighed heavily. "If so, it's the only improvement."

"Was the conversation of Madrid and London so much more sparkling than what you find in Antwerp? Does diplomacy have its social applications, then?" she continued gaily.

"If my wit *is* sharper, which I doubt, it's been honed by the wives and mistresses of great men. If tongues were blades, there'd not be a gentleman left standing in all Christendom. All of them would have been laid low by women—by ladies."

"Don't we merit some means of defending ourselves against male brutality?"

"None whatever. You were born with all the defenses you need. First you outsmart us, then you outlive us."

She chuckled darkly. "But at what a price, dear Pieter Paul. We have to bear you, in every sense of the word."

Suzanne could recognize a good exit line, particularly when she had uttered it herself. In any event, it was the moment when the *eau-de-vie* was produced by a servant—the time for the ladies to leave the dining room. As Rubens stood to help her from her chair, he allowed his mouth to graze her ear as he whispered hoarsely, "I want her."

Suzanne looked into his bold, old eyes, her face contriving to show both derision and mock surprise. Then, detecting that he was in no mood to be further trifled with, she became serious. "You understand, of course, that you'll have to marry her."

"If your father allowed such a thing, do you think she'd have me—willingly, I mean?"

She gave him no reply, but started to glide toward the door in the wake of her commodious mother. As she was about to quit the room, she caught the painter's eye. Her expression remained grave; but now, with brows raised, she put a silent question to him. Did he mean it? He nodded brusquely. He most emphatically did mean it. He wanted her.

326

The good, kindly, unworldly Fourment had taken note of the wordless exchange of glances between Suzanne and his old acquaintance, Rubens. He was not stupid. He believed he grasped the import of their looks, but found his deduction incredible. Certainly, this was not a subject that *he* could raise. The initiative lay with the painter. As was the custom, the three men gathered at Fourment's end of the long table in the cool dining room which was decorated by the Brussels tapestries he so successfully marketed.

They began to converse in a perfunctory way about Pieter Paul's recent travels to Madrid and London, a topic that was still a staple of casual chat in Antwerp where, when it came to that, anything Rubens did was a matter of obsessive interest. But because other things were on the painter's mind and on Daniel Fourment's, it was only Arnold Luden who maintained a mindless flow of talk, apparently oblivious of the more serious undercurrents swirling about him.

The two older men bided their time, each waiting for the other to find a way of bringing up the subject that consumed them both. Yet Luden would drone on in that sententious way that Suzanne had complained to Rubens of. At length, however, observing that neither of his companions was paying the least attention to his empty theorizing about the prospects for peace in the Netherlands and, as a logical corollary, the prospects for an upturn in commerce, he abruptly stilled himself and stared at them in turn. When, after perhaps a minute of silence had elapsed and neither seemed inclined to contribute a syllable to the post-prandial banter, he muttered sullenly, "Well?"

Fourment, startled from his bemused reflections, looked at Rubens and echoed his son-in-law. "Well?"

The artist, so rarely at a loss, boggled now. He felt like a man accused of heresy brought suddenly into the presence of the Grand Inquisitor. It was absurd. *Was* it absurd? Could he say precisely what he wanted to say? Did he really want to say it, or was he reacting to a dangerous impulse, a fleeting flash of passion? It was assuredly an impulse. But impulses were not common events in Pieter Paul Rubens' emotional history. And

327

when the impulse was to commit himself irrevocably to something so momentous as matrimony. . . . It was a hallucination. He was senescent. He was drunk. There had to be some rational explanation for so irrational a compulsion . . . Yet he knew that he must speak now or perhaps forever lose the occasion. If he spoke, there would be, could be, no retreat. The diplomat counseled caution. But the man, this aging, lonely man cried out for immediate and affirmative action.

For the second time in his long career, the demands of the flesh prevailed against the forces he took for intelligence. Pieter Paul remarked with a twinge of bitter humor that the Fourment family was involved in both cases. He decided. He took a deep breath. There was an unearthliness as he heard his own voice, as if it were disembodied, utter the horrendous phrase, "I would be honored, Daniel, if you gave me permission to court your daughter Hélène." Was it really *he* who said this stupendous thing?

Before Fourment had time to offer a reply, Arnold Luden gasped, "But surely you're joking, Maître Rubens." Then, evidently overcome by the enormity of his daring in making such a charge, Luden shrank, shriveled, clasped his arms to his lean side and bent his head low over his glass of *eau-de-vie*. He would like, Pieter Paul thought sympathetically, to be able to disappear magically from the room, from the earth.

The painter laughed testily. "Yes, Luden, it may sound like a joke. But it's not, I promise you."

"You assure me that you're serious, Pieter Paul?" Fourment inquired, grateful to his son-in-law for having stumbled so, for in doing this he had apparently righted the improbable conversation. "I'm asking you that in the interest of . . . the record, so to speak."

"It's not a joking matter, Daniel. I am most definitely serious."

Luden couldn't live with the images going through his mind. "But Hélène's only a child, in God's name," he wailed, his voice gagging.

"And I'm fifty-three," replied Rubens evenly. "Yes, I can tell

328

you that I'm even more aware of that discrepancy than you. I'm the one who's got all that age on him, after all."

Once again intimidated, this time by the artist's earnest determination, Luden looked away. "I haven't the right to speak."

"That is correct," said Fourment firmly, pleased to clear the air with a little self-righteous anger. "You haven't." Then he went on, addressing Pieter Paul, "Hélène is a woman. You have my glad permission to court her. You do my family honor."

Rubens gave his old friend a grateful smile, then looked at him quizzically. "You're certain of *your* feelings, Daniel. You don't want time to consider it?"

"Do you want time? Is that what you're getting at?" asked the merchant, suddenly wary.

"No, no," Pieter Paul replied hastily. "No, no. I'm absolutely sure. I've never been so sure of anything in my life. It's remarkable. Hélène is the most spectacularly beautiful mortal I've ever seen."

The compliment left the girl's father not especially moved. He was well aware of his daughter's beauty. Whatever it might be to Rubens, to him it was a simple fact of life, preferable to warts but not so gratifying as an improvement in trade. "There's just one stipulation, Pieter Paul. I shan't lift a finger in this matter beyond giving my permission."

"You oppose it?"

"How *could* I? How could any reasonable father set himself against such a magnificent marriage? But I won't support it. That wouldn't be fair. As Arnold here has so clumsily put it, there *is* the question of your ages. You have a son as old as she . . ."

"I could be her grandfather," said Pieter Paul with a little groan. "I know."

"I'm *not* unsympathetic, all the same. I know you'd be good and kind to her."

"I'd be princely," was the wistful rejoinder. "Not a whit less."

"I'm sure of it. All I'm trying to say is that I want the decision to be entirely Hélène's. *You* can plead your cause, but I won't."

"I'd have it no other way, Daniel."

"Suzanne will plead your cause," said Luden with bitterness.

"But would Hélène do as Suzanne tells her?" asked the father. He threw his stocky arms into the air. "Who the devil can predict what a woman will do? Sometimes I don't think they themselves know what they're going to do until they come to the very instant of decision."

If Hélène resembled her older sister in temperament, Rubens appreciated the precariousness of his position. He was liable to make himself the toy of a teen-aged girl. The whole thing, however, was so grotesque a distortion of common sense that he was unable to recognize the Pieter Paul Rubens he thought he knew. And for all that, he enjoying himself hugely. Which of them, he wondered, he or Hélène, was the quarry? Which of them was the hunter? He had to laugh. Lo, how was the mighty fallen.

In his imagination already the lawyer and *échevin* that he meant in time to become, Albrecht Rubens received with what he thought exemplary calm the news that his father intended to ask Hélène Fourment to be his bride. "I think you're the only person, papa, who can judge whether or not it's the right thing to do."

Pieter Paul was mildly dismayed by what seemed his older son's reaction of indifference. "Is that all you have to say about it?"

Albrecht was willing to concede, to himself, that it was odd he should have so little feeling. It would appear more natural to respond strongly, one way or the other. He might have been inclined to do this if he were as close to his father as he had been just after his mother's death. But now, with two years of continuous separation immediately behind them, no decision of Rubens' could concern him unless it concerned *him*, Albrecht. So he said blandly, "Yes, papa, that's all I have to say."

"You'd not resent her being in the house . . . living with us . . . with me?"

"I *like* Hélène, papa, the little that I know her. Why should I have any resentment?"

Rubens thought it wise not to press the point, not to try to find possible sources of antipathy. "And Nicolas? How do you think he'd feel?"

The youth pursed his lips, as he had seen his grandfather do when he was thoughtful. "Does it matter? Haven't you made up your mind already?"

"*I've* made up *my* mind, but I haven't yet spoken to Hélène."

Albrecht grinned. "Don't you think you ought to ask her first?"

The father considered the slight, pale youth who so closely resembled his mother. There seemed to be more of Philip Rubens in him than Pieter Paul—none, certainly, of the gallant Jan. "Perhaps you're right."

There was a long pause which the son finally terminated. "Is there something else, papa?"

Almost shyly, Rubens mumbled, "I'd like to have your blessing."

With wry solemnity, Albrecht laid a slender hand on Pieter Paul's shoulder. "Thy will be done," he said.

The next afternoon, Hélène Fourment was preparing herself to receive Maître Rubens in the tapestried sitting room of her father's comfortable, modest house. She was flustered. What girl in the first half of her seventeenth year wouldn't be just a little nervous after being apprised of the earthshaking knowledge that she would be proposed to by an old man? No matter what Daniel Fourment had said to the artist at luncheon the day before, Hélène felt herself to be still a girl, not a woman. And she was dithering now because she hadn't the least idea of how she should or would comport herself in the presence of the great man who soon would call.

Whenever the name of Pieter Paul Rubens came up in conversation in the Fourment house, stress was invariably laid on his "greatness." She would not have known how to define the term. She understood that it meant different things to different people. To her father, for example, and to her brother-in-law Arnold Luden, some portion of the attribution of greatness to Rubens doubtless derived from the fact that he was and had been for years an important purchaser of Brussels tapestries. He was a good customer. To Suzanne, Rubens' importance was obviously of a more personal nature; beyond this, Hélène didn't care to allow her imagination to venture.

For herself, she had never doubted his greatness. She hadn't considered it often. All of Antwerp knew that Rubens was a great man, rich, influential, erudite. She presumed, without caring much, that the entire world knew his name. Until she was told of his desire to marry her, Hélène had had no difficulty in believing in this popular belief. The intelligence that he was expressing an interest in her disturbed and threatened to dislodge her credulity. Important old men didn't fall in love with unimportant young girls. Or if they did, they had no desire to marry them.

It was comical, or it was tragic, or perhaps it was both at once. It was absurd, in any case. Of that she was sure. What did he know about her? Nothing save whatever Suzanne might have told him. How was it possible for an old man, a *great* old man . . . ? It was comical. And the comedy would end as soon as he became more acquainted with her. That seemed obvious. For in her own opinion, which she considered well informed, she was a silly, frivolous, flighty girl. She wouldn't have the remotest conception of how she ought to behave as the wife of Pieter Paul Rubens, who was known to have received in his magnificent house every dignitary from every country who ever visited Antwerp. He was better known by far than the military governor, than the burgomaster, than the archbishop. Only the Infanta Isabel was more famous than he. To come to this city without paying a formal visit to him was like going to Rome without paying a call on the pope. He was a landmark of Antwerp. For a prominent soul not to want his portrait painted by Rubens was like wishing to be buried in an unmarked grave.

332

What could Hélène Fourment, aged sixteen, do? What *should* she do? What *would* she do?

No, she was mistaken. It wasn't comical; it was tragic. Where lay the tragedy? For whom? For her, if she accepted his proposal? For him, if she rejected it? Oh, it was all so complicated, so confusing. She was unable to concentrate on a single aspect of the question; there were so many to be taken into account. Then, before she could collect herself, she heard a knock. He was here. She remembered her sister's instruction: "Be yourself." Who was that? It depended on the hour of the day, on her mood of the moment, on the weather . . . on the company she was in. It depended, above all, on the circumstances—whether she was able to control them or not. What in the name of God was she going to say to him?

Oh dear gentle God, he had flowers for her, all of them out of season, hothouse flowers, a colossal extravagance. He made a small, formal bow as he presented the bouquet to her, and said timidly, "I know that I must appear to you as winter does to the earth, my dear little Hélène, so I thought I should bring some spring along with me for moral support."

She stared at him in plain amazement. She hadn't anticipated a handsomely turned simile embellished with metaphor. What *had* she expected? A talking-to. That was it. He was so old, so avuncular or even paternal, that subconsciously she had prepared herself for a pat on the head, a packet of sweets, a condescending smile. So she was doubly flustered. She stood before him looking up into his kindly face, her arms clutching the enormous bunch of flowers, helpless in her befuddlement. She laughed. There was nothing else to be done. *He* laughed, and she noted with satisfaction that he possessed all his teeth—or at any rate all that showed. And the lines in his gutted features had been produced by smiles, by laughter—not by scowls and grimaces. These seemed good omens.

"Thank you for the flowers, *maître*," she said when she regained control of herself. "I wasn't laughing at you. I was laughing at myself." She remained motionless, forgetting what to do

333

with the bouquet—though in normal circumstances she would have known perfectly well.

He divined her problem. "Can't we call for a servant to put these in water?"

"They're very beautiful," she murmured, as if she hadn't heard him. "Do you know, *maître,* nobody has ever brought me flowers before?"

He allowed himself the self-indulgence of an elaborate frown. "How foolish of everybody. You told me you liked flowers. They become you. You belong in a garland of flowers."

"All the time?" she asked whimsically. "How amusing that would be."

He took the bouquet from her and went to the door that led to the servants' wing. A domestic responded at once to his summons, and relieved him of his fragrant burden. When he turned back toward Hélène, he found that she was seated. He took an armchair facing her and leaned back, crossing his silk-clad legs. "You know why I've asked to see you."

"I do, *maître.* Papa told me."

"And Suzanne told you?"

Hélène smiled involuntarily as she nodded. "Yes, *maître,* she did."

"I can imagine . . ."

"Oh, she said not a single word to your discredit, *maître,*" the girl protested. "To the contrary . . ." Her voice trailed off, allowing Rubens to wonder just what the older sister might have said of him. He tried to curb his vivid imagination.

"Well, well, I'm glad to hear that . . . Would you like me to make you a formal, kneeling proposal of marriage, Hélène, or would you, perhaps, agree with me that all I really need to say is what I need to say?"

She looked down, then raised her eyes to give him a childishly pitiable look. "I don't know what it is you need to say, *maître.*"

"That in the twenty-four hours since I last saw you, I feel as if I'd regained my youth. Just sight of you has done that for me.

334

I think I can't live without you, or certainly I could never again enjoy life, without your presence in it."

Hélène was embarrassed by the force of his feeling. She was unable to doubt his passion, but couldn't accept herself as the object of it. He frightened her. "You honor me too much, *maître*," she whispered. "There must be hundreds . . ."

He interrupted her with a peremptory lifting of the hand. "There are *not*. I've *seen* hundreds, possibly thousands of women in my travels. God alone knows how many women I've portrayed, dressed and undressed . . . I really meant no harm yesterday, Hélène, when I said you needed not a stitch to make you beautiful. It was the simple truth." He gave her an opportunity to comment about his behavior at table. She gave him nothing more than a replica of the blush she had shown him on the first occasion. "The point is," he went on, "that I couldn't honor you too much. If you accept me, you might honor *me* too much. This is an immensely important decision you have to make. But you know that."

To a girl who had never heard a word of flattery from any man before, the ardent attentions of this most admirable of gentlemen remained difficult to take at their face value. He *must* be lying. It just couldn't be Hélène Fourment to whom, about whom he was saying such things. Could she honor him? Was that possible? She recalled Suzanne's appraisal: "He's devoured by desire for you, but I told him he'd have to marry you to have you." She shuddered. Yet how to respond? Suzanne had also told her, "You'll never be offered a happier chance to enjoy the best of both worlds—an old husband who'll worship you, and enough money to lure a new one after he dies. You could even buy a lover." Her worldly sister's crudity distressed her, but the argument had been firmly established in Hélène's mind. A lover? "A woman," said Suzanne, "has to have a husband before she has a lover. Otherwise, she becomes a whore, not a lady." The words burned the girl's ears as she heard them again in recollection. It was all too much for her.

She clasped her plump fingers together, then released them

from each other, repeating this gesture of anxiety several times before speaking. "You're playing games with me, *maître*. Your phrases are meant to deceive me."

He shook his bald head very slowly, very deliberately, his hooded eyes sad and wise. "If anything, my dear Hélène, I deceive *myself* by imagining it possible that so glorious a creation as you are would consider an old veteran of life's wars . . ." He stopped himself, angered. "No, I ask you to forgive me. That's all wrong. Please forget I said it. I don't want either your sympathy or your pity. What I mean is that in the normal course of things, you should prefer a much younger man for your husband. What I'm asking you is very unusual. I wasn't trying to deceive you. I'll never deceive you."

His direct, earnest words moved her more than did his flowers or his compliments. She looked at him now as one child looks at another. He *was* old, but there seemed no frailty in him, no evidence of serious infirmity. Suzanne said that he suffered from gout, and added nastily, "But that doesn't affect him when he's lying down." Until this moment, "old age" had been, in Hélène's lexicon, synonymous with "decrepitude." That the word could also be associated with "husband" had never crossed her mind. It startled her to realize that she was neither shocked nor distressed by this novel idea when "husband" was juxtaposed with "Rubens." She didn't find him repellent. Her preoccupation was rather with her own deficiencies and feelings of inadequacy. She parried while she thought. "Why should I want to marry at all, at my age?"

He smiled dolefully. "Yes, you have plenty of time to squander."

"You think I waste my time?" Her tone was reproachful.

He found even her childish pout appealing. "I'm sure you do," he replied affably. "Have you anything more interesting, more important to do with your time than to waste it? Wasting time must be one of the most charming things in life . . . when one has the time to waste."

She was surprised. "You wasted your time when you were . . . younger?"

He sighed. "The opportunity didn't present itself very often, I'm sorry to say. But sometimes, here and there, I've found time to squander."

"Tell me," she cried delightedly. "Please tell me."

He was bowled over by the eagerness of her entreaty. In London, he had gone quite often with Balthasar Gerbier to the Globe Theatre. One of the plays they had seen had been Shakespeare's tragedy of the Moorish general Othello, who told his friends that he had won the love and eventually the hand of the beautiful Desdemona by telling her the story of his life—a tale of wars and wonders. Would a similiar account of his own career prevail against Hélène Fourment's compunctions? He had allowed literature to influence his art. Could it now influence his life as well?

They saw each other almost every afternoon. Pieter Paul sensed that he was gaining ground in his campaign. He sent her flowers and ribbons and lace; he thought it premature to offer her jewelry. Each time he called, she pressed him to continue the story of his life. He was touched and of course ravished that her interest in him, or at least in his narrative, failed to abate. Indeed, it grew, fed on itself.

There came a time, however, when the girl, who was becoming increasingly straightforward with him now that the presence of the great Rubens had become a custom, disclosed a certain dissatisfaction with his account. This was after he had described his marriage with Isabella, an abridgement that omitted mention of his late wife's collision with Anton van Dyck and his own deliquency with Suzanne.

Hélène had listened to his circumspect recital with appropriate respect. What disturbed her was that Pieter Paul, as he had finally persuaded her to call him, had re-created an Isabella she was unable to visualize. This was remarkable because the dryness and terseness of his evocations of her contrasted sharply with colorful descriptions of others he had known not nearly so well —the rich, the important, the powerful, the ridiculous people whose paths had crossed with his, and whom he brought vividly to life so entertainingly. But Hélène was unable to picture

Isabella from Rubens' narrative of their seventeen years together. She emerged from his descriptions as . . . an institution, perhaps, or a state of grace. But decidedly, Isabella Brandt did not assume the dimensions and warmth of an individual. Yet of all the mortals who had peopled Pieter Paul's exciting and exotic life, this one seemed to Hélène the most important.

She sought in herself the question that might elicit the information she required—but the fact was that she didn't quite know what she was looking for. Then, suddenly, she found the right query. "Did you ever paint her portrait?"

Rubens understood. "If you'll allow me, I'll bring you to my house tomorrow, and I'll show you the portraits I made of Isabella."

Hélène replied that she would like that very much.

Rubens would happily have taken her to his house that very afternoon, but he thought it prudent to prepare, in a devious way that he believed Richelieu would have approved, for her arrival. He was apprehensive that she might be overwhelmed by the size of his household staff, be intimidated by the prospect of being placed in charge of a substantial, smoothly functioning *ménage*. About the extent of his establishment, there was nothing he could do. But about its appearance, he could do and did a great deal. He instructed his domestics to remain as unobtrusive as possible during Hélène's tour the next day, a command they much resented, for they were naturally anxious to see the child who might soon become their mistress.

The servants were even more annoyed by Rubens' order that the house and rotunda and studio, normally maintained in the impeccable state that was the rule in Flanders, be deliberately disordered. Elsa, Isabella's former chambermaid, had achieved by the attrition of seniority the post of housekeeper. She alone dared to protest to her master that Hélène would form an entirely erroneous impression, would think her supervision inadequate. "She'll dismiss me."

"No," Rubens replied, rubbing his hands with glee, "she'll

think *my* supervision inadequate, which is just what I want her to think. I want her to feel that she'd not only be welcome in my house, Elsa, but that she'd be necessary." The housekeeper grudgingly agreed that the deception was a clever one, but she feared, nonetheless, for her security. Pieter Paul reassured her.

The exterior of the Rubens house in the Wapperstraat was familiar to Hélène. She had passed it often. The interior, which she entered now for the first time, was quite another matter. It alarmed her by its size and the richness of its decoration. The extraordinary state of untidiness was, as Pieter Paul had hoped, shocking to her. She was unwilling to believe that the meticulously groomed gentleman who had been courting her could bear to live in such squalid conditions. For the moment, she would contain her consternation. "It's very grand, Pieter Paul, very, very grand."

Before he could reply, Hélène saw a painting in which she immediately recognized the features of the artist as a much younger man, standing beside a seated woman in a bower of honeysuckle. This could only be the late Isabella Brandt. The girl moved with lithe grace across the large sitting room to confront this wedding portrait. Her eyes at first were only for the attire of the bride, for which the only description that seemed to suffice was "sumptuous." But for the woman concealed by this sumptuous adornment Hélène was able to feel nothing—certainly not that she was standing face to face with a dead but potentially menacing rival for Rubens' affection. It wasn't that she sensed in the picture of Isabella no presence of life, but rather that Isabella herself, at the age of eighteen or nineteen, seemed to Hélène far less developed a person than she thought herself in her seventeenth year. She saw no good reason for giving voice to this impression.

In the same painting, the artist had depicted himself as the man Hélène recognized. The features had been more taut twenty years ago than they were today. There was no trace of gray in the hair or beard or mustache. The flesh was firmer. But the eyes, the full mouth were the same. The expression on Pieter Paul's face in this portrait disturbed Hélène. He appeared sad or resigned—not happy, surely, not radiant. She continued her contemplation of the picture for a moment longer, still puzzled. Then it struck her. What was missing was the passion in the face of the Rubens she by now was so accustomed to. She kept the satisfaction of this realization tactfully to herself as she turned to him. "You have other portraits?"

"Of Isabella? Many. But most of them I don't like. She wasn't a good subject because she didn't like posing for me. She had little vanity. There is one, though, that captures her flavor, I think. Isabella despised it. She said it made her appear slatternly. It *is* informal." He drew Hélène across the room to the opposite wall on which hung a number of small portraits. She stopped before the picture of a small blond girl with eyes full of piquant affection. "Clara?" she asked him quietly.

"When she was four or five," he said with a nod, his voice dry with regret.

"She was beautiful."

"Yes, she was beautiful. She was beautiful until she was nothing."

What could Hélène possibly say to that? Sensibly, she elected to say not a word, but allowed him to lead her to another, smaller portrait of Isabella, this one plainly made a long time after their wedding. The girl was electrified by the transformation that had occurred in the woman's face during the interim. Here, she understood, she was confronted by a real woman, a *person,* full of force and humor and vitality. "She's alive there," she murmured a little fearfully, as if she were looking directly at a phantom.

"*Only* there," said Rubens, making no attempt to hide his sorrow. "And that's not enough."

Hélène sat down in a straight chair and stared at this little painting of Isabella. Age had improved the woman, put character in her face, added flesh as well as wisdom. But something else impressed Hélène; her intuitions, however, were surer than her capacity to identify them by name. What was it? Here was obviously a lovable wife, a lovable mother—but perhaps not a lovable woman? There seemed a hardness, a sternness, a resist-

340

ance in her nature as Pieter Paul had portrayed her. Was that good or bad? She had to make some observation. "She was a very strong person, wasn't she?"

"Mostly," he replied evasively.

"Mostly?"

"She was brave rather than strong. To marry me was an act of bravery. To marry me when she did, I mean. *She* had no choice, as you do."

"I don't understand what you intend by 'bravery,' Pieter Paul. You're not a monster, are you, beneath that handsome clothing? Were you cruel to her?" There was no note of accusation in Hélène's voice, merely curiosity.

"I think not."

"I think not, too. This isn't the face of a woman who's been mistreated. It's the face of a woman who's leading a rich, good life."

"Not always happy," he said quietly. "Not always. That's what you may *want* to see in the portrait, my little Hélène. You're trying to imagine from it how *you'll* look when you're thirty or so."

The idea that she would ever be thirty was so improbable that Hélène deigned it unworthy of comment. Instead, she made a half-turn and pointed to the wedding portrait. "Do you remember what you were feeling about yourself when you painted that?"

He was unprepared for that question. It opened up to him a view of territory he had abandoned. He was the more surprised because nothing Hélène had yet disclosed of herself could have alerted him to the possibility of her percipience. Yet it seemed clear that she knew she was touching a very sensitive nerve. There was something else: He was even more vulnerable to this child than he had thought. He immediately discarded this line of contemplation. Whatever her clairvoyance or his vulnerability, his commitment to her was complete. "I felt detached," he responded. "Why do you ask?"

"*Detached?* So short a time after your wedding, you felt detached?"

"That's what I said. The description doesn't satisfy you?"

"No. It's the wrong word."

"How would you know?"

She shrugged. "I'm just guessing, of course."

"What word, then?"

"Loneliness, I think," she replied without hesitation. "That's what I see in your eyes." She realized the terrible treacherousness of the ground she was treading, wondering how much, how far she might safely venture. "Were you always so lonely?"

"Always detached, yes. I never thought of myself as being particularly lonely." He paused and thought. "Perhaps that's because I was *always* lonely. I don't know." He had almost physically to repress his desire to seize this girl and crush her to him. "Separated. I think *that* may be the word. I felt separated."

"No, Pieter Paul, you felt *lonely*," she insisted. "Why do you avoid the word?"

"Because it makes me want to weep."

"Then weep. What's wrong with that? I do it all the time."

"No, no," he said sternly. "I weep only for joy . . . Will you give me cause?"

Hélène wouldn't allow him to corner her so easily. She brushed an errant strand of auburn hair from her flushed features. Her little smile was doubtful. "But wouldn't you feel separated from me too, even more than from Isabella? There are so many things you couldn't share with me, because there are so many things I could never understand." She rose from the chair and walked a few paces from him, then spun gracefully on the soles of her shoes to face him. "So many things I don't *want* to understand . . . politics, wars, diplomacy, great painting commissions. I know they're very important parts of your life, but they mean nothing to me. They could *never* mean anything to me." She folded her hands beneath her high, full bosom. "You see?" she concluded with a smile of defiance. "I'm just a silly girl."

"Indeed I *do* see, Hélène. I understand you perfectly."

The calm of his reply deflated her. "You *do?*" she asked plaintively.

342

"And I want to keep you just as silly and frivolous as you are right now. Your frivolousness is just what I need. I want the sound of your laughter in this empty house."

Hélène sniffed the air and looked about her. "What you want most of all in this house is someone who knows how to make your servants do their work . . ." She broke off with a little gasp of wonder at her rude temerity. For an instant, she had dared to behave as if she were Pieter Paul's equal. The idea alarmed her. She studied his face for sign of an adverse reaction and discovered a smile of most serene delight.

"You're absolutely right."

Her manner changed dramatically. "Well, of course I'm right. I'm not *altogether* frivolous, you know. I've been taught everything a good wife needs to learn."

"I'm sure you have."

"A neat house above all things."

"Above all things," he owlishly assented. "But full of laughter too. My house must be full of laughter."

"If you want to keep a house full of laughter, Pieter Paul, you'll have to keep a wife full of babies. Can you do that?"

He held his breath. "I'm eager to try," he finally said, and found himself trembling.

The time for her to make her decision was approaching. In Hélène's recognition of this fact came the realization that there was no decision to be made; it had already made itself. Rubens adored the girl, the child, in her; but he paid her the supreme compliment of treating the child as a woman. So the child *became* a woman. He understood her, he said. He knew that she had an intelligence upon which, until he came into her life, no one had placed a solitary demand. No one had even guessed at its existence.

It would be too easy for her to say, as one was supposed to say, that she loved Pieter Paul. In a curious fashion she did love him—for his need for her. No one had ever needed her before. But only to the man himself, when he had become her husband, might she confess that the need to which she responded with absolute and willing submission was physical, sexual.

Some would think it monstrous, that a girl of sixteen should seek the desire of an old man. So be it. Hélène Fourment savored Pieter Paul's ardor, *required* it, and she would have it. It was, after all, hers for the taking.

"May I show you the rest of the house?" he asked, his tone suddenly stiff and full of propriety. He was afraid he might have said too much to her too soon in their courtship. He damned his impatience.

"I've seen enough," she replied with a quaver.

"Shall I take you home, then?" He was beginning to sound desperate.

"If you must, I suppose."

"If I *must?*"

"I don't *want* to go home, Pieter Paul. I want to be nowhere except in your presence, in your life." She spoke so softly and so without having laid the groundwork for this wholehearted affirmation of everything he had hoped that for a long moment he was expressionless, as if he had either failed to hear her or failed to understand.

Then, like the sun emerging from a covering of black, fast-scudding clouds, his face exploded with happiness. He laughed. He bent over and kissed her sweet fingers. He straightened and began to dance by himself about the room. He returned to where she stood and took her hands. To the silent song of his elation, he swung her around and around. By now, she too was laughing with delight and relief—and perhaps with a trace of misgiving too, for difficult decisions always bring in their wake elements of doubt, second thoughts. But all of her emotions were to be from now on so inextricably intertwined with his, and his pleasure was so boundless, that Hélène gave no more than a fraction of a second to her little fears. *His* jubilation swept everything before it, like a tidal wave.

He whirled her in spiraling circles to the door. There he stopped, his breath short, his laughter gasping. He looked down at this precious pear, this plum, this peach. There were tears in his eyes.

344

She reached into her tightly fitted sleeve and gave him her handkerchief.

They were married most festively in December. The month of their nuptials seemed especially appropriate to Rubens and to those of his friends who were, variously, scandalized, repelled, offended, or envious of his having taken a child bride. Rarely had the small city of Antwerp been afforded a more promising and continuous subject for gossip. It was a mine that nearly everyone exploited.

From the outset, Hélène Fourment was happy. She forgave her husband for his little deception in making her believe his house was normally a shambles. He needn't have humiliated his servants, or put them to the trouble of creating all that disorder, she told him. She admitted that she had been somewhat intimidated by the magnitude of her new responsibilities; but once installed as the master's wife, she assumed with consummate prepossession the mantle this office automatically bestowed on her—because she knew she had him behind her for moral support.

She basked luxuriantly in the pleasure he took in her. She rejoiced in his kindnesses and his tendernesses, great and small, in his countless gifts—not least of them being all of the dead Isabella's jewelry, a collection of gems to which he added frequently. But most of all, as she had known she would, she delighted in his panting lust for her body. His artful passion would have aroused the most jaded courtesan. The unschooled Hélène lived for the frenzies of their love-making. Each moment of union was a revelation for her. She became addicted to his needs; they became *her* needs.

The early months of marriages between young and old have in common with those of similar ages the process of adjustment. All successful marriages become *folies à deux*. But when there is a great disparity of age, one of two developments occurs: The younger spouse seeks, whether consciously or not, to emulate the older one, or the reverse takes place. In the marriage of Hélène Fourment and Pieter Paul Rubens, *he* grew younger.

345

It was a phenomenon. All his old acquaintances were agreed about that—even those who regarded his decision to marry the girl a travesty of his wonted intelligence and who considered his subsequent behavior unseemly, even lunacy. He was disporting himself in 1631 in ways he would never have entertained at an age when such comportment was deemed acceptable. Balthasar Moretus, who had known Rubens longer and more intimately than any soul still alive, believed at first that the painter had entered his second childhood. But he was humbled and silenced by Pieter Paul's rejoinder: "I never *had* a first childhood, Balthasar. That's the glorious thing. *Now* I have the wisdom to enjoy a pleasure I might have just taken for granted thirty years ago."

He swore truthfully that he cared not a damn that his helpless adoration for Hélène appeared wholly out of character. He cared not a damn that his friends felt cheated—as if he had for his entire life been hiding from them an essential facet of his nature, a gluttonous appetite for *la volupté* and, more astonishingly still at his age, a genius for satisfying it. That he cared not a damn was the greatest wonder of all, perhaps, the most remarkable departure from the norm they knew. He was simply no longer the Rubens to whom everyone had grown adjusted, with whom they had been so comfortable for so many ingratiating years. This sudden transformation gave all the people familiar with him the apprehension that something terrible had suddenly happened to their vision. They looked at him, failed to recognize him; they rubbed their eyes and looked at him again. Still were they unable to see the man whose outlines were the same, but whose composition had been so drastically reformed. Balthasar Moretus compared the new Rubens to a page printed from pied type. All the right letters were there, but they made no sense. It just wasn't Pieter Paul Rubens.

Nor was it. He was unrecognizable even to himself. He was besotted with Hélène. He was beguiled. He was inebriated. He was amused. He was infatuated. He had been born again, in his fifty-fourth year. Her presence in his life had changed not only the name of the game but all the rules by which the game had theretofore been played. Nothing, absolutely nothing, was as it had been. Her entry upon his scene had been galvanic; it had touched everything, transfigured everything. The Pieter Paul who had been no longer existed.

This new man had occasionally to rub his *own* eyes when he looked at himself, thought about himself—so total was the alteration. It seemed to him as miraculous a thing as the alchemist's transformation of base metal into gold—with the critical difference that in *his* case there was no illusion. The miracle *had* occurred. He was living it. He had been utterly renovated.

In none of his activities available to public scrutiny did this metamorphosis reveal itself more clearly than in his painting. His attitude toward his profession was completely changed. He had always enjoyed the craft of painting because he had done it so well, so easily. But now he positively reveled in it, because it gave him the opportunity again and again to celebrate Hélène and his passion for her. He portrayed her. He parodied her. He disguised her. He translated her. He painted her in the richest of gowns. He painted her naked. He painted her as a temptress, tantalizingly half-draped in a fine fur wrap. In scarcely a picture to come from his hand during the ten years that followed their wedding did Hélène's face or form not figure in some way. She was never out of his eyes, so she was never out of his work. Her auburn hair, her face, her flesh, her blinding smile, her guileless grace were before his every waking vision; they were in every canvas he made. His days were strewn with the sweetest thoughts of nocturnal embraces, warm and eager. He had discovered in Hélène Fourment his fountain of youth.

He left her as infrequently as possible, took her with him whenever he left the city. He proclaimed his love and her loveliness to the whole world. Hélène, who had twice blushed when Pieter Paul had so mildly suggested that she needed no adornment to enhance her beauty, swam with drunken delight in the pleasure of his pleasure in painting her. She secreted not the smallest compunction when she came upon a picture of her magnificent body hanging on the wall of a private house, a town hall, a palace, or a church. Her flesh became ubiquitous.

To her sister Suzanne, who accused Hélène of having become an exhibitionist, she replied disarmingly, "I have a body my husband loves. I love to be loved. Should I care who knows it? Why, I'd walk the streets of Antwerp mother naked if Pieter Paul asked me to, and I'd enjoy it. Because it was something he wanted of me, something I could do for him." Her dark blue eyes danced. "And the *nights*, Suzanne, and the *mornings*, and the afternoons . . ."

As Rubens had recognized from his first sight of Hélène, she was one of his own creations come to life, a dream materialized. In this twilight of his life, which he happily and willingly and wittingly mistook for a dawn, he committed her fleshly divinity to his art. Each painting of Hélène was an act of love or a memory of love. He offered the world no explanation; none was needed. It was all right there, in every stroke of his brush. Hélène had brought life to his painting, brought his painting to life. *She* was his epic joy. He wept idyllically almost every day.

Although Pieter Paul insisted on trumpeting his adoration of Hélène to the world, he did his best to prevent that same world from intruding on his wonderful new life. As a rule, he was successful—but not invariably. During the last months of 1631, when his darling bride was great with her first child, the Infanta Isabel implored her privy councillor to come to her assistance. He obeyed with the greatest reluctance.

Maria de' Medici, having once again quarreled openly with Richelieu and once again urged her royal son to dismiss the cardinal from his service, had herself been banished yet again from Paris. Since Richelieu had by now made Louis XIII master of most of the powerful noble French families, the queen mother, who was fatter and dowdier but not a whit brighter than she had been in 1625, when Pieter Paul had last visited with her, sought refuge and comfort and possible assistance in the Netherlands.

The infanta was embarrassed by the Florentine virago's request for asylum; she granted it only at the insistence of Philip IV, who saw in the queen mother's defection an opportunity to

348

do substantial damage to France—at no appreciable cost to Spain. Rubens, annoyed by this importunity and impatient to be freed forever of official obligations, was not at his best when he saw Maria de' Medici. With fewer troops to support her querulous demands than even the powerless pope could boast, she inveighed bitterly against the treachery of the cardinal who had, she vowed, seduced her son. What she wanted was war, any kind of war that would drive Richelieu from office and bring mother and child back together.

Pieter Paul wanted peace, as he always had. Nevertheless, he detected in the queen mother's arguments something of the same possibility, to strike a blow against the cardinal, that the Count-Duke of Olivares had perceived. His letter to the Spanish first minister was no more recognizable as Rubens' handiwork than was anything else he accomplished after his second marriage. He wrote with unwontedly bitter hope that through Maria a civil war might be stirred up in France. He gloatingly conjectured about inducing Frenchmen to spill one another's blood. The anger in this missive was shameful, and soon after he had dispatched it, he was rueful. For what infuriated him was not so much the nation of France, nor even Richelieu (though the cardinal had blocked all of Rubens' attempts to contract for the completion of the great Luxembourg cycle), but the fact of having to involve himself once more in such questions. Fortunately, nothing came of this scheme.

During the next two years there were a few further interruptions of his privacy—an abortive mission of peace to The Hague, and several visits to Brussels to discuss with the aging and ailing infanta problems that were not a bit more soluble today than they had been in the past. But where, hitherto, he would have been willing to do anything in the pursuit of that chimera, peace, or at least its facsimile, today he just no longer cared a damn. The world would have to get along without him. He knew his limitations.

The death of the Infanta Isabel, at the end of 1633, brought the hope of a definitive ending to all of Pieter Paul's diplomatic and state obligations. He greatly mourned her passing, as did every Fleming, but there was more than a little consolation for him in the plausible notion that her successor, Philip IV's intelligent younger brother, the Cardinal-Infante Ferdinand, would not solicit Rubens' advice. Nor did he, more than casually. The convocation of the Netherlands' Estates-General, seeming (as had been the case in France in 1614) to acknowledge the inherent right of the governed to be consulted, terminated the artist's official career as a statesman. That this severance was accomplished rather abruptly troubled him little. His only connection with the new regent had to do with art. And he was amply satisfied to be no more than first court painter.

Hélène and her proliferating brood of infants were all the concern he wanted; his painting afforded him all the fame he wanted. The years of his twilight flew past his eyes like lightning flashes. Everything went wonderfully his way—or almost everything. At the end of 1634, shortly after he completed the nine superb panels to decorate the ceiling of the Whitehall Banqueting House and packed them off, he began to suffer more regularly from the gout that had victimized him only occasionally during the previous decade. He was pleased to be able to make use of his ailment as an excuse not to accompany the paintings to London, though he regretted breaking his promise to Charles I that he would see personally to their installation. He had no doubt, however, that when they were in place, they would be hailed as masterpieces. He was right.

In the spring of 1635, Hélène produced their third child, Isabella-Hélène, whose sister and brother, Clara and Frans, thrived in their parents' symbiotic love for each other and for them. Pieter Paul purchased the estate of Steen near the Flemish village of Elewijt. It boasted a handsome little château, medieval military style, complete with moat and drawbridge. The Rubens family spent most of the clement seasons there, for Hélène had expressed a growing weariness with the formality of life in Antwerp. He enjoyed playing the role of *seigneur* to the peasants rooted on the acreage he had acquired. He tried his hand once again at landscapes. He also created some genre scenes, particularly a *kermesse* as lusty as any the elder Pieter Bruegel had ever made.

But it was always to Hélène that his thoughts, his eyes, his brushes, and his heart returned. There was really nothing else of significance for him. He kept her full of babies, true to the promise he had made her. Their fourth, Pieter Paul, was born in March of 1637. By this time, the gout was chronic, with acute phases that impaired the use of his right hand—his painting hand. This first occurred at the very time when he had never been busier professionally. Philip IV had just commissioned him to create or attend to the production of more than a hundred pictures to adorn his new hunting lodge, the Torre del Parada, and for El Buen Retiro, another country retreat not far from the Spanish capital. With the assistance of every competent artist in Antwerp, he managed to accomplish most of the immense order.

He was in constant pain now, the anguish so great at times that he wept. Hélène suspected nothing of this increasing agony. She accepted his assurance that these tears, like all his tears, were inspired by his joy in her. Only during the first weeks of 1640 did his affliction become so terrible that he could no longer conceal it from her. He took to bed in March and left it only briefly, once to consult his notary. He wanted to be certain that his will was in order, that his dearest Hélène would be adequately provided for. She was to receive half of his entire estate. "You can find yourself a fine new husband with such riches as I'm going to leave you," he told her without a note of self-pity in his cracked voice. "You *must* remarry. I *want* you to."

She wouldn't listen to this kind of talk. She asked the regent to send his most competent physician to examine Pieter Paul, a request the infante eagerly agreed to, for Rubens was by way of being the greatest living ornament of Flanders. The doctor was optimistic. There was no known cure for gout, but remissions were frequent. Hélène took heart from the diagnosis; she believed what she wanted to believe.

On the morning of June 1, she awoke and turned to the beloved invalid at her side. "How is it with you, my heart?" She kissed his forehead.

"Well," he said dryly, "I've survived the night. That's become an important achievement."

"Nonsense. You're going to survive hundreds of more nights, thousands."

"Willingly, my dearest, as long as *you're* at my side," he replied. And though the pain he felt was excruciating, he meant every syllable.

She read the torment in his drawn features, and struggled to control her voice. She forced a smile. "You'll just *have* to." She leaned over him to kiss the withering cheek, and whispered, "I think I'm pregnant again."

There was no response, no movement.

"I'm pregnant, Pieter Paul," she reiterated, aloud, and raised herself to look at him. She touched and closed the open mouth, closed the empty eyes, and realized with a tremor of despair and loneliness that there would be no response. Had he heard her last words?

Describes his triumphs, conditions of his
time, his personal life, his philosophy, his
work as ambassador, and his life as an artist.